BONES

BONES

K.L. SPEER

BOOK 1 OF THE BONES SERIES

ISBN 979-8-9897440-0-8 (epub)
ISBN 979-8-9897440-1-5 (paperback)
ISBN 979-8-9897440-2-2 (hardcover)

For more information:
P.O. BOX 68014, Minneapolis, MN 55418
author.klspeer@gmail.com
www.klspeer.com

Bones is set in a brutal and violent post-apocalyptic world and contains intense violence, sexual activities on page, and graphic language. Since Bones is a healer, there are descriptions of blood, illness, and wounds. This book is intended for mature adults.

For a full list of content warnings
(will include mild spoilers), go here:
https://www.klspeer.com/content-warnings

To my twelve-year-old self
who always felt like an outsider
so she got lost in books and started
writing the first of many novels.
You never expected to be here,
but I wanted to tell you something.
We did it.

PROLOGUE

T he midday sun beat down on the desert sand. A young girl covered in dirt and dried blood lay where she'd fallen, too exhausted to get up. Above, a lone hawk circled. Two scrawny vultures had landed, stretching their fleshy necks to get a better look at her. One of them squawked, but she didn't move. The hawk circled again, then dove. The scavengers hopped sideways, letting out indignant screeches, and she pushed herself up. At her movement, the hawk changed course, soaring back into the sky. The vultures hadn't moved, still eyeing her hopefully. She glared at them.

"Fuck off," her voice cracked. "I ain't dead yet."

The huge birds stared with glittering beady eyes. A flash of anger filled her, and she bared her teeth and growled, swiping in their direction like an angry cat. The vultures took off in a flurry of noise and dust.

Now alone, she struggled to her feet. Her chapped lips stung, and her throat burned with thirst. She started trudging again, not in any particular direction. Just one foot in front of the other. Her stomach cramped. The last thing she'd eaten had been a couple small eggs she'd stolen from a nest two days ago.

The sun had moved halfway across the sky when a dust cloud appeared in the distance. She stopped walking, swaying as her legs trembled. Running was pointless; her pursuer could track anything. She took a deep breath and clenched her fists at her sides, steeling herself against seeing his face.

The ramshackle bikes skidded to a stop, and she squinted through the dust to see three bikes, three strangers. For a moment, she felt lightheaded with a strange mix of relief and disappointment. It wasn't him. The two on the sides revved their snarling engines as they looked her over in a way that made her feel cold. One was young, still a boy, and the other was a giant man. The man leered at her, flashing the crude chunk of gold he had in place of a tooth. But she paid attention to the one in the middle. Faded tattoos crawled up his neck, and he eyed her with a calculating gaze. The other two kept looking at him as though waiting for instruction.

For a moment, she hesitated. She could try to run. She could cry and scream. She could even try to fight. But her brother had taught her too well for that. He'd trained her to survive.

"You're small, but you're clever." She could hear Wolf's voice in her head. *"Folks see a kid and assume they're the smarter one. An' maybe they are, but anytime somebody underestimates you, you can use that."*

So she squared her bony little shoulders, stepped forward, and said, "I'm lookin' for work. I'm...I'm a healer, and I'm lookin' for work."

The man on the left snorted with laughter, slapping his leg, but the one in the middle just raised a single brow.

"That so?" he finally said in a lazy, dangerous sort of voice.

She clenched her ragged shirt at her sides to keep her hands from shaking. "Yeah. That's so."

"Just when you think you seen it all." The one on the left snorted again, his voice loud. He swung a leg over and kicked a wobbly kickstand down, his eyes on her. "C'mon, boss, we could use a little fun. How 'bout—"

A gunshot cracked across the dry, barren ground. She jerked backward, biting her tongue hard, but she didn't scream. The man who had dismounted glanced down at his bleeding shoulder in shock.

"The fuck—" he choked.

"Tell you what," the leader said, holstering his pistol, "I've been dreadful bored. So here's your chance. You fix Grip here, an' you're hired."

"Juck—" wheezed Grip, clutching his shoulder. He went down on one knee, his eyes rolling between her and the man who'd shot him.

The third biker laughed with a sneer, and she knew they expected her to fail. She stood quietly for a second, but then she moved forward.

"Juck!" Grip sputtered. "Juck, boss, I didn't mean to—" He

glanced at the young biker. "Vulture…help me, man—"

Both Juck and Vulture ignored him. Out of the corner of her eye, she could tell Juck's gaze had locked on her as she walked straight up to the bleeding man, reached out her skinny little arms, and placed her hands on his shoulder.

"The hell—" Grip got out, but then he sucked in a startled gasp.

Nothing happened. At least, she knew that's what it looked like, but a second later, the bullet pushed itself out of Grip's shoulder like a worm coming out of the dirt. She spared a glance at Juck to see shock and excitement creeping across his face. The bullet dropped to the sand in an almost silent thud, and she let go, staggering backward but somehow remaining on her feet. She tried to hide the way her entire body shook with chills by clasping her trembling hands in front of her. In the silence, Grip stared open-mouthed at her, his beefy hand gingerly touching the fresh pink scar where the bullet hole had been.

She looked at Juck, and Juck smiled. She held his eyes, unsure if she should feel relieved or not that she wasn't going to die today.

"You're hired," Juck said, his voice soft. "Come here, girl."

She didn't hesitate this time. She left Grip where he sat still gaping and went straight up to Juck's bike. She lifted her freckled face and studied him as he studied her. He looked to be in his late forties, hair and beard beginning to grey. He had ruddy, wrinkled skin from the desert sun and a pleasant enough expression, but something about him set her on edge, something dark.

"Look at those eyes," Juck said. "Never seen eyes that green before."

Her stomach twisted, and she fought the urge to shift on her feet. The third biker, Vulture, studied her from behind Juck. He looked a little younger than Wolf, maybe sixteen or seventeen. His dark blond hair curled at the ends, and his face was handsome, but he stared down at her, his nose wrinkled in disgust.

"Gods, she's all bones," Vulture mocked.

He wasn't wrong, but her face reddened. She'd been skinny before, but two weeks in the desert with practically no food had reduced her to almost nothing.

"Without bones, you'd be nothin' more than a puddle of muck on the ground, boy," Juck said, his voice a quiet rebuke.

Vulture flushed and scowled.

"What's your name, girl?" Juck asked.

She swallowed hard, but her name stuck in her throat like a rock. The girl she'd been was as good as dead, so who was she now? "Don't got one."

"How old are you?" Vulture asked, still scowling. "Seven?"

She flashed him a fierce look. "I'm ten, asshole."

Vulture snorted, and she clenched her fists hard enough to make her nails bite into her palms.

"Don't got a name, huh?" Juck smiled. "Well, you do now, Bones."

He moved quickly, just like when he'd drawn his gun and shot Grip. She tensed when he grabbed her around the waist and lifted her, but she didn't fight. He settled her onto his bike in front of him and gripped his handlebars, his arms closing her in like steel bars.

"Let's git," he said, a triumphant smile playing across his face. He revved the bike, then took off with a jerk.

She gripped the seat, clinging to the cracked leather, and didn't look back.

"The gods sent an angel, all for me," Juck said reverently in her ear.

She didn't correct him, but she knew Wolf would have laughed himself sick at the thought of her being an angel. The wind whipped the tears out of her eyes and left them somewhere behind along with her name.

She was Bones, Wolf was gone, and the only kind of angel she could ever possibly be was an angel of death.

CHAPTER 1

Twelve Years Later

U nfortunately, I wasn't going to bleed to death.

The blood trickling down my face for hours from the big gash in my temple had stopped. If it'd been anyone else, I would've called that a good sign, but I wasn't sure what was coming for me. There was a damn good chance I was better off slowly bleeding to death in the dark.

I leaned my head back, letting it thud against the metal wall. I sat on the floor of an empty safe, just large enough for me to sit with my legs crossed. Zip ties secured my hands behind my back, the plastic leaving raw welts on my wrists.

If you're captured, don't fight 'em. They'll think you're weak. Use that against 'em.

I know, Wolf. I panicked, ok?

The mercenaries had snuck up on my sad little camp under cover of the thick trees. I hadn't seen them until they were on top of me, and instead of playing dumb like I should have, I panicked.

If you're outnumbered, do not try to fight, Wolf growled.

There'd been six of them and one of me, but I did manage to fling red-hot coals in one asshole's face and leave my only knife buried in another's thigh.

Never give up your only weapon! Wolf barked.

Gods, will you shut up already?

If I'd kept my head, they probably would've locked me in a regular room, but since I fought and injured them just enough to piss them off, they threw me in this godsforsaken safe.

The worst part was not knowing *why*. Did they know me? Did a bounty for me exist already? Or was I just lucky enough to get picked up by traffickers? I smiled humorlessly. Gods, wouldn't that be fitting?

The dim light and lack of interaction made it difficult to tell how much time had passed, but I would guess I'd been in here for more than a day. My stomach ached with hunger and my throat burned with thirst. Had they forgotten about me? Had they all been killed in a fight? Had I been left to waste away in a metal coffin?

I'd fallen into a half-asleep daze when a noise by the door startled me. I sat in the pitch black, my heart pounding and adrenaline flooding my veins, but the door didn't open. The scraping sounds and muffled voices continued for a long time, and dread began to pool in my stomach. The mercs didn't have any trouble locking it when they threw me in here. My eyes widened in sudden realization. These people weren't *unlocking* the safe, they were *picking* it. I strained, trying to hear the conversation, but a soft clicking sound made me freeze and then all the gears turned, and the thick door swung open. I forced myself to slump over with my eyes closed and my heart in my throat.

A bright light shone right on my face and a strangled exclamation cut through the silence. Hands reached into the safe, grabbing my arms and dragging me out to lay on the cold floor. Someone spoke in a harsh, angry whisper I couldn't make out, but a body knelt beside me and cut the zip ties around my wrists. The blood rushed back into my hands. I wanted to lash out, to run, but I remembered now, Wolf's voice thundering in my head. I cracked my eyes open, squinting in the light. Shadowy figures filled the room, but they sure as hell weren't the mercs. I tried to focus on the scraps of whispered conversation I could hear.

"—believe that little fucker lied. There's nothing here!"

"—end well. Fuck!"

"—leave her. We gotta get outta here."

The person beside me reached out, and I instinctively flinched. They withdrew and set the flashlight on the floor, illuminating a handsome male face. He looked somewhere in his mid to late twenties with a strong jaw covered in light stubble. His brown eyes—gentle eyes —widened in concern, and that told me all I needed to know.

"—not gonna hurt you." He reached a hand out to me again. "Can you walk?"

I nodded, shaking. I tried to push myself up but then sank back with a hiss of pain. He fell for it. His brow drew together in concern, and he seized my arms, helping me to my feet. I wobbled on one foot, keeping my other foot raised as though it hurt to walk on. He ducked under my arm, supporting my weight as I pretended to limp. Maybe my leg was fine, but I didn't have to pretend to need his support. Thanks to the blood loss and hunger, the room wouldn't stop spinning, forcing me to lean on him. The other shadowy well-armed figures bled out of the room, scouting ahead. Their guns glinted in the dim light as we crept down the hallway, and all five of them blended into the shadows with their dark clothing.

A cool breeze blew in from the open window at the end of the hall, and I studied it as we grew closer. It looked big enough for me to fit through and a flat roof stretched out below it. Perfect. My companion and I brought up the rear of the group, and the other four passed the window and turned down the next hallway. Once we reached the window, I doubled over, moaning in pain. He fell for it again, hook, line, and sinker, crouching down to look at me.

"Hey, are you—"

As soon as he crouched down, I threw my shoulder into him, hard. I glimpsed the surprise on his face as he went down, tripping over my foot that I'd placed behind his, but I ducked through the open window, dropped onto the roof, and ran. My bruised body screamed in protest and my head swam, but the flood of adrenaline helped me push past it. My feet pounded across the concrete. Behind me, I heard bodies drop onto the roof in pursuit. I didn't dare look back. The edge of the roof loomed in front of me, and I didn't pause, throwing myself into the darkness and praying to any gods listening that I would land on something besides the ground.

I collided hard with a ramshackle patched-up tin roof and pain stabbed me through the chest making me gasp. My knees and palms burned as I tried to get a grip on the tin, slicing my skin on the sharp edges. I slid way too close to the edge before I finally stopped myself.

A body landed with a thud on the roof somewhere nearby, and I pushed myself up and took off again. The pain in my chest twisted with each breath, but I didn't have time to examine it. No one yelled at me to stop, but they were trying to steal me from the mercs, so that made sense. I wished they *were* yelling so I could have some idea of their location.

The small buildings in this town sat almost on top of each other, sharing walls to reduce building materials, which meant I could easily run across the roofs but there wasn't much cover. I jumped a crumbling stove pipe and made a sharp turn left. I couldn't see my pursuer anywhere. I needed to get to the ground. It'd be easier to disappear—

A furious shout rang out and then gunfire erupted behind me.

I swore, flinging myself to the roof on my stomach. Bullets sprayed around me, but a stolen glance revealed it wasn't the mysterious gang pursuing me. The mercs poured onto the roof.

The gang scattered, ducking for cover and returning fire. I swore again, trying to crawl forward on my stomach. I did not want to get stuck in the middle of a gang war. *Again.*

The gunfire moved away, and somebody let out a strangled scream. I started to scramble to my feet. I just needed to get off this damn roof before—

A body slammed into me, crushing me back down against the roof and knocking all the air from my lungs.

"Don't move," a voice growled in my ear.

His weight pinned me to the roof. I finally gasped in a lung full of air, and then bullets sprayed around us again, tearing up the tin roof. I tried to kick away from my captor, panicked.

"Don't *move*!" he hissed again.

I gritted my teeth to keep the whimper from getting out and forced myself to go still. As soon as the gunfire eased, he moved, dragging me in a crouch behind the remains of a brick chimney. His hand gripped my arm like a vise. I couldn't get a good look at his face, but somehow I knew it was the one who'd tried to help me earlier.

"Get her back!" The scream came from somewhere behind us. "Find her! Get—"

Gunfire swallowed up the rest, and I prayed to the gods somebody put a bullet in that merc.

I took advantage of the moment and tried to wrench my arm free. He moved so fucking fast and suddenly trapped me with my face against the crumbling chimney and my back against his chest. His arm wrapped around my neck in a chokehold and tightened. I panicked and clawed at his arm, black spots dancing in my vision.

Do not fucking panic! Wolf barked.

I slumped in his hold, pretending to pass out. He relaxed his arm so I could breathe but continued to hold me against his body. As soon as I could, I sucked in a breath and twisted my chin so I could sink my teeth into his forearm. He swore as he wrenched free, and I tasted blood. I tried to duck under his other arm, but suddenly bullets slammed into our hiding place. The noise deafened me. Pieces of brick-and-mortar flew everywhere. Both of us dropped back down behind the sorry shelter of the chimney. He grabbed a handful of my jacket and yanked me toward him. I braced for a blow, but instead, he swung me around to trade places, giving me more cover from the bullets.

I didn't have much time to process that before he let out a strangled gasp that told me he'd been hit. He fell forward onto his knees, his hands grabbing at his gut, and slumped on top of me. I shoved at him as his weight crushed me for the second time, and he rolled off onto his back beside me. I struggled up to my knees, trying to peer around the chimney when a hand snagged my jacket. I snarled as my gaze snapped back down to him. Couldn't he just die already?

"Road past Ace's is clear," he groaned out each word, but his eyes stayed sharp on my face. "Run."

I hesitated. He was *still* helping me? Of course, it could be a trap, but even in the dim moonlight, I could see the dark blood oozing out between his fingers. I could smell it, thick and coppery.

"Run!" he growled.

I didn't move. His eyes narrowed in confusion as I stared into them. I could hear Wolf's voice screaming at me.

Get the fuck outta there!

The few small broken pieces of me that still cared seeing a person in pain cut like glass under my skin. I could run and save myself, but if I did, he would die. I hissed through my teeth, but I moved forward, prying his hand away from the wound and pressing my own hands against his bloody stomach.

"Leave me," he groaned in pain. "Run."

His face paled, blood dribbling between his lips as he coughed. I'd seen death on people's faces more times than I could count. Death had a way of revealing people's true natures. Some people begged, some threatened, some tried to bargain. And this idiot I didn't even know was dying and *still* trying to help me. I hated him for it.

He started trying to talk again, grabbing at my hands.

"Shut up, dumbass," I hissed at him, pressing harder at his wound.

He cried out in pain, but his cry cut off as the familiar warmth spread from my chest down my arms and into his stomach. The bullet had gone clean through his gut. Normally a death wound, but not tonight. I could feel his body mending beneath my fingers, all the muscles and organs knitting themselves back together. His hand curled over the top of one of mine, squeezing gently, and I glanced up to see his eyes full of awe. The wound closed shut, leaving what I knew would be a fresh pink scar, and all the warmth left me.

My head spun as I sucked in a breath and shivered, chilled like I just jumped into an icy river. His lips formed a question, his voice hoarse and his eyes still lit up with amazement.

"Who—"

Time to go.

I jerked away. His hand fell back to his stomach, his fingers searching for a wound that was no longer there. I started to stand, listening for gunfire, ready—

Something cracked into the back of my head like thunder, and everything went dark.

Angry voices cut through me as I regained consciousness. My head throbbed and I cracked my eyes open, a pained groan escaping through my teeth, and everything went silent. I blinked at the sky just starting to lighten into a pink dawn above me. Then the sky disappeared, blocked by three male faces staring down at me, and my heart seized in terror.

I rolled and they lunged. I managed to get to my knees but stalled when the world spun so violently that I thought I might be sick. Hands seized my arms and hauled me up to my feet. I kicked out, but strong arms banded around me, pinning both my arms to my sides. I threw my head backward, aiming for his nose, but I wasn't quite tall enough. My throbbing head connected with his collarbone, and stars burst in my vision. Before I could recover, he yanked my upper body back while shoving his hips into mine, forcing me onto his knee. The more I fought, the more he leaned back, pulling me with him until just the tips of my toes touched the ground. I thrashed, but he was firmly centered, and I had no leverage. I gave up, helpless fury burning in my eyes.

A dark-haired man stepped right in front of me, and my panicked gaze focused on his face. He looked older than my twenty-two years, maybe nearing thirty. His dark eyes matched his unruly black hair. They snapped with angry golden sparks as he glared at me, reminding me of the dark grey chunk of flint I'd stolen to make my campfires. A long scar ran up his left cheek, stopping just underneath his eye.

"Juck's secret weapon," he said, his voice low and hard.

The roaring in my head threatened to swallow me. So the mercs had known. They'd known me, which meant somebody had talked. I thought I'd have more time, I thought I'd be able to get farther away—

"Lot of stories make more sense now," he continued, "like Juck's *immortality*."

I glared at him, and he glared right back. A giant muscled man shifted into view. He had dark skin and black hair buzzed close to his scalp. His arms crossed but despite his intimidating size, he met my gaze with a calm, steady expression.

"What are you?" the first man demanded.

I broke away from that intense gaze and stared stubbornly at the trees behind him. Gods, I'd been free for two weeks. Two. Defeat tasted bitter in my mouth.

"Mac!"

Both men's hands twitched toward the guns on their hips as a young person came hurtling through the trees toward us, all gangly arms and legs.

"Trucks are moving out. Mercs," he spit out rapid fire.

"Get to the rovers," the black-haired man, Mac apparently, said. "Load up."

He turned his back on me and stalked into the trees. The one holding me released me, dropping me back to the ground. He switched to holding my left upper arm, and I shot a glance up at his face to meet the brown eyes of the one I'd so stupidly healed. I glanced away, tensing further when Muscles stepped forward and grabbed my other arm and the two of them started dragging me along after Mac. I couldn't see the town anywhere, just trees. I squinted up at the sky, trying to get a read on our location, but it just made my head hurt worse.

We stepped out into a clearing. Mac climbed into a fortified off-road vehicle with two seats in the front and a bench seat in the back, and it purred to life. A second one behind it already idled. My two guards dragged me up to the one Mac waited in and shoved me in the backseat. Released from their grip, I started scrambling over the seat trying to escape out the other side, but Muscles caught my ankle and yanked me back. I tumbled onto the floor of the rover but managed to kick out hard with my free leg as I fell. I caught Muscles in the chin and felt a sick sort of satisfaction when he swore and spit blood.

"Will you fucking hold onto her?" Mac snapped, twisting to glance back at the commotion.

Muscles swore some more and jerked me toward him by the ankle. I slid across the floor, and he hauled me up by the arms and leaned in. His dark brown eyes glittered as blood dribbled down his chin.

"You wanna get tied up again?" he growled, his grip on my arms tightening.

I dropped my eyes as my stomach twisted. My wrists still ached with welts and bruises from being zip tied for so long in that safe. Satisfied, he shoved me back and someone behind me hauled me up into the seat right next to them. I scooted away for some space, but then Muscles climbed in, crowding me back. He wiped the blood from his chin, glaring at me. To avoid his angry gaze, I glanced to my right only to see Brown Eyes studying me. I dropped my eyes to the floor and tucked my hands into my lap to hide how they trembled. The adrenaline had faded, leaving me nauseous and shaky.

"On your go, Alpha," a female voice crackled over a radio.

The rover peeled out, the second one following close behind. We traveled on a near-overgrown dirt road that snaked through the woods. The rover bounced over the rough terrain, making the gash on my head throb. The backseat fit two, not three, making me wedged between the two men, my skin crawling from the sudden onset of physical closeness. I tried to make myself as small as possible, but I couldn't avoid the way their thighs and shoulders pressed against mine. My shoulders curled inwards until I hunched forward on the seat. I kept my eyes trained on my scuffed-up boots. We drove in silence for a while, but I could *feel* the questions brewing.

I took a moment to catalog my injuries. The back of my head pounded from being knocked out, but at least the big gash in my temple had stopped bleeding. Small but painful cuts covered my palms from the tin roofing. The left side of my chest under my shoulder hurt the worst. I remembered landing hard on something sharp when I jumped off the roof. I pulled my thick plaid shirt back, wincing as it caught on something, and warm blood started trickling down my chest. I wasn't able to see the wound, but it was still bleeding.

"What's your name?" Brown Eyes spoke over the engine. He sounded curious and not demanding.

I hesitated, debating whether stubborn silence would be worth it. Probably not.

"Bones," I muttered.

I didn't look up, but in the silence, I assumed all of them had the same surprised expression most people got when they heard my name.

"Bones?" Brown Eyes repeated.

Muscles snorted. "Funny name for a pretty little thing."

"That pretty little thing near knocked your teeth out," Brown Eyes said.

I stole glances at both, tensing. Muscles glared daggers at him, but Brown Eyes grinned. I stared back down at my feet.

"Sounds like a bounty hunter's name," the young boy in the front seat chimed in, twisting around to peer back at us.

"Shuddup, Jax," Mac ordered.

The boy scowled but turned back around.

"Got a surname?" Brown Eyes asked.

"No," I lied.

"Ok," he said. "So how'd you heal me, Bones?"

I gritted my teeth and tried to focus past the pounding in my head. "I'm a healer," I muttered.

"Yeah, you're gonna need to explain that a bit more," he said. "Because I've never met a healer who could do what you did."

I caught a glimpse of Mac's eyes in the rear mirror and glanced away quickly. "I have—" Gods, help me. "Powers."

A short silence fell before Muscles repeated, his voice suspicious, "You have magic healing powers?"

My temper rose, but I forced it back down. "Yes."

"Magic healing powers?" Muscles said again, even more skeptically.

"Ask your buddy why he's still breathing if you don't believe me," I snapped.

"I mean, I got no explanations," Brown Eyes said. "It sure as hell seemed like magic."

"Maybe it was a trick," Muscles said.

"If it was, it fuckin' hurt," Brown Eyes replied.

"I don't do fucking tricks," I muttered.

"So you have magic healing powers."

Gods, if Muscles said that one more time, I would jump out of this rover.

"How?" Brown Eyes asked.

"Fuck if I know," I ground out.

"Have you always had them?"

"Yes."

Silence fell again. I could sense them all exchanging looks, but I just folded myself further in half, my elbows on my knees and my hands clasping behind my neck. If I hadn't so *stupidly* healed Brown Eyes, I probably could've passed myself off as Juck's runaway whore or something. Not like that'd be far from the truth anyway. But now they'd seen what I could do and there was no way in hell they would let me go.

"I'm Trey," Brown Eyes spoke up again.

I didn't move, didn't acknowledge I'd heard him at all.

"Griz is the one still spitting blood," Trey added, amusement clear in his voice.

Muscles growled on the other side of me, but it sounded half-hearted at best.

"Mac is drivin' and that's Jax up there," Trey continued.

I still didn't move. My dry eyes felt like they might crumble to dust in my head. After a few minutes, someone nudged my shoulder. I tensed as I peered up, but Trey held out what looked like a granola bar wrapped in wax paper. My stomach cramped in hunger at the sight of it. I took it, my hands trembling, and bit off a small piece. I wanted to inhale the whole thing, but I knew that wouldn't end well, so I nibbled a few bites before holding it back out to him.

Trey frowned. "You can eat all of it."

"I'm done," I said, then trying not to sound too desperate I asked, "Do you have any water?"

Trey reluctantly took the granola bar and pulled a battered metal bottle out of his pack. I tipped it back, gulping down the water. I had to force myself not to drink it all, but when I tried to give it back, Trey shook his head.

"It's ok. You can drink it all."

I didn't need to be told twice.

"Can you heal yourself?" Griz asked.

I looked at him, but he was looking at the gash on my head.

"No."

Griz gave me a look I couldn't quite read and then glanced down at my shoulder. "Did you get shot?"

I curled my shoulders inward, trying to shrink away from his gaze. "No. Just a cut."

"That's a lot of blood for just a cut," Griz muttered.

"It's nothing."

They didn't say anything more. We drove and drove through the endless woods, nothing but trees and mountains as far as I could see. Where the hell were we going? I had no idea what sort of holds existed out here in the mountains. I wanted to ask, but it was safer to stay quiet and small and just observe.

Of all the half-assed plans—

Shut up, Wolf.

I didn't know what to think of these people. Mac knew I'd belonged to Juck, they'd been looking for his "secret weapon," and I'd be willing to wager that didn't mean anything *good.* So far they hadn't hurt me too much besides knocking me out. Trey seemed to care about my well-being, but I knew all too well one person caring didn't mean shit.

Exhaustion crept over me, and I tried hard to fight it, but I dozed off several times before jerking awake, startling both men next to me every time.

"Bones, it's alright if you sleep." Trey murmured, which only made me try harder to stay awake.

Stay alert, Wolf snapped.

Despite my best efforts, it wasn't long before the exhaustion won and pulled me under.

CHAPTER 2

I jerked awake with a gasp. Next to me, a body jolted and on the other side, somebody swore. My heart pounded in my throat, and it took me a few seconds to remember where the hell I was. The sun had sunk below the trees, bathing the sky in orange streaks. The rover had stopped, but I still couldn't see anything but trees. The wide-open space of the desert often made me feel exposed, but here, swallowed by trees, I felt trapped.

"Jumpy little thing," Griz muttered and I flushed.

Mac and Jax hopped out as the second rover pulled up beside us.

Griz grabbed my arm and pulled me out, gripping tighter as I swayed a little. Gods, I hoped this dizziness passed soon. The second rover's crew unloaded beside us, two women and one other man. The driver—a woman with long black hair pulled back into a ponytail— stared me down with a look of pure hatred in her bloodshot eyes. I took an involuntary step backward, treading on Griz's foot.

"Bring her over here," Trey called, pulling a battered first aid kit from the back of the rover.

Griz pulled me over to where Trey set the kit on the hood of the rover, standing in the headlight. The woman turned away and began unloading supplies. Unease swirled in my stomach. Griz dropped my arm, standing next to me with his massive arms crossed while I tried to remember if I'd ever seen that woman before.

"Come sit down and unbutton your shirt so I can take a look at that wound on your shoulder," Trey said, gesturing toward a large rock.

All thoughts of the woman went straight out of my head.

"It's just a scratch," I snapped, trying to keep the anxiety out of my voice. I gripped the collar of my shirt, pulling it tighter across my chest like it might somehow protect me and trying to hide my wince of pain from doing so.

"Look, Bones, I'm not trying to make a move on you," Trey said patiently, "but that's not just a scratch. Your shirt is wet, which means it's still fuckin' bleeding. That wound needs to be cleaned and maybe stitched. You know that."

I glared at him, heat rising in my face. "I can do it myself."

"You can't even see it. C'mon. You want Griz to sit on you?" A smile quirked at the corner of Trey's mouth. "Because we can do this the hard way."

He rolled up his sleeves and in the bright light of the headlights, I caught a glimpse of the bite I'd given him. My teeth marks were stamped onto his skin as a new pink scar.

Griz took a step forward and my entire body tensed. I didn't understand why they were making such a big deal out of a stupid wound. They were trying to intimidate me, and they were succeeding. When he took a second step, I panicked. I took off like a terrified rabbit, but apparently Griz anticipated that. He lunged and caught my arm, jerking me to a stop. The rest of the group went quiet, and I could feel everyone's eyes on us. My heart pounded and my stomach churned with a swell of fear. I kept my eyes on the ground. I wasn't sure what they meant by the hard way, but maybe if I made it difficult enough they'd give up. Surely it wouldn't be worth the trouble, right?

Trey must've signaled to everyone somehow because they all went back to their tasks, ignoring the three of us.

I flinched when Trey reached toward me, and he withdrew his hand. I hated that I did it, that I couldn't control the way my body reacted. My face burned.

"We're not gonna hurt you," Griz murmured next to me, still holding my arm.

"I can do it myself. Just let me do it," I tried again, hating the desperation leaking into my voice.

"Hey." Trey's voice gentled in a way that made my throat tighten. "Bones, look at me."

"I swear it's nothin'. Just give me a bandage, and I can take care of it."

"Bones, c'mon, look at me."

I lifted my eyes, but I couldn't quite look Trey in the face, so I stared at his hands instead. He stood a step away, keeping his gestures slow and non-threatening. He had workers' hands, calloused and rough, but he kept his nails neatly trimmed. The sun had browned his skin and highlighted the small white scars peppered across his hands. He raised one hand, and I tracked the movement as he tucked his wavy brown hair back behind his ear to keep it out of his face. I met his gaze finally and hated the gentleness that somehow still existed there. His brown eyes, framed with long eyelashes, met mine.

"I know you've got little cause to trust us." Trey pitched his voice low enough just for me to hear. "But I owe you my life, and I swear on that debt I'm not gonna hurt you. That wound is bleeding a lot, and I just want to stitch it up. Will you let me do that?"

"What'll you do if I don't?" I tried to sound defiant, but I just sounded scared.

"Keep pestering you until you change your mind." He smiled.

I didn't return it and his face grew serious again.

"We aren't gonna force you, Bones. I was just kidding about Griz sitting on you."

"I wouldn't sit on you even if he told me to," Griz added. "I'd probably break you in half."

"I'm not the best healer and I sure as hell can't do what you can do. But I can stitch a wound." Trey paused a second, then added, "I can't just do nothin' when somebody is hurt. You seem like you feel the same way."

The silence stretched as I stared at him. I knew he meant that moment on the roof when I'd looked into his eyes and decided to heal him instead of running. I didn't like that he'd somehow seen those thoughts on my face. I could usually hide what I felt better.

"Please, Bones," Trey added, still in that soft voice. "I'm not gonna hurt you."

Maybe *he* wouldn't, but a life debt only carried so far, and I wasn't *just* afraid of being hurt.

Choose your battles, Wolf snarled.

I swallowed hard and unbuttoned the plaid shirt, my shaking

fingers moving fast before I could change my mind. Griz released my arm again as I pulled the shirt off my left shoulder and let it drop, revealing my upper chest and the bloodied tank underneath. I tried to steel myself, but Trey's low exclamation still made me wince.

"What the *fuck*?" Anger snapped in his voice, but his hands were gentle as he shifted my flannel over more.

Griz sucked in a sharp breath, and my face burned. In the center of my chest a large, crude "J" had been branded into my flesh. It started at my collarbone and ended just above my breasts, the rough skin raised and an angry red, clearly a semi-recent wound. It was impossible to miss, but then that had been the point.

"Did Juck do this to you?" Trey's voice dropped to something quiet and dark.

I didn't answer him, figuring that was pretty fucking obvious. I wished I could just sink into the ground and disappear.

"Does that burn need some kind of treatment?" Griz asked.

His gruff voice sounded gentle, and I flicked my eyes up, surprised. His gaze remained calm and steady, but it looked like actual concern shone there. I glanced at Trey, but he'd turned toward the woods, a muscle in his jaw flexing. I shook my head.

"Does it hurt?" Griz asked.

"Not really," I lied. It ached all the time, but I didn't want to admit that.

"How long ago did this happen?" Trey spoke again, his voice rough.

I tried to swallow past the lump in my throat. "Couple weeks."

A brief silence hung around us.

"Uh." Trey cleared his throat. "Ok. This gash in your shoulder is gonna need some stitches. Looks like a piece of that shitty roof stabbed you. You want a swig?"

He held out a bottle I numbly took. He unrolled a leather satchel full of basic healer tools. Relief and surprise made me lightheaded. At least he didn't seem like he would ask any more questions. I took a drink and handed it back, my eyes watering as it burned all the way down.

"I'm gonna pour this over the wound, alright?" Trey waited until I nodded before pouring the amber liquid over my shoulder, catching the excess with a clean rag.

My body jerked in pain. Griz made a sympathetic noise through his teeth. Trey handed me back the bottle again, and I took another large drink as he started stitching me up. He worked confidently like he'd done this a few times before. The alcohol took the edge off, but it still hurt like hell. Griz took the bottle from me as Trey worked, taking a swig himself.

After Trey tied the stitches off, I shrugged my flannel back on as quickly as I could, buttoning it all the way up to my chin. Relief swept over me, but then Griz handed Trey a clean rag and a fresh bottle of water.

"Now I'm just gonna clean this up." Trey gestured toward the gash in my head as he poured the water on the rag.

I tensed again as he rested a hand on my temple, holding my head still as he cleaned the dried blood off.

"Looks like it's scabbed over pretty good. Shouldn't need stitches," Trey mused as he dabbed at the ugly gash.

"What happened there?" Griz asked, taking another drink of alcohol.

When I didn't answer, Trey's eyes flicked to mine again. "What happened here?" he repeated.

"The mercs," I muttered.

"This is a deep gash, and it bled a lot." Trey gently wiped the rag down the side of my face where I could feel stiff dried blood coating my skin. "You're fuckin' covered in blood. They didn't even try to patch you up?"

I fought the urge to snap something about how most people didn't give a shit.

"Did they hit you with something?" Griz pressed.

"Obviously," I muttered.

Griz raised an eyebrow, but the corner of his mouth twitched.

"The fuck were they gonna do if you bled to death?" Trey asked, anger coating his voice again.

"Well I didn't," I said, hoping they got the message that I did not want to talk about this.

"How long were you in that safe?" Griz asked.

"I dunno."

"Fuckin' mercs," Trey muttered.

Well, we could agree on that at least.

"Alright. Let me see your hands." Trey tucked the bottle under his arm and held his hands out, palms up.

I hesitated before putting my hands in his. He gripped my hands, tilting them to catch the light of the headlight and leaning close to examine my shredded palms.

"Shit," he murmured. "You did a number on these. You better take another drink 'cause I'm gonna have to clean these cuts out."

He glanced back up at my face. In the growing dark, I could ignore the other bodies moving just out of sight. Even Griz seemed to fade away from where he stood at my shoulder. Trey's hands tightened on mine as his eyes shone with something like regret.

"I'm sorry," he murmured, and I knew he wasn't talking about the cuts on my palms. "We had no idea the weapon was a person. We never would've done it if we'd known."

I jerked my hands away, feeling cold.

"I can clean these myself," I snapped, averting my gaze.

For the first time, he didn't argue. He just handed me the bottle of alcohol. I gulped down another mouthful and then gritted my teeth and poured the alcohol over the slices, relishing the burning pain. As I set the bottle down, my eyes smarting, Trey moved in again, wrapping my hand in a clean bandage before I could protest. Then he paused for a moment, pushing my sleeve up to look at the welts on my wrists.

"Gods, those ties were tight," he muttered, continuing the bandage up my wrist. As he pushed my sleeve up further to tie it off, dark bruises came into view, and that muscle in his jaw started flexing again.

"Are you hurt anywhere else?" Griz examined the bruises on my arm too.

"No."

The two of them exchanged a look, but Trey just grabbed the bottle and held his hand out. "I'll do your other hand."

I gave him my other hand, swearing through my teeth as he poured the alcohol over the exposed wounds.

By the time he finished, the camp had been set up. Jax had cooked something in a small fire and the smell made my mouth water. Trey cleaned up the supplies and Griz brought me over to the fire, gripping my arm a little more gently. He gestured for me to sit and then took a seat on my left as I glanced around. Across the fire from me sat the woman from before. I met her gaze to find her still glaring at me with hatred. I dropped my eyes, feeling my heart rate pick up. Did I know her? Had I met her before? I wracked my brain but came up empty.

Griz handed me a tin plate with some steaming meat and potatoes on it. I fumbled to grip it with my bandaged hands, and then nearly dropped the whole thing when the woman across the fire erupted.

"So that's it?" she snarled, leaping to her feet and stabbing a finger in my direction. "We're just gonna stitch her up and feed her like nothing happened?"

"Sit down, Lana," Griz snapped.

"*Sit down, Lana?*" she parroted back at him, her voice rising. "My brother is *dead* and that's all you have to say?"

Dread fell over me like a thick blanket.

"We'll have time to grieve once we get home." Griz's voice gentled. "Right now we gotta follow orders."

"Our *orders* were not to save this bitch," Lana raged, tears glimmering in her eyes. "We were supposed to bring back the weapon—"

"She *is* the weapon," Trey interrupted from a few feet away.

In the silence, everyone stared at me, and I stared at the crackling fire.

"No," Lana snarled, moving suddenly.

My gaze shot up to her. She'd drawn a gun and pointed it straight at me.

"We couldn't even bring his body back! I had to leave my brother on the fuckin' roof, with the fuckin' mercs! I can't even *bury* him. And it's her fuckin' fault."

"Lana!" Trey held out a hand. "Put the gun down."

"Blood for blood." Lana's hands didn't shake, but her voice did.

I stared up at the gun, but I couldn't deny that I felt as much relief as I did fear. Wolf snarled, but gods, I was just so damn tired. Then Mac appeared behind Lana, his gun pressed against the back of her head.

"Put it down," Mac ordered, all scary quiet as his eyes sparked in the firelight. "We're seein' this through."

Lana bared her teeth at me like a wildcat. Tears shone in her eyes, but finally, she lowered the gun. Mac took it from her and then Trey joined as they marched her back behind the rover. In the silence, I waited in resigned misery to hear the gunshot signaling her execution, but it never came.

"Eat," Griz said next to me.

The food smelled amazing, but it'd been a long time since I ate actual food. I ate as much as I could, stopping when my stomach roiled. I set the plate on the ground by my feet and wrapped my arms around myself.

Mac, Trey, and Lana returned after the fire had died down. Lana still glared at me with glittering hatred, but she stayed silent. Mac and Trey resumed eating like nothing had happened. I eyed them, feeling curious despite my best efforts. If anybody had challenged Juck like that, they'd have been dead before they got a handful of words out. Or just close to dead so Juck could have some fun. The small bit of meat and potatoes I'd eaten turned to rocks in my stomach. My fingers touched the scar on my chest.

"Was he shot by the mercs?" I asked Griz.

Griz glanced at me, surprised. "Yeah."

I let the weight of that sink over me. If I hadn't run, her brother would probably still be alive. Blood for blood. I thought of Wolf and a chill ran down my spine.

"That's Raven on Lana's left," Griz added, nodding toward the other girl on their crew. She had long black hair on one half of her head and a shaved scalp on the other side. She continued to ignore me, and I didn't mind.

"Sam is the one over by the kid." Sam had close-cut blond hair and a short beard. He appeared to be teasing Jax who scowled at him.

I gave a brief nod, and Griz lapsed into silence again. He cleaned his plate and then eyed my still full plate.

"You should eat more."

I shook my head. "I'm done. You can have the rest."

He eyed me for a few seconds, but then shrugged and took my plate and dug in. I studied him. He wore a light jacket, but the bulky muscles in his arms showed through the fabric. The dark chocolate brown of his skin glowed in the firelight. There was a soothing calmness to his quiet, steady presence that annoyed me. I didn't want to feel calm, nothing about this should make me feel *calm.*

Once Mac and Trey had finished eating, everyone moved to their bedrolls. Griz pulled me up by the arm and led me behind a tree to relieve my bladder. I fumbled with my pants, but Griz kept his gaze elsewhere. When we returned to camp, he paused, looking at Mac.

"She can use Exo's bedroll," Mac said.

Rage flashed across Lana's face. Exo must've been her brother. She opened her mouth but before she could speak, I did.

"No. I don't need...no."

Mac stared at me hard, then shrugged. Lana just turned her back and climbed into her bedroll next to Raven. The other woman put her arm around Lana's shoulders while fixing me with a glare. Mac came and took my arm from Griz, his grip painfully tight. He brought me back to the rover and told me to climb in. After I climbed into the backseat and sat, he took my right arm and zip tied my bandaged wrist to the metal bar of the rover. Trey came up and watched him, a frown on his face.

"This really necessary?" Trey asked, low.

"I'm not taking any more chances," Mac snapped back. "And you aren't either."

Pain and guilt flashed across Trey's face, and he didn't argue. I tried to pretend I wasn't paying careful attention. The tension between the two of them pulsed like a live wire. Trey was the weak link, the one who cared just a little too much. If I could use that, maybe I still had a chance. Mac finished tightening the zip tie, tight enough that I couldn't slip my bandaged hand free and strode back toward the fire. The welts on my wrist burned. Trey seemed to hesitate.

"Trey?" I whispered, letting a tremor into my voice.

He moved closer to the rover and looked at me with wary eyes.

"I—"

"What's up, Bones?"

"I'm sorry. About Exo," I whispered.

Trey stayed silent, and I had to fight the urge to glance up at his face. I willed my eyes to fill with tears and let them fall. He put a hand on my knee, and I managed to keep from flinching. When I glanced up through the tears, his face had softened.

"It's not your fault," he said.

I watched him as the tears continued to fall from my eyes, trying to pick the best course of action.

Careful. I heard Wolf's stern voice. *Don't overdo it.*

The alcohol warming my blood gave me courage, so I started mumbling too quiet for him to hear. His brow furrowed as he tried to make it out. I let out a small sob and kept going. He stepped closer and leaned into the rover, trying to hear me.

"—should have let her shoot me. Why—"

His fingers snaked around my free wrist, catching my hand that was attempting to pull the knife out of the holster on his belt.

My gaze snapped to his face, fear tightening in my gut. His eyes were sharp, but he looked *amused.*

"Like I said, I owe you my life," he said, refusing to release my wrist, even as I tried to jerk free. "So I'm gonna pretend you weren't just trying to steal my knife."

I dropped the act, swearing at him through my teeth. He quirked a half smile and let go of my wrist, stepping back out of reach. I glared at him, wishing again I'd left him to die on the rooftop.

"Night, Bones," he called as he walked away, leaving me alone in the dark.

ᎶᏕ

The night was cold and long. I tried to get my hand free for hours, even going so far as to debate dislocating my thumb to see if I could slip out of the zip tie, but I didn't think the angle would work. So instead, I just fucked up the bandage and rubbed even more of the skin on my wrist raw as I jerked against the tie. I didn't dare sleep. Even with a rotating guard, I didn't trust these people. Sure they needed me alive, but I knew far too well what sort of pain could be inflicted without killing.

By the time the sun rose, my teeth were chattering, and my eyelids felt so heavy. When Griz came to cut me free, he noted my bloodied wrist and then glared at me. I glared right back.

"C'mon," he snapped after he cut through the tie, "climb out."

My numb and stiff legs gave out on me as I tried to obey. He grabbed my arm, keeping me from falling out on my face, and grumbled to himself. The camp bustled with activity, everyone packing up to leave. Griz stuck me by the dying fire.

"Gimme your wrist." He glared. "I'll fix the bandage."

Too tired to argue, I gave it to him. He re-wrapped the bandage as I shivered. Lana seemed to be ignoring me today. I wished I could do the same, but I didn't trust her. I kept an eye on her as she helped load up the rovers and nearly jumped out of my skin when someone draped a jacket across my shoulders. Trey didn't stop to see if I kept it, he just moved past and climbed into the rover to start it. I wanted to throw it at him, but I knew better than to give up the warmth out of spite. So I pulled it on, checking the pockets and scowling when I found them empty.

Too soon, Griz took me by the elbow and brought me back to the rover. I climbed in and found myself sandwiched between Griz and Trey again. I ignored them both.

"On your go, Alpha," a female voice I realized must be Raven crackled on the radio, and the rovers moved out.

Like the previous day, exhaustion pulled at my eyelids. I fought it as long as I could, but it wasn't long before I blinked, and the sun jumped to the middle of the sky. I squinted at the unending sea of trees, trying to get my bearings. My shivering had eased, and I was slouched over on—

Whatever momentary calm I'd woken with evaporated as I realized I was curled into Trey's side, my head on his shoulder. I jerked upright, but there was nowhere to go to get some space. Trey turned his head to look at me, but I just folded myself in half again despite the pain in my shoulder from the movement. I stayed that way for a long time, dozing until the rover slowed. I sat upright to see we'd driven up to a metal gate blocking the dirt road. Jax hopped out with a ring of keys, unlocking the gate and shoving it open. The rovers drove through, and Jax locked it behind us before clambering back in. We drove through three more gates like that, and I started feeling queasy. Wherever we were going was well protected, but I couldn't help feeling like they were locking us *in.*

We went steadily up, and the trees thinned a little. When we crested a ridge, I caught my first glimpse of the hold nestled in the trees and surrounded by high walls that looked like metal. A massive watchtower sat in the middle. My heart sank. I'd never seen a hold so well protected. It looked like a damn fortress.

"Home sweet home," Griz said.

"You ready?" Trey asked.

I stole a glance at him, but he was looking at Mac. Mac's gaze flashed to me in the rear mirror, and a muscle jumped in his jaw. My stomach sank at the tension filling the air. Whatever waited for us at the hold, it wasn't going to be good. I knew I should give Trey his jacket back, but I found myself clutching it tighter to my body like it might protect me.

"Let's do this," Mac replied, his voice tight.

Mac roared up to a metal gate that creaked open. I stole one last desperate glance at the woods before they disappeared behind the huge wall towering over us. The second rover followed close behind, and I heard the metal gate slam shut.

Buildings made of logs, wood, and metal filled the hold. People milled through what looked like a small marketplace. When the rovers drove up, most people stopped to look. A few people approached, an older tall woman leading the way. She had a leather belt over one shoulder that had two holstered pistols in the front and what looked like a giant knife holstered at her hip. Faded tattoos covered her wrinkled and weathered skin, and her grey dreads were pulled back by a scarf. Her eyes studied me, sharp as a hawk. No emotion shone in those eyes, just calculating judgment, and my stomach twisted at how much that look reminded me of Juck. Three men with impressive-looking guns stalked behind her. Most holds I'd encountered had some sort of council of leadership, but this show of force made this hold look more like the desert garrisons run by the violent warlords Juck often worked with.

The rovers came to a halt. Mac stepped out and approached the woman, tipping his head. Trey and Griz climbed down, Griz pulling me out with him. He hauled me a few steps away from the rover and then stopped, his grip tightening on my arm like a warning. Mac spoke to the woman in low tones, and she replied. I couldn't hear what they said, but the energy seemed to shift toward something ugly. I stared at my feet, waiting, and tried to prepare myself as best I could.

"Bring her," the woman finally called in a clear, cold voice that made me want to shiver.

Griz jerked me into motion. We filed up to the watchtower, passing through a fortified door. Guards watched us pass, holding automatic weapons that would've made Juck—

No. I gritted my teeth. I didn't have to waste my thoughts on him. Not anymore.

We went down a long circular flight of stone stairs that led to a dingy hallway. The woman and her guards entered a dim room with straw on the floor, but Griz and Trey stopped in the hallway. Mac took my arm from Griz, and the three of them exchanged a look heavy with significance. My heart stumbled into overdrive, but then Mac yanked me forward, leaving Trey and Griz in the hallway as the door swung shut.

The small room smelled of blood and vomit and fear, and my hands started trembling. A single chair stood in the center of the room covered with straps and buckles capable of holding someone down no matter how much they screamed and strained to get free.

"So, Mac," the woman said, smiling in a way that made my skin crawl, "you promised me your informant was trustworthy. You swore this trip would be worth the cost."

She paused, but Mac didn't say a word. I stole a glance at his face. He stared at the woman, standing rigidly like a soldier. An expressionless mask hid whatever emotions he felt, but as he gripped my arm, I could feel both our hearts racing.

"A quiet covert operation to retrieve Juck's secret weapon." Her sharp gaze swung to me, and I fought the urge to shrink back. "And what have you brought me? A fortune of gasoline gone, half our supply of ammunition used up in a rooftop firefight, one of my men dead, and a scrawny girl with 'magic healing powers?'" Her voice dripped with scorn.

"Bones could be a powerful asset," Mac said. "There's a reason Juck called her his 'secret weapon.'"

"How about a demonstration?" The woman clapped her hands together, her smile growing wide again.

My stomach lurched.

"You can give us a demonstration, right, Bones?" The calmness of Mac's tone clashed with the hardness in his eyes.

I knew it wasn't a question.

C'mon, Wolf growled in my head. *You're not helpless, dammit!*

"Yes," I got out in a hoarse whisper, fumbling to unwrap my bandaged hands.

The woman's smile showed all teeth now. She beckoned us forward, and Mac pulled me along with him. I dropped the bandages into the hay and prayed the queasy feeling in my gut wasn't showing on my face. The woman drew a wicked-looking knife from the holster on her belt and Mac released my arm. Two of her men stepped forward to grab Mac by the arms, holding him still, and my lungs turned to stone. I had a flash of memory back to the baking hot desert, the glint of Juck's pistol, and the smell of Grip's blood. The woman continued smiling ear to ear as she raised her arm and slashed Mac's stomach clean open.

Mac doubled over as much as he could with the men holding his arms. Blood stained his shirt red and ran down his pant legs. I blinked and for a moment it wasn't Mac standing there bleeding out in front of me. I moved forward in a panic, grabbing him as the men released his arms. I stumbled under his weight, but I managed to get him down on his back. His hands pressed against the wound, but the straw on the floor beneath him turned scarlet.

I ripped his shirt up and pulled his hands away from the wound, replacing them with my own. The hot, slippery mess of organs pulsed against my hands, threatening to spill out onto the dirty floor. Mac panted hard through his teeth, fear and death creeping into his wide eyes. My powers felt fainter than I hoped, but the comforting warmth swept down my arms and into Mac.

"It's ok. You're ok," I whispered to him.

His eyes locked on mine as the blood flow eased, and my powers wove his body back together. When only a fresh, pink scar remained, I let go. I wrapped my shaking arms around myself, noting Trey's jacket was now covered in Mac's blood.

The woman moved forward from where she'd been hovering near my elbow and ran her hand over the scar on Mac's stomach. Mac lay still on the floor, panting.

"Incredible," the woman murmured. "Does it hurt?"

Mac swallowed, his nostrils flaring. "Not anymore."

The woman turned to me, taking my face in her hands. A sugary scent washed over me as she leaned closer. It clashed with the sharp tang of blood. She tilted my head down, inspecting the scabbed gash on my head.

"You can't heal yourself?" she asked, suddenly soothing and calm like a mother talking to her child.

"No."

Mac pushed himself up to sit, and with the way the woman tilted my head, I could see his hands trembling. His body had healed, but my powers couldn't replace the blood he'd lost.

"Don't stand up too fast," I told him.

He gave me a nod but didn't say anything as he stood, swaying just a little bit, but he made it to the wall and leaned on it for support.

The woman still studied me, her eyes bright and calculating. "Could you do it again?" She stroked my hair as though I were a pet.

My panic spiked and I forced myself not to look at Mac. "I need… I need rest," I stammered. "I can only do it so much."

"How much?" she pushed.

"I…I don't know—"

The woman turned to one of her men, cutting me off.

"Sax, bring me Hojo."

The man gave a sharp nod and disappeared through the door. The woman let go of me and stood, pulling out a cloth and wiping Mac's blood from her knife. I climbed to my feet, brushing bloody straw from my pants. My mind balked at every scenario running through it, and I couldn't help glancing toward Mac. He still leaned on the wall, but he was standing. I had a strange flash of relief that at least she wasn't going to hurt Mac again and frowned, disgusted with myself.

Mac met my eyes, staring at me hard as though trying to communicate something, but before I could even begin to try and figure it out the sound of a metal door clanging open sounded in the distance. Someone started yelling in a hoarse, furious voice.

Sax returned, dragging a dirty, gaunt man with wild, ratted hair. He threw him into the chair and started buckling him in. The man thrashed and kicked, but Sax overpowered him. Bile rose in my throat, but I forced myself to swallow it down.

"Madame," Hojo barked, "you fuckin' bitch."

Madame smiled and stalked toward him. She angled the knife and set it against the man's arm bound to the chair. "We're gonna have some fun, you and I," she said, then she leaned in and whispered, "You shoulda killed me instead of him."

"I didn't—" Hojo started, but the words cut off in a scream.

I couldn't help the strangled noise that escaped through my teeth as she sliced into his arm. Hojo's scream grew louder as she moved the knife up toward his shoulder, cutting so deep I could see the white of his bone. Blood spilled down his arm and into the straw.

"It wasn't me!" he howled. "It wasn't me!"

Madame ignored him, turning those cold eyes back on me. "Go ahead, Bones."

Hojo sobbed and spat out every curse word in the book as I laid shaking hands on his bloody arm. The warmth remained, but using it ached like a sore muscle. The bleeding eased and the skin began to knit itself back together, slower than before, but still steady. Hojo's sobs quieted as I healed him, and I could feel him studying me. Madame hovered close again, watching. Finally, the wound closed. Madame bent over Hojo's arm, and I couldn't contain my gasp of horror as she sliced his arm open again. Hojo's scream made my ears ring.

"Again." Madame smiled.

I did it again. I had to choke back a sob when next she crushed Hojo's fingers in an iron clamp, but I healed those too. One of her men took an iron bar and smashed Hojo's leg until the bone broke. I healed that too, tears spilling from my eyes as Hojo screamed and cursed and spit. They tortured him for hours, and I healed him every time, the pain from doing so turning sharper. Madame spoke to him a few times, a mixture of taunting and questioning. I wanted to tell her if he knew anything, he would've spilled it all by now, but I kept my lips pressed tight together.

My power flowing through me started to feel like claws shredding me from the inside. Sweat stung my eyes, and when I swiped a sleeve across my running nose, it came back bloody. Mac watched me, his dark eyes glittering. I got the impression Madame was testing him as well as me, and I gritted my teeth, trying to make myself numb.

Madame slashed her knife through Hojo's neck, and I managed to heal the deadly wound before I stumbled and fell to my knees, vomiting bile into the bloody straw. My body shook as I heaved. Above me, Hojo sobbed.

"Get her up," I heard Madame say.

Somebody hauled me to my feet. The room spun. Madame said something but I couldn't focus on the words. A sharp stinging slap to my face made me gasp.

"Again," Madame ordered.

She plunged the knife into Hojo's chest. Hojo let out a pained wheeze. Madame pulled the knife back out and smiled at me.

"Or he dies."

I lurched forward and fumbled at the wound. Hojo's eyes closed, his face twisted in pain. I tried to find any remnant of my power inside me, but nothing remained but wisps of smoke. The room tilted, darkness creeping into the edges of my vision. I tried to focus on Hojo, tried to blink past the darkness, but then, nothing.

CHAPTER 3

M urmured words were exchanged over my head. I'd never felt so *drained.* I tried to open my eyes, but I couldn't seem to remember how.

Red silk fluttered across my vision. A warm wet cloth wiped my face. I heard the sound of water pouring and tried to turn my head to look. Pain spiked behind my eyes, and I groaned.

"Hush now," a soft voice said, "you're—"

But everything faded away again.

"I didn't want to," I whispered through chapped lips and chattering teeth. I had no idea what I was saying. Was this a dream?

"I know," a male voice said gently.

Fear sliced through me, and I managed to focus on a face framed in wavy brown hair. He smiled a little, but sorrow lingered in his gentle eyes.

"It's ok, you're safe," he murmured.

I furrowed my brow, staring at him. My brain waded through thick mud as I struggled to remember his name. Trey. His name was Trey. Gods, I felt like death. Was I dying? A fresh wave of chills rattled through me, and my breath caught in panic.

"What's wrong with me?" I managed to say through my chattering teeth.

"You have a high fever," Trey said and his mouth twisted in a worried frown.

His face swam in my vision for a second. "I don't get sick."

"Ever?" he asked, his eyebrows raised.

"Never." I grimaced. "It feels awful."

A grin crossed his face. "Yeah, it does, doesn't it?"

I licked my dry lips. Gods, I was so thirsty. As if he'd heard my thoughts, he grabbed a small wooden bowl of water. He slid one hand under my head and lifted it just enough so I could drink from the bowl that he brought to my lips.

"Maybe this has somethin' to do with your powers then," Trey muttered thoughtfully. "Mac said you healed until you passed out."

Hojo's screams filled my head along with Madame's cruel smile and my breath caught. My eyes welled up and overflowed. Trey glanced back at me as he set the bowl down and alarm flashed across his face.

"What's wrong?"

"I tortured him," I sobbed.

"No, Bones." Trey's hand wrapped around one of mine. His eyes met mine. "You healed him. Madame tortured him."

"I can't...I can't do it again. Please...please don't make me do it again."

"I'm so sorry," he said, soft and pained. "This is my fault."

"Why can't I just do good?" I choked out through the sobs. "I don't want to hurt people. I always hurt people. I'm never gonna do enough to make...make me *good*."

"Bones, you are good—"

"I'm not!" I interrupted. "I can't...I can't do enough. It's too much —"

Pain stabbed behind my eyes, and I squeezed them shut. My head swam as though I was spinning in circles.

A clattering noise. Voices.

"Is he dead?" I tried to ask, but I couldn't tell if I spoke or not. I needed to know, but I couldn't remember who—

Someone's hand rested on my forehead, and they gave a muttered curse. "She's still burning up."

Something ice-cold pressed against my face and I tried to jerk away, but it followed me.

"It's cold," I mumbled, my teeth chattering as I tried to raise my hand to push it away.

"I know," a voice said as a hand captured my wrist and pulled it back down, "but we gotta bring your fever down."

"I don't get sick," I tried to say, but the room spun faster and faster.

"It's alright, Bones," the voice said, "just try to sleep."

⟋⟍

"Clarity, I'm telling you, I could! I could get you out."

"Trey, stop," a soft, feminine voice spoke. "I can take care of myself."

"Clarity, you nearly *died*." Trey's voice sharpened. "I can't—"

"She's waking up."

I cracked my eyes open. Red silks draped across the window, swaying in the breeze. Trey's face appeared, his eyes wide and concerned.

"Bones?"

I parted my lips and they cracked.

"Water?" I croaked.

Another face appeared, and I stared at a beautiful girl about my age dressed in a skimpy red silk slip. She wore her curly black hair done up on top of her head in a pretty, delicate style. She held a bowl of water to my lips, and I gulped it. I'd never been so weak before. I tried to hold the bowl of water steady, but my hands shook so much water started sloshing over the sides. The girl, Clarity I guessed, covered my hands with hers, helping me hold it still.

"Easy," she said in a sweet, gentle voice. "Don't drink it too fast."

After I drank, I collapsed back onto the silken pillow, exhausted. Memories flashed through my mind, and it took all my control to keep my emotions in check. Madame had tortured that man. Just to see what I could do, how far she could push me. And I'd done everything she'd asked. I thought if I could escape Juck, I'd be free of that *evil*—

"Bones?" Trey's hands wrapped around one of mine.

I jerked away from his touch. He let go, guilt flashing across his face.

"Bones. It's ok. You're safe."

A raspy sarcastic laugh crawled out of my throat like a wheeze.

Safe? Safe didn't exist for me.

"You're safe," Trey said again, and I had to fight the urge to scream at him.

"Get out," I rasped, still refusing to meet his gaze.

He stood quietly for a moment. "I'm so sorry," he finally said, soft and pained, and the tone of his voice almost triggered a memory, but nothing came.

I glanced down at my hands to avoid looking into those deep brown wells of pleading emotion. I expected to see the blood and gore and vomit still staining my hands, but they'd been wiped clean. I wore a skimpy shirt with a plunging neckline that highlighted the brand on my chest in a way that made my skin crawl. My fingers twitched with the urge to cover the awful mark, and I twisted them together to keep from revealing that weakness.

"Bones?"

"Trey." Clarity came up behind him, touching his shoulder. "I think you should go."

"I'm not just leaving her here—"

"Just go wait outside, ok? We'll be down before the bell."

They stared at each other for a moment, conversing with only their eyes. Finally, Trey sighed and strode out of the room. Clarity approached, the side of the thin mattress dipping as she perched on the edge of the bed.

"That was a horrible thing Madame made you do," she said.

"Is he dead?" I mumbled.

She hesitated a moment, and I knew the answer before she gave it. "Yes."

I finally looked up. Her brown eyes looked like Trey's, but her skin was darker, more bronzed than tan. Up close I could see the healing bruises on her too-thin face and arms. I could guess where we were. I'd been in enough brothels to recognize this as one. I struggled to sit up, relieved when she didn't move to help me. I leaned back against the cool rough wall, my eyes drifting around her room without actually seeing it.

I couldn't get the sound of Hojo's screams out of my head. Juck had been endlessly cruel and tortured countless people, including me, but he'd never used me to torture anyone else. I closed my eyes, furious at myself for not seeing this possibility. Yes, he'd called me his secret weapon, but I'd never thought of myself as an actual weapon before. I'd never had my healing twisted and abused like that before.

One of the first things Juck ever told me was that if people knew what I could do they would hurt me and use me. My stomach churned. I fucking hated it when he was right.

Clarity cleared her throat delicately, and I came back to the red silk room with a pained start.

"Trey and Mac brought you here last night. You were unconscious. I cleaned you up as best I could."

I watched her eyes flicker to where the "J" burned into my chest, and my fingers twitched again with the urge to cover it up.

"I am not a healer," she continued. "You were not injured that I could see, but you were burning up with a fever. I wasn't sure what to do, but Trey and I stayed with you all night. We tried to cool you down with cold washcloths, and your fever finally broke this morning around dawn."

She paused and then reached out and placed a gentle hand over mine. "Are you ok?"

No. I wanted to say. *No, I was not ok.*

You gotta be stronger. You hear? Be stronger. Wolf's voice echoed in my head.

"I'll be fine," I lied, pulling my hand free.

Her eyes looked sad as though she could see everything I wasn't saying. "My name is Clarity. I don't blame you for not trusting us, but there *are* good people here." She paused. "Mac and Trey are good people."

I couldn't resist the sneer that crossed my face, but I stayed silent. After a moment of studying my face, she sighed.

"How do you feel then?" she asked, her voice brisker. "Does anything hurt?"

I paused. My entire body ached like I'd received a beating. That warm kernel of power in my chest felt small and weak. My hands still shook, and nausea turned my stomach, but I wasn't about to tell her any of that.

"I'll be fine," I repeated.

Clarity's eyes narrowed on my face, and I had to look away. Her eyes looked so similar to Trey's.

"Trey said you're to report to the clinic as soon as you're able. Would you like a bath before you go?"

A bath? I peered up at her in surprise, and she smiled.

"One of my johns gifted it to me. We don't have hot water, but you can get yourself clean."

"That'd be nice," I said.

I got to my feet and the room spun, but I managed to follow her into an adjoining room I hadn't noticed before. A large tub stood in the room on what looked like clawed feet. A crude pipe stuck out of the floor with a single spigot attached to it. She started the water and then pointed at a chipped ceramic tray beside the tub.

"There's soap here. Mist is our soapmaker and she's very talented. Mine is peppermint scented. There's a towel on the hook. Your clothes are here." She gestured at a drying rack in the corner, and I noticed, surprised, that my pants and flannel were both clean. "I couldn't salvage your shirt," she apologized. "But you can have the one you're wearing." She hesitated for a moment, studying me as I leaned on the door for support. "Do you need help?"

"I can do it," I said stiffly, hoping I told the truth.

"Ok," she said, but her brow furrowed. "I'll just be in my room. If you need something, just yell."

I managed to get myself undressed and into the tub. The ice-cold water soothed my aching body. I didn't mind the cold. I'd spent a decent amount of time at an oasis as Juck traded with warlords. I taught myself how to swim in the cold, clear waters and tried to pretend those precious calm moments weren't paid for in other people's blood.

The soap smelled amazing. I scrubbed my hair and entire body twice, wincing at the disgusting color the water turned. I worked quickly, unsure of how much time I had. When I climbed out, I felt better just being *clean*. I wrapped myself in the towel and hesitantly looked at my reflection in the small round mirror hanging on the wall. My face was thinner than I expected, and I grimaced at myself. My normal tan from the desert sun had faded to a sickly pale, all my freckles standing out against my skin. The angry red of the gash in my temple caught my attention, and I examined the thick scab before finally meeting my own gaze. My green eyes stared back at me, looking so damn *empty*.

I looked away from my eyes and down at the stitched-up gash on my shoulder. Trey's neat stitches were still in place and thank the gods it showed no sign of infection. I steeled myself and dropped the towel lower to reveal the brand on my chest.

It'd been over two weeks, but the sight of it still made my eyes burn with tears. My fingers traced the thick, reddened skin and a traitorous tear slid down my cheek. I tried to block them out, but I couldn't stop the horrible memories of being pinned to the ground, screaming and begging as Juck approached with the glowing red metal fencing twisted into a rough "J" shape. I would never forget the sound and the smell of the hot metal burning into my skin. Afterward, Juck had been overly attentive and gentle, like he wanted to earn back my forgiveness.

Up until I repeatedly stabbed a knife in his chest anyway.

I turned away from the mirror, swiping the tears from my face.

You can't change what's past, so move on, Wolf growled in my head.

My palms looked a lot better, only a few of the deeper slices remained scabbed, the rest nearly gone. The bruises on my arms and legs faded to an ugly yellow.

I pulled on my clothes, including Clarity's revealing shirt, but I put my flannel over top and buttoned it up to my chin. The worn shirt had a big gash in it from where the roofing had cut through me, but I could mend it. I finger-combed my wet hair and left it down to dry. The thick dark brown waves had grown long, reaching past my collarbone. It looked so shiny. I couldn't remember the last time I'd been able to fully wash my hair.

"Bones?"

I jumped at Clarity's voice.

"You doin' ok?"

I opened the door and left the bathing room instead of answering. She smiled at me, scanning my clean appearance.

"Here, I found you some new socks." She held out a pair of handmade knitted socks.

"What do I owe you?" I asked without taking them. Whatever she wanted in return for all of this, I just hoped I could pay it.

She looked surprised. "Nothing."

I narrowed my eyes, confused. "What?"

"You don't owe me anything, Bones," she said. "I was glad to help. Especially since you saved Trey's life."

I shifted, trying to make sense of it. Did she think she owed me since I saved Trey? Were we even now? I tried hard to avoid owing people anything.

"Ok." I took the socks.

"You think you can make it to the clinic ok?" she asked as I pulled on the socks and my worn boots.

I wasn't sure how far I'd have to go or what awaited me there, but I nodded. I knew I didn't have a choice. No matter how nicely phrased, I never got an actual choice.

ೲ

Clarity led me down the rickety stairs. I had to lean on the railing, but she took slow steps, most likely for my benefit. We passed numerous scantily dressed people. Most of them stared at me with bold curiosity. A few even smiled or winked, but behind their schooled expressions, their eyes looked about as empty as mine.

The main floor of the brothel dripped in garish luxury. Painted gold trinkets covered the walls and dusty fake plants filled the room. A few worn and stained plush rugs covered the creaky wood floor. Candles dripped wax onto every surface. More half-naked people lounged on faded couches.

"We don't open for another hour," Clarity murmured. "I'd let you stay longer, but I need to start getting ready."

"It's fine."

Clarity led the way outside where Trey leaned against the building, frowning down at his feet. His head jerked up when he heard us approach and he straightened, his eyes widening at the sight of me. My face warmed under his scrutiny, but then Clarity turned and startled me by grasping both my hands in hers.

"If you ever need anything, you know where to find me," she said, her voice low and serious.

I met her gaze and regretted it at the sight of the same gentleness I'd seen in Trey. She squeezed my hands and then let go. She turned to Trey and threw her arms around him in a tight hug that he returned. When she pulled away, she gave him a sweet smile.

"See you later, Trey. Glad you're back."

Trey's answering smile looked soft and sad. Clarity didn't linger, turning and hurrying back into the brothel. I glanced at Trey, curiosity pricking at me despite my best efforts. Were they lovers? He watched Clarity vanish and sighed as the door shut behind her before meeting my gaze.

"Are you ok?" he asked.

"I'll be fine," I repeated the lie shortly.

"You look nice."

I looked away and didn't respond. In the early morning light, the hold bustled with activity. A group of people, including several children who couldn't have been older than eight, passed by wielding shovels and crude axes. A few chickens darted through the dirt, chasing bugs and squawking. We were surrounded by ramshackle structures, and most of the people looked tired, hungry, and dirty. All the brothels I'd seen had been in the poor districts and that seemed to be true here too.

"Bones—" Trey started, but I cut him off.

"Where's the clinic?" I asked, swinging my gaze back to him.

He studied me and didn't respond.

"Trey," I snapped irritably. I was still weak and tired, and the air had warmed enough to make me sweat under my flannel. I didn't want to stand here any longer than I had to.

"It's on the other side of the hold," he said finally. "It's a long walk. You sure you can make it?"

I tried to choke down my annoyance. "I said I'll be fine."

Trey didn't look convinced, but thankfully he just led the way. I trailed behind him. It wasn't long before the whispers started, and I dropped my eyes to the heels of Trey's boots. I tried not to hear what they said, but I heard "magic" thrown out more than once. Word had spread fast. I wasn't used to so many people knowing what I could do. I'd spent the last twelve years trying to be invisible, and now all this attention on me felt borderline painful.

This was the largest hold I'd ever seen, and we hadn't walked far before my legs started feeling dangerously shaky. I forced myself to keep pace with Trey, stubbornly refusing to admit how difficult I found this trek. Sweat trickled down my back as my breathing grew heavier. Still, I kept my jaw clenched shut. Trey's silhouette in front of me seemed to sway. I could do this. I was fine. I just—

"Bones!"

I cracked my eyes open, confused to see Trey leaning over me.

"Hey, it's ok. You just passed out."

I ignored Trey's offered hand and hauled myself up to sit from where I'd been lying in the dirt. Several people had stopped to stare, and

I felt their gazes on me like unwanted hands.

"I'm fine," I said, trying to push myself up to my feet.

Trey grabbed my elbow, helping me up, but he didn't let go after I stood. I tried to jerk my arm free, but his grip tightened.

"Bones, you just *passed out*."

I hated the concern on his face.

"I'm *fine.*" I tried to yank my arm free again.

"I want to help. Will you let me help you?" he asked softer.

"I've had enough of your *help*," I snarled and this time when I jerked away, he let go.

I started trudging forward again, hoping I went the right way. I still felt sick and dizzy, but I kept going. My throat ached with thirst, and I wished I would have drunk more of the water Clarity had offered.

"Why didn't you just take me to the clinic last night?" I muttered.

Trey didn't answer for a moment, and I almost turned to make sure he followed. "We figured you'd feel more comfortable if Clarity got you cleaned up. Rather than me and Mac."

I didn't know what made me more uncomfortable, knowing I'd been vulnerable in their presence or knowing I believed they hadn't taken advantage.

Don't trust 'em, Wolf snarled. *You know better.*

I stumbled, and Trey caught my elbow again.

"I'm fi—" I started to mumble, but then I twisted and retched, barely missing his boots.

Trey held me up and snapped an order at someone. After I finished retching up the small bit of water and bile in my stomach, he ducked his shoulder under my arm and half-carried me over to a spot of shade. He sat me down and crouched in front of me, pressing his palm against my forehead.

"Shit, you're burning up again," he muttered. "I'm sorry, Bones, but we gotta take this off," he added, his fingers hesitating on the top button of my flannel.

"No." I gripped his wrist with my shaking hand.

"It's really not that noticeable, you know," Trey tried, his tone light.

"Don't say that," I mumbled, trying to focus as the world spun around me. "He'll make it bigger."

Trey's face darkened. "He's dead if he tries," he said in a voice quiet and hard as steel.

Red flashed across my vision. I panted through my teeth, my fingers slippery with blood. Juck's empty eyes stared at me as I pulled the knife out of his chest. The sickening squelch made my stomach turn.

"He's already dead," I said. "He's not tryin' anything anymore."

Trey pulled my arms out of the thick sleeves. I blinked, wondering when he'd gotten all the buttons undone.

"Bones?"

I opened my eyes. When did I close them? Trey stood over me, his brow furrowed in concern.

"Can you get on the horse?"

I squinted up at him, confused. Sure enough, behind him a horse snorted out a breath and tossed its head.

"You get on, and I'll pass her up to you," someone said.

I watched Trey pull himself easily up onto the horse's back, impressed with the graceful movement. Then strong hands seized my upper arms, pulling me to my feet, and I panicked, flailing.

"If you give me a bloody lip again, I will drop you on your skinny ass."

The hands turned me around and when I met Griz's eyes, a stupid part of me relaxed. Despite his gruff, annoyed tone, Griz crouched and gently swept an arm under my knees and lifted me up.

Somehow the two of them got me on the horse. I twisted a handful of its mane in my hands and clung to it as my head spun. The horse swung its head back, huffing curiously at my pants. Trey said something to Griz, but the words sounded jumbled. Then his arms closed around me, urging the horse forward. I tipped backward with the movement, thudding into Trey's chest. He wrapped one arm around my waist, holding me against him, and the warmth of his solid body behind me felt *nice*. My head rolled to the side, coming to a rest on his chin. I shouldn't be doing this, I knew, but I couldn't remember why. Maybe Wolf would be mad?

I promised myself I'd figure it out later as my eyes drifted shut.

⁊

"That's not what I fucking asked, Trey. Did you know?" A clipped, angry voice.

"Mac, listen godsdamnit. She tried to hide it. I barely got her to let me patch up her shoulder 'cause she didn't want us to see it."

I opened my eyes. I was lying on a mattress. A single electric bulb dangled from rickety rafters. My head throbbed, but adrenaline started shooting through me like a drug. I closed my eyes again before anyone noticed.

"You shoulda told me," Mac growled.

"Mac, I didn't—"

"You didn't what? You didn't think it was important to tell me Juck fuckin' *branded* her like an animal?"

"It wasn't my story to tell." Trey sounded angry. "I thought you of all people would understand that."

The silence crackled with emotion.

"He *branded* her?" someone else finally asked.

"Burned a big 'J' right into her chest," Griz growled.

"I doubt that's all he did," Trey said darkly.

"Fuckin bastard."

"I think he's dead."

"Good."

"You met him once, right?"

"Yeah me and Griz."

I couldn't tell who was speaking anymore, but I didn't dare open my eyes or move.

"Hated him from the moment I laid eyes on him. We didn't see her, though."

"Yeah, well, he woulda kept her hidden I bet."

"Didn't the Reapers deal in slaves?"

"Mostly." I recognized Mac's voice. "The slavers hired them to deliver people purchased by warlords. But they also scavenged and bartered anything worth something and you could hire them to do just about anything so long as you were willing to pay for it."

"Was it the Reapers who tracked down that woman who ran away from the warlord near Salt?"

"You mean hunted her down and tortured her before turning her over half-dead? Yeah. That was them."

I had to clamp down on the memories that suddenly surged through my mind. The sound of the woman's screams, me breaking down and begging Juck to stop, the beating I received for daring to question his decisions.

"What did Madame say?"

"That she's our responsibility."

"Oh great," someone said sarcastically.

I cracked my eyes open just enough so I could see who was talking, hating that I couldn't keep track.

"Another fucking test?" Griz frowned.

"It's my fault." Pain filled Trey's voice.

"Trey, don't," Mac said. "She's just pissed we actually delivered."

"What she did last night—" Trey started.

"I know," Mac cut him off.

"Mac, I can't—" Trey tried again.

"*I know*," Mac repeated even firmer, but he didn't sound angry.

"Gods, won't this be fun." Sam crossed his arms, frowning.

"Is she gonna die?" a young voice asked. "What'll Madame do to us if she dies?"

"Nah, Jax, she's not gonna die. I'm sure she just needs rest," Trey said.

"Lana's gonna lose her shit," Griz muttered.

"We need to set up a rotation," Mac said. "Trey, you—"

"I got it," Trey interrupted. "You can—"

I tried to be quiet as I shifted, my arm tingling from my position, but the floor underneath my mattress creaked loudly and all five of them stared at me.

"Welcome back," Trey said.

I pushed myself up with shaky arms, feeling far too vulnerable lying down. My head still pounded, but the rest of me did feel better. I scanned their faces, my stomach dropping as I noticed their eyes flicking to my chest. I glanced down, and my panic swelled at the sight of my shirt's low neckline displaying the brand on my chest.

"How you feeling?" Trey strode over and crouched next to the mattress. "And if you say you'll be fine one more time, I'm gonna give you a narc."

My heart leapt into my throat at the mention of the heavy drugs. I knew I didn't manage to contain the terror when Trey's eyes narrowed on my face, studying my expression.

"My head hurts," I said fast before he could ask any questions.

"Can I?" He reached out toward my forehead, and despite feeling uncomfortable I nodded. He pressed a large warm hand to my forehead and then let out a relieved sigh. "Fever's gone. You want some water?"

"Where's my flannel?" I whispered.

"Right here." He reached behind me, plucking my flannel shirt from the floor and handing it to me. "I'll get you some water."

I pulled my shirt on as fast as I could and buttoned it up to my chin without looking at the silent group standing at the table watching me. My skin crawled at the attention. When Trey came back with a chipped ceramic mug of water, I took it gratefully.

My gaze shot up when Mac moved forward to stand behind Trey, his arms crossed over his chest. I couldn't help glancing down to his stomach, the memory of the giant gash in his gut and the fear in his eyes racing through my mind.

"We gotta talk," Mac said.

"Come on, Jax." Griz steered the young boy outside with Sam following, leaving me alone with Trey and Mac.

Trey twisted to look up at Mac, but he didn't look confused, just resigned. I took a large gulp of water and tried to hide my anxiety.

"Madame would like to offer you a job here as healer for the Vault," Mac said, his hands clenching and unclenching at his sides.

I narrowed my eyes. "And if I decline?"

Something like discomfort flashed across his stoic face. "That's not an option."

I wasn't expecting anything else, but the heavy wave of hopeless dread washed over me again.

"You can stay here at the clinic," Mac continued after it became clear I wasn't gonna ask anything else. "There's a loft." He gestured up at a rickety ladder I hadn't noticed before. "Upstairs can be your lodging. You can have whatever's here left from the previous healer. Madame had a stash of narcs." He motioned toward a dingy safe that had been recently placed in the room judging by the absence of dust on it. "Trey and I have the key, so you can ask us to open the safe when you need one. Madame wants you under guard to make sure you're...cooperative."

I made a scornful noise under my breath and those sharp eyes narrowed on me.

"You've been officially added to my crew," he said bitterly, letting me know how he felt about *that* decision, "and yes, I expect you to be *cooperative*."

I bristled but managed to keep my mouth shut.

"You will replace Exo. You'll be under our protection and answer directly to me or Trey, but you will follow my rules. I don't tolerate any of my crew causing harm to each other or putting each other's safety in jeopardy."

I resisted the urge to look at the bite mark on Trey's arm.

"Madame will have—" he hesitated for the briefest moment, "—special projects for you from time to time. But if you follow orders, you can make a real place here."

After last night I knew what sort of "special projects" I'd be expected to do. I couldn't torture anyone like that again. I *couldn't*.

You'll do what you have to to survive, Wolf growled.

Angry tears burned my throat. A small part of me had hoped this would be different, and I hated myself for it. They may have treated me better, but nothing had really changed. I'd exchanged Juck for Madame, the Reapers for Mac's crew. With Juck I'd been forced to watch people I *could* save die, and here I'd be forced to heal people who'd probably *prefer* to die than experience endless torture. Gods, I would never be able to atone for anything. Why couldn't I just heal people without hurting them?

I knew I should keep my mouth shut, but my temper got the best of me.

"So that's what you two did, then?" I asked in an impudent tone I knew would not end well for me. "Followed orders? Just torture a few people here and there?"

Trey recoiled, but Mac's expression turned dark.

"Watch your mouth, Bones," Mac snarled.

He sounded so much like Wolf that I saw red. "Or what?" I snarled right back. "You'll tell Madame that I'm *uncooperative*?"

"Bones, we're trying to help you—" Trey tried to interject.

"I don't want your fucking help!" I leapt to my feet, my voice raising. "I never wanted it! I don't want to be a part of your fucking crew. I didn't ask for any of this!"

I raised my arm, preparing to hurl the empty ceramic mug at his head, but Mac darted between us and seized my arm. The cup shattered on the floor by our feet, and I gasped as Mac jerked me closer, his flinty eyes glittering.

"*We* are not trying to help you, *Trey* is trying to help you. I didn't ask for this either, but it's done, and I sure as hell am not gonna let you endanger any more of my crew with your attitude. You wanna be uncooperative? Fine by me. I'll give you up to Madame. She loves sending people to the whipping post."

"Madame or *you?*" I hissed, trying to wrench my arm free.

I thought I saw the hit I expected coming and flinched, but Trey grabbed his shoulder and yanked him away, whispering to him. Mac shrugged him off, still glaring at me, but he stayed back.

"Rations are handed out at dawn and dusk at the bells. You don't go anywhere without a guard, and if you even think about trying to get through the wall, Madame will make you wish you were dead. And then you'll have to answer to *me*." He gave me a final glare before he turned on his heel and slammed the door behind him.

In the silence, Trey let out a long sigh.

"I'll be outside if you need anything," he said before following Mac out the door.

I clenched my jaw hard to keep from screaming in frustration as angry tears pricked at my eyes. I wished I'd let Trey bleed out on that rooftop. I wished I'd let Mac bleed out in Madame's dungeon. Mostly I just wished Lana had shot me.

Survive, Wolf snarled.

I closed my eyes and took several deep breaths, trying to get my raging emotions back under control. It didn't work much, so I cleaned up the shattered mug at my feet and started stomping around the small clinic, taking stock of what supplies I had. Judging by how much dust and cobwebs covered everything, the clinic had been empty for a while. The few mismatched cabinets in the kitchen contained a random assortment of medical supplies like IV tubing, scissors, a worn stethoscope, tourniquets, needles, and neatly folded bandages. An ornate hutch held various tiny bottles labeled in spidery handwriting and a few ancient bottles of pills with faded print. The steel sink in the corner actually worked, with cold clear water gushing out when I turned the knob. A wood-burning stove stood in the other corner, and large pots to heat up water hung on the wall. A faded leather chair sat near the cabinet. It had a footrest and a headrest and as I stepped on the lever by the floor, I discovered it moved up and down too. I also found a notebook with notes about patients and procedures and recipes for various ointments and tinctures. Whoever had been the healer before me had put in a lot of work to keep the clinic neat and organized.

I eyed the small safe. I'd occasionally had narcs to use on the Reapers, but they were a luxury and a liability. Nine times out of ten, they were stolen and used recreationally unless Juck kept them locked up in his tent. I tried lifting the safe. It didn't budge. At least somebody would have a hard time getting it out of the clinic.

Three small windows in the loft let in some sunlight. I couldn't see anything but the sky, but I liked the natural light. I tried flipping the light switch near the door, peering up at the single-bulb head hanging from the ceiling. Nothing happened, but I knew the hold had power because there'd been lights on in the watchtower. I climbed up the loft ladder to find a less dirty square where the mattress must have been, a small dresser, empty except for a few spiders, and a wooden chair.

I stood in the middle of the loft, a lump in my throat. This could have been something special. I had my own clinic. I *could* do good here, but would it even count with all my "special projects?" I remembered the awe I felt the first time I healed, my childish excitement that I could ease suffering. It seemed so simple then, but instead I'd been forced to hide my power my whole life. Now I finally didn't have to hide, but I was...I was *torturing* people.

If my brother could see what I'd become, he would be horrified.

I shoved that rogue thought back into the dark depths of my mind where it belonged. All I could do was keep going, even as the thought filled me with a bone-weary exhaustion. I had to keep going. I had to keep trying to make up for all the blood on my hands, it was the only option, and it was my burden to bear. I would find a way out of here. In the meantime, I just had to play along.

I scared the shit out of Griz when I threw open the door, sweeping a cloud of dust outside. He peered inside coughing as I dumped out my bucket of dirty water, noting my progress at cleaning everything.

"Lookin' good," he said before returning to his chair, leaning it back to balance on two legs with a rifle resting on his knees.

I stared at the gun, my stomach turning. I wasn't sure if he had it to keep me *cooperative* or to keep other people away.

"You need anything?" he asked, and I noticed he was watching me study his gun.

"No," I snapped, stomping back inside to tackle the loft.

CHAPTER 4

I was working on banishing all the spiderwebs in the loft when
the door opened with a crash.

"Bones!" Griz called.

Adrenaline spiked through my body, and I clambered down the
ladder. Griz stood in the middle of the clinic with a man holding a young
boy in his arms. The boy's features were sunken and pale, and his chest
terribly still.

"He's been sick," the man said, his voice panicked. "Fever. But
now he won't wake up."

I moved before he even finished speaking, taking the boy from his
arms and laying him gently on the exam chair. I struggled to find his
pulse; it was so faint. He was burning up, his small body shutting down. I
glanced at Griz, unsure of the rules.

"Can I use my power?" I asked, hoping I sounded calm and not
near tears.

Griz looked at me like I'd grown two heads. "Yes—"

Relief surged through me, and I didn't wait to hear the rest. I laid
my hands on the little boy's shoulders and concentrated. That kernel of
warmth ached like a sore muscle, but it responded as I directed it into the
child's small body. I heard the man gasp as color flooded back into the
little boy's face. The warmth flowing through me eased and then
vanished, and the boy took a great shuddering breath and opened his

eyes.

"Dad?" he asked.

The man gathered him up in his arms in a tight embrace. I had to turn away, emotion threatening to undo me. The man thanked me, his voice shaking.

"Bring 'em sooner next time," I said, turning back around once I knew I wouldn't do something stupid like cry.

The man looked startled by my cold response, but he just nodded and promised he would before leaving with his child in his arms. I wiped the counter clean.

"Why'd you ask if you could use your power?" Griz asked, his voice curious. "Did Madame say something?"

I turned my back to him and started to rinse out the rag. "No."

"So why'd you ask?"

"I wasn't…I wasn't sure if it was allowed."

"What do you mean *allowed*?"

"Juck wouldn't let me use it on anyone but him," I muttered.

I didn't turn around so I couldn't see his expression, but he sounded angry when he growled, "That fucker."

I stayed facing the sink, bracing myself on the cool metal. As the adrenaline faded, the confusing swarm of relief and anger overwhelmed me. I'd been terrified I'd be forced to watch that boy die in front of me, knowing I *could* save him. Like I had time and time again. The fury at Mac and his crew for dragging me here remained, but I also couldn't deny the grateful tears pricking behind my eyelids.

"So you were just Juck's personal healer?" Griz asked.

"No. I was the healer for everyone," I muttered.

In the long pause, I waited for the question that came next.

"So what'd you do for the rest of 'em if you couldn't use your powers?" Griz finally asked.

Shame burned hot in my face. "As much as I could, like a regular healer, but mostly I just watched 'em die."

"Did they know you had powers?"

"No," I said, then amended, "not until a few weeks ago, anyway."

When Juck had brought me back to his gang and introduced me as the new healer, the startled outrage on everyone's faces wasn't unexpected. I *did* expect him to give them an explanation, but instead, he just walked away, pulling me with him. The angry murmurs followed us, and I didn't understand why he wasn't telling them that I wasn't just a kid, that I had healing powers. I was trying to gather the courage to ask when he dragged me into his tent and told me I could only use my healing powers on *him*.

"You're my lil' Angel," he had said softly, stroking my hair. "Don't tell anybody else what you can do. If they knew, they'd hurt you an' use you up, but I'll protect you, alright, Angel?"

He seemed kind at that moment, and I peered up at him, wondering if my earlier assessment of him had been wrong. He smiled as I met his eyes, but the coldness there made my skin prickle.

His hand stroking my hair seized a fistful, holding my head still in a painful grip that made me gasp. "You don't touch anyone 'less I say so. You hear me?"

I heard him loud and clear.

I wasn't sure why I kept talking, but I did. "One of Juck's men brought me any medical textbooks he could find, and I read them over and over until I memorized them. The rest I learned from experience." I took a deep breath and rubbed the dampness out of my eyes. "I need some supplies. Soap for starters. Some alcohol for sterilizing—"

I turned around as I listed, and faltered when I realized Trey stood next to Griz. I wasn't sure how much he heard. I looked away and forced myself to continue like I didn't care.

"Blankets, a flashlight if you have 'em, some cots, and a change of clothes."

Griz nodded but then glanced at Trey. I followed his gaze, feeling my stomach drop at the unease on Trey's face.

"Griz can work on getting those supplies," Trey said quietly. "But Madame wants to talk to you."

The hair on the back of my neck rose and I fought the urge to shudder. I tried to keep my face blank, but I inwardly panicked. I couldn't torture someone again. Gods, I *couldn't*.

Trey held something out to me. "Here. Found you a different shirt."

I took it, unfolding it to see a simple sleeveless black shirt with a high neckline. I turned my back to them and unbuttoned my flannel shirt, the cool air a relief on my sweaty skin, and pulled the new shirt over top of Clarity's thin tank top. It covered the brand on my chest perfectly. I didn't thank him as I turned back and followed him outside, but gratitude clogged my throat. I didn't want anyone to see the brand, but I especially didn't want Madame to see it. The less ammo she had against me the better.

"She just wants to ask you some questions this time," Trey said as we walked like he wanted to reassure me.

I didn't reply, focusing on steeling myself.

You can survive this, Wolf ordered in my head. *Do what you gotta do to survive.*

☙

Madame sat at a table, her fingers drumming on the surface. On her left sat a woman with a shaved head. Beside that woman sat Sax, the man who'd dragged Hojo out for Madame to play with last night. On Madame's right sat an older man with an ugly scar on his cheek. It looked like some creature had taken a large bite out of the side of his face. Next to the older man sat Mac. I avoided his gaze.

"Take a seat, Bones," Madame commanded. "We have some questions for you."

Trey strode up to the table and pulled out a wooden chair across from Madame. Reluctantly, I followed and sat. Trey stood behind my chair, hands clasped behind his back. I tried to ignore the panicky feeling of being trapped.

"Hello, Bones," the older man started, his voice warm. "I'm Nemo and over there is Zana. We're a part of Madame's council. Zana oversees the guards and law enforcement, and I oversee agriculture and manufacturing."

Based on the look on Madame's face, she either disliked Nemo or Zana or both. It surprised me to hear she had a council, especially after she'd met us at the gate with armed men like a warlord. She didn't seem like the type to share power.

"So you were Juck's healer."

It wasn't really a question, but I answered him anyway, "Yes."

"What happened to The Reapers?" Madame asked.

I swallowed hard. "There was a rebellion."

"No shit," Madame said. "I want to know why."

I hesitated, squeezing my hands together in my lap under the table. "Most of the Reapers didn't know about my powers. Juck only let me heal himself and the couple men who knew. One of his men was trying to stage a coup, so he told the Reapers about my powers, and they turned on Juck."

"Vulture tried to take over, didn't he?" Madame pressed and I had to force myself not to react that she knew his name.

"Yes."

Madame eyed me with that sharp gaze, and I fought the urge to shrink. "Were you fucking him?"

I tried to keep calm, but my palms were sweaty and my face hot.

"No," I lied.

She raised an eyebrow, not falling for it. "Were you fucking Juck?"

I clenched my fists so hard my nails bit into my palms. I tried to answer while at the same time trying to shove down a flood of horrible memories clawing their way up my throat.

"No." I finally got out, using all my energy to keep my expression blank.

"Is he dead?" Madame asked.

"Yes," I said, unable to keep a bitter sort of satisfaction out of my voice.

"What about Vulture?"

Vulture stared at me from where he lay sprawled on the floor, bleeding heavily.

"Bones—" he wheezed.

I dropped the bloody knife and it fell into the sand with a soft thud.

"Angel, you did it." Vulture grinned despite the bullet wound in his shoulder. "You killed the bastard."

I backed away, gulping in panicked gasps.

"Angel?" Vulture pulled himself up, his face twisted in pain. "It's ok, baby, you did it. He—"

I backed farther away toward the tent door and I saw the moment he realized I was leaving him there. I wasn't expecting the hurt on his face to look so raw and real, but it hardened into hatred.

I turned and ran from the tent into the dim light of evening. His furious yell followed me, but the screams and cries of the injured and dying swallowed the noise.

"I don't know," I admitted. "He was badly injured."

Madame tilted her head, her eyes sharp, and I dropped my eyes back down to the table.

"You didn't heal him?"

"No."

In the silence, they all considered me, the healer who left an injured man to die. I could feel the shame crawling up my neck, my stomach turning at the memory of my hands gripping the bloody handle of the knife in Juck's chest.

"How long were you in the Reapers?" Zana asked.

I chanced glancing at her. I would guess her age to be somewhere around thirty. Her nose was pierced with a crude silver ring, and her muscled arms were covered in tattoos. The front of her uniform had multiple sheaths of knives, and I didn't doubt she knew how to use them. Something about her reminded me of a few of the female Reapers, hardened and dangerous. I met her gaze to see her raise an eyebrow at me, and I quickly dropped my eyes again.

"My whole life." This lie fell more easily off my tongue. "I was born there."

"Parents?" Madame asked.

"Dead." Another lie.

"Siblings?"

"No." I didn't dare look at any of them, willing my lie to be steady and convincing.

"So why did Wrangler have you locked up in his safe?" Madame pressed.

I hesitated again, my stomach twisting. I didn't have to lie about this. "I don't know. They knew who I was. I guess…I guess one of the Reapers must've talked."

"Do we know who was coming to collect?" the old man asked Madame.

Madame frowned. "No."

"Wrangler doesn't know who took her," Mac spoke up for the first time, his voice flat. "They didn't know Exo. They'll figure it out eventually, but we have some time."

"Wrangler knows better than to make a move against me." Madame smiled, sending a shiver down my spine.

I tried not to panic as my mind whirled. Someone had been looking for me. It could've been a Reaper. Gods, I prayed it was a Reaper. I'd even prefer it to be Vulture coming for revenge. I couldn't begin to entertain the idea of it being someone else. Not without totally falling apart. Under the table, my hands twitched anxiously.

"If Vulture is alive, he'd be looking for me," I said, unable to keep my voice from shaking.

"The Reapers are broken," Zana inserted with a sneer, "even if it is Vulture, they've got maybe a dozen people left in one piece. I doubt he'd be a real threat."

Nemo watched me. I tried to school my expression into something neutral.

"There's always the possibility a Reaper used their knowledge of Bones' powers to join a different gang," he said. "The Voiceless were in the area. So were the Crows."

A shudder went down my spine. The Voiceless were a fanatic religious group who devoted themselves to the gods. The seven leaders had their lips stitched crudely shut with thick black thread so they could only speak to the gods or some shit. I'd had nightmares about their faces after first seeing them. They portrayed themselves as the saviors of the world, but I'd seen firsthand the horrible things they did to people in the name of the gods.

The Crows were a rival gang to the Reapers. Their leader, a woman named Seven, had hated Juck. If one of the Reapers had joined the Crows, Seven would be delighted to track me down and take me for herself just to spite Juck's ghost. Neither option would be good, but the Voiceless would definitely be worse.

"Are there more powered people?" Madame asked.

"Not that I've seen." *Just be calm. Breathe.*

"Was Juck looking for more?" she pushed.

"Yes."

"Is that why he was so far North?" Nemo asked.

"Yes," I said again.

Only me and Vulture knew the real reason Juck had been traveling farther and farther. He'd been chasing stories of miracles and unexplainable things, but that's all they'd ever turned out to be—just stories.

"You were born with this power?" Zana asked.

"As far as I know," I said.

"How did you figure it out?" Nemo sounded genuinely interested, but my stomach plummeted.

"I found an injured dog and when I picked it up, its wounds

healed." My voice shook, and I hoped no one noticed.

"Fascinating," Nemo murmured.

A short silence fell where I prayed no one would ask any more questions about my past.

"I assume Mac gave you all the details about your new job?" Madame asked as though I had any say in this.

I nodded.

"Good. Mac, have your informant keep an eye out for who comes looking," Madame added. "I want to stay ahead of this, you hear me?"

"Yes ma'am," Mac said.

"I want a round-the-clock guard on her," Madame added, staring at me. "We don't want our precious treasure to get lost."

I swallowed hard and stared at the table, but that must have been our dismissal because Trey grabbed my arm and pulled me up and out of the chair. Mac followed and the three of us left the room. Even in the hot sun, I still shivered. I let Trey tow me along by the arm, focused on trying to keep all the dark, awful things I kept pushed deep down in my memories from clawing their way out. Before I knew it, we arrived at the clinic. Trey released my arm and moved to whisper to Mac. I stood where he left me at the metal exam table, staring down at it without seeing it.

It couldn't have been him.

It couldn't.

I hadn't heard a whisper of him in a long time now. I was sure I'd shaken him off.

"Bones."

A sharp voice startled me, and I looked up to see Mac glaring at me. "Is there someone else looking for you?"

All the blood rushed out of my face. "I don't know."

Mac stalked around the table toward me, and I tried to hold my ground, but as he approached, I couldn't help taking a step back.

"I meant what I said before," he said in a dangerous voice. "I'm not risking any more of my people for you. So if I find out you're lying…"

His threat trailed off, but an icy numbness filled me.

"You'll what?" I asked, but my voice had none of its earlier bite. "Burn another letter into my skin?"

Horror flashed through his eyes. "No," he said harshly. "I'm not

Juck."

I turned away, staring at one of the windows in the loft. My throat ached trying to hold back the tears that begged for release. I couldn't figure out why they all kept acting so shocked at Juck's cruelty. As far as I'd seen, Juck acted the same as most people with any little bit of power. Madame sure as hell wasn't any different.

"Bones," Trey said, "it's not gonna be like that—"

"Get out," I interrupted, making my voice as harsh as possible. I did *not* want to cry in front of them, and I wasn't sure how much longer I could hold myself together.

Trey took a step toward me, but Mac grabbed his arm, halting him.

"Griz is outside if you need anything," Mac said, and then they left.

I climbed up to the loft and folded myself into the darkest corner. I wrapped my arms around my legs and let go of everything fighting to escape, crying as silently as possible until my head pounded.

Survive, Wolf growled.

Why? I wanted to scream at him. *What is the godsdammed point?*

CHAPTER 5

The bell rang, signaling dinner rations, but I didn't leave the clinic. I'd pulled the mattress back up to the loft. It hadn't been easy by myself, but I'd refused to ask for help. Jax had dropped off some worn but clean blankets, so I made up the bed. Under the mattress I slid an old rusty pair of scissors I found in the cabinet and felt better having a way to defend myself. I placed a candle next to the mattress and heard the door open.

"Bones?" Griz called. "You hear the bell? It's dinner time."

"I'm not hungry," I snapped at him from the loft.

He peered up at me, his brow furrowing. Then he just stepped back outside and shut the door. Relieved, I laid down on my mattress. I'd placed it against the wall but angled it so I could see the ladder. I figured I could probably pull the ladder up with me at night too, adding another layer of protection. I stared at the darkening sky out the window, lost in my thoughts. Then the door opened again.

"Bones?"

I scowled, recognizing Trey's voice. I sat up on the mattress, but I didn't answer. I heard him come in, shutting the door behind him.

"Bones? I brought dinner."

I let out a heavy sigh. "I'm not hungry," I repeated, my voice dull.

The single light bulb turned on, blinding me. I swore under my breath, squinting past the white spots in my vision and listening as Trey's footsteps crossed the room, and then the ladder shifted as he began to climb. I crossed my arms across my chest and waited. His head popped up a second later, all smiling brown eyes.

"Electricity turns on after dark. Can I come in?" he asked.

I debated telling him no, but I feared he'd just come in anyway. So I shrugged. He seemed to take that as a yes, and climbed up, holding two packs of something wrapped in tin foil.

"C'mon." He smiled as he crossed the small loft to sink onto the floor next to my mattress. "They had fresh butter today. You don't wanna miss that!"

A wave of nausea hit me at the mere mention of food. "I'm really not hungry."

He set the packets down, unwrapping them both and ignoring me. It looked like a thick slice of bread with some cooked meat and, as promised, butter.

"See I know you're lying 'cause you haven't had anything to eat since yesterday." He nudged one of the packets closer to me. "An' you're practically skin and—" He paused, his eyes flashing to my face in sudden realization. "—bones."

I glared at him, daring him to ask. He pressed his lips together, but the corners twitched up.

"Just a few bites," he wheedled, "c'mon, Bones."

"If I eat a few bites will you leave?" I snapped.

He grinned at that. "Yep."

I grabbed the bread and took a bite. I couldn't remember the last time I'd had butter, and the rich flavor that melted on my tongue tasted like heaven. I forced myself to take another bite before I lost my nerve. As I swallowed, Trey grinned at me like I'd just made his day.

"Good job!" he cheered.

I threw the rest of the bread at him. He caught it and took a big bite, still grinning.

"Now go away," I growled at him.

He shook his head, laughter dancing in those warm eyes. "I didn't say *when* I'd leave."

I glared at him.

"Don't tell me you'd rather sit up here by yourself." Trey grinned. "You'd miss my sparkling personality."

"Like I'd miss a hole in the head," I shot back at him.

He laughed and took another bite of my bread, apparently not at all bothered by me.

"You should try the deer steaks," he said between bites. "They're not bad."

"What happened to the last healer?" I asked instead.

Trey sobered. "Madame executed him after Viper, her partner, died."

I wasn't exactly surprised. "How'd Viper die?"

"He got real sick with a fever. Lotta people died."

It sounded like the same sickness that killed off so many of the Reapers a few months before everything went to shit. Juck had boasted about being untouchable, and only I knew he'd fallen ill, and I'd healed him. I'd spent many nights sobbing in the crude medical tent over sick folks gasping for air and begging their forgiveness after they breathed their last breath. Vulture had acted sorry for me, but I knew he'd just been calculating how to use me and the Reapers' deaths to fuel his takeover.

"She thinks Viper was poisoned. That…" He hesitated. "That man, Hojo? Madame got it in her head he was the one who carried it out."

I could practically hear my heart thudding heavily in my chest, shame twisting my lungs into knots.

"We've been without a healer since then," Trey continued. "Nobody wanted to volunteer after that."

I stared at a spot on the wall. I didn't blame 'em. I wasn't sure what was worse. Not having healing powers or having them and not being allowed to use them. Either way, you had to watch a lot of people die, and that stuck with you.

Trey's arm moved toward me, and I flinched out of habit. He jerked his hand back.

"I wasn't gonna hit you."

I shifted uncomfortably, avoiding his eyes and hating the heat creeping up my neck.

"Bones, I'm *never* gonna hit you." He sounded sad and it made me furious.

"Madame—" I started angrily, but he interrupted.

"What Madame did last night was fucking *evil,*" he said, his voice low and earnest. "I'm not gonna lie to you and say everyone here is a good person. But I won't ever lay a hand on you, I swear. Nobody in our crew will. Mac is real strict about that kinda shit. And if anybody messes with you, they'll deal with us."

I thought back to Mac grabbing my arm, the rage in his eyes, and how I thought he would hit me. *Sure. I'll believe that when I see it.*

After a beat, Trey sighed and sat back again. "What I was gonna say was, I don't think you'll have to worry about ending up like our old healer. He obviously couldn't do miracles like you."

I tried to swallow past the lump in my throat. My eyes burned. *Miracles.* No, I wasn't afraid of being sentenced to death. I was too valuable to be executed, and there were plenty of things worse than death. I learned that lesson while still a child.

"Seriously, you should try these steaks," Trey said again, his voice lighter.

"If I eat them, will you go away *immediately*?" I snapped.

"Deal," Trey said with a giant grin.

I rolled my eyes and took a bite, ignoring how my stomach churned. I managed to eat most of one of the steaks before I had to stop. I clenched my jaw and tried to convince myself I was fine.

"You ok?" Trey asked, looking up from his food.

I lurched to my feet and darted around him, sliding down the ladder. I barely made it outside before I hurled up everything I'd eaten into the dirt.

"Whoa," someone said. "What the fuck?"

The clinic door opened and slapped shut behind me.

"What's goin' on?"

"I dunno," Trey answered.

They gave me some space as I finally managed to stop heaving, to my relief. A handkerchief appeared and I took it without looking at who offered it, wiping my mouth. My face burned again. I hated looking weak like this. I straightened and forced myself to turn around to see Sam standing beside Trey. He was shorter but built the same, lean and wiry. His blond hair was buzzed close to his head and a short beard covered his jaw.

"You ok?" Trey asked again.

"Fine," I snapped.

"Yeah, looks like it," Sam said dryly. "I often puke my guts out when I'm fine."

I couldn't even muster the energy to glare at him. I tried to offer the handkerchief back, but Sam shook his head.

"Nah, you keep it."

I shoved it into my pocket and ducked my head, letting my hair shield my face, and tried to slide past them back to the clinic. Trey moved to block me.

"What's going on? Are you sick?" he asked.

"No."

Trey gave me a look of disbelief, and Sam's eyes narrowed. I desperately wished they'd let me just go back inside and leave me alone.

"I'm fine, I swear," I snapped.

"C'mon, Bones," Trey said more firmly, "what's going on?"

"Are you pregnant?" Sam asked.

"Gods, no." I couldn't contain the horror at the thought.

"So what's goin' on then, Shortcake?" Sam pushed.

I bit the inside of my cheek hard, refusing to react to the nickname. Trey gave Sam a look, raising an eyebrow, but he didn't comment either. Gods, I almost missed the Reapers. Sure they were all violent assholes, but at least none of them pestered me like this.

"It's nothing. This always happens when I haven't eaten for a long time. I'm fine."

Sam crossed his arms. "Whad'd'ya mean 'always'?"

"Gods, will you just let it go?" I snapped.

This time when I pushed past them, they let me, but they both followed me inside. I bit back a scream of frustration.

"Out with it, Shortcake," Sam threatened. "You're a part of this crew now, and we need to know why you're gettin' sick. Don't make me get Mac. He gets real pissy when we disrupt his beauty sleep."

I gave him an incredulous look. What the fuck? Why were they making me talk about this? Were they worried I wouldn't be able to do my job?

"I can heal just fine," I snapped. "It's not gonna affect my work, alright?"

Trey and Sam exchanged a look I didn't understand.

"We're not asking just 'cause of that," Trey said, studying me far too closely. "We're asking 'cause we want to make sure you're not sick."

"I already told you I'm not sick!" I cried, frustrated.

"So explain it then," Sam demanded.

I glared at them both. They weren't gonna let it go. I wrapped my arms around myself, ignoring the pain in my shoulder as the stitches stretched.

"Juck didn't let me eat when I pissed him off. It happened all the fucking time so it's not a big deal. I know how to deal with it. I just have to eat small amounts of bland shit for a while until my body adjusts and then I'll be *fine.*"

The silence crackled with tension.

"He starved you when he was mad?" Sam asked.

"It's not a big deal," I said again, feeling defensive.

"It *is* a big deal," Trey said, and I flinched at the anger in his voice. "How long would he make you go without food?"

"I dunno. It varied."

"But long enough that you get sick when you try to eat?"

"I can still work just fine."

"No, Bones! That's not what we're upset about." Trey let out a frustrated breath. "You never should have been treated like that."

My throat closed up. I didn't want to go down that path. Dwelling on it wouldn't change anything. I just had to keep going.

Survive, Wolf agreed.

"Nobody is gonna do that here," Sam said. "Not while you're in our crew. What kinda bland food do you need?"

I stared at them, anger creeping back over me. I did not fucking understand them at all. "So torture is fine, but starving somebody isn't?"

"No torture is *not* fine," Trey snapped.

"Trey," Sam warned.

They glared at each other for a moment before Trey heaved a frustrated sigh and turned back to me.

"What kinda bland food do you need?" he repeated Sam's question.

I stared at the two of them for a moment before giving up. "Broth is the best," I muttered.

"We can do that," Trey said.

"Yep. Gimme a few minutes," Sam said before slipping back out the door.

I didn't miss the warning look he gave Trey before he left though. I didn't need to know exactly what it meant to know that I did *not* want to be a part of it. Trey sighed again and scrubbed a hand over his face.

"Sorry I pushed you to eat too much," he said.

I stared at him, my thoughts tumbling all over each other. As horrible as being with Juck had been, at least I knew what to expect from him and the Reapers. I hated feeling so off-balance here, hated not knowing how to predict what would happen.

Trey opened his mouth to say something else, but the door burst open, startling us. Two giant men stumbled in, both of them bleeding everywhere and shouting drunkenly about it. I started moving, relieved at the familiarity of snarling at them to shut the fuck up and sit. I knew how to do this.

I didn't care for the details, but they wanted to tell me the whole story. A knife fight with a couple rusters, whatever that meant, broke out at a place called Mootzie's. The two men looked like they did some sort of hard labor, judging by their bulky muscles and numerous scars. The first one stood taller with thick stubble on his face and a tattoo near his left eye. He'd taken a knife to the side, but the gash wasn't too deep. The other had a large, bushy beard, and tattoos all up and down his muscled arms. He'd grabbed a blade with his bare hand and nearly sliced his fucking fingers off. I told the one with the gash on his side to put pressure on it while I dealt with his buddy's hand. It was a mess, sliced muscles and tendons and blood and dirt everywhere. I wrapped my hands around the wound, and they finally quieted as the warmth spread from my hands into his injured hand. They stared open-mouthed when I let go. The man opened and closed his hand. If I hadn't had my powers, he would have lost at least one finger, but instead, a long pink scar spanned his entire hand.

"Fucking hell," he slurred. "Blaze, look at this."

They peered at his hand and then up at me, their eyes wide.

"Fuck," Blaze agreed.

"Get off my chair so I can take care of your friend," I said.

"I'd let you take care of me any day, doc," he said, leaning forward and giving me a grin. "You wanna get a drink with me?"

"No," I snapped. "Now get off."

"I could get off—" he started, wiggling his eyebrows with a grin, but Trey cleared his throat. "Alright, alright, Mason." He slid off the chair, but before I could move, he grabbed my hand. "Name's Zip. If you change your mind about that drink, lemme know."

I jerked my hand free, turning to Blaze. "Alright, you're next."

Blaze's shallow wound only needed a few stitches, but he wasn't too pleased that he had to deal with a needle. As I gathered my supplies, I asked Trey in a low voice for a narc. He raised his eyebrows, looking confused, but he unlocked the safe and handed me one anyway. I prepped it and tucked it in the band of my pants where I could reach it fast.

"Why don't I get the magic?" Blaze growled, his eyes on the small needle in my hands.

"Because this is barely anything," I snapped at him, trying to move his arm out of the way. "Stop being such a baby."

"Fuck that!" Blaze bellowed, taking a swing at my head.

Trey moved, but I ducked, grabbing the narc and stabbing it into his meaty thigh with more force than necessary. He blinked down at it, his string of curses slurring as the drug hit him. When he toppled back into the chair with a heavy thud, I let out the breath I held. Trey had halted an arm's length away from me. I moved my glare to Zip who stood next to the table watching. He raised his hands and backed away.

"Do what you gotta do, Doc," he said.

They stayed silent as I stitched the wound closed with steady hands. After I got him bandaged, Zip lifted his unconscious buddy over his shoulder.

"Hope I see ya around, Doc," he said with a grin.

I didn't answer, turning to wash my hands in the ice-cold water.

"Why didn't you use magic?" Trey asked from where he stood by the table.

"I figured I should save it for emergencies," I muttered, exhaustion creeping into my bones. I'd never reached my limit before when I only healed Juck and sometimes Grip and Vulture. I didn't even know I had a limit. Now I did, and it'd be stupid not to conserve my power.

"Like when some idiot gets shot in the gut on a rooftop?"

I looked over at him as I shut off the water. He grinned at me, leaning on the table, his expression so open I could practically hear his invitation to tease him back. *C'mon, play with me.*

My heart clenched and I turned away as I started disinfecting my tools with a bottle of alcohol.

"Why'd he call you 'Mason'?" I asked.

"That's my surname," he answered.

"What's a ruster?"

"People who live in the slums."

The door opened again, and Sam entered. He held up a steaming tin mug.

"Here you go, Shortcake. Wasn't sure how much broth you wanted," he said. "I can get more if you want."

Shortcake. Well, the Reapers had called me much worse.

"Here, I'll finish cleaning up." Trey moved next to me, reaching for the tools in my hand.

I handed them over, feeling uncomfortable, and took the mug from Sam, sipping it while watching Trey tell Sam what just happened. When he got to the part where Blaze took a swing at me, Sam's face darkened.

"Sorry I wasn't here to help," he said.

Before I could say anything, Trey beat me to it. "She didn't need any help," he said, grinning at me. "She was prepped with a narc and knocked him out as soon as he tried to hit her."

Sam's face broke into a wide grin. "Atta girl."

I stared at them over the mug. Did they want something? Was that the reason they were being nice? None of this made any sense and I hated feeling on edge as I tried to figure it out.

"What do you want?" I asked sharply. "You think I'm gonna suck you off for this or something?"

They both looked at me with matching startled expressions.

"Gods, what?" Sam asked.

"What? No!" Trey said at the same time.

"I mean, not unless you want to," Sam added with a smirk that vanished with a grunt when Trey elbowed him, hard.

A part of me relaxed, but the anger remained. "Why are you doing this then? What the fuck do you want?"

"Doing what?" Sam asked, rubbing his side and glaring at Trey.

"All of this!" I shook the half-empty mug at them.

Sam's brows drew together as he stared at me, but pity filled Trey's face and it only made me angrier.

"Don't," I snapped before he could say anything. "I don't need your help."

"We know," Trey said, his eyes gentle. "Just 'cause you don't need help doesn't mean you gotta do everything by yourself."

"You're part of our crew now," Sam said.

My brow furrowed.

"We take care of our own," he added like *I* was the stupid one.

"I got one of your crew *killed.*"

"You didn't kill Exo," Trey said, even as sadness flashed through his eyes. "Exo disobeyed orders."

"Yeah, that's not on you." The pain in Sam's voice was clear, but he seemed to force a grin. "I mean, would I have preferred to avoid a fuckin' nighttime rooftop chase where I nearly fell through that damn tin roof and lost my favorite knife? Yes."

"All I know is you sure as hell didn't have to save my life, but you did it anyway." Trey's face was still serious.

"And all *I* know is you're one of us now. So you can quit the lone wolf bullshit." Sam crossed his arms, but he was still grinning.

I stared at them, clutching the mug. "There's no way you *all* feel like that."

Mac and Lana's angry faces flashed through my head. I hadn't seen Lana since we arrived at the hold, and I dreaded the next time we ran into each other.

They looked uncomfortable for the first time.

"Well, no." Trey allowed.

"Not everyone can be as smart as us," Sam smirked.

"But everyone is loyal to Mac. They'll follow orders even if they don't like it," Trey added.

I didn't believe that, but I didn't argue. I couldn't afford to believe it, no matter how good it sounded.

Don't let your guard down, Wolf agreed.

So I just sipped my broth and watched them argue over how to organize my tools. It wasn't long afterward that Griz came to take over. Trey and Sam cheerfully told me goodnight and Griz took up his spot outside the door. The sudden silence didn't feel quite as welcome as I thought it would.

I scowled at myself. *Get it the fuck together.*

I climbed up the ladder and with a lot of effort managed to pull it up into the loft with me. I straightened, panting but relieved. I toed off my boots and climbed under the blankets on my bed. The lumpy mattress was the most comfortable thing I'd slept on in a long time. The blankets smelled clean, like soap. I had an entire *house* all to myself. After twelve years of sleeping in tents, this felt almost luxurious. There was no sand in the bed or my hair, no danger of the wind whipping a pole out of the ground, and no other person whose presence was a constant threat. I didn't have to fall asleep terrified of what he might do in the middle of the night.

It was so close to what I'd pretended not to want for twelve years. It was so close to an actual home.

C'mon, you're smarter than that, Wolf snarled.

I know. I know.

Madame summoned me again two days later. I'd spent the past couple of days healing and organizing. Most people who walked into the clinic just needed a few stitches or some medicine. I could tell the people here had grown used to patching themselves up and that most continued to do so despite having a healer again. I didn't blame them for not trusting me. I used my downtime to sort through the previous healer's supplies. Sam brought me broth for every meal and my stomach slowly adjusted.

Griz and Sam were both inside the clinic, talking to each other as I tried hard to ignore them. They acted more like brothers than crew mates, constantly joking with each other. And gods, they were *loud.* When the door opened, I turned, and my heart sank at the sight of Mac. I hadn't seen him since Madame's interrogation, and I wasn't excited to see him now.

"Madame wants you," he said.

Griz and Sam went quiet as I put away the tools I'd been cleaning. I hoped they didn't notice how my hands had started trembling.

"Where's Trey?" Sam asked.

"In the bunkhouse," Mac responded.

I pretended not to notice the looks they were exchanging. There was some unspoken shit happening. I finished my work and turned back around, wiping my sweaty palms on my pants. Griz and Sam were both frowning, but they didn't say anything. Mac just glanced at me and strode out the door, expecting me to follow.

Mac led the way a few paces ahead of me. The closer we got to the watchtower, the more my hands shook, and I tried to steel myself. As soon as Mac opened the doors, we could hear the screams, and they only grew louder as we descended the stairs. My panicked urge to flee felt like it was choking me. If I turned around and moved quietly, Mac might not even notice—

As though he heard my frantic thoughts, he turned and stared at me, that muscle in his jaw ticking. I stopped in my tracks. When he strode up the stairs toward me, I panicked and retreated up a step, but he caught my forearm in a tight grip.

"What the fuck?" I seethed, yanking against his grip.

"You really gonna tell me you weren't thinkin' about running?" he said without even looking at me.

I clenched my jaw to keep my mouth shut, but I wasn't sure if I was holding back from cursing at him or begging him for help.

A middle-aged man sat restrained in the chair. Madame had already carved his arm up like she'd been too impatient to wait for me before starting. His screams echoed off the walls as he sobbed and swore he didn't know anything. Mac dragged me in and shut the door. Madame barely spared a glance at us, which made me feel even worse. She didn't seem worried that I would refuse to come.

I tucked myself into the corner, rubbing my arm where Mac had grabbed me. Mac leaned against the wall a few steps away, his face blank. The man in the chair screamed again, and I wished I would have run. What would Madame do if I refused to heal him?

Do what you gotta to survive, Wolf snarled.

Madame didn't ask that many questions. Mostly she repeated ones like *who do you report to?* And *where did you get that gun?* Questions I didn't quite understand and tried not to think about too much. I didn't want to be involved in whatever was happening at the Vault. I just wanted to keep my head down and get the fuck out of this place as soon as I could.

When Madame called me up to heal the man's many wounds, I hesitated, watching her face. Once she realized I hadn't moved, her cold gaze narrowed on me.

"Bones," she repeated in a dangerous voice, "you need some motivation?"

Several of her men chuckled, and my stomach dropped. I pushed off the wall and moved forward. The man stared at me with fear in his eyes as he sobbed. I wrapped my hands around his arm and called on my healing powers. He gasped as they began to flow into him, but I couldn't look at him.

You fucking coward. That wasn't Wolf's voice. That was mine.

Madame hovered behind me as I worked and again that sugary sweet smell drifted around me, mixing with the smell of blood and urine in a way that made my stomach turn. Her men prowled around the chair like wild animals. They watched Madame torture the man, eyes bright with excitement. After the third or fourth healing, two of them surrounded me as I tried to retreat to my corner.

"You know, I think I got something I need you to take a look at, Bones," one of them leered.

I tried to move past him, but the second one blocked me.

"Me too." He grinned, licking his lips. "Been hurtin' me so bad."

"C'mon, sweetheart, help me out." The first leaned over, grabbing my wrist and yanking me toward him.

I tried to jerk away, furious, but Mac appeared at my side and grabbed the man's arm. He didn't even say anything, he just stared him in the eyes with an expression that made goosebumps rise on my arms. The man sneered, but I could see the fear he tried to hide. He dropped my wrist, and I darted back to my corner.

"Calm down, Mac." He spit in the hay. "We're just havin' some fun."

"Not with her you're not," Mac said, his voice cold and hard.

The two of them muttered some more but retreated to where Madame was sawing off one of the man's fingers as he screamed.

I stared at the hay and tried to feel numb, to shove my mind out of my head and let it float away like I'd done so many times with Juck. Mac came back to lean on the wall, a lot closer to me than he'd been before, but I didn't look at him. The next time I stepped forward when Madame called me, he followed like a protective shadow. Madame's men glared at him and muttered to each other, but no one tried to grab me.

Madame eventually killed the man by slicing his throat and dismissed us. It didn't seem to matter how many people I'd seen killed because it still made my heart lurch into my throat when she struck that death blow. The man's body slumped in the chair, blood dripping onto the floor, and I stood there staring, my brain stuck on the stupid thought I didn't even know his name. Mac grabbed my elbow and started hauling me out, and I let him, my legs weak and shaky.

Once we got a safe distance from the watchtower, Mac stopped and turned to me. I kept my eyes down, trying to hide the fact they were brimming with tears, and attempted to calm my ragged breathing as I waited for whatever he wanted to say. But he didn't say anything. He stood there silently for so long that fear began creeping in. When I couldn't take it any longer, I finally peered up at him. In the dim light, I could tell he was looking at me, but I couldn't see his expression.

"You good?" he asked in a low voice.

I stared at him. *Good?!*

Fury brought me back to my senses. "Fuck you, Mac," I hissed at him before I wrenched my arm free from his grip and pushed past him, striding toward the clinic.

He didn't try to stop me, but I heard him follow me a few paces behind.

When I angrily threw the door open, I faltered on the threshold. Trey, Griz, and Sam were standing around the exam table. All of them turned toward me.

"Bones—" Trey's eyes were wide with concern as he moved forward.

I pushed past him, storming to the ladder.

"Bones?" he called after me, but I didn't stop.

I heard the door open and shut again as Mac followed me inside. I retreated to the corner where they couldn't see me and stripped out of my blood-covered clothes, throwing on Clarity's thin tank top and the extra pants Jax had brought over. I wished I had a sink up here so I could clean the blood out of my clothes without having to go back down where the four men spoke in low angry tones. I debated just letting the blood stain my clothes, but I didn't feel like seeing the reminder of what I'd done every time I got dressed.

Clenching my jaw, I grabbed my dirty clothes and went back down the ladder. Everyone stopped talking as soon as I did, and my cheeks heated, knowing the brand on my chest was visible. I tried my best to ignore them, going straight to the sink and dumping my clothes in. I turned the water on, lathered my hands with soap, and scrubbed viciously until my skin stung. Behind me, the four men resumed talking.

"He didn't know anything," Mac said.

"I knew that was a personal vendetta," Sam muttered.

"Keep an eye on Dale and Pike," Mac said. "They were real interested in Bones."

My spine stiffened, but I didn't turn around.

"What do you mean?" Trey asked.

"They tried to make a pass at her."

I bit back a furious scoff at Mac's phrasing.

"Bones, you ok?" Trey appeared at my elbow, and I flinched, anxiety still thrumming through me. "Sorry," he added, "I didn't mean to scare you."

I ignored him, moving on from my clothes to the blood streaked up my arms. He stood quietly beside me, watching me try to scrub my skin off my bones.

When Trey spoke again, the softness in his voice made my heart clench. "Bones, are you ok?"

"I'm fine," I lied through my teeth.

He frowned, but I looked away, checking my reflection in a metal pot to make sure I got all the blood off. I rinsed the rag out and draped it on the side of the sink before gathering up my wet clothes and pushing past him again to go back to the loft. No one tried to talk to me as I disappeared upstairs again. I draped my wet clothes on the single chair to dry and crawled onto my mattress, pulling my worn blanket over my head. The four of them stayed downstairs talking quietly for a long time as I lay curled in a ball, trying to forget the sound of the man's screams. Eventually, I heard Mac, Griz, and Trey say goodnight to Sam who had the night watch.

"Night, Shortcake," he called, but I didn't respond. When he flipped the single bulb off, it was a relief to be plunged into darkness.

CHAPTER 6

*T*he little girl looked about three years old. She clung to her mom, wailing as the slavers tried to rip her away. Her mom screamed, but none of the slavers even batted an eye. They finally got them pulled apart and the Reapers shoved the woman into the back of the truck. The screaming didn't stop though, and I desperately wanted to cover my ears.

Juck came striding back to his bike where I stood, a wide grin on his face and I knew he'd managed to barter a higher price.

"C'mon, Angel," he said cheerfully, swinging onto his bike. "Time to go."

I climbed on behind him and pressed one ear against his back, trying to muffle the screams a little. It didn't work. Even the overwhelming roar of all the bikes didn't drown her out, and the woman continued to wail. Normally they quieted after a while. This one didn't. Panic started building in my chest.

Just stop, I longed to plead. Stop before they hurt you. Please!

After a couple hours, Juck had enough. He raised an arm, signaling to the truck and my heart dropped.

"She's probably gonna stop soon." I couldn't help blurting out.

The whole procession came to a stop and Juck swung off the bike. He paused for a moment, staring at me.

"You questioning me, Angel?" he asked.

I swallowed hard and shook my head.

"Good. Then you can come watch." His eyes glittered.

I swung off the bike, feeling sick. Grip opened the back of the truck and the woman began screaming even louder as they hauled her out. Juck forced her mouth open and as he began to cut out her tongue with ruthless efficiency, he met my eyes and smiled. Blood gushed from her mouth and her cries became garbled noises and I twisted, retching into the sand—

I jerked upright. It took me a moment to orient myself and to register that Sam stood downstairs shouting my name.

"Bones!"

"I'm fine," I choked out.

"Put the ladder down right now." He sounded pissed.

I glanced at the ladder lying on the floor, and a sudden anxiety filled me. "Why?"

"Now, Bones!"

"I'm sorry if I was loud—"

"I swear to the gods if you don't put the ladder down right now—"

I threw off the blanket, wiping at my wet face, and slid the ladder back down. As soon as it hit the floor, I scrambled back to my mattress, pressing against the wall. Sam shot up the ladder, scanning the loft with narrowed eyes as he strode toward me, and I tried to brace myself.

"I'm sorry. It was just a nightmare," I said as fast as I could manage. "I'll be quieter—"

"Wait, what?" He stopped, his brow furrowing as he stared down at me.

"I'm sorry," I repeated, my voice wobbling.

Sam crouched where he stood so he could look me in the eye. "I'm not mad. I thought someone was up here hurting you."

I stared at him, embarrassment mixing with the anxiety and the lingering horror from my dream. "Oh."

"Gods, did you think I was mad 'cause you were too loud?"

I dropped my eyes, my face burning.

"You were screamin' at someone to stop." His voice had an edge to it.

My dream surged back to my mind, the memories of what followed trying to play out in my head. If only cutting out her tongue had been the worst thing Juck did to her. I covered my mouth with a shaking hand, willing myself not to be sick.

"Breathe in through your nose," he instructed. "Slowly."

I did, and bit by bit my stomach settled. In the dim light of the moon coming in the window, I couldn't see his expression, but he stayed put and didn't try to touch me.

"Just for the record, none of us are ever gonna be mad 'cause you woke up screaming, but we *are* gonna need to make sure you're alright."

"I said I was fine," I muttered.

"Yeah, you say that a lot," he retorted, and I saw the flash of his teeth as he grinned. "So far you haven't been fine even once."

We sat in silence for a while, and I tried to wrestle myself back under control so he would go away.

"You have nightmares a lot?"

I had them almost every night, but I shrugged.

"I dunno if anybody's told you, but Mac handpicked this crew. To join, we each had to swear to live by a certain code, knowin' that breaking the code meant exile or execution. Part of that code is not causing harm. Nobody in this crew is gonna hurt you."

I didn't know if that made me feel any better.

"Madame is a fucking bitch," he said, "but she lets the crew leaders govern their own people. That's how Mac carved out a place for us—a safe place. And you're in it, ok?"

I thought about Clarity and her bruises, Hojo's skeletal body, and the man who'd died screaming just a few hours ago. I wanted to ask Sam what about them, but I had no high ground to stand on. I'd stayed with Juck for twelve years while he hurt and killed people. Besides, I wasn't staying here, so I shouldn't even care.

"I'll let you get back to sleep," Sam said. "But can you leave the ladder down? I promise, no one is gonna get in here."

I gave a short nod and that seemed to satisfy him. He stood and headed to the ladder.

"Night, Shortcake," he called over his shoulder.

In the silent darkness, I laid back down and stared anxiously at the ladder until exhaustion pulled me under again.

৬৩

I spent the next several days in fear of the door opening, dreading Mac returning to summon me back to the watchtower, but the days continued to go by with no sign of him. More people started coming into the clinic, keeping me busy in a good way. Being able to freely heal people felt like a balm on my soul, but also left me confused. I hated Madame and everything that happened under the watchtower, but as I used my powers more a long-dormant part of me seemed to awaken and stretch, and it felt *good*. I tried to tell myself that I was quickly growing attached to the clinic because I'd never had my own space before, but it didn't change how I felt about the small wooden building.

Mac's crew confused me even more. I didn't know what to do with them, and they would not leave me alone or *stop fucking talking*. Trey, Griz, and Sam were almost always in the clinic getting in my way. They joked and teased and asked stupid questions and didn't seem to care when I refused to participate or snapped at them to get the fuck out and go bother someone else. They didn't act like guarding the clinic and keeping an eye on me was a job. Sometimes I had to remind myself Madame ordered them to be here. They were guards, not friends, no matter how friendly they acted.

Jax didn't come to the clinic often, and when he did he seemed to be delivering things. He stayed quiet around me, but I often heard him chattering at the others outside. Sam called him "the kid," "Trey Jr.," and "blondie." He didn't seem to mind the nicknames, except for "the kid." I often heard him shouting "I am fifteen! I'm not a kid!"

Sometimes I caught a glimpse of his sandy blond hair and my heart would leap before I remembered where I was.

I spotted Lana a few times from a distance, but I could still feel the scorching heat of her glare. Raven still hadn't said a word to me, but the woman could speak volumes with a single twitch of her eyebrow. She'd made it clear she disliked me, but I expected that. Neither of them had taken a guard shift yet, and I couldn't help wondering how they were given out. Did Mac assign shifts or did they volunteer? I glanced outside from where I was bandaging a man's leg in the clinic. I'd taken to leaving the door open due to the heat. As much as I was curious about how Mac distributed shifts, I wasn't about to encourage the two idiots currently challenging each other to see who could balance a stick on one finger the longest by asking.

"Cheater!" Trey yelled, the stick wobbling on his finger, but he laughed as he dodged the pinecones Sam tossed at him.

"What? I'm just tryin' to clean up Bones's yard." Sam caught me watching them and winked.

I flushed and looked back down at my work. This could not be more different from being with the Reapers. They hated me at first. They thought Juck had lost his damn mind making a ten-year-old kid the gang healer. On good days they just ignored me, but most of the time they were cruel. Once I got older, they got more friendly, but not in a nice way. Then Juck made it crystal clear no one, *no one,* was allowed to touch me and they went back to keeping their distance. Only two had been something like friends, and they both paid the price for it.

My heart clenched at the memory as I glanced back outside. Sam and Trey had abandoned the stick and circled each other, fists raised, but they were both grinning as they taunted each other. When they started throwing punches, my fingers stalled wrapping the bandage. They moved lightly on their feet, throwing jabs and spinning and ducking and laughing the whole time. It wasn't long before Trey had Sam in a headlock, a move I recognized from being trapped in it on the roof, and Sam tapped out. They broke apart grinning and wiping sweat from their faces.

The blacksmith I'd been bandaging cleared his throat, and I just about jumped out of my skin. My face flamed. I'd forgotten about him. He eyed me with a slight smile, clearly knowing why I'd gotten distracted.

"Sorry," I mumbled, tying off the bandage.

"S'alright," he said. "Mac's crew is one of the best Safeguards we've got."

"Safeguard?" I asked before I could rein in my damn curiosity and shut my mouth.

"Crews that go outside the hold and do reconnaissance or make trades," he explained. "We're pretty self-sustaining here, but we have to go on supply runs or make trades every so often. It's always dangerous when you're dealing with valuable resources. Sometimes they gotta fight off raiders."

I needed to know this information for my escape. That's why I asked. Not because I wanted to know anything about them. "How many Safeguard crews are there?"

"We're down to two now. Mac's crew and Hawk's crew. We had a third, but they went on a mission, and well, none of 'em came back."

The Reapers had often clashed with small crews. Usually over resources, but sometimes all it took was a stupid argument. Sometimes they attacked small crews just for fun or to blow off steam. The spaces between holds and garrisons were no man's land, ripe for anyone to control if they had the gun power and the stomach for it. Juck had both. The Reapers had ruled the desert for the past decade, partly thanks to me. Juck and his immortality were infamous. He could receive a fatal injury and come back in just hours for revenge. My stomach churned.

"Now that you're here, we won't have to make so many to get medicine or medical supplies," the man continued. "That's always been our biggest need. Once the snow falls, it's pretty impossible to get in and out of here so we gotta stock up for winter."

I tucked that bit of info away too. If I wanted to get out of here, I'd have to do it before winter or wait until the snow melted. I rattled off some instructions for how to keep his wound clean and he thanked me with a grin before heading out to chat with my guards. Trey and Sam had both stripped off their shirts and my eyes lingered on them. I'd seen countless bodies working as a healer, and you'd think I'd be immune to getting distracted by them. But I couldn't help admiring their wiry muscled bodies gleaming with sweat in the sunshine. They were both handsome, but my eyes kept straying to Trey. From this distance, I couldn't see the scar on Trey's stomach, but I knew it existed. I wondered if I ran my hands across his tanned skin, would I feel it beneath my fingertips?

I gave myself a firm mental shake and forced myself to get back to work.

ᘒᐤ

Almost two weeks passed before Trey came in one morning and told me we were taking a tour of the Vault. I frowned at him, trying to hide my anxiety. Trey hadn't given me any reasons to be afraid of him, but that sort of command made alarm bells start blaring in my head.

"I'm busy," I said.

"C'mon," he replied, "you need to know where everything is."

"I don't care."

"I got a couple horses all ready," he continued like I wasn't digging my heels in.

"I'm not going."

He sighed, his eyes pained. "Bones, please. Mac asked me to do this, and I really don't want to force you."

But I will if I have to. I heard the unspoken subtext. I glared at him for a few more seconds, debating making this into a big fight out of sheer stubbornness.

Choose your battles, Wolf barked in my head.

"Fine," I said through my teeth.

He let out a breath, his eyes brightening again. "Alright, let's go."

I followed him outside where two horses waited already saddled up. I paused nervously. I knew I'd ridden a horse with Trey when I first got here, but I'd been unconscious for most of it. I didn't have any experience with horses. Not many people had them in the desert. Finding enough food for them proved difficult and most people owned bikes. Scavenging parts for bikes didn't take much work, and thanks to the boiling sun, the solar panels that powered the engines stayed charged.

Trey noticed I'd stopped. "You comin'?"

I didn't move, hating to admit I didn't know what to do.

He turned and strode back over to me, his brow furrowed. "What's wrong?"

I swallowed my pride. "I don't know how to ride a horse."

Understanding dawned in his eyes and he smiled that gentle smile. "Oh! Well, I'll teach you. C'mere."

I followed him over, feeling more nervous as we got closer and I realized exactly how *big* the horses were.

"This one is Violet and this one is Marigold." He gestured to the two horses.

Violet was dark brown, and Marigold was a golden palomino. Marigold lowered her head and nudged Trey in a move that seemed affectionate.

"You're riding Violet. She's very gentle."

Violet swung her head toward me, and I stopped in my tracks.

"You're ok," Trey said. "She just wants to say hello. Here, hold your hand out, like this." He demonstrated reaching forward with one hand, offering the back of his palm to the horse who sniffed it.

He turned back toward me, reaching out to take my hand and tug me forward. I let him, but my heart pounded in my chest. I held my free hand out like he did, and the horse's whiskers tickled my skin as she sniffed me. I stared at those massive hooves and couldn't help picturing how they could crush a human foot or a skull. Once Violet stopped sniffing, Trey pulled me forward again, going alongside the horse to stop at her side.

"Hey Vi," Trey said in a calm, even voice as he stroked the horse's shoulder. He raised my hand he held and set it on the horse's warm side. "You try."

I stroked my hand down the horse's side. Her coat felt warm and soft under my fingers. Violet swung her head back again, staring at me and huffing at my shirt.

"Don't approach a horse from behind. I mean, Vi will be fine 'cause she's gentle, but some horses will feel threatened," Trey continued with a wry smile. "Trust me, it's a real good way to get kicked. Now that you've greeted the horse, you can mount up. This is called the horn." He reached up and grabbed the part of the saddle sticking up. "You hold onto this, put your foot here in the stirrup, and then push up and swing your other leg over." He demonstrated, moving with a practiced ease, and then smiled at me from on top of the horse. "To get off, you do the same thing, just in reverse." He swung one leg over, holding onto the horn and lowering himself down to the ground.

Violet ignored us and snagged a mouthful of grass.

"Your turn."

I had to stand on my tiptoes to reach the horn, but I managed. I got my boot in the stirrup, a little awkwardly, and then pulled myself up the way Trey had done. I wasn't as fluid as Trey, but I did it, a flutter of accomplishment coming to life in my chest.

"Nice." Trey grinned up at me. "Here I'll adjust the stirrups a little. Your legs are a bit shorter than mine."

I moved my feet so he could adjust the straps until I could reach both more easily. He slipped them back on my feet and then stood, surveying me.

"How do you feel?" he asked.

I wasn't sure exactly what he meant. "Fine?"

He chuckled. "Shoulda seen that one comin'." He grabbed the reins and handed them to me. "Hold these with one hand. Keep 'em loose. You don't need to worry too much about steering 'cause Violet will follow me, but all you do is move your hand with the reins in the direction you want her to go."

He moved over to Marigold and mounted, taking the reins and checking on me one more time. "When you want the horse to go, you just squeeze gently with your legs or tap with your heels. Don't kick 'em unless you want 'em to take off. To stop, you just pull back on the reins like this." He showed me. "Alright, ready?"

I wasn't sure, but I nodded anyway. He grinned and Marigold started out, Violet following along behind. Fluffy clouds filled the sky and the breeze was pleasantly chilly, carrying the sharp scent of pine trees with it. Birds sang in the trees and chickens clucked on the ground. Drops of dew coated the grass and made the ground sparkle in the sunlight. We took a left toward the main gate, and hope fluttered in my stomach for a moment. Were we going outside the hold?

"This is the main gate," Trey said, stopping in front of it. "There's only two. This one and a smaller one on the other side of the Vault."

A dozen armed guards watched us. Trey waved, greeted a few by name, and quickly got pulled into a conversation. My hope of going outside the wall died. I stayed quiet, eying the massive gate made from a giant sheet of dull grey metal like the walls. One person wouldn't be able to open that thing. There had to be some sort of pulley system or something. I wanted to look closer, but a few of the guards noted me studying the gate so I quickly glanced away toward the middle of the hold where the horrible watchtower loomed.

The watchtower was an enormous structure, looming over the entire hold from a small hill. It was made of concrete, and while weathered, it showed no signs of disrepair like some of the other buildings. I wondered what this place had been. The watchtower, the wall, and some of the other bigger buildings had clearly been built in the Before.

"What's a pretty girl like you doin' in a place like this?"

I startled and Violet startled with me, sidestepping. One of the guards had approached.

"Whoa, sorry." The man raised his hands in a gesture of surrender, chuckling.

He looked to be in his thirties, and while his expression was pleasant enough, his energy made me nervous. Something about his thin face reminded me of a weasel.

"Bones, right?" he finally asked when I didn't say anything. "I'm Lem."

I gave him a short nod, hoping that would satisfy him. He grinned, stepping forward and grabbing Violet's reins in a move that made me tense.

"How are you doin' this morning?" He rested his free hand on my knee.

I wanted him away from me, but I forced myself to unclench my jaw and speak as civilly as I could manage. "Fine."

"You ever want a fun night, you should join us at Hydro."

"No."

"I haven't even told you what it is yet!" he still spoke lightly, but his eyes darkened.

I pulled the reins to the side, hoping he would release Violet, but he didn't.

"I'm not interested," I said a little louder.

"I bet we could change your mind if—"

He cut off as Trey rode Marigold almost directly into him, forcing him to let go of Violet and jump backward, cursing.

"Oh sorry, Lem," Trey called out, but his expression was dark. "Didn't see you there."

Lem glared at him, straightening his jacket. "Watch where you're fuckin' goin', Trey."

"You meet Bones? You hear she officially belongs to Mac's crew?" Trey leaned forward on the saddle horn, and I couldn't see his face, but something like fear flashed through Lem's eyes as he glanced between me and Trey. "She's one of ours now, and we're keepin' a real close eye on her."

That sounded like a threat, but as Lem glowered and took a step back, I guessed it wasn't for me.

Trey reached out and tugged on Violet's reins. "Have a good one, Lem." He didn't let go of Violet, keeping her close beside Marigold as we moved away.

I didn't look back, but I could feel Lem's eyes on me and it made my skin crawl. I rubbed my knee, trying to erase the sensation of Lem's hand touching me.

"Sorry 'bout that."

I glanced up at him to see that muscle ticking in his jaw as he scanned me.

"Lem's a creep, but he shouldn't bother you again."

"Is everybody scared of Mac?" I asked before I could think better of it.

"Mac's given people a good reason to fear him if they cross him,"

Trey replied.

In the silence that followed, I mulled over what Trey had said to Lem, my temper growing the more I thought about it. I didn't *belong* to Mac. I remembered Sam saying Madame let the crew leaders govern their own people. Maybe that's what Sam meant when he said I was in Mac's safe place. Well fuck that. I wasn't a nice shiny trophy for them to display. I'd been that before, and I wasn't doing it again.

"We take care of our own."

"You're in the crew now, so if anybody messes with you, they'll deal with us.

I hated that tiny part of me that thought maybe they said that shit because they actually saw me as a person.

Don't trust 'em, Wolf snarled.

"This is—" Trey started, gesturing at a large building, but I couldn't keep my damn mouth shut.

"Mac doesn't *own* me," I snarled in a pretty good impression of Wolf.

Trey halted Marigold and looked at me with eyebrows raised. "What?"

"I'm not a fucking *possession*."

"I know?" Trey's brow furrowed. "Why—"

"What you said to that man," I snapped, hating that my voice wobbled. "I don't give a fuck what Mac thinks, but I don't—"

"Bones," Trey interrupted, looking exasperated, "that's not what I meant."

I pressed my lips together, glaring at him. He sighed and glanced around us as he shifted Marigold even closer to Violet so he could lower his voice.

"Look, the way things work here is…not ideal," he said, his eyes never leaving mine, "but Mac doesn't think you're a possession. You're a member of his crew, of *my* crew. An' we want people to know that 'cause it'll keep assholes like Lem from harassin' you."

I believed that's what *Trey* believed. I wasn't so sure about anyone else.

"We don't want our precious treasure to get lost." Madame's cruel voice ran through my head.

Gods, I was so fucking tired of being a *thing*.

"Bones."

I glanced up at Trey, trying to stuff down all the emotions clogging my throat. His eyes were serious, but he gave me a small crooked smile.

"I heard you tell Lem no. If somebody won't take no for an answer, you got me as backup, alright?"

That made my eyes burn with a confusing swell of emotions, and I had to duck my head, letting my hair fall forward and shield my face. Trey cleared his throat before continuing.

"As I was sayin', this is the garage where we keep the rovers and some other vehicles. We don't use 'em around the hold. They're still running on gasoline, so we gotta conserve it," Trey explained. "We use horsepower inside the walls."

Once I got myself under control I peered up at the big wooden building. Half of it seemed to be well-maintained and the other half falling apart. In one corner an entire fucking tree poked through the roof. It surprised me to hear they still used gasoline. Finding vehicles that ran on gas and still worked was rare. In the desert, everyone used solar power to avoid paying the outrageous cost of gasoline. The Reapers loved to raid for gasoline because the payout was huge.

Trey turned to go alongside the garage on a smaller dirt road. The horses' hooves kicked up a cloud of dust that coated the nearby evergreen trees and made my mouth taste like mud. As we went around the garage, another large building came into view. This one looked newer with walls of corrugated metal and a tin roof.

"That's the barracks." Trey gestured to several training fields where a group of people jogged. "This is where the guards train. The lower level guards sleep in the barracks, but the crews get their own smaller bunkhouse." He motioned toward the cluster of smaller buildings between the barracks and the garage. These were small old wooden cabins. A couple had boarded up windows, but Trey stopped in front of number four which looked neatly maintained with old glass windows still intact. "This one's ours. So if you ever need to find us, there's usually at least one of our crew in there."

As I glanced up at the cabin, Lana's face flashed in the window before she dropped the curtain back down. I looked away, my heart pounding.

Trey turned Marigold around and pointed at a cluster of trees in the distance. "The clinic is just behind those trees, so we're actually pretty close."

I realized I could see the corner of the clinic roof between the trees. My closeness to their bunkhouse brought me a tiny bit of comfort, which immediately made me irritated at myself.

Don't let your guard down, Wolf growled.

A handful of larger, nicer homes surrounded the watchtower. I assumed Madame lived in one of them, but I wondered who had the rest. Maybe the council members I'd been introduced to, Nemo and Zana? Madame's sneer floated through my mind.

"How long has there been a council?" I asked as we moved down the dirt road.

Trey looked surprised and then delighted that I asked a question, and I immediately regretted it.

"Not too long."

I didn't miss the way his voice lowered carefully or the way he brought Marigold closer to me and Violet again.

"There was a rebellion about twenty years ago, and the unrest from it never died. About five years ago, Madame announced the council to try an' make nice. She appointed Zana and the people elected Nemo."

I wanted to ask more questions, but I pressed my lips together. If the council was a compromise, it seemed reasonable to assume they didn't have a ton of power. I just needed to get a feel for the hierarchy here. I didn't need all the details.

Trey waited for a moment, looking disappointed when I stayed silent, then urged Marigold to continue.

We moved South and Trey showed me the horse stables, the farm, the fields, and the small pens of livestock. Pigs and goats and several cows milled about in pens. Chickens roamed free everywhere. In the fields, people harvested the crops, a working tractor made hay bales, and fruit trees grew everywhere. There were mostly apple trees, but some pear, plum, and cherry trees as well. More people worked harvesting the fruit and packing it into crates.

It took us over an hour to reach the far south end of the hold. There we found the manufacturing district, a giant old warehouse housing a variety of ancient machinery as well as the butcher and the tannery. I knew before Trey pointed it out that we had to be near the slums. The wide dirt road changed to a narrow footpath choked with weeds. Trash and debris littered the ground. I understood why they were called rusters, as most of the ramshackle huts were made from rusted sheets of metal. A dirty child stood in front of one, coughing as she watched us pass.

I didn't miss the way Trey's expression darkened when we rode past the brothel.

I caught a glimpse of the second gate that led out of the Vault and my heart sank. It seemed to be permanently closed. I couldn't be sure from this distance, but it looked like it had been boarded shut.

"Last count we took, there were three hundred and seven people here," Trey said as he urged Marigold on. "We don't get many people coming from outside. Most of the people here have been here for generations."

"What was this place?" I asked, glancing up at the watchtower again.

"Best we can guess it was built to be some kind of shelter for the end of the world. I don't think they ever made it here though. It was just sitting here empty for gods know how long before the founding members stumbled on it. Whoever it was, they built the bigger buildings, some of the houses, the wall, and planted all the fruit trees."

I glanced up at the apple tree we rode under. Small red apples weighed down the branches. Trey reached up and plucked one off the tree and then held it out to me with a grin. I took it from him and watched as he grabbed another, wiped the dust off with his sleeve, and then took a bite. I copied him and took a cautious bite. It tasted sweet and tangy.

Trey finished his apple, tossing the core to a group of chickens. I nibbled mine slowly, still nervous about being sick, but my stomach stayed calm. I'd been eating more solid food due to Sam's pestering, and so far I hadn't been sick. I never would've guessed from looking at him that Sam would be such a mother hen.

"Seems like your stomach is adjusting," Trey said.

"Yeah."

"That's good." He sure sounded genuine.

I didn't know what to say, so I just bit into my apple again.

We passed a series of solar panels hooked up to a massive generator. The panels looked old, but well cared for, and Trey continued, "The builders also set up the solar power generator and all the plumbing. Originally there were workin' toilets and everything, but the pipes were so eroded the founders decided to let them be and put in the outhouses. All the original buildings have water and electricity though, like the clinic. We keep the power turned off in most buildings during the day so we don't drain the generator. Yours should be on all the time now, though. Me and Mac convinced Madame you would need good lighting to work." He flashed me an easy grin.

We rode past a water spigot that a line of people stood at, waiting to fill up jugs and bottles. I'd seen a couple spigots scattered around. Most of the people waiting looked like they'd come from the slums, which made sense. I doubted they had any plumbing or electricity in those shacks.

I *was* surprised, however, to see Nemo walking toward the spigot carrying two large plastic jugs.

"Well howdy, Trey, Bones," he said with a kind smile, and I tried not to stare at the awful scar on the side of his face. "What are you two up to?"

"Just givin' Bones a tour of the Vault," Trey said with an answering smile, then he looked at the jugs in Nemo's hands. "Your water go out?"

"No." Nemo set one of the jugs down to lift his hat and run a hand through his greying hair. "I'm just helpin' some folks out who have trouble carryin' these jugs." He chuckled. "Old age comes for us all."

Trey smiled back and asked him about the harvest, and I took the opportunity to study Nemo. I couldn't guess his age from just looking at him. He could've been in his late forties or early sixties. The scar didn't help. My eyes traced the puckered, rough flesh, wondering how it happened. It really did look like an animal took a bite out of the side of his face. He had weathered skin, but his dark blue eyes were clear and full of a similar warmth to Trey's. He stood about as tall as Trey and lean and wiry. He met my eyes, and I flushed at being caught staring, but he just smiled.

"Well I better get a move on," he said, lifting the empty jug again. "You two have a nice day, now."

As we rode away, I realized I'd seen Nemo a few times now doing more manual labor than I'd expected a member of the council to be doing. I sure as hell had never seen Madame or Zana out working. I wondered if Nemo knew what Madame did down in that dungeon room. Feeling nauseous, I tossed my apple and tried to focus on Trey again.

A small market was set up on the East side of the hold, and next to that sat a huge, long building Trey identified as the kitchens and canteen. A series of small workshops billowed smoke from their chimneys to the North. I noticed the blacksmith I'd bandaged a few days ago. He glanced up from his work, smiled, and waved, which Trey returned and I pretended not to see.

I realized with relief we'd made a full circle and the clinic appeared again. Noon had passed, and I desperately wanted to be done interacting with people. When we arrived, Sam and Jax were kicking an old faded ball around outside. I dismounted, my legs aching, as Trey greeted them. I tried to slip past them unnoticed to go inside, but of course, all three of them followed me in, Trey and Sam talking loudly.

"You show Bones where everything is?" Sam asked.

"Yep," Trey responded.

"*Everything?*" Sam asked.

Trey rolled his eyes. "Alright, no, I did not show her the place where you shot that cougar."

"Why not?" Sam asked, outraged. "It's an important part of the hold history!"

"You were piss drunk and you got off a lucky shot," Trey retorted.

"I saved the whole fuckin' hold from that cougar." Sam glared at him. "Bravely risked my life and limbs. And this is the thanks I get. Can you believe this bullshit, Jax?"

Jax rolled his eyes in an exact imitation of Trey, and Sam pounced on him, wrestling him into a headlock while they both yelled and Trey laughed.

I opened a cabinet to hide the smile I was fighting.

CHAPTER 7

I must have gotten kinda used to all the noise because the next morning I woke up and the silence made me uneasy. I went down the ladder and peered out the front door, but no one sat in the chair in front of the clinic. I squinted into the morning sunlight, but I couldn't see any sign of Mac's crew. Anxiety prickled my skin and I shut the door and busied myself getting ready for the day. Maybe Madame had decided I didn't need a full-time guard anymore.

This is a good thing. The sooner they trust you, the sooner you can try to get the fuck out of here.

My stomach growled. Sam hadn't brought my broth. The morning bells had rung a while ago, and I didn't feel like braving the canteen by myself. So I forced myself to ignore my hunger and sat to continue reading the previous healer's notebook. I hadn't gotten very far when the door opened. I looked up to see a man slip inside. He turned toward me and I froze at the sight of one of Madame's guards who'd "made a pass at me," as Mac put it. I caught a glimpse of the other one standing outside as though guarding the door. My stomach twisted in fear. I could wager a guess at what came next.

"Can I help you?" I asked, setting the notebook on the counter.

The man gave me a grin that made my skin crawl and raked his gaze up and down my body. "Oh, I think you can, baby."

Fuck.

I forced myself to stay where I stood, watching him. The eager anticipation in his eyes made me want to be sick. Finally, he started prowling closer. When he got a little further from the door, I lunged around the exam table, trying to get to the exit. He moved quick as a snake, snagging me around the arm and shoving me against the wall, hot foul breath in my face and hands groping my chest. I got an arm free and swung at his face with my whole body. The meaty part of my fist connected with his nose hard, just like Wolf had taught me, and I heard the audible *crack*. He hissed in rage and pain and stumbled back. I tried to dart around him, but he tackled me to the floor, blood still spurting from his nose.

"You bitch," he snarled.

I kicked him *hard* in the groin, and he swore as he crumpled. I scrambled across the floor, managing to get to my feet again.

I made it just a few steps from the door when it opened, and his buddy darted in like he'd heard the commotion. I changed directions, trying to get to the loft ladder, but the second man tackled me to the floor. I twisted, managing to rake my fingernails down his face, leaving bloody lines, and he jerked his head back swearing. I tried to scurry out from under him, but he lunged, putting his full weight on my legs, and caught my hands, pinning them to the floor.

"You like it rough, huh?" he said, grinning down at me even as blood welled up from the scratches I'd given him. "I thought so."

"Get off me!" I hissed, bucking my hips, but I couldn't move his bulk.

"I think that bitch broke my nose," the first asshole said from where he'd finally managed to stop moaning about his balls.

"Quit whining, Dale," the one on top of me said. He stared down at me and grinned again. "It's no fun if they don't fight."

Bile rose in my throat. I strained to get away, breathing hard, but he didn't move.

"I think we're gonna have some fun," he said, his eyes glinting.

Dale appeared beside us, glaring down at me. "Careful where you stick your dick in this one, Pike. She might bite it off."

I snarled at them. Panic started to take hold of me, even as I tried hard to fight it.

"S' alright, Bones. I like my women wild," Pike said. He peered up at Dale. "Hold her arms."

I tried to fight, but Dale pinned my arms down. Panic made me struggle for each breath now, desperate and furious tears welling up in my eyes. Pike leaned down, his foul breath hot on my face.

"Don't worry, baby." The victory in his eyes made mine overflow. "I can make you feel real good."

His mouth slammed down on mine, and I squirmed, desperately trying to turn my head. He kissed me roughly, one hand sliding up my shirt, and for a moment I was back in the desert, sobbing and begging as Juck pinned me down.

I managed to catch his lip in my teeth, and I bit down as hard as I could. He yelled and the foul taste of his blood filled my mouth. When he pulled back, I was viciously pleased to see I'd ripped his whole fucking lip. I spit a mouthful of blood at him.

"Told you she was a biter," Dale sneered.

I barely had time to gasp in a breath before Pike's fist connected with my face. My head snapped to the side, the pain blinding me. He hit me again and I tried to move my arms up to shield my head, forgetting Dale had them pinned. His next blow connected with the healing gash on my temple and the pain burst through my head like a flare. When I finally focused on the room again, Pike had his pants undone and was fumbling with mine. He grinned as I struggled to stay conscious. I blinked and Juck's face leered down at me again.

No! Gods...

Somebody tackled him off me and they went rolling like fighting cats. A roar of noise deafened me, and I tried to focus on the blur of movement, but everything went dark.

ᘒ

Pain jerked me back. A body was leaning over me, something pressed against my head.

I panicked, flailing. I tried to sit up, but someone's hands pinned my shoulders to the floor. I gasped in a frantic breath and started kicking.

"Bones! Bones, it's Mac!"

I froze, blinking up at him. It wasn't Dale or Pike. Mac crouched over me and his eyes glinted.

"You're safe. Stay down. You're hurt," he said, his voice sharp as cut glass.

I shoved his hands off me and got up on my elbows again before he even finished speaking, my eyes darting around the room. Pain stabbed through my head, but I didn't see the men anywhere. I glanced down at my legs, relief making me even dizzier that my pants were still on.

Mac reached for me again, but I scrambled away, getting to my feet and staggering back to lean against the wall as the room spun. He got to his feet and stepped toward me, but then stopped and stood still, fists clenched at his sides, and a terrifying glare on his face.

"I'm not gonna hurt you, Bones," he said. "That gash in your head split open again." He held up a bloodied cloth he must have been pressing against my head. "You should sit."

I could not fucking sit right now. All my instincts screamed at me that I needed to be on my feet, I needed to be able to run if necessary. I took deep breaths, trying to get past the dizziness, but I kept smelling that foul breath, kept feeling their hands on me, kept seeing Juck's face. My head hurt like hell. I touched the side of my head underneath the gash and sure enough, my trembling fingers came away bloody.

"You want a narc?" Mac asked his voice quiet steel.

"No!" I snapped, far too quickly.

I finally met his gaze to see him looking at me with one eyebrow raised. I swallowed my pride, panic roaring through my veins.

"Please, Mac, no drugs."

He stared at me for a long time, but finally, he just nodded.

"Alright. No drugs." He took slow steps toward me and held out the bloodied cloth. "Put some pressure on that. Looks like it's gonna need stitches this time."

I took the cloth and pressed it to my head as the room continued to spin. "I can do it."

He looked me in the eyes, so close I could see the ring of golden sparks around his pupil. "Thought you said you couldn't heal yourself."

"I can't," I tried to snap, but my voice shook, "but I can give myself a couple damn stitches just fine."

His gaze narrowed into a glare, but before he could speak, the door crashed open. I jumped and Mac spun on his heel, his hand on his gun. Then he dropped his hand back down with a scowl.

"Dammit, Trey, I almost shot you."

Trey didn't even pause, barreling his way over to me in a determined fury. I retreated a few steps, my body acting on instinct, and he immediately stopped, scanning me. His mouth pressed in a tight line and his eyes hardened.

"I shoulda killed 'em," he said in a low, harsh voice.

"Lana?" Mac asked.

"With Griz by the gate." Trey met his gaze.

Mac nodded. "I'll deal with it."

"Lana?" I asked as Mac slammed the door on his way out.

Trey studied my battered face, but he didn't meet my eyes. "She volunteered for guard duty."

I read between the lines, my stomach dropping.

"I'm sorry," Trey said, his voice rough. "She said she wanted to make things right. I thought I could trust her."

Clearly, you've never lost a brother, I wanted to say, but I didn't.

"What'll happen to her?" I asked, remembering what Sam had said about their code.

"If she's lucky, exile."

I didn't care what happened to Lana, but I couldn't help the dredge of memories his words brought up. Lucky? Exile was far from merciful. I started shuffling toward my supplies, trying to ignore the way the room tilted.

"The fuck are you doing?" Trey demanded. He stepped forward but then paused again.

"Gonna stitch up my head," I muttered.

I made it one more step before he blocked the way, but he didn't touch me.

"Sit your ass down," he said, pointing at the chair.

"I can—"

"Please, Bones." His voice cracked with emotion. "Please let me do it."

The sharp pain in his voice killed any fight I had left.

"Fine." I got myself up on the chair.

He went to the sink, scrubbing his hands, before gathering up the supplies. When he moved back beside me, he lifted a clean wet rag. "You ready?" he asked.

I nodded, dropping the bloodied rag I held to my head and he began to dab the blood off. I had a brief moment of deja vu, remembering him doing this exact same thing in the light of the rover headlight.

"I'm sorry," he said again in that rough voice. "I shoulda been here."

I stared at the wall and didn't respond. I didn't know why he cared so much. I wasn't his responsibility. When he finished cleaning the blood, he threaded the needle with steady hands. Against my better judgment, I flicked my gaze up to his face just as he glanced at me. I wasn't sure what shone in those brown eyes, but it made me feel wobbly inside. I looked away, clenching my fists hard enough for my nails to bite into my palms.

Trey rested one hand on the side of my head, holding me still as he started to stitch me up. It hurt but I welcomed it—anything to chase away that stupid feeling in my gut. I counted the stitches he made out of habit.

After he tied the final stitch off, he scrubbed off his hands and then climbed up the ladder. I slid off the chair, watching as he threw my mattress and blanket down from the loft.

"What are you doing?"

"You shouldn't climb up and down the ladder when you're hurt," he said, jumping down and dragging the mattress into the empty corner.

I looked up at the loft, my one piece of safety, and frowned. Trey caught my expression.

"I volunteered for guard duty." He gave me a crooked grin as he climbed the ladder again. "If anybody comes through that door and even looks at you funny, I'll shoot 'em."

I didn't thank him, but that tight knot in my chest eased a little.

"What're these for?"

I looked up to see him holding the rusted scissors I'd stashed under the mattress. A lot of help they'd been up in the loft.

I shrugged, feeling dumb. "Just in case."

"Here."

He clambered down the ladder and then bent and fiddled with his boot. When he stood he held out a small holstered knife.

"Take this. It's small, but it's real sharp. It should fit in your boot. Sorry, I shoulda thought to make sure you had somethin' for protection."

I took it, surprised he trusted me with a weapon, small or not. I flicked it open, and I could practically hear Wolf's growl of approval. It was well-made and sturdy. As I studied it, I noticed my hand. Every single one of my fingernails had dark red blood under them. I remembered raking my nails down Pike's face and fought a sudden wave of nausea.

"Does anything else hurt besides your head?" Trey asked as he threw my blankets back over the mattress.

My whole body ached, but I knew how to ignore it. I tried to push away the flashes of memory that kept trying to invade my head and shoved the knife in my pocket.

"No," I lied, hoping he'd stop fussing. I headed to the sink, turned the water on, and tried to scrub the blood out from under my nails.

"You want to lay down and rest for a bit?"

"No," I repeated. I couldn't get all the blood out from under my nails. I lathered my hands again, hating how they shook.

Trey approached and my entire body tensed.

"What are you doing?" he asked, and gods, I was not going to fucking cry.

"Trying to get the blood off," I said through my teeth.

"Bones, your hands are clean."

"It's under my nails," I snapped.

He peered back down at my hands, realization dawning on his face. "I see. Here, hold on." He rummaged through the drawers until he found a small scalpel. He held his hand out, palm up. "Can I see your hand?"

My skin crawled at the thought of being touched, but even I had to admit my hands shook too hard for me to try and scrape the blood out myself. Reluctantly I placed my hand in his, and he curled his warm fingers around it, holding mine still. I watched as he scraped the blood out from under my nails, rinsing the scalpel in the sink as he went. I tried to breathe evenly, fighting back the tears that ached in my throat at the strange overwhelming intimacy of the act. He let go as soon as he finished and I retreated. His eyes followed me, but he just disinfected the scalpel for me and hung it up to dry.

"How about you sit for a minute?" he said as he dried his hands.

"No."

He frowned and opened his mouth to argue, but at that moment the door opened and Griz came striding in. He stopped in his tracks and swore when his eyes landed on my face.

"Lana?" Trey asked.

"Exile," Griz answered. "All three of 'em."

I leaned against the exam table and focused on breathing in through my nose and out through my mouth. Griz opened and clenched his fists at his side as he studied me.

"I should've killed him," Trey repeated in a low voice.

"Trust me, he wasn't in great shape," Griz said with a grim smile.

The door opened again, and a woman stepped in, holding her bloodied arm against her chest. She stopped at the sight of me, her eyes darting between me and Griz and Trey.

"Is…is this a bad time?" she asked.

"No," I said before Griz or Trey could say anything, "it's fine. You need stitches?"

"I, uh, I think so," the woman said. "Stupid knife slipped when I was cutting the soap."

I went back to the sink, washing my hands and my face for good measure, relishing the feel of the cold water on my swelling eye and cheek. When I turned around, the woman studied my face. I remembered Clarity mentioning the soapmaker, but I couldn't remember her name.

"Are you alright?" she asked.

"Looks worse than it is," I tried to say lightly, but my voice sounded wooden even to my own ears. "Have a seat." I gestured toward the exam chair as I got out my tools.

She frowned and glanced at Trey and Griz as she sat. "What happened?" she asked them.

"Lana paid two men to attack Bones," Trey answered, his voice dark.

She looked back at me, her eyes wide. "Because of Exo?"

"Yeah," Trey sighed.

"Exile?"

"All three of 'em."

I moved to her side and focused on disinfecting the gash in her arm, trying to ignore them. My hands still trembled, and I attempted to steady them by sheer force of will. Trying to stitch a wound with shaking hands was shitty for everyone involved.

"I'm sorry, Bones," the woman said. "My name is Mist by the way."

I flicked my eyes to hers. She smiled, and I dropped my gaze again, wishing people would stop fucking talking to me. For a few minutes, I thought I got my wish, working in silence. I finally got her all prepped and sat on the stool, bending over her arm with my needle ready. I took a deep breath, relieved to see my hands were steadier.

"Is the lavender ok?" Mist asked.

I looked up, confused.

"The soap," she clarified with a smile. "I have different scents if you don't like it."

"Oh," I said, "no, I…I like it."

She beamed. "Oh good. I was— *fuck*." She winced as I made the first stitch.

"Sorry," I murmured.

"S'ok," she sighed. "My own fault for not watching what I was fucking doing. I was gonna say I hoped a nice calming scent would be good for the med clinic. So I tracked down some wild lavender."

That thoughtful act made emotion flood me again. I stayed bent over her arm so I didn't have to worry about my face. "Thank you."

"You're welcome." I could hear the smile in her voice. "I'll put it on my foraging list then."

"Where do you forage?" I asked, hoping I sounded normal and not like I was fishing for information.

"In the woods," she said cheerfully. "Hawk takes me once a week."

It took me a second to remember Hawk was the leader of the other Safeguard crew. I tucked that information away.

"The rainwater barrels still working?" Trey asked.

Mist grinned at him. "Like a charm." She looked back at me and caught me glancing between them. "Trey helped me build a couple rain barrels for making lye. Now I don't have to trek down to the river and fill up buckets."

I nodded like I understood, which I didn't. They continued to chat about various things, and I let their voices fade into a pleasant background noise. After I finished, she thanked me warmly and said goodbye to all of us. Trey took my supplies and began to sterilize them. Griz wiped down the table as I washed up.

"Bones, I really think you should rest a beat," Trey tried again.

"No," I repeated.

The door opened again and a woman with a wailing baby came in. Her gaze narrowed on my face, but she glanced at Trey and Griz and didn't comment. The baby was refusing to use one of his arms, screaming when I tried to examine it. I wrapped my hands around his little arm, and he quieted as my powers healed the injury to his elbow. When I let go, the baby waved both arms in the air, smiling at me through the tears still in his eyes. The woman sniffled and picked him up, pressing a kiss to his head of short dark curls.

"Thank you!" She stepped into my space and hugged me, which made me stiffen. "Are you ok?" she whispered in my ear.

I nodded, feeling so fucking uncomfortable. She gave me a sharp look like she didn't quite believe me as she pulled back.

"Can I bring Jet back tomorrow?" she asked louder, shifting the toddler on her hip. "To make sure everything looks good?"

I blinked, confused. "Um, sure."

"I'll see you tomorrow then. Thank you, Bones."

She shot a sharp look at Trey and Griz as she left, and I realized she suspected that one of them had hurt me. The immediate urge to defend the two men surprised and annoyed me, and I pressed my lips together.

"There will be an announcement put up on the newsboard," Trey said as I trudged back to the sink and washed my hands. "So people will know what happened."

Great. That probably meant more people asking questions. My head seemed to pound in time with my heartbeat.

"Bones—" Trey started.

"No," I snapped. Gods, I did not need to sit and rest. I needed to keep moving.

"I'm gonna check on Mac," Griz announced. He gave me a stern look when I glanced at him. "Bones, you should at least sit for a minute."

"I'm fine."

Griz shook his head at me as he left. "Gods, you are stubborn as a mule."

"I'm half tempted to just give you a narc," Trey muttered after the door shut.

I snapped my gaze to him, panic bursting in my chest. "No. I can't have narcs."

"Why not?" he asked, crossing his arms.

"They hurt me."

He raised an eyebrow and I prayed to the gods he wouldn't ask any more questions. He didn't look like he believed me. It wasn't exactly a lie. I didn't have any explanation for what happened when I was drugged but *hurt* was the best word I could come up with.

"Promise me." My voice sounded higher than normal. "Promise you'll never give me a narc."

"What if you're really injured?" He crossed the room until he stood across the exam table from me. "I don't know if I can keep that promise."

"Trey." Gods, how could I convince him? "I swear to you that me getting a narc is worse than any pain I could ever experience."

He frowned. "What happens?"

"I...I can't really explain it. It's just...bad."

He studied me, his brow slightly furrowed. "Alright," he finally said, "I promise."

I let out a shaky breath, but he wasn't finished.

"*If* you take a few minutes and rest."

I glared at him. "I am *fine*."

"Bones," he said in a sharper voice, "you do realize why I can't believe you when you say that, right?"

The door opening again rescued me. An older coughing man came in, followed by a man limping, his face lined in pain. Relief made me dizzy as I went back to work, trying to ignore the curious looks I got with my fucked up face. Before I finished with the man who'd sprained his ankle, several more people came in with minor injuries. The clinic didn't empty for a couple hours, but as the last person filed out, Trey followed and flipped the sign on the door to "Closed."

"What are you doing?" I asked.

"The clinic is closed." Trey leaned out the door and said something to someone I couldn't quite make out. When he came back in and shut the door behind him, he gave me a stern look. "You're hurt and you need to rest."

Panic rose in my throat. "I need to—"

"It can wait," Trey cut in.

I didn't know how to explain that I had to keep moving, that staying busy was the only thing holding me together.

"Who's taking the night watch?" I asked, hoping to distract him.

"Me."

I frowned. "You've been here all day."

"I hope you're not gettin' tired of me," he teased, but it didn't quite reach his eyes. "I'm gonna be staying here for a while. Think of it like a permanent security detail. Griz and Mac are gonna bring a mattress over."

I froze. My eyes darted between him and the door. Would he sleep in the clinic with me?

"I'll set up over here by the door," Trey added, his voice softening like he could sense my panic.

Was I relieved or terrified? I wasn't sure. Both?

"Oh," I managed to say.

We stared at each other for a few breaths, but the stillness felt unbearable. I needed to do *something*. I moved to the sink, grabbed the old plastic bucket underneath, and filled it with water.

"What are you doing?" Trey asked, an edge to his voice.

"Cleaning." Somebody had wiped up most of my blood from the floor, but it needed a good scrubbing.

"Bones," he sounded exasperated, "this is not resting."

"I don't need to sit on my ass," I snapped at him.

I heard him approaching, and I tensed. He reached past me and turned the water off. The soft sleeve of his flannel shirt brushed my arm. "What are you gonna clean?" he asked quietly.

"The floor."

"Let me do it." He lifted the bucket out of the sink.

"I can do it," I argued.

"I know you can," he replied, grabbing the stiff bristle brush from under the sink, "but you don't have to."

I glared at his back as he strode away and got down on his hands and knees to scrub the floor. *Godsdamnit.* I settled for rearranging the shelf of tiny bottles. I caught Trey giving me an annoyed look, but he didn't say anything. He finished the floor before I finished my task. Reaching up to grab the bottles on the tallest shelf made my shoulders and arms hurt. My body was starting to ache, and I knew I would be hurting worse tomorrow, but right now I needed to keep moving.

"Let me get it."

He startled me, appearing behind me out of thin air.

"Sorry," he said when I jumped. He grabbed the bottles off the high shelf, setting them down on the counter for me to organize. "I can put them back up. Just tell me where."

I scowled but directed him on where to put the small bottles. With his help, we finished the tedious job far too quickly. I scanned the small room, trying to figure out what to tackle next. The windows needed to be cleaned, but they were so high up and I wasn't sure if I could—

"Bones, will you sit for a godsdamned minute?" Trey's voice sharpened.

"I am *fine*," I growled at him.

That muscle jumped in his jaw. "What's goin' on?"

"I have work to do."

"You can take a break."

"I don't *want* to."

"Why not?" he pushed.

"Just let me work." I could hear the edge of desperation in my voice.

"Why do you need to keep working?" He stepped closer, and the urge to flee crashed over me.

"Trey, *please*." I retreated back a step.

He stopped in his tracks, studying me. "Does it help?" he asked. "Staying busy?"

I stared at him for a moment, then gave a jerky nod, my throat tight.

"Ok," he said, surprising me. He glanced around the clinic like I'd just done, and then his face brightened. "Um, well, I was actually wonderin' if you could help me with something?"

I waited, feeling anxious again.

"I ripped my favorite jacket pretty bad. I've been meaning to sew it, but well, my stitches aren't anywhere near as neat as yours." He glanced up at where his stitches held my head together. "Would you mind?" He met my gaze again and smiled. "You don't have to, that's just the first thing I thought of."

"Yeah," I said, "I can do that."

He grinned, and the warmth of it made my breath catch. "I'll ask Griz if he can grab it."

He strode over to the door and stepped outside. I heard them talking, so apparently Griz guarded the clinic outside. When he stepped back in, he said cheerfully, "Griz is gettin' it for me. Mac is meetin' with Madame right now, but they'll bring a mattress over later."

Griz returned with the jacket a minute later. He scanned me again, but then just let himself back out. I pulled out the thread I'd found while organizing. The dark green color of the thread clashed with the brown of his jacket. I held it up to show Trey.

"This is the only thread I have."

He smiled. "That's fine. Doesn't have to match." He moved over to the sink and rinsed out the bucket he'd used to clean the floor before filling it back up with soapy water. "I'll do the windows while you do that."

I glanced up at the windows, surprised. He must have seen me examining them earlier. He climbed up the loft and started wiping the windows down as I sat in the exam chair and started sewing his jacket back together. I kept catching myself watching him work. He could barely reach most of the window, which meant I never would've been able to without climbing on something. Trey was at least six inches taller than me. Maybe more. I hadn't grown much taller than I'd been at ten. Vulture used to call me petite, but I knew from reading medical textbooks that it was more likely stunted growth from malnutrition.

I focused on making my stitches small and neat. Sewing fabric was easy compared to sewing skin. I used to hate mending as a kid, but mostly because I *had* to do it as a girl. I'd never admit it out loud, but I ended up grateful for all that mending when I started sewing bodies back together.

Trey came back down the ladder grinning. "Windows are clean," he said as he took the bucket to the sink and dumped out the dirty water.

I finished sewing the tear in his jacket a few minutes later and after inspecting my work, I got up to show him. Even after just a short while of sitting, my body felt stiff and sore, and I knew from experience tomorrow would be worse.

I thought I'd managed to calm myself down, but when the door opened, I jumped like I'd touched an electric fence. Trey startled at my reaction, his hand going to the pistol at his hip. Griz stopped in the doorway with a steaming mug, his eyebrows raised as he glanced between us. My face flushed hot.

"Sorry, man," Trey apologized, dropping his hand from the weapon.

"S'alright." Griz stepped inside and approached with the mug. "Here, Bones."

I took it, grateful for the warmth of the cup that seeped into my icy hands, but then I realized something. "The bell didn't ring."

"I sweet-talked Neena into givin' me a cup early," Griz explained. "You didn't get breakfast."

I stared hard into the steaming mug of broth. Godsdamnit, I would not cry.

"Lemme know if you want any more."

The gentleness of Griz's voice almost unraveled me, and I had to turn away before I lost it. I sipped my broth and pretended to study the shelf of tinctures, my eyes burning.

"Be right back with your mattress," I heard Griz add to Trey before he left.

Thank the gods Trey didn't try to talk to me, resuming his post by the door. A few minutes later Griz and Mac showed up with a mattress and blankets. I hovered on the other side of the exam table, watching as they set up Trey's bed near the door. Mac glanced up at me and approached. He stopped on the opposite side of the table, fidgeting. The scar on his face seemed to stand out more than usual from his tan skin.

"I'm sorry," Mac said in a low voice. "Lana was one of mine and I take full responsibility. She's been exiled, along with the two men she hired to attack you."

I eyed him.

"How are you feeling?" he added.

"Give you one guess," Griz interjected.

A tiny spark of amusement flashed through Mac's eyes. "Fine?"

"You got it!"

I crossed my arms across my chest.

"For a healer, you sure do a shit job at taking care of yourself," Mac said.

I glared at him, struggling to keep my temper in check.

"I closed the clinic," Trey said. "I'm gonna make sure she rests now."

"I am—" I started, but Mac held out a hand, his palm facing me.

"Do not say 'fine,'" he said sharply. "You're not fine. You were attacked and almost raped."

I cringed away from his blunt words, my breath catching.

"Gods, Mac," Trey muttered.

"Pretend I'm the doctor. I'm asking you if you're alright. You wouldn't want a patient to lie to you, would you?" Mac pushed, leaning toward me, both hands on the table. "I know Trey stitched up your head, but are you hurt anywhere else?"

I pressed my lips together, horrified that my eyes welled up with tears.

"Bones," Mac's grey eyes seemed to soften, and that was worse than his glare, "c'mon. Talk to me."

"I know how to handle it," I spit out, hating that my voice shook.

He frowned, but then the understanding dawned darkly on his face. "Will you talk to Trey? Or Griz? Someone you trust?"

"Trust?" I exploded, my hold on my temper snapping. "Like how you said I could *trust* your fuckin' crew? Trust like this?" I gestured to my face. "I'm so fuckin' sick of you all pretending that you're so *different*. For the record, I'd rather still be with Juck. At least he never pretended to be somethin' he wasn't." That was a bald-faced lie, but I wanted to lash out and hurt them.

Sure enough all three flinched.

"I said I can handle it. Now leave me the fuck alone!"

The silence after my tirade seemed deafening. Trey and Griz weren't looking at me, both standing tensely and looking pained. Mac, however, held my gaze with an intensity I couldn't quite name, a muscle in his jaw ticking.

"Alright," he finally said, "g'night."

With that, he turned and strode back out.

Griz sighed and followed Mac. "Night, Bones."

I wrapped my arms around myself. In the wake of that burst of anger, my hands shook, and my eyes still burned. I wished Trey would leave so I could let myself cry, but the bed by the door was a stark reminder he wasn't going anywhere.

"Bones, I'm so sorry—" Trey started, his voice quiet and rough.

Gods, I couldn't do this.

"I'm goin' to bed," I interrupted. I didn't wait to see his reaction, I just turned and stormed over to my mattress. The dinner bell hadn't even rung yet, but I didn't care. I pulled off my boots, not looking in Trey's direction, and burrowed under the blanket. Safely hidden, I held my breath as the tears escaped, rolling down my face and dampening the mattress.

In the silence, I heard Trey let out a heavy breath. "I'm gonna lock the door and turn the light off," he said quietly. "I'm just over here if you need anything." He paused for a moment. "Or if you want to talk."

I didn't answer, trying to let out my breath quietly, muffling my shaky gasps by pressing the blanket over my mouth. I squeezed my eyes shut, pain lancing through my head. I didn't want to *talk*. I didn't want to *be here*. I didn't want to *be*.

You can't let them win. If you fall apart, they win, Wolf growled.

Shut up, I snarled back. *You don't get to talk 'cause you're not fuckin' here.*

I wished all of this was just one long nightmare and any moment now Wolf would shake me awake. He'd be scowling, annoyed that I woke him up again, but he'd still wrap an arm around me and hum the song our mom used to sing until I stopped crying and fell back asleep.

But I'd wished the same thing almost every single night for twelve fucking years. Wolf wasn't here. This was real, and my brother was gone.

CHAPTER 8

The next morning, I woke up stiff and so sore I had to hobble around the clinic. When Sam brought me broth, he stopped short at the sight of my bruised face.

"Fuck," he swore, setting the broth on the table and starting toward me.

My legs moved to put the table between us before my brain caught up, which made him halt in his tracks. My face heated, and I felt stupid. I knew he wasn't going to hurt me, but my brain was stuck in flight mode.

That's a good thing, Wolf snarled. *That's how you survive.*

"Shortcake," Sam said, but I refused to look at him.

"I'm fine," I said, getting out the tools I used most so I could have them ready.

I could feel his eyes on me, but I kept my head down. I hated how on edge I felt.

"C'mon, Shortcake, can I just take a look at that gash in your head? I want to check Trey's stitchin' job." Sam's voice sounded calm, but it had a sharpness to it.

"It's fine." I glanced sideways at where Trey stood leaning against the wall and watching us.

"Has anybody even checked you for injuries besides your head?"

I finally looked at him, my eyes blazing. "Yeah, *I* did. *I'm* the healer, and I'm sayin' I'm *fine.*"

"If only you were known for tellin' the truth," Sam deadpanned, glaring back at me.

"Fuck off, Sam," I snapped.

"Why are you limping if you're fine?" he pushed.

I swallowed hard, working to keep my emotions under control. "I'm just a little bruised."

Sam's face twisted. "Gods, I—"

"Stop," I snapped at him desperately. "What's done is done. Just *leave* it."

"Sam," Trey finally spoke up, gesturing toward the door with his head.

Sam let out an angry sigh but turned and strode to the door with Trey following. I could hear them talking heatedly outside, but Trey came back inside alone.

"He's just worried," he said, leaning back against the wall, one leg raised and pressed against the wall behind him. "He wants to make sure you're alright." He paused. "We all do."

You didn't seem to care about that when you fucking dragged me here, is what I wanted to say, but didn't.

He sighed. "I know this is fucked up. I'm sorry we dragged you here."

He hesitated and I couldn't resist glancing at him, unnerved that he said almost exactly what had been on my mind. He stared at me, brown eyes almost golden in the beam of sunlight he stood in.

"I wish things were different—*really* different—but they're not. Not yet."

I looked away. I didn't know what that meant, and I wasn't going to ask. He was quiet for a while and I started to hope that maybe he'd stay that way.

"Lana betrayed all of us, and we're all dealin' with it in our own way," he said, crushing my hopes for silence. "Mac and me, we've tried real hard to make this crew a safe space, but we're just a few people in hundreds and there's only so much we can do." He took a deep breath. "What happened to you yesterday was awful, and I don't blame you for not trusting us. But...and I'm real sorry if I'm bein' a pain in the ass, *but* I'm just gonna keep reminding you that you are a part of this crew and that means something to all of us."

Gods, I wished he'd stop talking. I continued to ignore him, wiping down the counter for the third time in a row just to have something to do with my hands.

"I hope you know—"

The door opened and I could have cried from relief to see a pale-faced man stumble in.

Trey quieted and I busied myself with healing the man's injuries. After he left, Trey tried to continue talking to me between patients, but around the noon hour he seemed to accept that I wasn't going to respond and fell silent.

Thank the gods the day was busy with a near endless stream of sick and injured people. It seemed like the people of the Vault were warming up to my presence. Most of them still watched me with suspicion, but they still came. More than half of the people made comments about my face, but they were surprisingly kind. They seemed to know what happened, so I guessed that meant Madame had put up a notice.

The woman with baby Jet came back and introduced herself as Leda. I checked Jet over, but I slowly realized she seemed more concerned about *me*.

"Everythin' looks good," I said, but when I glanced up she held out a small wrapped parcel.

"I made a strawberry cake and brought you some." Leda smiled.

"O-oh," I stammered. "You didn't have to do that."

When I took the parcel from her, she gripped my hand for a moment. "I saw the notice." She pitched her voice low. "I just…well, I just wanted you to know there are good people here and we're so grateful for you." Her eyes glittered with tears. "I'm sorry for what happened."

I didn't know what to say, but she didn't seem to mind. Leda squeezed my hand once more before letting go and scooped up Jet who had started to fuss.

"Time for his nap." She smiled at the little boy. "Thanks again, Bones."

I stood at the exam table staring at the door after she left, feeling bewildered.

"Leda's one of the good ones," Trey spoke up from where he stood near the door. He smiled when I looked at him.

The door opened and Clarity stepped inside. I hadn't seen her since the day I'd woken up in her room at the brothel. She had a fresh ring of bruises around her neck, but she smiled. I waited on edge for her to react to my face, but she didn't say anything.

"Hi, Bones," she said like we were old friends, then smiled at Trey. "Hey, Trey."

"Hey, sis."

I looked between them in surprise. "You're a Mason?"

"No," she replied. "We had different dads, and mine wanted me to take his name, so I'm a Reed."

"The only thing our dads had in common besides likin' our mom was that they were both assholes," Trey said.

I didn't care. I really didn't. "*Were*?" I heard myself ask.

"Mine died in a bar fight," Clarity explained with zero remorse.

"Mine died in an animal attack outside the hold," Trey added.

"Do you have any other siblings?"

"Mac." Clarity smiled, and I blinked in surprise.

"Our mom adopted Mac when he was seven, so he's part of the family too," Trey explained.

"We almost had a little sister, but our mom died in childbirth." This time I could hear the pain in Clarity's voice. "The baby died too."

I kept my eyes on the tools I was sorting. Childbirth scared the shit out of me, and I hated helping with births. Thankfully there hadn't been a whole lot of childbirth in the Reapers. Most of the bikers who ended up pregnant came to me for herbs that would end the pregnancy. Not many wanted to try to raise a baby in the middle of a bloodthirsty desert gang.

"I gotta run an errand for Mac," Trey said. "I'll be back in a bit. Griz is outside."

After he left, the silence lingered until I finally glanced up to meet Clarity's gaze. She gave me a gentle smile.

"Trey told me what happened," she said. "I can't believe Lana betrayed you all like that."

I hated the guilt that stabbed me. If it weren't for me, Lana and Exo would both still be here.

"Are you ok?" she asked.

My eyes went to the ring of bruises around her neck. She clearly knew what men were capable of doing.

"I could heal those bruises for you," I found myself saying.

She looked surprised. "You don't have to do that."

I shrugged. "Bruises are pretty easy." I hesitated for a moment.

"Are you hurt anywhere else?"

She smiled, but her eyes looked sad. "Just a little sore."

This exhaustion reached all the way down to my bones. I knew exactly what she meant, and I'd be willing to bet whoever hurt her hadn't been exiled or punished in any way. Gods, I wanted to do *something.*

"Can I heal you?" I asked, holding her gaze.

"Sure."

She sat on the chair and I laid my hands on her neck. It took little effort to direct that warmth through her skin, taking away the bruises and the lingering pain I sensed in several parts of her body. When I stepped back, she smiled despite the tears shining in her eyes.

"Thank you, Bones."

I shrugged, swallowing hard.

"Trey hates that I work in the brothel," she added, sliding off the chair.

I went back to pretending to organize the tinctures, but I listened.

"My dad owed a debt and died before he could pay it, so Madame sent me to the brothel to work the remainder off. Trey keeps trying to get me out, but I don't have any other place to go." She smiled sadly again. "Mac offered to let me join his crew, but I've never been physically strong and I get sick a lot. And the brothel isn't so bad. We stick together and try to help each other out."

"How old were you?" I asked.

She hesitated for a moment. "Twelve."

I had to fight to swallow past the nausea. A fucking kid working in a brothel. That could have been me. Probably would have been me if I didn't have this power.

"Mac doesn't hate that you work in the brothel?" I couldn't resist the jab at Mac.

Clarity blinked, her brow furrowing slightly. "I don't think he *likes* it, but he respects my decision."

Oh. I didn't know what to say after that.

"Anyways, I just wanted to see how you were doing."

"I'm fine," I said, but more weary than snappy. I met her eyes and let a tiny bit of vulnerability show. "It's nothin' new."

We exchanged a look that spoke more than words ever could. She understood, and so did I, and we both hated it.

"I know you don't know me that well," she said in a low voice, "but I *can* vouch for my brothers. They're good men."

I looked away again. "If anyone is ever hurt at the brothel, just send for me. Doesn't have to be an emergency."

She paused for a moment. "I will. Thank you, Bones."

After Clarity left, I had a few moments of silence before a woman came in. Griz followed her inside, and the way he watched her made me tense. She looked harmless—thin, and frail—but she watched me hungrily with a strange light in her eyes.

"You have a gift," the woman said before I could say anything. She tilted her head, a birdlike movement.

"Can I help you?" I asked.

She smiled, and I noticed her pupils were blown wide like she was high on something.

"Angel," the woman murmured reverently.

I felt the blood leave my face so fast the room swam. "Don't call me that."

"The Voiceless were right." Her face shone with awe. "The gods have sent their Angel to save us."

"The gods sent you to me, Angel. You are mine to wield how I see fit; you hear me?"

I sucked in a desperate breath through my nose, trying to quell the nausea.

"I seek your blessing, Angel!"

The woman started toward me and I retreated quickly, but Griz grabbed her before she got more than two steps in. He had to carry her out as she fought, but he managed.

"No!" she wailed. "Angel, please!"

As soon as the door shut behind them, I fled up to the loft and tucked myself into my corner, my back to the wall and my knees drawn up to my chest. My hands trembled as I fought waves of nausea.

Angel.

I hated that Juck still had so much power over me. I wanted him to be gone, out of my memories, my fears, my nightmares. I hated that one word could reduce me to this because I could only hear his voice saying it. I wasn't sure if most people knew Juck had once been a part of the Voiceless. He often fervently talked to me about the Voiceless and the gods when we were alone. He said he left due to a disagreement, but sometimes I wondered if that was true. He seemed to go out of his way to keep the Reapers and the Voiceless from crossing paths despite believing he had been chosen as a new god by finding me in the desert.

Angel. He'd groaned it in my ear when—

I clapped a hand over my mouth again, determined to not be sick.

Griz's head popped up over the side of the loft and I jumped with a gasp.

"Sorry," he said, "you ok?"

I nodded, wiping my wet cheeks and hoping he didn't notice as he pulled himself up the rest of the way into the loft. He sat against the wall several feet away from me.

"Don't know why I keep asking you that when I know you'll just lie," he said, but he didn't sound mad.

I tried to take a deep breath, tried to fight off the tears that welled in my eyes and tried to pretend he wasn't there. Out of the corner of my eye, I could see him watching me.

"You run into the Voiceless before?" he asked.

I shook my head. "Just seen 'em from a distance. And heard things."

"Did they know about you?"

I shuddered. "No."

He looked thoughtful. "Word's out about your powers now though. Mac's contact says people have been asking around about you."

Gods, if he was trying to make me feel better, he was doing a real shit job of it.

"I don't know much 'bout their beliefs, but if they think you're some sorta angel—"

I tensed.

"You really don't like that word, do you?"

I didn't answer him.

"Is that what they all believe? Megs is batshit crazy, so I never know."

Honestly, I wasn't sure either. I only knew what Juck told me. According to Juck, the Voiceless believed that seven gods rose from the ashes of the old world and made themselves known. Seven prophets were chosen, one for each god, and they served the gods until death. Followers had to commit themselves to the Voiceless to prove their devotion, paying them absurd amounts of tribute and occasionally carrying out horrible violent acts when the gods demanded it. Only the true believers knew the names of the gods, and after death, their souls were taken by angels to Paradise. The rest of us were doomed to suffer in eternal damnation. Juck's big disagreement was that he believed the gods were *not* immortal, and that new gods would rise to replace them. He thought finding me in the desert anointed him as one of the new gods, but I thought it was all bullshit.

I shrugged.

"So who used to call you that?" he asked. "Juck?"

Whatever expression crossed my face must have been confirmation enough because his expression darkened. We sat in silence while my heart returned to a normal rhythm.

"Me and Mac met him once," he said, "during a trade deal. Didn't like him much."

"When?"

He looked surprised that I asked a question. "Must've been about six years ago? The Reapers had a stock of propane tanks and we needed some…along with everybody else."

I swallowed hard. "I remember that."

His eyebrows rose. "You were there?"

"I was supposed to stay in his tent, but I snuck out."

"To see the trade meeting?"

"No." The words tumbled out, surprising me. "I tried to run away."

"Ah," he said, watching me. "Is that why he was in such a rage that last day?"

Gods, why was I talking about this? I stood, brushing off my pants. "I should get back to work."

"Clinic's closed," Griz said, not moving from where he sat on the floor.

I fixed him with a sharp look. "Why?"

"So you could have a break."

I didn't know what to do with that. "I'm—"

"Fine," Griz finished, shaking his head with a grin. "Yeah, I know."

I glared at him and made my way over to the ladder.

"You know it's ok to not be fine sometimes," he called as I descended.

I ignored him, going to the door and unlocking it. When I opened it to flip the sign, Sam sat outside, carving something from a piece of wood with a knife. He looked up at me and grinned.

"Break over, Shortcake?" he asked.

I flipped the sign to open and shut the door without responding.

After the dinner bell, Sam came in with my mug of broth and a piece of bread, and the other woman in Mac's crew, Raven, came in with him.

"Hey, Raven," Griz said, an edge to his voice, "what's up?"

Silver piercings shone from Raven's eyebrows, nose, and lips and her body was lean and muscled like a fighter. Her blue eyes locked on me, and she smiled, but it definitely wasn't friendly. I wasn't sure what she thought about what Lana had done, but I knew they'd been friends.

"Do I need a reason to be here?" she drawled.

Sam stepped around her and handed me my mug and bread. "Just ignore her. She's in a mood."

Raven laughed, sauntering through the clinic and eyeing everything. "I just want to see what all the fuss is about. If I gotta follow all of Mac's new rules, I should at least get to see why."

I didn't know what she meant, and I didn't like it.

"What rules?" I asked shortly.

She met my gaze again. "Oh you know, keep Bones safe. Report any chatter about Bones. Make sure Bones has her special broth every day. Have eyes on Bones at all times." Her eyes cut to Griz who glared at her.

"Watch it, Raven," Griz warned.

"What?" She widened her eyes innocently. "I'm just trying to do my job, Griz."

"You know Madame's orders," Sam said, and from his expression, this wasn't the first time they'd had this conversation.

"All I know is we used to be the top pick for missions and now we just sit around watchin' *her*." Her lip curled. "I'm fucking sick of Hawk's crew getting all the good jobs. We haven't left this shithole in *weeks*."

"You want to complain, go take it up with Mac," Griz growled. "Or better yet, go tell Madame how you feel."

She smirked. "Yeah you'd like that wouldn't you, Griz?"

The door opened and Trey walked in. He stopped at the sight of so many people and scanned everyone. "We havin' a party?"

"If only," Raven said.

"We're *all* just leavin'," Sam said.

Raven rolled her eyes but strode out the door without another word. Sam and Griz exchanged a look with Trey and followed.

"Night Bones!" Griz called over his shoulder.

Trey gave me a wary look. "What was that about?"

I shrugged and went back to sipping my broth. I actually appreciated Raven saying all that. I didn't want to be involved in their hold politics, but if my presence caused drama in the crew, I wanted to know about it. I didn't want to get caught unaware again.

"Did Raven say something?"

"Raven said a lot of things."

"Like what?"

"Like you all have better things to do than watch me and the clinic."

"Oh." He looked relieved, and I narrowed my eyes at him, wondering what he'd been nervous about. "Well, she can take that up with Madame."

I finished my broth and moved on to my bread. I hated this nauseating mental back and forth where one moment I thought maybe they cared and the next I thought they were just following orders.

"Oh I brought you something," Trey said.

I eyed him with suspicion.

He pulled out a slightly crushed handful of dandelion flowers from his jacket pocket. My breath caught. He laid them on the exam table, and I knew he'd continued talking, but I wasn't listening. I stared at the small, cheerful yellow flowers, overwhelmed with the flood of emotion sweeping over me.

"Bones?"

I glanced up at Trey, startled when I realized he'd moved closer. He looked at me with concern.

"You ok?"

I nodded, gazing back at the flowers. My heart ached, and I didn't think before I whispered, "My brother used to bring me these."

He stayed quiet for longer than I expected, and I then remembered with a lurch of terror that I'd told Madame and everyone else I didn't have any siblings. My mind raced with how to fix it. Maybe he didn't remember that.

"Sounds like a good brother," Trey said.

I looked up at him warily, but he just smiled. I couldn't tell if he remembered or not, so I just left it. His eyes warmed, and something in my chest cracked like a seed breaking open to take root.

"They're my favorite," I confessed before I could think better of it, and his smile widened.

"I'll keep an eye out for them for you then."

"You don't have to do that," I said, fidgeting with the leaves.

He stepped even closer and nudged my shoulder with his. "I want to."

I gave him an exasperated look. "Why?"

"Cause you like 'em."

I scoffed and picked up the little flowers. The fuzzy yellow petals flooded me with memories, Wolf's teasing smile as he held out the flowers, trying to coax me into forgiving him, Wolf promising he'd be back soon from his hunting trip and that he'd bring me a dandelion.

"You want to go for a walk?" Trey asked, startling me back to the present.

I looked up at him. We stood so close, but it didn't make me panic. His eyes held mine, so open that it seemed like everything he felt was right there, laid bare like windows to his soul. I couldn't hold his gaze for long, terrified of what I might see. My rationale that his kindness *had* to be some sort of act was wearing thin.

He still watched me, waiting, and I remembered he'd asked me a question. A walk? This seemed like a question where the answer meant a lot more than just taking a stroll. The panic surged through me like a splash of cold water on my face. I took a few steps away, pretending to straighten the drying tools on the counter.

"I think I'll just go to bed," I said without looking at him.

"Ok." He sounded disappointed and it bothered me more than I liked to admit. "You need any help closing up?"

I shook my head.

"Alright then. I'll step out so you can change."

I slipped out of my pants and shirt, pulling on the oversized ragged T-shirt and thin shorts I slept in. I climbed into bed and then sat there, unsure if I should call out and tell him he could come back in or not.

Before I could decide, he knocked and called, "You good?"

"Yep."

He came back in and gave me a slight smile before retreating to his own mattress, kicking off his boots, and taking off his shirt. I tried to pretend I didn't notice his strong arms, the golden brown of his skin from the sun, and the way the lean muscles in his stomach formed a V that disappeared into his pants. My heart beat faster, ignoring me as I tried to calm it down. Trey turned toward me, and I barely remembered to stop staring before he caught me.

"Night, Bones," he said as he flicked off the light.

It took me a long time to fall asleep.

CHAPTER 9

I woke up to the sound of screams.

I jerked upright, scrambling to get out of Juck's tent before whoever was attacking us lit it on fire. My feet hit the freezing hardwood floor, shocking me awake. The sliver of sky I could see through the windows was still dark.

"Hold on," Trey said to me, holding out one hand for me to stay put. He hadn't put on a shirt, but he had his gun drawn as he cracked the door open to peer out.

"Trey!" I heard Mac shouting. "Fire in the slums!"

"Fuck." Trey holstered his gun and grabbed his shirt.

He glanced at me as he threw it on, but I was already moving. I pulled my pants on and stuffed my feet into my boots. When we darted out of the clinic, we could *see* the flames even from this distance. Most of the hold seemed to be running toward the south end of the Vault. Trey and I joined them, coughing as thick smoke filled the air. When we finally reached the slums, I gasped at the sight of at least half the homes burning. Screams echoed from more than one of the burning buildings and Trey's head snapped in that direction.

"Bones!" Sam yelled from where he crouched over a body on the ground.

I looked back at Trey to see him looking at me, even as both of us moved in opposite directions.

"Be careful," I blurted out, and he paused for half a second, something soft flashing through his eyes.

"You too," he said, and then he ran.

I had to force myself to focus, pushing past the huge swell of fear that swept over me at the sight of him running toward the fire. I ran to Sam to see him holding a severely burned woman who was sobbing.

"Get all the injured in one area," I said to Sam, shifting into a familiar medic mode. It wasn't the first time I dealt with a large disaster with multiple people injured. At least this time I could actually save people's lives.

"Got it." Sam leapt to his feet and ran.

I crouched beside the woman, taking her hands. My healing power eagerly rushed down my arms and into her body, and the blisters and burns healed before my eyes. Griz appeared, carrying an injured man, and I switched to him as soon as the woman's injuries healed. The woman sobbed her thanks as she sat up, and I gave her a short nod before focusing on the man's burns. More people started bringing the injured over to me, and I lost myself in the work of healing every single one. The many injuries ranged from small burns or smoke inhalation to people gasping their last breaths, their bodies barely recognizable. I focused on the latter and tried to get the severely injured healed first.

Sweat trickled down my face. I could feel the heat of the fire, even from a safe distance away. Most of the hold had formed a bucket brigade from the nearest outdoor water spigots and worked together to pass and throw buckets of water on the fire. It didn't seem to do much until several of Madame's men showed up with long thick hoses that they connected to the spigots to spray water on the fire. They seemed reluctant to help, muttering things about "fucking rusters," which made my blood boil.

Even with the hoses, it wasn't until sunrise that the fire began to finally die. I kept finding myself searching the nearby faces for Trey, but I didn't see him anywhere. I tried to ignore the worry that settled like a stone in my stomach. I finished all the severely injured and moved on to the moderate to mild injuries. It hurt now, like the final times when I healed Hojo. I swiped my sleeve across my running nose to see blood and bit back a curse.

"Bones!"

I glanced up to see Sam running toward me, and my heart sank when I realized he had an injured child in his arms. I quickly scrubbed my nose with my sleeve, hoping I got most of the blood.

"She tried to hide under the bed," Sam gasped, his voice hoarse. "Trey got her out. We never would've found her if her sister hadn't seen her go under there."

Trey. He must be ok, then. I quickly grabbed the girl's burned hands. It *hurt*. My healing power had dwindled to a thin thread, but I gritted my teeth and kept going.

"Your nose—" Sam started, alarmed.

"I'm fine," I snapped, ignoring the blood trickling from my nose again.

The golden warmth inside of me flickered. The little girl was healing, but slowly—too slowly—and then my power sputtered, leaving only wisps of smoke. Panic started roaring through me as I tried again, but there was nothing there. It was gone. The girl started crying, a thin wail that sounded like it came from far away. Her disfigured face blurred in my vision.

No! I can't run out now. Gods, please!

I reached for that power again, desperate, but everything tipped sideways and—

☙

I shivered so hard my teeth rattled in my head. Something about this felt familiar.

"—drink something. C'mon, Bones."

Mac's angry face came into focus. He always seemed angry when he looked at me.

"Bones," he said sharply, "try to drink."

I realized I was lying on my mattress in the clinic. Mac's hand slid under my neck, lifting my head as he brought a mug of water toward my lips. I managed to get a few swallows of water down. Daylight streamed through the windows of the clinic. My throat and lungs burned as though I'd inhaled a shit ton of smoke—

I stiffened in horror, my eyes snapping up to Mac's face. "Did she die?" My voice came out raspy.

Mac lowered my head and removed his hand from the back of my neck, seeming to hesitate as he stared at me with those dark grey eyes. I squeezed my eyes shut as they flooded with tears, already knowing the answer.

"It's not your fault," I thought I heard Mac say, but I must have been dreaming because it *was* my fault.

"No." Mac's voice came out even sharper, startling my eyes back open. "You saved thirty-six people, Bones. You healed until you fuckin' passed out. You did everythin' you could."

"She was just a kid," I choked out.

"You did everythin' you could," he repeated, and he sounded like he believed that.

He had a bandage wrapped around his forearm. I reached out, intending to wrap my shaking fingers around it, but he grabbed my wrist and yanked my hand away. My eyes shot back up to his face.

"No," he snapped, glaring down at me.

Tears started rolling down my face, and the angry lines of his face softened to confusion.

"What's—" he started to say, but words bubbled out of me.

"Please let me heal you," I sobbed. "Please. I know you don't like me, but I gotta...I gotta...let me do *somethin'*, please—"

"Bones!" His voice was a quiet command as he leaned in, holding my gaze. "You need to rest. It's just a small burn." He hesitated for a moment, and I felt his thumb ghost over the inside of my wrist. "And I don't dislike you. I just don't want you to burn out again."

The clinic door opened and shut, and Mac released my wrist and moved, his form blurring as the room spun. My tears trailed off as I shivered. My fingers fumbled for my blanket, but I couldn't find it, and then warm hands wrapped around mine.

"I know you're cold," a gentle voice said next to me, "but we gotta bring your fever down."

I squinted to see Trey kneeling next to me, his eyes soft and concerned.

"Why are...what...what—"

I paused, trying to remember what I'd been about to ask. I focused on his face and suddenly realized he was *safe*. Tears filled my eyes again as relief overwhelmed me.

"You're ok," I whispered.

He smiled, his eyes warming. "I'm ok."

"You scared me," I mumbled, my eyes drifting closed. "I didn't see you."

"You worryin' about me now?" he asked, his gentle voice teasing.

"Yes," I replied, exhaustion crashing over me.

"I'm alright, Bones," he murmured.

I couldn't decipher the intense emotion in his voice. I wanted to open my eyes to see his expression, but my eyelids were too heavy.

"Don't leave," I tried to say, but shivers violently wracked my body.

A gentle hand smoothed my hair back from my sticky, sweaty face. "I'm not goin' anywhere, darlin'."

෨

I startled awake at a loud crash.

"Ah fuck," someone groaned.

"Sam!"

I turned my head to see Trey sitting beside my mattress looking away from me with an exasperated expression.

"Did you seriously just break that?"

"Well, I thought the lid would stay on!"

I followed his gaze to see Sam standing by the exam table, holding a glass lid and looking guilty. The jar I kept clean rags in lay in pieces on the floor. He met my eyes and was visibly startled to see me awake and staring back at him.

"Sorry, Shortcake," he sighed. "I'll find you a new one."

"Hey," Trey said from my other side. "How you feelin'?"

I looked back to find him studying me. "What happened?"

"You saved a shit ton of people, and then you passed out." He paused. "You had a high fever again. I'm wonderin' if you sorta burn out when you use up all your power and it makes you sick. Cause this was just like last time."

Last time, when I helped Madame torture Hojo to death.

"Did that little girl die?" I mumbled.

"Yes."

I closed my eyes, guilt sweeping through me.

"Bones," Trey's hand curled around mine and squeezed, "you saved so many people. You did everything you could. It's not your fault."

I still failed.

"Would you blame me for her dying?"

My eyes popped open. "No."

"If I'd found her sooner, she might be alive," he countered.

I set my jaw. I knew what he was doing, and I didn't like it. "It's not the same thing," I muttered.

"Why not?" he pushed.

"*You* did all you could." The whispered words tumbled out of me. "I couldn't do enough."

"Bones," the gentle way he said my name made my eyes well up, "you might have remarkable power, but you're still human. You have limits."

"It's never enough," as soon as I said the words, I wished I could take it back.

"What *would* be enough?" he asked slowly, studying me.

I swallowed hard. This was headed toward dangerous ground. "I want to get up," I said instead.

He hesitated but then nodded. "Ok, just take it easy."

I sat up and realized Sam must have left. Just the two of us remained in the clinic. I frowned, a hazy memory floating through my head. "Was Mac here?"

"Yeah, earlier," Trey answered. "Why?"

My eyes narrowed. "Was I sayin' shit?"

Guilt flashed across his face, his eyes widening. "No."

It was so obviously a lie I almost laughed, but the fact he lied made it pretty clear I'd said something I wouldn't be happy about. I glared at him, torn between wanting to demand he tell me and wanting to pretend it never happened.

"Come on," he said, getting to his feet and holding his hands out. "I bet you'll feel better if you get some fresh air."

I knew he wanted to distract me, but being distracted sounded kind of nice. I gave him my hands, letting him pull me up. I didn't miss the delighted surprise that flashed across his face, but then the room spun as I stood, and I gripped his hands tighter instead of letting go.

"Dizzy?" he asked.

"Yeah."

"Let me know when it passes," he said, holding my hands and waiting.

"I'm ok," I said after the room seemed to settle.

He released my hands, but only to tuck my arm in his. I stiffened, which made him pause, but I didn't pull away. After a few seconds, he started walking slowly, reaching out to open the clinic door, and I walked with him.

"What time is it?" I asked.

"'Bout time for the dinner bell now."

I frowned as we stepped outside and sure enough, the setting sun lit up the sky with a deep orange color. I'd been out for about twelve hours. If Trey was right and this happened every time I used up all my power, I'd have to be careful.

The air still smelled like smoke and burnt wood. "The fire out?"

"Yeah," he sighed. "Lost about half the homes in the slums though."

"What'll happen to those people who lost their homes?" I asked, feeling uneasy.

"Same thing that happens any time there's some sort of natural disaster," Trey said and his voice had a dark edge to it. "Madame won't do shit and the rest of us will scrounge up materials and help 'em rebuild."

So many questions spun through my mind. I wanted to ask him how he could stand to work for Madame, how he justified the things she did, and why he stayed here at the Vault.

Instead, I kept my mouth shut.

Even if I didn't get an up close and personal look at what Madame did to people in that awful dungeon room, I'd heard enough small pieces of conversation to know unrest simmered here. I had plenty of experience with unrest, and if I wanted to survive, I needed to just keep my head down and stay the fuck out of it.

Survive, Wolf agreed, startling me. He'd been quiet lately.

"How many people died?" I asked.

"Seven." Trey's free hand came up to rest over the top of my hand on his arm and squeezed. "Would have probably been triple that if you hadn't been here."

Guilt mixed with something soft and warm in my chest.

"*But* we aren't talkin' about the fire anymore. We're gonna do somethin' else."

"What?" I asked warily.

"You'll see," he said with a grin.

We were headed for the barn, I realized. A prickle of fear ran through me. I knew better than to blindly follow a man somewhere isolated. Trey let go of my arm to pull the big doors open and then tugged me through. Even with Wolf snarling warnings in my head, my feet followed him inside, but my body had tensed so much that when Trey turned toward me, I flinched. He paused, studying my face in confusion.

"You ok?" he asked.

I nodded, but he frowned.

"There's a nest of kittens in the hayloft," he explained. "You want to see 'em?"

Surprise and something unbearably soft overwhelmed me for a moment. Kittens. He wanted to show me kittens.

I nodded again, not trusting myself to speak.

"Here, you stay here and I'll bring a couple down." He grinned, and the warmth of it made me feel even more unsteady.

I waited as he disappeared up the ladder. The barn smelled like oats and animals, but it wasn't unpleasant. Tools and various pieces of equipment lined the walls in an orderly fashion. Trey let out a curse from somewhere up above me.

"Trey?"

"I'm fine. Just this little one has a strong bite." He came down the ladder, grinning and climbing easily despite holding a kitten in each hand. "Reminds me of someone else I know."

I scowled at him and his grin widened.

"You want the little one who bites or the sleepy one?" he asked, approaching me.

I reached out and took the little one from him. I had a point to prove now. The kitten had grey stripes and hissed as I took it from him. It glared at me with blue eyes, baring its teeth as it growled. I placed it on my chest directly above my heart and covered it with my sleeves so it didn't feel so exposed. Trey raised his eyebrows as the kitten quieted.

"Are you using your powers?" he playfully accused.

"No," I said indignantly. "It's just scared. You gotta give it somewhere to feel safe."

"Hmmm," Trey hummed, a corner of his mouth twitching up.

"What?"

"Nothin'." He grinned.

"*What?*" I glared at him.

"It's just good advice," he said, but his grin softened into something that made soft and terrifying feelings stir to life in my chest.

My heart started beating faster and my cheeks warmed.

"Never woulda thought you were a secret wild kitten tamer."

"It doesn't need to be tamed," I shot back. "It just needs to know you aren't gonna hurt it."

Gods, that smile.

"You're right," he murmured.

If he didn't stop looking at me with that soft, warm gaze, I would do…something, something stupid. He wasn't standing that close to me, but every part of my body buzzed with awareness of him like I stood where lightning was about to strike.

"Where were you tryin' to go?" Trey asked.

My brow furrowed in confusion.

"When the mercs found you," he clarified. "Where were you going?"

Oh.

"I didn't really have a plan," I mumbled.

He looked taken aback. "You didn't?"

"I just wanted to get far away." I could feel my cheeks warming again.

His eyebrows raised. "So you just set off into the mountains without a plan?"

Gods, he sounded like Wolf right now. "I was doin' just fine."

His lips twitched. "You and I have *very* different definitions of 'fine.'"

I glanced back down at the kitten. It had calmed enough to poke its head out from under my sleeve, sniffing curiously. I shifted to hold it with one hand and used a finger to stroke the top of its head. After a minute, a rattling little purr filled the room. I looked smugly up at Trey.

"How did you do that?" he demanded.

"If you pet it like this," I continued stroking its head, "it feels like a mama cat licking it and it's comforting."

"You are full of surprises, Bones."

"I had…I knew someone really good with animals once." Why was I constantly telling him more than I meant to? My stomach twisted in panic.

He studied me with his head tilted as though he could sense my chaotic emotions, and I dropped my eyes to the kitten he held and frowned.

"You're bleeding."

He glanced at his hand. "Oh, yeah that's where that one," he gestured at my kitten, "bit me."

"Can I heal it?" I asked.

His eyebrows raised. "You don't have to. I don't want you to push yourself too hard."

I gave him an exasperated look. "I think I can handle it."

One side of his mouth tilted up in a crooked smile. "Alright."

I stepped closer, freeing one hand to cover the small wound. My healing power ached, but it took just a few seconds to heal. Trey smelled good, I realized as I stood close to him, like my lavender soap and the oil he used to clean his gun. As soon as the wound vanished, I quickly stepped backward.

"What'd you mean when you said it would never be enough?"

The sudden change in topics made me nauseous.

"It's...nothing," I lied.

"You can tell me," he urged.

"I...I just..." Gods, those damn brown eyes made it hard to think straight. "I have a lot of blood on my hands."

He frowned.

"I have this...this power to *heal*...but I keep...I keep *hurting* people. I don't know...I don't know if I can heal enough...to make up for it."

"Are you keeping score?" he asked, but not in a mocking way. He studied my face, his brow furrowed as though he wanted to understand.

"No. I don't know. I just...I want to...I need to balance the scales."

"What scales?"

"The...scales." I gestured vaguely with one hand, my face heating.

"Do you feel responsible every time you can't heal someone?"

"I've watched so many people die," I whispered. "People I could've saved with my powers."

"You said Juck didn't let you heal other people."

"I could have...I could've *tried*."

He shifted closer. "What would have happened if you did?"

I swallowed hard, terror fluttering in my stomach. *He's gone. He can't hurt you.* But gods, if Juck had caught me trying to heal someone—

I sucked in a breath through my nose as my stomach churned.

Why the fuck was I talking about this?

"I should get back to the clinic."

Disappointment flashed through his eyes, but it vanished as quickly as it came. "Ok," he said.

On our way back, I made sure to walk at least an arm's length away. It seemed like every time I got close to him, I ended up saying way more than I meant to. Why did he slip through my defenses so easily? I couldn't pretend I didn't have any feelings for him. I could feel them trying to put down roots and grow.

Griz and Sam stood in front of the clinic arguing about something, and I'd never been so glad to see them. They immediately pulled Trey into the argument, and I slipped back into the clinic.

Don't— Wolf started.

I know, I interrupted. *I know.*

Juck's grip on my jaw tightened.

"You belong to me," he hissed, spittle hitting my face. "All of you."

"Juck, please!" I got out, choking on sobs. "I'm sorry—"

The blow caught me across the face, and I fell back onto his bed with a cry. He loomed over me, crawling over my body to press a kiss on my neck. He still wore his bloodstained clothes.

"Gods, Angel, you make me so crazy," he murmured against my skin.

With every word, my body stiffened more. He'd never spoken to me or touched me like this before, but I'd never seen him this angry before either. His hand slid up under my shirt, and I started to panic.

"Juck, stop," I sobbed, trying to push him off.

"Did you beg him to stop?" he snarled in my ear. "Tell me you didn't fuck him."

I couldn't manage to get any words out, my breath coming fast and panicked. I shoved harder against him, but he didn't move. Wolf's training suddenly seared through my head like my brother was screaming at me to fight. I balled up my fist and punched him in the side, aiming for his kidney.

Juck grunted in pain. He half rolled off me and I tried to scramble out from under him, but he lunged and wrestled me back. This time he pinned my arms under his knees as he straddled me. The look on his face made pure terror flood me.

"I spent years protectin' you, keepin' you safe and cared for, and this is how you thank me?"

"Juck, please!" I begged.

"The gods sent you to me, Angel. You are mine to wield how I see fit; you hear me?"

"I'm sorry! Please don't—"

He hit me across the face again and I gasped, stars exploding across my vision. As I struggled to focus, I felt him yanking my pants down my thighs and I started screaming—

"Bones!"

I shot upright, panting in the darkness.

"It's alright, Bones," a soft voice murmured. "You're in the clinic. You're safe."

"Trey?" I asked shakily, my mind still stuck in the nightmare.

"I'm right here." The mattress dipped as he sat on it next to me.

I reached out blindly until my hand touched his bare shoulder. I planned to jerk away as soon as I figured out where he sat, but I couldn't seem to make my fingers move. His hand came up to rest on top of mine and squeezed, the warmth of his skin seeping into mine.

"I'm here," he murmured. "You're safe."

A strangled sob escaped my lips. I leaned forward until my head rested on his arm and he went still. I knew I shouldn't be doing this, but I just so desperately wanted to be comforted.

After about a minute, he let go of my hand to brush my tangled hair from my tear-streaked face. His fingers moved gently against my skin. I wasn't sure what it said about me that I found it so much easier to be close to someone like this in the dark. He wiped the tears that trailed down my face with his thumb.

"You're safe," he murmured again. "Juck's not here. He's dead. He can't hurt you anymore."

I squeezed my eyes shut, but it did nothing to stop the fresh batch of tears streaming down my face. I *did* feel safe with him here, and that knowledge didn't scare me as much as I knew it should.

He moved away, and I almost begged him not to go before I realized he was just shifting to sit beside me. His arm wrapped around my shoulders, and I immediately curled into him. We sat that way for a long time before my tears finally eased, but I was struck by the realization I didn't want him to go back to his own bed. His gentle, comforting touch was like a drug and I wanted more. I fought with myself for a while, but my defenses crumbled down, brick by brick. It wasn't long before I gave up and started to lay back. He immediately dropped his arm, but I caught his hand and tugged gently, trying to pull him down with me. He seemed to hesitate.

"Bones, you sure this is ok?" he asked. "You're awake right?"

"I'm awake," I said, my voice hoarse.

I tugged on him again and this time he came with me. I scooted over, giving him room to slide in next to me. He still seemed cautious, even once he lay beside me, so I went ahead and curled into his chest. His arms lightly wrapped around me.

"Promise you'll tell me if you want me to go back to my own bed?" Trey murmured.

"I don't want you to go back to your own bed," I said into his chest, enjoying the feel of his warm skin against my face.

He huffed a quiet laugh and his arms finally tightened around me. "Alright. I'm not arguing."

Wrapped up in his arms, the horror of my nightmare—my *memory* —began to fade. I closed my eyes and listened to his heart thundering in his chest. I waited for him to start pushing for more. I waited for his hands to start wandering. I waited for him to take what he wanted. Even after his heart slowed and his breath evened out in sleep, I still waited. I fell asleep waiting for him to turn into every other man I'd known.

CHAPTER 10

I woke before dawn.

I stiffened when I realized I lay in someone's arms, but when I lifted my head to see Trey still sleeping next to me, my entire body relaxed. I watched him for a while and my heart felt raw, like an exposed nerve. I'd never met anyone like him. I'd never struggled so hard to keep my distance. Yes, he was handsome, but he was also kind and gentle and patient—so patient.

I wanted to stay here until he opened his eyes. I wanted those beautiful eyes to warm at the sight of me like they always did, despite how much I pushed him away. I wanted him to smile and pull me tighter and kiss me.

You gonna do this again? You know how this ends, Wolf warned.

I tried to block them out, but Wolf seemed to release the memories with his words. A gentle touch against my skin, fevered kisses stolen in the cool dark desert, a secret smile offered across the bonfire, a fragile hope stirring in my chest, and then nothing but blood and horrifying screams and the tears that streamed down my face as I begged, *begged,* Juck to spare him.

My spine locked up. I wanted to scream at Wolf to shut up again, but I couldn't. He was right. I couldn't do this again. I couldn't watch the life fade from those brown eyes because of me. I'd taken this too far, and now I had to fix it. Gods, how could I fix it? Nothing I'd tried had worked so far, and I could only think of one other option.

I had to make him hate me.

The grief that swept over me physically hurt, but I forced myself to bear it.

Numbly, I slid out of Trey's arms. He mumbled something and rolled over but didn't wake. I shoved my feet in my boots and cracked the door open just enough to squeeze through. The morning bell hadn't rung yet, but people were up and making their way toward the canteen. I pulled my hood up over my head and fell in line. As I approached the canteen, the bells rang, and people began filing inside. I'd never shown up here before. Sam had been bringing my food to the clinic since that first day. I followed the crowd inside, glancing around.

The canteen was a long rectangular building. Inside there were rows and rows of wooden tables and benches. At the front was a large window where people stood handing out food. Behind them, an enormous kitchen stretched out. I slipped into the line and shuffled forward with the crowd until I reached the window. A man I'd never seen before handed me a warm tin foil packet without even looking up. I took it along with a crooked metal fork. Then I moved out of the way, searching around the room until I found him.

Zip sat talking and laughing with a bunch of similarly giant muscled men. I'd seen him around a few times since I'd healed him. He and his friends were rough and crude and prone to getting into stupid fights, but folks stayed out of their way. Most people didn't mess with them. So I took a breath and made my way over to sit next to him. The whole table went silent, staring at me in surprise, but Zip's face broke into a wide grin.

"You change your mind about that drink?" he asked.

"Yeah, I did," I said, hoping my voice didn't sound as dead as it felt.

He threw a brawny arm covered in tattoos around my shoulders. A leather tie pulled his dark hair back from his face. He had deep-set eyes under bushy eyebrows and a thick beard. The weight of his arm felt suffocating, but I forced myself to bear it.

"Glad to hear it." The smugness in his voice made me bristle.

"Bones?"

All of us looked up to see Trey standing at the end of the table. His eyes narrowed on Zip's arm around me, his jaw tight. A few paces behind him, Mac and Griz stood with grim expressions.

"Everything alright?" he asked.

I forced my expression to stay neutral. "Yeah, fine."

Zip's arm tightened around me, and he grinned toothily at Trey. "You heard the doc."

Trey's face darkened. He gave me a closer look, obviously trying to find some sort of distress in my expression. I hoped none of the turbulent emotions in my chest were showing on my face. I raised an eyebrow.

"You need something, Trey?" I asked.

A muscle jumped in Trey's jaw, but he just shook his head and strode away. I watched out of the corner of my eye as they all went and sat at another table. I could feel their eyes on me, but I ignored them. I desperately wanted to shove Zip's arm off me, but instead, I unwrapped my tin foil package and took a small bite of the eggs and potatoes.

"So, you wanna grab a drink tonight?" Zip asked.

I took another small bite, making him wait. "Sure."

Zip's grin widened. "I'll pick you up after the dinner bell, Doc."

I made an affirming sound, and when I didn't say anything else, the men's conversation resumed.

They were all loggers, I discovered as I listened, which explained the muscles. They went outside the wall armed with their axes and brought back wood for building and burning. I tried to keep from looking too interested about groups going outside the wall.

I managed to eat over half of my breakfast. *Sam is gonna be so proud.*

Irritation flooded me at the thought that just popped into my head. Why the fuck would it matter what Sam thought?

Once they were close to finishing up their food, I slid out from under Zip's arm.

"See you later, then."

As I strode away, I pretended not to hear the hoots and hollers coming from his buddies. I made it maybe five paces outside before Trey appeared at my side, and I steeled myself.

"The hell was that about?" he asked.

I gave him a sharp look. "What?"

He glared at me, that muscle jumping in his jaw again. "You know what I'm talking about."

I kept striding through the hold. "I don't think it's any of your damn business, Trey."

He grabbed my arm, forcing me to come to an abrupt stop. His eyes were dark. "Bones, last night—"

I jerked away, glaring right back. "Meant nothing."

The hurt that rippled across his face hit me straight in the heart. "Nothing?" he echoed. "You're really gonna tell me that meant nothing?"

"You took advantage, and I don't want it to ever happen again." I put as much spite and malice into the lie as possible, and he took a step backward like I'd slapped him. I followed, stepping into his space.

"I asked you—" he tried to say, his voice rough.

"Don't. Ever. Do that again," I hissed.

I didn't wait for his response, I just turned on my heel and strode away. My throat ached, trying to hold back tears, but I kept seeing the hurt in his eyes. The guilt and shame threatened to drown me, but I would rather he hated me for being a total bitch than watch him die. I managed to keep it together until I got to the clinic where I climbed up to the loft, sat in the corner again, and let myself cry for a few minutes, big ugly sobs shaking my shoulders. But after a few minutes, I forced myself to get up and go wash my face. I didn't deserve to grieve losing him any longer than that.

When I reached the sink I stopped and stared at the wall. A new mirror hung over the sink. It had a little shelf attached to the bottom and on it sat a tiny green glass bottle with a dandelion in it.

My eyes burned again so I washed my face, letting the ice-cold water soothe my swollen eyes. I stared at my reflection after I toweled off my face, avoiding the flower. My red, puffy eyes stared back at me. My face had filled out more since I'd studied my reflection in Clarity's mirror. I looked healthier—well, less sickly. The swelling around my right eye had gone down, leaving an ugly yellow bruise. Trey's neat stitches still held the gash in my head together, but I would be able to remove them in a few days. I turned my head to the side, examining the lighter bruise on my jawline, before meeting my own eyes again. I tried to see the ten year old girl I'd once been, but there was no trace of her in my hollow green eyes and bruised face.

When the first patient came in the door, I got a glimpse of Trey sitting outside. He stayed outside the whole day, both of us pretending not to notice each other. I watched the sun move across the sky with an increasing sense of dread. Too soon the bell rang for dinner. I didn't go, my stomach rolling uneasily. When the door opened, I jumped, but Sam stood there with a steaming mug of broth and my dinner ration.

"Hey." He moved into the clinic and set my food on the exam table, then stood there with his arms crossed.

I ignored the food, picking up the mug and sipping it. The warm broth helped calm my stomach.

"I was surprised to see you at the canteen this morning," he said, his voice suspiciously casual.

I didn't say anything, shame cutting through me that he witnessed me treating Trey like shit.

"You still want me to bring your food here?"

"I can get it myself."

He eyed me for a moment. "Didn't Zip try to hit you when you healed him?"

"That was Blaze."

"Right, my bad."

I wished he would leave, but he just stood there and stared at me.

"Do you need something?" I snapped.

"I'm just tryin' to figure out if you went and found the first big, ugly hunk of muscle you saw or if I'm supposed to believe you actually *like* Zip?"

"It's none of your fuckin' business." I glared at him.

"It's my fuckin' business when it involves my best friend." He glared right back, his voice angry.

I dropped my eyes and took a big drink of my broth, hoping it would wash down the lump in my throat. None of them could hate me as much as I hated myself.

"What the fuck are you doing, Bones?" His sharp voice cut through me.

The door crashing open saved me, and Zip's massive form filled the doorway. I set the mug down and noticed Sam had one hand on the gun at his hip. I stepped in front of him, blocking him from Zip's view as I walked to the door. Zip seemed like the type to take that kind of threat seriously.

Behind Zip I could see Trey sitting in the chair, watching with narrowed eyes. I ignored him as I stepped out with Zip and pretended I didn't feel his eyes boring into my back as we left.

We went to Zip's favorite dive, a grungy shack with "Mootzie's" over the door. Zip ordered two mugs of moonshine, a bitter brew that burned down my throat and into my empty stomach. It seemed like all the loggers were crowded inside, and they greeted Zip raucously. Soon everything grew blurry around the edges. Zip laughed next to me, an arm wrapped around my waist. He ordered us another round. Then another. After the third, I realized I didn't care that Zip's hands were all over me. It felt nice, not caring. Gods, how long had it been since I'd been drunk?

Zip and I got separated for a bit when the dive began to fill up with people. I made my way over to the bar to get another drink.

"Bones?"

I turned to see Hawk, the leader of the other Safeguard crew. I'd stitched up a small wound on his arm a few days ago.

"Hey," I said, and I must've sounded a lot more friendly than normal judging by the surprised look on his face.

"I was hoping to see you again." The surprised look turned into a flirtatious smile.

"You better not be bleeding." I raised an eyebrow.

"Not bleeding." He held his hands up in surrender, laughing.

"Good 'cause I'm off duty."

He stepped closer, scanning my bruised face. "Damn, I saw the newsboard but—"

An arm snaked around my ribs and pulled me back until I was pressed up against a broad chest.

"Hey, Hawk," Zip said, his voice a low warning.

The realization dawned on Hawk's face, the flirtatious smile vanishing. "Hey, Zip."

"Bones, you want another drink?" Zip asked.

"Have a good night, you two," Hawk said before vanishing back into the crowd.

"I don't share, Doc," Zip said low into my hair, the threat clear. "Now c'mon, I'll get you another drink."

I went with him, letting him hold onto me like he feared someone would snatch me away. I hated it, but I knew how to play this role. I'd wagered he would be jealous and possessive, which meant if I was with Zip, nobody would mess with me either.

Well, except for Zip.

I practically chugged my next drink.

Zip started playing a game of cards with me perched in his lap. As

I glanced over Zip's shoulder, I met flinty grey eyes and froze. Mac and Griz sat across the room at a table. They each had a drink in front of them, but both of them watched me with narrowed eyes. I looked away, my temper rising. Gods, why couldn't they just leave me alone?

Zip laid down his cards and swore when he lost again. Even with my dulled senses, I could tell a fight was brewing, and I didn't want to patch him up again.

"C'mon, Zip," I caught his face to get his attention, "let's go."

Zip's bleary gaze landed on me, startled like he'd forgotten I was even there. A wicked smile curled under his beard.

"Keep yer cards, Blaze," he slurred, standing. "I got better things to do."

I slid off his lap when he stood, but then he grabbed me and jerked me up into his arms to kiss me hard. Blaze and his buddies jeered and heckled him, but Zip just pulled back with a grin and steered us toward the door, his hand on my ass. Mac and Griz watched us go. I pretended not to see them.

Zip led me out of the dive and then roughly pressed me up against a shack, his lips hard and demanding against mine. The moonshine made it easy to surrender as his hands roamed down my body. Gods, I hoped Mac and Griz hadn't followed us out. I forced my thoughts away from them as I dug my nails into Zip's shoulders hard enough to make him growl. I didn't want him to be gentle. For once I wasn't trying to forget about other rough hands. I wanted to forget the gentle ones that had held me last night. I didn't want to think about Trey. I didn't want to think at all.

I woke up with a start.

Next to me, Zip snored, his naked body half draped over mine. I didn't recognize the tiny shack I'd woken up in, and I scanned the room. There wasn't much to see, a few pieces of homemade wooden furniture, a dirt floor, and the pile of furs we were laying on. I slid out from under Zip, waves of nausea rolling over me. My head pounded as I collected my clothes. There were several new bruises on my body. I hadn't wanted gentle, and from the bits and pieces I could remember, I'd gotten my wish. Hopefully, he'd been too drunk to notice the brand on my chest.

I dressed as quickly and quietly as I could manage. Thank the gods, Zip didn't even stir. When I stepped outside, the sun hadn't even fully risen yet, but the light sent stabbing pains through my head. I made it a few steps before puking into the frosty grass.

Wolf stayed silent in my head. I debated poking at him, demanding he express his disapproval, but I couldn't find the energy. I stumbled back to my clinic, stopping to retch a few more times. Gods, what did Mootzie put in that shit? When I opened the door to the clinic, my heart skipped a beat in my chest at the sight of Trey sitting on the chair by the door, still dressed and awake. I forced myself to continue inside. He stared at me as I toed off my boots, his jaw tight.

"You look like shit," he said.

I flashed a vulgar hand signal as I went around him to collapse onto my bed. The silence felt full of tension. I wished he would leave.

"Why you doin' this, Bones?" he finally asked.

I swallowed hard, refusing to lift my face from the lumpy mattress. I needed him to be mad. I could deal with mad. I could not deal with the hurt in his voice.

"Go away," I mumbled.

"You gotta know," Trey continued like I hadn't even spoken, "dammit, Bones, you gotta know I care about you. I'm sorry you feel like I took advantage of you. I was trying real hard to make sure you didn't —"

"Go. Away." I lifted my head enough to spit the words at him.

He stared me down. "You wanna know what I think?"

"No."

He continued anyway, "I think you let me in just a little bit, and now you're pushing me away 'cause you're scared."

"You're wrong."

"I don't believe you—" he started, but I didn't let him finish.

"What? You think you're special 'cause I saved your life and let you into my bed? Well, you're not. Now leave me the fuck alone!"

In the silence, he stared at me, hurt and anger replacing the warm kindness I'd grown so used to seeing on his handsome face. I held his gaze, eyes blazing. Finally, he just stood and let himself out. I collapsed back onto my mattress and swallowed the bitter tears aching in my throat.

I don't care, I repeated in my head like a magic spell from a storybook. Maybe if I said it enough times it'd come true. *I don't care.*

It felt like I'd just closed my eyes when someone shook me roughly awake. I jolted, looking up to see Mac glaring down at me.

"Madame wants you," he said.

Fuck.

I crawled out of bed, my stomach churning for more reasons than just being hungover as shit. Mac leaned against the exam table and waited as I washed my face, hoping the cold water would help. I waited on edge for him to say something about last night, but he didn't say a word. I wasn't sure what was worse.

When I was ready, he led the way, staying a few paces ahead of me as I tried to keep up. My anxiety grew with every step.

We went straight down the stairs back to that horrible room with the straw floor and I tried to steel myself. Madame stood inside with two of her guards. My stomach sank when I recognized the woman strapped to the chair. It was Mist, the soapmaker. She looked like she'd put up a fight, her face battered and bloody, but her eyes blazed angrily.

"Oh good, Bones, you're just in time," Madame purred. "Mist is being very uncooperative."

I had to fight to keep from retching right there. The room reeked like blood and that sickly sugary scent. Mac closed the door behind him and stood in front of it. The suffocating feeling of being trapped did not help.

"Fuck you, bitch," Mist spit at Madame.

Madame smiled. She drew that all-too-familiar knife and stalked around Mist, looking thoughtful.

"Where should we start, Bones?" she mused.

I stayed pale-faced and silent, but she didn't seem to care. Eventually, she stopped and brushed Mist's light hair away from her ear.

"Who gave you the order?" Madame asked in a low, deadly voice.

Mist just snarled at her. Madame grinned and then with one swift motion, she sliced Mist's ear clean off.

Mist cried out and jerked as blood spurted. I took a step forward instinctively, horrified, but halted when Madame held out her hand for me to stop. Madame walked around to Mist's other side and pulled her hair back from her other ear.

"Who gave you the order?" she repeated.

Mist gasped in ragged breaths, but she still didn't speak. I saw Madame move and closed my eyes so I didn't have to see her slice off Mist's other ear. The noise that came out of Mist's mouth made the hair on the back of my neck stand on end.

"Bones."

Madame's sharp voice forced my eyes open. She gave me a hard look as Mist sobbed through her teeth beside her, blood running down her neck.

"I want her to be able to hear me, but don't bother trying to make her look pretty," Madame ordered.

I moved forward woodenly and placed my hands on either side of Mist's bloody head. I couldn't meet her eyes, shame blazing through me like a fire. My healing stopped the blood and closed the wounds, but her ears were still gone.

"Can you hear me, Mist?" Madame demanded.

Mist spit a mouthful of blood at her, and I jumped as Madame plunged her knife through the palm of Mist's hand. Mist screamed and out of pure desperation and panic, I looked at Mac.

I can't do this. I screamed inside my head.

He met my frantic gaze with his steady one. I didn't know him well enough to know his tells. Did he hate this as much as I did? Did he not mind watching Madame torture people? I was near tears, but his face stayed expressionless.

I gave up and looked away. Madame tortured Mist for several hours. She just kept asking the same question, and Mist refused to answer. I didn't know what the question meant, and I sure as hell wasn't gonna ask. I healed Mist when Madame instructed, avoided eye contact, and tried to pretend I was somewhere far, far away. Finally, Madame signaled to the guards to take Mist back to her cell.

"Bones, you go and make sure she lives to see another day," Madame commanded me. "I'm not done with her yet."

Mac and I followed as the two guards dragged Mist's limp body down the hallway. There were more cells down here than I'd thought. And most of them were occupied. Scrawny faces pressed themselves against the bars, watching us walk past. I kept my eyes down, trying to avoid looking at them.

The guards threw Mist into her cell and then stepped out, gesturing at me with a sneer. I slipped through the open door and knelt at her side to place my shaking hands on her bloody arm. She wasn't conscious, but I healed her injuries and took away the pain. I couldn't make her ears grow back, but at least she could still hear. Hot tears fell on my hands as I leaned over her.

"I'm sorry, Mist," I breathed. "I'm so sorry."

She didn't wake up, but her breathing had evened out. I got to my feet, wiping my dirty, bloodied sleeve across my face before I turned around. Mac stood outside the bars a few steps away from the guards, watching me, his face still expressionless. The guards locked the door after I stepped out and led the way back down the hall. I followed them numbly, Mac at my side. As we walked past the cells a sudden voice rang out, startling all of us.

"Hey, you!"

I looked up with Mac and the guards to see a man hanging on the bars of his cell. Unlike the others I'd seen, he didn't look gaunt and sick. He wore simple clothes, but he was muscled in a way that would make most people steer clear of him. His unkempt black hair hung down in his face. I met his sharp almond-shaped eyes and my heart stopped. He was staring straight at me as though he *recognized* me.

"Shuddup," one of the guards said, smacking the cell bars with the butt of his gun.

The man fell back, his arms raised, but he didn't look away from me. I ducked my head and hurried after the guards, but I could still feel his eyes on me until we went up the stairs and out of sight. My heart pounded in my throat, but the guards didn't seem to have noticed so I kept my mouth shut. I didn't recognize him at all. He wasn't a Reaper. If he'd met me before, I had no idea how or when.

I hated the way the bright sunlight outside highlighted all the blood coating my hands and clothes, revealing the horrible things I'd done in that room. I didn't wait for Mac, I just made a beeline for the clinic. I desperately wanted to get out of these bloody clothes and wash off the blood and grime coating my hands. I caught a glimpse of Mac following behind me as I threw the clinic door open and stormed inside. Anger crackled under my skin.

I went right to the sink, scrubbing my hands with more force than I needed. The lavender soap did nothing to calm down my raging emotions and made me feel more guilty for what I'd done to the person who so carefully crafted it. Tears welled in my eyes, but the door opened behind me and I knew Mac had followed me inside, and I sure as hell was not gonna cry in front of him.

"Did you know that guy?" Mac asked.

"What guy?" I asked through my teeth, playing dumb.

"The one in the cell."

"No."

It wasn't a lie, but in the silence, I could tell Mac didn't believe me.

"He looked like he knew you."

"I don't know him, Mac."

I finished scrubbing my skin raw and turned around. Mac leaned with his back against the table, arms crossed over his chest, watching me. I had the sudden urge to scream at him.

"What?" I snapped instead.

Mac stared at me like I was a riddle he wanted to solve. I glared back at him, waiting.

"I'm not ok with it," he said in a low voice.

"Ok with what?"

"The torture," he clarified.

"Congrats on not being a monster," I spit out.

One corner of his lip turned up. "I could tell you were wondering."

"Great. Thanks for letting me know you're not ok with the horrible thing you're forcing me to do."

His amusement disappeared. "I'm not forcing you to do anything."

I scoffed. "I would not *be here* if you hadn't brought me here *by force.*"

He shifted, but his grey eyes narrowed. "You're not the only one who doesn't have a choice, Bones. Maybe if you stopped trying to be a godsdamn martyr, you'd see that."

He turned on his heel and slammed the door behind him before I could come up with a response.

CHAPTER 11

Only one day passed before Mac returned. I was in the middle of healing a child who'd broken out in red scabby spots and a fever. When the door opened and he strode in, my stomach dropped. He didn't say anything and leaned against the wall by the door, waiting. I finished my work, endured the tearful mother's gratitude, and then went to the sink to wash my hands. Mac stayed silent behind me, most likely still pissed, which was fine by me. I turned around as I dried my hands, expecting to see him still brooding by the door, but sucked in a startled gasp to find him right behind me.

"What—"

"I'm gonna ask you one more time," he said in a soft voice that made a chill walk down my spine. "Did you know that man in the cells?"

"No!" We were back to this again? I couldn't help yielding back a step, bumping into the sink, but he followed, towering over me. "I told you, Mac, I *don't know him.*"

He stared down at me, his face still expressionless and his eyes so dark they looked as black as his hair. Something must have happened. Something big.

"Why are you still asking me that?" I demanded. He stood just inches away from me, trapping me against the sink.

"Because somehow last night he escaped the watchtower, and nobody escapes the fucking watchtower without help."

I glared up at him, but internally my heart pounded. If he didn't believe me, how would I prove that I had nothing to do with it? Trey could back me up, but *would* he after the horrible things I said to him? Not to mention that I wasn't happy to hear that man escaped either. I didn't know who he was, and I didn't want to find out.

"Madame is on a warpath, and maybe the guards didn't notice how he looked at you, but I sure as hell did. He *recognized* you."

"I know. I saw it too," I snapped, deciding impulsively that honesty would be the best choice in this situation. "Maybe he saw me before with the Reapers. I don't know. But *I* don't know him."

He stared me down for so long that I had to resist the urge to fidget.

"If you don't believe me, why don't you ask Trey if I was here all night?" I caved to the urge to break the silence.

"I already did," he replied.

My heart sank. Of course, Trey would use this to his advantage. I'd hurt him and gave him the perfect opportunity to hurt me back.

"He said you were here all night," Mac added.

It took me a second to register what he said. My brows knit together in confusion. "What—" I forced myself to push past my desperate need to understand why Trey hadn't seized this opportunity and focused on the *other* reason for my confusion. "Then why are you in here using your scary asshole act on me?"

His eyes widened, surprise flashing through them before he narrowed them again. "Because I want some answers."

"Well I've got none," I snapped.

"I want to know why you looked so scared when you saw him recognize you."

My mouth went dry as my mind spun with how to answer him. He studied my face, and I had a terrible feeling that if I lied, he would know.

"I try not to be noticed. By *anyone*." I managed to get out.

"Why?"

My mind raced with how to avoid giving him the real answer while also not lying. "It doesn't usually end well."

"What do you mean?" he pushed, and I didn't have to fake my temper surging through me.

"Don't play dumb. You know exactly what I fuckin' mean." I gestured at my bruised face.

Something that looked an awful lot like regret flashed across his face. Behind him, the door opened, and a man limped in with a bloody bandage around his leg. He paused in the doorway when he spotted us, me standing with my back to the sink and Mac looming over me.

"This a bad time?" he asked.

"No," I said.

"Yes," Mac said at the same time.

I gave Mac an annoyed glare and stepped around him. "No. It's fine. You hurt your leg?"

The man eyed Mac nervously. "You sure—"

"It's fine," I repeated. "Mac was just leaving."

The man's eyes widened and he glanced at Mac again. I refused to turn around to see Mac's expression, but I imagined he looked less than pleased that I was throwing him out of the clinic.

"See you later, Bones," Mac said smoothly, surprising me. He stepped around me and strode to the door, disappearing through it without a look back as though we'd been discussing the weather.

I took a deep breath and turned back to the injured man. "Let me take a look."

In the weeks that followed, Trey didn't speak to me unless necessary, though he still guarded the clinic. Every day he went outside at dawn and stayed there until dark when he came in and went to bed. Sometimes Griz or Sam would take the day shift as they traded off helping rebuild the homes that'd been lost in the slum. I continued to find dandelions on the shelf under the mirror, but I never acknowledged them. My face healed and people finally stopped staring. I hardly saw Mac at all except for the couple of times he came and summoned me back to the dungeon to help Madame torture people. Neither of them was Mist, and I couldn't find the courage to ask if she still lived. Mac and I didn't talk at all on those walks to and from the watchtower, and I managed to resist the urge to look at him when the torture sessions ripped more of my soul to shreds. The man who'd escaped had apparently vanished into thin air.

In the mornings I went to the canteen with Zip and the loggers and at night I went out drinking with them. When I got home, I always found a mug of broth and my dinner ration on the exam table, but I didn't see any of Mac's crew at Mootzie's again. Most of those nights ended with me waking up in Zip's shack. If he ever noticed the brand on my chest, he didn't mention it, though I doubted he noticed much due to how drunk he got. Not that I had any room to judge because I got shitfaced every night so I wouldn't freak out about Zip's hands on my body. I lost any weight I'd managed to put on my bones from throwing up in the mornings. It was a shit routine, and I knew it, but it was better than staying and seeing that hurt on Trey's face.

Raven started coming by more often. Unlike the others, she didn't even try to hide her anger at what I'd done to Trey. I attempted to ignore her, but her words often stuck in my heart like barbs.

"Don't know what you see in that hulking beast," she said by way of greeting as she stepped through the door one afternoon.

I assumed she meant Zip, but I pressed my lips together and continued doing laundry in the sink.

"But I don't know what the fuck Trey sees in *you* either," she continued.

I scrubbed my dirty clothes with more force than necessary.

"You know you're lucky you have *magic healing powers,*" her words dripped with scorn, "otherwise you'd be completely worthless."

"Do you need something?" I snapped, turning to face her, soapy water dripping off my hands.

Raven widened her eyes. "I'm just doing my job, Boney."

"Which is what exactly?" I glared at her, refusing to comment on the nickname. "I don't need help. So go do something else."

"Can't." She smiled, showing all her teeth. "I'm on guard duty."

"Then go guard *outside.*"

"Maybe I don't want to." She picked up a pair of forceps near the sink and clapped them together at me.

I forced myself to clench my jaw shut and turned back to the sink, scrubbing the blood and vomit from my clothes.

"He must be *really* good in the sack, is that it?"

"What?"

She leaned on the counter, watching me with a sharp light in her blue eyes. "Zip," she said like I was stupid.

"I'm not talking to you about Zip," I said through my teeth.

"You know most people just go to the brothel when they want to get laid," she continued like I hadn't said anything.

The fury that rushed through me broke through my self-control. "I don't go to fucking brothels where most of the workers there don't have any other choice."

She raised an eyebrow, her voice taunting. "Oh, I touched a nerve. Guess you would know since you were Juck's whore."

I flinched and hated that I showed that weakness in front of her. "Get out," I snapped.

"Make me," she sneered.

I whipped around to face her, fury blinding me, but the door abruptly opened, and Sam entered. He scanned both of us, quickly reading the energy in the room, and then strode forward to grab Raven by the arm.

"Alright, I'm relieving you of guard duty," he said firmly, pulling her toward the door.

Raven jerked free. "Fine. I have better things to do anyway."

She slammed the door hard, making the windows rattle. I turned my back on Sam and went back to washing my clothes, trying to blink back furious tears. I heard Sam slowly approach.

"What'd she say?" he asked sharply.

"Doesn't matter," I muttered without turning around.

"Shortcake, that's—"

"I'm not talkin' about it," I interrupted. "Leave me alone."

"Bones—"

"Go *away,* Sam,*"* I tried to say fiercely, but my voice broke, which I *hated.*

After a brief silence, he let out a heavy sigh. "Alright. I'll be outside."

I waited until I heard him walk to the door and step outside, shutting it softly behind him. In the silence, I gingerly touched the horrible brand hiding under my shirt. The hot, angry tears escaped, and I let them fall. I hated Raven, but she spoke the truth. I'd never be able to escape the things Juck had done to me. Even if he hadn't marked his cruelty into my skin, he'd left scars on my very soul.

***

"Angel!"

My spine went rigid, but I didn't turn around from the stall of fresh herbs at the market. I recognized Megs' voice. She still came around every so often, trying to get into the clinic to see me. Sometimes she made it inside, but most of the time whoever guarded the clinic told her to get lost.

"Angel, please! I beg you for your blessing!"

At my side, Sam snorted. "How come you never ask me for a blessing, Megs?"

In the silence, I could just imagine her blinking owlishly in confusion.

"The gods have sent—" she tried.

"Yeah, yeah," Sam interrupted, "we know the spiel. Sorry, we're fresh outta blessings. Come back next week."

I stood frozen, holding a sprig of mint and listening for the sound of her footsteps drawing nearer. Instead, I heard her mumble something and shuffle away. I glanced at Sam, unable to hide my surprise.

"What?" he said. "I know how to de-escalate a situation."

I raised my eyebrows.

"Sorry, shoulda realized you wouldn't know what that means. It's responding to people in a way that *doesn't* make them want to hit you."

"Everything you say makes me want to hit you," I said dryly, the words slipping out of my mouth and surprising me.

He looked surprised too, but he grinned. "Yeah well, that's a *you* problem."

I rolled my eyes and went back to picking through the mint. I needed to make more tinctures to treat nausea and upset stomach. Once I had what I needed, Sam stepped up and paid. I knew Madame gave Mac some sort of stipend to purchase ingredients and tools necessary for me to work. I started small, but over time I added more things I needed, and no one ever questioned my purchases.

As we walked back to the clinic, my anxiety grew with every step. I knew Trey would be replacing Sam later and in a few hours Zip would

—

"So *are* you an angel?" Sam asked.

Nausea curdled in my stomach. "Don't call me that."

"Why not?"

I had to unclench my jaw so I could answer. "Because I don't like it."

"How come?"

"Just don't," I snapped.

"Why?"

Gods, did he *want* me to hit him? I picked up my pace, but he matched my steps.

"Some girls like bein' called 'Angel'," he pushed, unrelenting.

"How would you know?" I glared at him.

He clutched his chest like I'd stabbed him. "Shortcake, what are you implying?"

I ignored him.

"I'll have you know I'm a high commodity around here."

"Funny, seems like I'm the only person you ever talk to."

"I talk to lots of people!" He grinned.

"Then how 'bout you go talk to one of them and leave me alone."

"You'd miss me," he said.

"Let's try it and see."

"You *wound* me!" he said dramatically. "I'm delightful!"

"You're *annoying*."

"Shortcake, you tryin' to break my poor lil heart?"

"If your heart's anywhere near as thick as your head, I think you'll be fine."

"Hey!" He sounded genuinely indignant now. "That was mean!"

I rolled my eyes, but to my surprise, I had to fight the urge to smile. He grumbled and whined about how mean I was, but for the first time in weeks, he didn't seem angry at me. It felt like a breath of air after being underwater.

We'd made it halfway back to the clinic when Trey came running around a shack and barely managed to avoid crashing into Sam.

"Whoa—" Sam started, catching him by the shoulders.

"It's Clarity," Trey gasped. "She's hurt."

The three of us sprinted the entire way to the brothel. Trey tried to fill us in as we ran. A regular client of hers liked to get rough. There had been an incident just a couple weeks before I arrived where he nearly killed her. He'd been banned from the brothel for a while, but they missed his coin enough to let him return.

"How bad is it?" I asked, trying to ignore the painful stitch in my side as I ran.

"It looks bad." Trey's voice sounded tight with pain and fear. "I can't tell though."

I tried to prepare myself for the worst, but my stomach still dropped at the sight of her when I entered her room. She lay on her bed, another brothel worker sitting beside her, dabbing her bloody face with a cloth. I could hardly recognize her swollen face and she breathed raggedly, her nostrils flaring like she struggled to get enough air into her lungs.

I dropped everything I held on the floor and rushed up to her side. Her head turned toward me, but she didn't say anything. I didn't say anything either, just took her hands and began to work. The golden warmth seemed to flow to every part of her body, healing a multitude of injuries. Slowly the bleeding stopped and the swelling on her face receded. Her breathing evened out. She started trying to mumble something to me, but her eyelids drooped.

"It's ok, Clarity," I murmured, squeezing her hands. "Just rest."

She managed to squeeze my hand back a tiny bit and then her eyes closed. Once she'd been healed, every small scratch erased, I set her hands back down on her stomach. When I looked up, the girl who sat on her other side stared at me, her mouth open in awe. I dropped my gaze, feeling uncomfortable.

"How much does it cost?"

The whispered words had me looking back up. The girl looked nervous, but she swallowed and asked again, "How much does it cost?"

"Nothing," I said, my throat tight.

Her eyes widened and she glanced between me and Trey and Sam. "Can…can you help me with something?"

I followed her back to her room, noting she shared it with four other girls. It was small and cramped and smelled sour, very different from Clarity's single room decorated with red silks. Two girls slept in their beds, and the other three beds were empty.

"I have this rash," the girl said in a tiny whisper, "itches somethin' fierce. I keep scratchin' it til it bleeds."

She showed me the rash, and it took just a couple of seconds to heal it. The simple act left her in tears.

"Thank you," she whispered. "Thank you."

"You can always come get me if you get something like this again," I told her, unable to keep the emotion from my voice. "Please tell the others."

"The previous healer wouldn't treat us." She sniffled, wiping at her eyes. "Said we were worse than rusters. He'd drop off some bandages and medicines but that was it."

"I'm not like that," I said, furious at the thought of refusing to treat someone because they worked at a brothel. "Tell the others they can come anytime. Or I can come here."

"Thank you, Bones," she whispered again as I slipped out the door.

The weather turned colder. I started going for walks along the wall whenever I had free time, trying to covertly examine the layered metal sheets between me and freedom. I could feel the pressure of time building. It wouldn't be long before the mountains filled up with snow, and then I'd be stuck here until spring. The walls were made of giant sheets of metal welded together and overlapped in layers. It must have taken forever to build, but it stood impressively solid. I couldn't find any holes or spots that looked a little weak. The smaller gate on the other end of the hold had been chained shut with multiple padlocks and some pieces of wood nailed across it for good measure. The only way out was through the guarded gate.

The loggers got sent out for an extended trip to bring back more wood for winter. I thought about trying to sneak out with them, but Madame kept me so busy torturing people for four nights in a row that I missed my opportunity. I wondered if she did it on purpose.

The first night of Zip's absence, I didn't know what to do with myself. I cleaned the entire clinic just to have something to do since I didn't want to go to Mootzie's by myself. As I dumped out a bucket of dirty water outside, I noticed two small children darting through the shadows. I moved slower, watching them out of the corner of my eye. They followed a drunk man who stumbled down the path eating his dinner ration. He dropped about half of his food, and the children darted out to pick up every tiny crumb. Something in my chest twisted. As I stood there outside, pretending to work, I noticed more. They moved like tiny ghosts with hollow faces and empty eyes.

"You need help?"

I startled, looking at where Trey sat in the wooden chair by the clinic door, watching me.

"No," I said, going back inside and slamming the door.

When Sam brought me my mug of broth and meal ration, I asked him about the kids.

"They're orphans," he said. "They're too young to work, so they have to beg or scrounge for food until they're big enough to join a workforce, the guards, or a crew."

I frowned. "They can't get food at the canteen?"

"Only working folks can get food at the canteen." His voice didn't waver, but *something* flashed in his blue eyes.

"What about the kids who have parents?"

"If the parents can work, they're allowed a little extra for their children."

I thought about all the food I'd passed up and the guilt ate me alive. After he left, I quickly divided my ration into half a dozen small packages, leaving just the broth for myself. I gulped down the broth and then shoved the food into a bag that I slung over my shoulder. When I stepped outside, Trey looked up at me, surprised.

"I'm just runnin' an errand," I said. "I'll be back in a few minutes."

He frowned at me. "What errand?"

"A personal one," I snapped. "I'll be back, ok?"

I strode off without waiting for an answer. When I couldn't see the clinic any longer, I slowed, watching the shadows for the tiny figures. The first one took off when I got close. I didn't have much luck with the second, so I started leaving the little packages on the ground near their hiding spots. I tried to do it stealthily, slipping through the shadows like they did. I wasn't sure what Madame would do if she caught me, but I doubted she'd be happy about it. I never saw any of the children take the packages, but when I would glance back, the ground would be empty.

By the third night, the children stopped running from me. They didn't approach, but they stayed put, watching me with giant, hungry eyes. I tried to give my small meals to different kids every night, spreading the food around to as many children as I could. Some were so young it hurt to see them.

On the fifth night, I tried talking to them. Not directly. I didn't want to scare them off. But when I would set the food package down near them, I would talk in low tones, keeping my eyes on the ground.

"I'm Bones. I'm the healer. If you're ever sick or hurt, come to the clinic."

Another few nights passed before the first tiny person slipped through the clinic door so quietly I didn't hear them, and when I turned around, I nearly jumped out of my skin. A little girl stood inside, her clothes hanging off her thin frame. Her pale blue eyes took up most of her face. When I jumped, so did she, retreating a few steps toward the door.

"It's ok," I blurted out, trying to think of a way to keep her from running. I sank until I sat on the floor, crossing my legs in front of me. "You just scared me a little."

She stopped moving backward, eyeing me. I could tell she had a fever just by looking at her flushed cheeks and glassy eyes.

"I'm Bones," I said. "What's your name?"

She didn't answer for a long while, but I forced myself to wait.

"Apple," she whispered.

"Hi, Apple," I said. "Are you hurt? Or sick?"

She chewed on her lip for a few seconds, but then pulled her filthy sleeve up to reveal an infected gash in her arm.

"Ouch," I murmured. "That looks like it hurts."

She hesitated, then nodded.

"Did you know I can do magic?" I asked. "I can make that go away. You wanna see?"

Her eyes got even larger. I waited and after about a minute, she took tentative steps up to me. I held out my hands, palms up, and let her place her injured arm into my hands.

"It won't even hurt," I whispered. "Watch."

I gently wrapped my fingers around her arm and sent that warmth down my arms and into hers. She jumped when it flowed into her, her eyes widening in surprise, but didn't pull away. Her little mouth fell open as she watched the oozing wound slowly close up and disappear, leaving a small pink scar. I let go as soon as it healed, folding my hands into my lap. She touched the scar with a filthy finger and then looked back at me, her eyes clear again.

For a moment we stared at each other. She had to be about five or six years old with dirty blonde hair and those huge blue eyes. I wanted to ask her how she got that wound, what happened to her parents, and where she slept at night, but I knew that would just scare her away. So I just stayed quiet and unmoving until she backed to the door before cracking it open. She spared a glance outside, checking for Trey, I assumed. A second later she vanished.

The next night, Apple brought two little boys with red, infected eyes nearly crusted shut. It took some convincing before they let me heal them, but once the first one went, the second one quickly followed. Apple even gave me a tiny, shy smile before the three of them slid out the door.

I sat on the floor for a few minutes after they left, tears pricking in my eyes. I never would have been able to do something like this with Juck. I still wasn't *happy* to be here, but this felt like something *good.* I could do something really, truly *good* here. Something no one else cared to do. I took a deep breath, my mind made up. I wasn't gonna stay, but I *could* stay through the winter. I could find a way to deal with my soul being shredded during torture sessions if it meant I could make sure these kids survived until spring.

It snowed for the first time three days later. When I set out for my evening "errands," huge flakes of snow drifted through the air. I'd only seen snow once before, so I walked a little slower, holding my hand out and admiring the snowflakes that landed on my thick mitten. Apple met me in the narrow alley between the stables and the blacksmith where we'd arranged to meet that night. The number of kids kept growing. I'd started saving half of my breakfast ration to divide up with my whole dinner ration, but it still wasn't enough. I learned from talking to them that in the summer and early fall, they could eat fallen fruit from the fruit trees and sneak a few vegetables from the garden or a couple of eggs from a chicken nest. Now that winter approached, those options had disappeared. The chickens who ran free through the spring, summer, and fall had been confined to a coop in the giant barn. All the fruit trees had been stripped bare and the fields barren. And despite my help, every night only a third of them got food. They took turns fairly well, but I knew sometimes fights broke out after I left because I healed the injuries.

Apple had become a tiny leader of sorts. She organized the kids into groups, ones who got food and ones who needed healing. I passed out the food and then set to work healing all the scrapes and burns and bruises and rattling coughs. I always used my powers, no matter how small the wound. I doubted they would voluntarily show up for stitches.

"It's a good thing Madame gave Mac that chance," an older boy named Atlas said as I healed his twisted ankle.

I peered up at him, my brow furrowed. "What chance?"

"The chance to save Trey."

"What?" I asked, my heart pounding.

"He got arrested. Mac bartered to get him out."

"Why was he arrested?"

"I dunno." He shrugged. "But she was pissed. She wanted to execute him."

My mind spun as I tried to absorb that information. Why hadn't I heard about this?

"Trey was part of the uprising," Apple added in a whisper from where she'd appeared by my elbow.

My skin prickled. "The uprising?"

"There are people who want to take down Madame," she whispered.

I'd figured out that much. As much as I tried to stay out of it, I couldn't help hearing the questions Madame asked during torture sessions. It wasn't much of a reach to assume she was trying to root out rebels, and of course, Trey would be a part of it. He was exactly the kind of hopeful dreamer rebellions snatched up for their cause.

"So wait, what chance? What did Mac do?" I whispered back.

"Mac said he'd go get Juck's secret weapon and give it to her if she let Trey go." Apple's eyes were so serious in the dim light.

My heart sank. "And she agreed to that?"

Atlas shrugged again. "Everybody wanted the secret weapon. We thought it was gonna be a magic potion."

"No, you thought it was gonna be a magic ring," Apple corrected him.

Atlas scowled at her. "It coulda been. There's magic rings in stories."

Apple didn't look convinced.

"But it's good she gave 'em the chance, 'cause we got you," Atlas said with innocent confidence.

I tried to smile, but I wasn't sure I managed it.

"You're not the only one who doesn't have a choice, Bones. Maybe if you stopped trying to be a godsdamn martyr, you'd see that." Mac's words ran through my head.

A new thought struck me, and I went cold all over. Was Trey still a part of the rebellion? Would I enter the dungeon one night and see Trey in that chair? Would I be forced to watch Madame carve him up until he screamed? I couldn't…I couldn't—

"Bones?" Atlas whispered, jolting me out of my panicked thoughts. Both he and Apple were staring at me with wide, anxious eyes.

"You ok?"

I wrestled the panic down, feeling shaky. "I'm ok. How do you know all of this?"

"We hear things," Atlas said.

"And see things," Apple added, her eyes haunted.

Gods, I didn't want to know what sort of things these kids had been exposed to. I took a breath and forced myself to focus on the task at hand. I finished healing Atlas and moved on to a tiny, frail girl with a sprained wrist. Her hands were icy cold, and without a second thought, I grabbed my mittens out of my pocket and put them on her small hands after I finished. I needed to figure out a way to clothe these kids better. None of them had appropriate clothing for the upcoming winter. I wondered if I could get away with having them sleep in my loft at night.

"Oh, Bones!" Apple chirped. "Look what I found!" She pulled a perfect tiny acorn out of her pocket and presented it to me, beaming. "It's for you!"

"Thank you," I murmured, taking it from her freezing little hand. "That's—"

The sound of footsteps crunching through the snow from one end of the alley made all their little heads snap up. A figure stepped out of the darkness and they took off like a flock of startled birds. Only Apple stayed at my side, near vibrating with fear and a strange protective anger. I stepped in front of her to shield her, but Trey stepped out of the darkness, eyes wide as he watched the kids disappear.

"Is this what you've been doin' every night?" he asked.

I got defensive. "Why?"

He looked startled at my tone. "Cause I'd have helped you if you asked."

I clamped down on the rising well of emotion in my throat. "I don't need help."

Those sad brown eyes cut like a knife. "Bones, c'mon. How long are you gonna do this?"

"Leave Bones alone," Apple spit from where she clutched my shirt. She reminded me of that fierce little kitten I'd held in the barn, all adorably puffed up but ready to bite.

Trey looked down at her and smiled, a real genuine smile I hadn't seen in weeks. "Well, hi." He crouched, resting his long arms on his knees. "I'm Trey. Who are you?"

"I know who you are." She tossed her hair back, and I had to fight the urge to smile. "I'm Apple an' *I'm* the one who helps Bones."

Trey nodded, his face grave. "Oh, ok. I apologize, Miss Apple. I was just wonderin' if I could help Bones too."

She frowned at him.

"I'm thinkin', if I helped too, we could feed even *more* kids every night," Trey continued.

Her eyes widened, and she glanced up at me. I kept my expression even, unsure of what to say. She squinted back at Trey.

"You gonna give up your ration too?" she asked.

I had to bite back a curse. Trey's brow furrowed in confusion for a second before understanding crossed his face. He glanced sharply up at me. "You're giving up your ration?"

I glared at him, my stomach churning. "Where else am I gonna get food?"

"I dunno, I thought you worked out a deal or something with Madame." He stood up and stepped closer. "How much of your food are you giving up?"

Apple's cold fingers dug into my side. I rested my hand on top of her head, trying to comfort her. "I don't think that's any of your business," I said.

"Bones." He rubbed his forehead in a jerky, frustrated motion. "Godsdamnit."

Panic started to creep in. What if he tried to stop me? What if he told Madame?

"Bones?" Apple whispered.

I forced myself to calm down, turning my back on Trey and kneeling to face her. She looked scared and I hated it.

"I'm gonna go talk to Trey," I said softly. "It's gonna be ok. I'll see you tomorrow, alright?"

She nodded, casting another worried glance up at Trey before turning and disappearing into the darkness.

I took a breath and stood, turning to Trey, steeling myself. His eyes met mine, shining soft and warm again, and I hated how they made me feel wobbly.

"I'm not gonna stop feeding them," I hissed. "You can't make me."

"I know," he said.

I blinked, surprised. I'd been expecting him to fight me on this.

He stared at my bare hands. "Where's your mittens?"

I flushed. "I gave 'em to one of the kids."

He held my eyes as he stepped closer and reached toward me. I narrowed my eyes, but he just gently took my cold hand. "Let's go back to the clinic where it's warm."

I paused, confused. "Ok." Shouldn't he still hate me?

He didn't let go, tugging me along with him as he turned and headed back to the clinic. I knew if I yanked my hand back, he'd let go, but for some stupid reason, I didn't. Back in the clinic, I expected him to drop my hand but if anything, he gripped it tighter. He led me to the wood stove before he stopped and turned, his face full of emotion.

"Bones, you don't have to hide the soft parts of you. Not from me," he murmured. "No matter what's goin' on between us, I will *never* use them to hurt you."

I stared at him, rooted to the spot by those words. I didn't understand how he *knew* the things that scared me without me saying it out loud. He stepped closer, still holding my hand, and I just continued to stand there staring as he caught my other hand too.

"I was never gonna make you stop feeding them," he said. "All I want is to make sure you don't kill yourself trying to save everyone else."

"I'm not gonna kill myself," I scoffed weakly.

He brought my icy hands up to his lips, blowing warm breath onto my fingers. I knew I should pull away. I knew I should say something cruel to push him away, but I couldn't.

"You know what I think about almost every night?" he murmured.

I could've sworn he pressed his lips briefly to my knuckles, but I wasn't sure. I thought I'd ripped out all the feelings I had for him, but I could feel them there again, tiny shoots uncurling and stretching upwards.

"I think about your face when Lana pulled that gun on you. You looked *relieved.* You were gonna just sit there and let her kill you. An' all I knew was that I couldn't let that happen."

My eyes burned and I blinked, trying to get ahold of myself, but the words spilled out. "You should hate me."

"Would you believe me if I said I tried?" That crooked smile ghosted across his lips.

"Trey—"

"Let me help you," he interrupted. "You wanna be with Zip? That's fine. Be with Zip. But please, Bones. Please stop pushin' me away. I'm never gonna try to make you stop caring, ok? It's one of the most beautiful things about you." He smiled. "Even though you try so damn hard to act like you don't care at all."

He let go of my hands and stepped back, leaving me chilled. I tried to think of something to say, but my brain had dropped clean out of my head.

"I'll talk to Mac about the kids, ok? See if we can work out a way to get some extra food."

"No," I said sharply and he frowned, but I continued before he could protest, "Let me talk to Madame. I'm sure I can work out a deal."

He studied me for a moment but nodded. "Alright. I'll let you handle it. Anything else?"

"I want to let 'em sleep in the loft," I blurted out. "There's plenty of room, and they're so small, and it's gettin' so cold. I can—"

"Ok."

I fell silent, staring at him.

"Ok," he repeated. "I think that's a great idea."

"Ok," I echoed. I hoped I didn't look as off-balance as I felt.

"Have you been eating *anything* for dinner?"

I winced. "My broth."

He shook his head at me, but he smiled. "You dumbass."

I tried to glare at him, but I wasn't sure I managed it.

"Can we be friends?" he asked, holding out his hand like he wanted to shake.

I hesitated, but before I could find the strength to resist, I put my hand in his again. His warm fingers curled around mine and gave it a firm shake.

"Friends," I whispered and his face transformed into that sunshine smile.

Gods, I wasn't sure I could hate Mac for dragging me here now that I knew why. I remembered the tension between Mac and Trey on our journey back to the Vault. I remembered Trey saying if they'd known Juck's secret weapon was a person, they wouldn't have taken the job. I doubted Mac would say the same if the alternative was Trey's death.

I didn't like the realization that Mac and I were more similar than I thought.

The next morning I went to see Madame. I'd never attempted to see her without being summoned, so I wasn't sure she'd see me, but when I spoke to the guards at the entrance of the watchtower, they beckoned me inside. Madame sat at a desk in her office with a map in front of her. She scanned me as I came in, her eyes as cold as always.

"What is it, Bones?"

"I want to use the orphans as my messengers," I said, keeping my voice steady and respectful. "That way people can get messages to me or send for me if they need help and I can send messages and medicine to people. It's not fair of me to keep Mac's crew tied up. They've got better things to do."

She eyed me for a moment. "You give those kids anything and you'll never see it again."

"I thought of that. An' I thought maybe if I could offer them shelter and food at the clinic, they'd be more willing to work for me."

Her eyebrows raised. "You want to house and feed the orphans at the clinic?"

"I know your policy is that only working folks can get rations," I chose my words carefully. "I want to put them to work. I need the help, an' they need the food and shelter. Everybody wins."

She leaned forward, steepling her hands together. "Those kids become a vital part of our workforce once they're big enough."

I swallowed down the fury rising in my throat. She didn't want to take care of these kids, but she still expected them to work for her once they got older. "This could be a temporary thing. They could work for me until they're old enough to move on."

In the silence, I held my breath. I didn't have a backup plan, and I had no clue what to do if she said no. Finally, she nodded.

"Alright. I think your plan could work. But you'll be responsible for them, you hear? They step out of line and it's on your head."

"Yes ma'am," I agreed, relief coursing through me.

"Tell Mac to find some supplies. I'll tell the canteen you're allowed to feed them."

I walked outside and despite the cold wind, I felt warm inside and out.

CHAPTER 12

The first night only a dozen of the children showed up to sleep in the loft. Apple was the first through the door, looking positively gleeful. The blankets Griz and Sam had scrounged up were tattered and threadbare but better than nothing. And to see the kids' reactions, you'd think I handed them the world.

Hearing the kids sleeping above where I lay on my mattress comforted me. Their little whispers and sleep mumbles meant they were safe and warm. Trey came in, kicking snow off his boots, and I sat up. In the dim glow of the wood stove, he noticed me and smiled. I crawled out from under my blanket, shivering, and crossed the room toward him.

"How many kids showed up?" he whispered, glancing up at the loft.

"Only about a dozen," I whispered back, frowning.

"More will come," he assured me, "once word spreads."

"I hope so," I murmured.

He shrugged out of his jacket, hanging it on the hook by the door, and bent to shake the snow out of his wet hair, turning his waves into loose curls. "It's still coming down out there."

"Trey?"

He glanced up at me through his damp curls, and my breath caught for a moment at how the firelight reflected in his eyes and played across the planes of his face. He was strikingly handsome. I tried to ignore my feelings for him wrapping roots around my heart.

"Thank you," I whispered, my voice hoarse with emotion.

His smile was so sweet and soft. "You're welcome, Bones."

⟋⟍

More kids did come, slowly—then as the weather got colder, all at once. Somehow we managed to get every kid who showed up a bed, and they didn't seem to mind that they were squished into the loft, sleeping on top of each other. Once people noticed the kids sleeping at the clinic, many of them started bringing extra food and clothing. Their generosity startled me. I thought no one else cared, but the people kept proving me wrong.

Leda and baby Jet came by almost every day. Leda had an eye for organizing and soon the loft upstairs had a semblance of being a bedroom. She even got Griz, Sam, and Trey to build some makeshift bunkbeds.

"I've wanted to do something about these kids for a long time now," Leda told me one day, Jet perched on her hip chewing on a wooden teething ring. "I wish we had a school, but Madame won't approve a building for one."

A school *was* a good idea. I'd learned how to read at the small schoolhouse in our hold, and I would've been fucked if I hadn't. I wasn't surprised Madame didn't think it was necessary though. So long as she had bodies for labor, she didn't seem to give a shit about the rest.

"Bones?"

I snapped out of my thoughts with a jolt. Leda stared at me, one eyebrow raised.

"I'm sorry, what did you say?" I asked, my face heating.

"I was just sayin' that Trey seems to be taken with you." She gave me a sly grin, her teeth flashing white against her dark skin.

I kept my face blank. "He's working."

She raised her eyebrows. "Oh is that all?"

I shrugged, trying to push away the memory of Trey's arms around me as I fiddled with things on the counter. "I'm with Zip."

"Yeah, I heard about that."

I wasn't brave enough to look at her, but I could hear the disapproval in her voice.

"All I'm sayin' is I've known Trey since he was in diapers, and I've never seen him so focused on someone before."

When I glanced up to glare at her, she just grinned.

"It's just his job," I said, my voice a little sharper.

Before she could respond, the door opened and Trey strode in, kicking snow from his boots and shaking it from his hair. He smiled at both of us, taking off his jacket before coming over, something in his hand.

"Hey Leda," he greeted her. "Thanks for all your help getting the beds situated upstairs."

"Of course." Leda smiled, then she glanced at his hand. "Whatcha got there?"

Trey's ears went a little pink. "Oh, I made something for Bones." He placed one of my small green glass bottles on the table with a single dandelion flower inside.

As I looked closer, I realized the flower was carved out of wood and painted a cheerful yellow with the stem green.

"Can't get the real ones now, so I figured this could stand in for 'em during the winter."

My heart felt impossibly tight and too big all at once. I picked up the little wooden carving, trying my hardest to keep my expression even, but I struggled. When I looked up, both Leda and Trey smiled at me.

"Thank you," I said, trying to pretend my voice didn't wobble.

"You're welcome, Bones," Trey murmured.

I knew if I held his gaze I would cry, so I turned and walked over to the mirror, setting the little dandelion carving on the shelf. It *did* add a little bit of sunshine. I washed my hands in the sink as an excuse to hide in the corner a little longer, pulling myself back together. When I came back to the table Trey had moved over to his mattress to take his pistol apart and oil it. He glanced up once and smiled warmly at me before focusing on his gun. Leda shifted Jet to her other hip and gave me a smug grin.

"*Definitely* just his job," she leaned in to whisper to me.

I rolled my eyes.

She laughed, her dark curls bouncing. "I'm heading home. I'll see you two later."

Trey gave her a wave. After the door shut behind her, silence fell but it wasn't uncomfortable. Trey focused on cleaning his gun. The few kids upstairs whispered to each other. A cheerful fire crackled in the wood stove, bathing the spotless clinic in a warm orange light.

The comforting feeling of *home* hit me straight in the heart.

You know better, Wolf said, but he sounded a little quieter than normal.

It'd been almost two weeks since Madame last summoned me to the dungeon. I could pretend that wasn't a part of my life. I could pretend that this was my home, where I wanted to be, that Trey—

I shoved those thoughts back down. I didn't have the luxury of indulging in silly fantasies. Zip would be back soon, and Madame would summon me any day. That was the reality of my life and pretending anything different would just make it hurt worse when it got taken away.

໑

The loggers came back a week later, several teams of large horses hauling giant logs. I didn't see Zip for a few days still, as they continued to work chopping and distributing the wood. When someone burst through the door five days after the loggers got back, I assumed it was Zip. I turned from where I stood by the stove with a pit in my stomach, but it wasn't him. It was the partner of one of the other loggers, his face panicked.

"Silver's sick," he blurted out. "Been sick since he got back, but it's gettin' worse. Can you come, Doc?"

I nodded, grabbing the med kit I'd put together. Trey waited outside and immediately took the heavy bag from me as we walked through the snow. Silver's partner, Marsh, walked so fast I had to trot to keep up. The temperature barely changed between outside and inside as we entered, the ramshackle walls doing almost nothing to keep the cold out. Inside, their shack reminded me of Zip's, but more furnished. Silver lay on a pile of furs, his normally tan face pale. His breathing sounded more like a gurgle. I made my way to his side and Trey followed so he could set the med kit down next to me.

"Silver?" I asked. "Can you hear me?"

His eyes stayed on the ceiling, unfocused.

"How long has he been like this?" I asked Marsh.

"He wasn't feelin' great this morning, but when I came home from workin' he was like this."

I took Silver's vitals with my worn instruments, my stomach churning with dread. A person declining that fast meant a serious illness. I laid my hands on Silver's sweaty shoulders and let my power flow into him.

It felt...*off.* I frowned as I continued to channel that warmth into him. Slowly his color came back, and his eyes focused on me, but it took a lot more effort than it should have. I kept going until his breathing sounded normal again. When I let go, my hands shook, and getting to my feet took an unusual amount of effort. I'd just finished packing up my med kit when Atlas came running through the door.

"Bones, there's a bunch of people sick," he gasped. "Got at least five people asking you to come."

Fuck.

Dawn broke before I stumbled back to the clinic. This sickness was spreading so fast. The kids had been bringing me messages and summons all day, and I was barely keeping my head above the water. I wanted to keep going, but Trey had threatened to throw me over his shoulder and carry me back if I didn't take a break to sleep.

"Just a couple hours of sleep, alright?" Trey said, my med kit hefted over his shoulder. "Then you can head back out."

I nodded, too exhausted to argue.

As we entered the clinic, the sound of labored breathing and rattling coughs reached us, and I darted up the ladder to the loft. A little boy named Cloud met me at the top of the ladder, his eyes huge and scared.

"They were ok at dinner," he whispered.

I sank beside the closest one, placing my hands on the little boy's thin shoulders as Trey crouched beside me.

"Are you feeling ok, Cloud?" Trey asked.

"Yeah." Cloud's voice trembled. "Am I gonna get sick too?"

"If you get sick, I'll heal you," I said. "You're gonna be ok."

He nodded, but he still looked scared. The sick boy finally took a breath without wheezing and opened his eyes.

"Miss Bones?" he whimpered.

"It's just Bones," I murmured. "You're ok. You got sick, but I'm healing you."

Cloud followed us to all five of the sick kids, and some of that fear melted away in his eyes as he watched me heal his friends.

"How do you do that?" he whispered at one point.

"I don't know," I answered, too tired to come up with anything else. "I just can."

"I wish I could do that too," he said and had to bite back the urge to tell him that no, he didn't want this.

"Well, you're a big help taking messages and medicine for me," I said instead, and when I glanced at him, he had a shy smile on his face.

On the last kid, Cloud sucked in a sharp breath, causing both Trey and I to look up at him.

"Your nose is bleeding, Bones," he said, his voice rising in alarm.

"It's ok." I hoped I sounded reassuring. "I'm ok."

Trey shifted beside me, pulling out a handkerchief. He met my eyes, his gaze concerned, but steady. "Ok if I get that?"

I nodded, feeling uncomfortable, but I didn't want to let go and stop healing this last kid. I wasn't sure I'd be able to start again. Trey dabbed at my nose, wiping away the blood in a strangely intimate gesture. Once I finished, I pulled my hands away and chills wracked my body. Cloud's eyes widened further.

"She's gonna be ok, Cloud," Trey said, wrapping an arm around my waist to steady me. "She just needs some rest."

"Cloud, go tell the other kids." Gods, I was so tired. "Tell 'em to come back here right away if they don't feel good."

Cloud nodded and darted down the ladder. One of the kids I'd healed started to cry. I looked in her direction and started to stand, but Trey's arm tightened around me.

"No, you're taking a rest," he directed.

"But—"

"Bones."

"I should stay up and see if any more sick kids come." I leaned on him, still shivering.

"You have to rest," Trey chided. "Remember how sick you got when you burnt yourself out?"

I grimaced.

"C'mon. Let's go down the ladder, you can lie down, and I'll keep an eye on the kids, ok?"

I nodded. I hated resting with people still sick, but as I shakily made my way down the ladder, I couldn't deny my body was nearing burnout. Trey made sure I drank some water and tucked me in like a child.

"I'll keep watch," he murmured. "Just rest, ok?"

I tried to mumble in agreement, but I fell asleep almost as soon as my head hit the pillow.

He let me sleep for three hours before he woke me back up and I started rounds again. It took just two days for hundreds of people to get sick. The more I healed, the more I believed this had to be the same disease that killed so many of the Reapers. Just like before, medicine had no effect. Only my healing powers made a difference. Last time I hadn't been able to use my powers on anyone besides Juck and Vulture. This time I saved almost everyone, but it took a huge toll on my body. I barely slept, dragging myself from shack to shack, healing until I reached the edge of burnout. We started taking a horse, usually Violet, with us on rounds because, by the time I finished, I couldn't even walk.

There was something so *unnatural* about this illness. Every other disease I'd ever healed felt natural, no matter how severe. I'd read about viruses and germs, and I knew they were made of the same materials as human bodies. This was different. It didn't feel normal. It felt *alien*, like an oozing darkness, and when my healing power connected with that darkness, it fought back. Instead of healing a sickness, it was like I waged a battle every single time.

Zip fell sick a couple of days after Silver. When I healed him, I didn't miss how his eyes kept flicking to Trey waiting by the door before narrowing on me again with suspicion. I hadn't seen him since before he left, and I had to fight the feeling that I'd done something wrong. He didn't say anything, but unease still swirled through me the entire time I healed him. He demanded a kiss before I left, and I obliged, hoping it would ease the anger he'd voiced that I couldn't stay and take care of him. He made a show of it, kissing me while his hands roamed my body. I hated it, but I let him.

The muscle in Trey's jaw ticked when we stepped outside, but he didn't say anything as he wrapped an arm around my waist and helped me stumble over to Violet.

The sickness didn't discriminate. Madame fell ill and so did all of the council. I bounced between the slums and the large nice houses and everywhere in between. I healed Madame with six of her men standing behind me with guns ready in case I got any ideas. I had plenty of ideas, but there was no need to threaten *me.* Trey standing in the room was all the motivation I needed to obey orders. I knew if I tried anything, Trey would do something stupid and heroic and end up dead.

I was healing Nemo when Trey swayed in my peripheral vision. I glanced at him to see a sheen of sweat on his pale face. He noticed me examining him and gave me a lopsided smile with glassy eyes.

"Why the fuck didn't you tell me you were sick?" I snapped at him, still funneling my healing power into Nemo.

"I was gonna," he mumbled.

I turned my attention back to Nemo. He was breathing easy now, that strange dark spot of sickness I could sense shrinking beneath my powers. In just another minute I smothered it and it vanished. I let go feeling relieved.

"Thank you, Bones," Nemo rasped .

I nodded and got to my feet, ignoring the way the room spun, and strode over to Trey, laying my hand on his forehead. I grimaced at how hot he felt. He shivered.

"Let's get you back to the clinic." I glared at him.

I wasn't too exhausted. I'd only been working for a couple of hours, and we hadn't even had to call for a horse yet. I hovered at Trey's side as we left for the clinic, noting his shivering was growing worse. Thank the gods it wasn't a long walk from Nemo's place to the clinic. When we made it through the door, Trey collapsed onto his mattress. I went to crouch next to him, but he held up a hand, halting me.

"No. Go drink some water first," he said through chattering teeth.

I muttered some choice words but did what he said. If this sickness had taught me anything it was that arguing with Trey was like arguing with a brick wall. I gulped down a glass of water, glancing up at the loft. It looked empty, most of the kids spent all day checking on folks for me. After I finished my water, I returned to where he still sat upright, watching me.

"Gods, lay down." I shoved his shoulder as I kneeled beside him.

He obeyed, and I pulled the worn blanket up over him and then unbuttoned his shirt enough to lay my hands on his bare chest. As the warmth of my healing powers flowed into him his hand came up and curled around mine, just like he'd done when I'd saved his life on the rooftop.

"Feels like sunshine," he murmured, his eyes half closed.

I scoffed under my breath.

"It does." His eyes had closed all the way now, but his hand tightened around mine. "S' beautiful. Just like you."

My cheeks warmed; I didn't answer, but he fell asleep just a second later. I healed him until that inky darkness vanished. Then I gently freed my hand and sat back on my heels, gazing down at him. His hair fell over his forehead into his eyes, so I brushed it from his face. He leaned into my hand, mumbling nonsense, and I let myself sit there and cradle his face for a moment. A light stubble grew on his jaw, scratchy against my skin as I stroked my thumb up his cheek.

I don't know what the fuck Trey sees in you. Raven's cruel words ran through my head.

Honestly, I didn't either.

"Bones," he mumbled in his sleep, and for some stupid reason my eyes filled with tears.

"Get some rest," I whispered, stroking his cheek once more before I pulled away.

As soon as I stepped outside, I heard my name being called. I looked up to see Cloud running toward me.

"Mac is sick at the bunkhouse," he gasped when he reached me. "Where's Trey?"

"He's sleeping inside. He got sick, but I just healed him. Can you go find Griz or Sam and ask them to meet me there?"

He nodded . "You need a horse yet?"

I paused. My body felt bone tired, but not to the point of struggling to walk...yet. "Might need one soon," I admitted.

He set off to fulfill his tasks and I made my way to the bunkhouse. I'd only been inside the place where Mac's crew all lived together a few times and they'd all been in recent days to heal Raven, Sam, Jax, and Griz. It wasn't anything too special. Just a tidy narrow cabin with a small living area and a little kitchen. Two rows of bunk beds filled the largest room where everyone slept. When I came inside, kicking the snow from my boots, Jax popped out of the bedroom, wide-eyed.

"Oh good, Cloud found you. Mac's real sick, Bones."

He didn't look too good himself. I'd only just healed him last night and he still looked pale.

"It's ok, Jax." I shrugged out of my coat. "You should lie down on the couch, ok? I'll go take care of Mac."

"Ok." He sounded relieved as he sank down.

I grabbed a blanket from the back of the couch and tucked it around him. He curled up on his side, his blond hair sticking up in every direction.

"Thanks, Bones," he mumbled.

I had to resist the urge to smooth down his hair. He was the same age as Dune—

I bit the side of my cheek hard enough to taste blood and strode toward the bedroom. I could not go down that mental path right now.

Mac lay on his side, shivering hard with his eyes closed on one of the lower bunks. I perched on the side of the mattress, placing my hand on his forehead. He was burning up, even hotter than Trey had been. His eyes cracked open and blinked at me in confusion.

"Bones?"

"It's ok," I murmured. He wasn't wearing a shirt, so I pulled the blanket down just enough to bare his muscular chest, noting the numerous scars on his tan skin. "I'm gonna heal you."

He went quiet, but his eyes stayed open, staring at me as I healed him. It was starting to hurt now, and I hoped Cloud found Griz or Sam. I'd probably be able to still walk after this, but I'd need a horse for sure after the next—

Mac's fingers brushed my cheek, and I startled out of my thoughts.

"What's the matter?" I asked, worried by the pain in his eyes.

His hand dropped heavily back down to the bed. "M' sorry," he mumbled.

"What for?"

"All of it."

I stared down at him, my mind racing. I wasn't sure what to say. "Mac—"

"S' not ok," he mumbled. "I never shoulda brought you here."

I sighed, remembering all our earlier fights and what the kids had told me. "I know you didn't have a choice, Mac."

"I couldn't let Trey die." His eyes were so anguished.

"I know."

"He's my brother."

"I know, Mac. It's ok."

Guilt filled me. He wasn't telling me anything I didn't already know, but I also knew he was only saying these things because he wasn't in his right mind.

"M' not ok with it," he said, sounding desperate again.

"I know," I tried to soothe him. "You told me, remember?"

"No." He seemed to grow agitated. "M' not ok with what she makes you do."

"I know, Mac. It's not your fault."

"It's ok if you hate me," he mumbled and the pain in his eyes was so sharp.

"I don't," I said, surprised to realize it was true.

"It's ok, you should—"

"Mac," I interrupted him, leaning forward so I could make sure I caught his gaze. "I don't hate you."

He stared hard at me with pained grey eyes, his brow furrowed, but didn't say anything.

"I don't hate you, Mac," I said again, softer, and something like relief flashed across his face.

I focused on healing him again. That spot of sickness fought back fiercely, sapping more of my strength than I'd anticipated.

Mac's hand gripped my wrist and I startled. "You know you're one of us right?"

"I know. It's ok, Mac—"

"No." He squeezed my wrist. "Listen. You're part of my crew, my family. We take care of each other."

"I know—"

"I'm not gonna let anybody hurt you again." His voice was raspy and I couldn't tell if it was from emotion or the fever. His intense eyes held mine.

I wanted to tell him to not say shit like that, to not make promises he couldn't keep, but instead, I just forced a slight smile. "I know. I believe you."

That seemed to settle him and he relaxed. I continued healing, and after a few minutes he seemed to doze off and his hand fell from my wrist. I let out a relieved breath, my head spinning and not just from healing. I wasn't sure what to think of that entire conversation. Thankfully Mac stayed asleep because it took almost an hour before that spot began to shrink.

"Bones?" I heard Griz calling from the front room.

"Back here," I answered.

Griz strode in, stopping at my shoulder. I glanced at Mac's face to see his eyes were open again and looking a lot clearer.

"How you feelin'?" Griz asked Mac.

"Been better," Mac mumbled.

"Feels like getting kicked by a horse, don't it?" Griz said.

"You weren't jokin'." Mac closed his eyes again.

I finally managed to smother the sickness and the relief made me dizzy. I held onto the bed for support as I stood. My legs trembled under my weight.

"You ok, Bones?" Griz asked, taking my elbow.

I let myself lean into him, and he wrapped his arm around my waist to support me better. "I can do a few more."

"Alright," he replied.

"Bones?"

I stopped and looked down at Mac when he said my name. His face was still pale, but to my relief, his eyes were sharp again.

"Thank you." His voice was gruff but sincere.

I nodded, wondering if he recalled anything he'd said and half hoping he didn't. "Get some rest."

CHAPTER 13

The entire hold got sick except for me, but I'd never been sick that I could remember, not from normal illnesses anyway. The burnout fever didn't seem like it counted. Two months of absolute hell passed, but finally, the sickness receded. About a dozen older people and a handful of others died before I reached them, but it would have been a hell of a lot more if I hadn't pushed myself to the brink of burnout every single moment. If I hadn't brought the kids into the clinic, most of them probably would have died alone in the snow.

"C'mon, Shortcake," Sam said as I leaned on the wall for a moment, trying to get the room to stop spinning, "time to go back."

"Just one more," I argued, wiping my sweaty face with my sleeve. "I can do one more."

"Bones," Trey warned, "you're done."

"I gotta keep on top of it," I snapped. "It's startin' to let up, but if I relax now, it might surge again."

"There's a huge fucking difference between relaxin' and laying down for a couple hours before you pass out," Sam challenged, looking as exhausted as I felt.

The woman and her five small children huddled in their bed of blankets on the floor and watched us argue. All six of them had been ill, but I'd healed them all.

"I could make you some food," the woman tried.

"Thank you, Miss Shaw," Trey said, "but what Bones needs is to go sleep for a while."

Before the woman could respond, the door burst open and Apple came racing in. "Trey, Clarity is sick!"

The flicker of fear in Trey's eyes gave me the adrenaline boost I needed. "Let's go."

As we left the shack, Mac came striding up. "I heard Clarity is sick. Sam, you go take a break. I'll cover for you."

"Fine, but make her rest after Clarity," Sam said, glaring at me.

I glared back at him and as he stepped backwards, he raised two fingers pointing at his eyes and then pointed at me with one. I rolled my eyes and turned toward the horse, but a smile tugged at my lips.

"I'm gonna run ahead," Trey called, taking off with the med kit.

"Bones, c'mere," Mac ordered, "I'll give you a boost."

He knelt next to Violet and gestured at me to put a foot in his clasped hands, and I used him as a step to mount the horse. We'd been on friendlier terms since I'd healed him, but I still wasn't sure how much he recalled from when he'd been sick. I wrapped my cold fingers in Vi's mane, focusing on not falling off, but Mac didn't take the lead like Griz and Sam normally did. He swung up on the horse behind me like Trey often did. I stiffened in surprise, and he stilled.

"This ok?" he asked. "You look like you might fall off."

I *felt* like I might fall off, so I just nodded.

He reached around me to take the reins and then loosely wrapped an arm around my waist as he nudged his heels into Vi's side and clucked his tongue at her to start moving at a fast walk. I sat stiffly for a while, but exhaustion and cold pulled me back to sag against his warm chest. His arm tightened around me.

"You doin' ok?" he asked.

"Just tired," I mumbled. "Gotta get to Clarity first though."

"K, but you're restin' after her, got it?"

I hummed in agreement, fighting my heavy eyelids.

"Don't know what we woulda done without you," he said. "We probably woulda lost half the hold by now. I'll never be able to thank you enough for saving us."

I didn't know what to do with that. Mac wasn't usually one for handing out compliments.

"Something's off about this sickness," I muttered after a bit.

He stayed quiet for a moment. "I thought so too," he finally said in a low voice. "Seems like the loggers brought it back. A couple of 'em visited a bar in Farbanks and they were the first ones sick."

"Shouldn't be this hard to heal 'em." My eyes closed on their own accord, sleep calling me.

Mac said something I didn't catch, and when I didn't respond, his arm just tightened around my waist. I could've sworn only a couple of seconds had passed before Mac shook me awake, and I blinked blearily at the brothel in front of us. Mac swung off the horse then helped me down. I rubbed my eyes hard and tried to wake up a little as I followed Mac inside. We went up to Clarity's room and found Trey crouched at her bed, looking stricken.

Clarity's breathing rattled in her chest and sweat beaded on her pale face. She stared at the ceiling, muttering nonsense.

"She's not responding to me at all," Trey said in a tight voice.

I crouched on the other side of the bed and placed my hands on her bare bony shoulders.

"Clarity?" I said. "It's Bones. Can you hear me?"

She just continued to mutter, her eyes darting around. I gathered my strength and pushed the faint remnants of my power into her. The cases all ranged in severity, but Clarity was the worst case I'd seen yet. As healing her drained my powers, I started to get scared I didn't have enough left. The little girl I'd been unable to heal after the fire flashed through my mind, and renewed determination filled me. I would not let Clarity die. Warm liquid trickled across my lips and I tasted blood. Trey glanced up at me from the other side of the bed and swore.

"I'm ok," I muttered, focusing on the color returning to Clarity's face.

Trey shifted and held up a handkerchief. "Mac."

I blinked, about to reassure Mac he did not have to wipe my nose, but he took the handkerchief and kneeled beside me. It surprised me to see he didn't look uncomfortable.

"May I?" he asked.

When I nodded, he gently dabbed the blood from my nose. He had to do it again several times when blood started trickling out again, but he never hesitated or complained. Again, the intimacy of the simple act overwhelmed me.

"Trey, she's gonna be ok," Mac murmured.

I glanced up to see Trey's face creased with worry, and I started praying that Mac was right as more blood dribbled from my nose.

After what felt like forever, Clarity focused on my face. Her brow furrowed in confusion.

"Bones?" she whispered.

"S'ok," I rasped, "you're sick, but I'm healing you."

"Clare?" Trey leaned forward.

"Trey," she whispered, her head rolling to see him, "hi."

"Hi," he said back, his voice thick with emotion.

"Hey, Clare Bear," Mac said from beside me.

Her eyes widened at the sight of Mac, but a tiny smile played on her lips. "Hi, Macaroo."

I had to fight the urge to smile. *Macaroo?*

"Sorry," she murmured.

"Don't say that. You got nothin' to be sorry for," Trey scolded.

"Scared you again." Her voice was so faint.

"We're your big brothers. It's our job to worry 'bout you," Trey said with forced lightness.

Those words stabbed right through my heart, and I must have made some sort of noise because both Trey and Mac focused on me.

"Bones," Mac snapped.

"I'm almost done," I growled. I could feel the sickness shrinking, yielding to the warmth of my powers. "Let me work."

Thank the gods he listened, though he hovered at my shoulder, watching and waiting. Finally, the last speck of darkness gave way, and I let go. Immediately warmth fled my bones, and I started shivering so hard my teeth rattled. Trey looked between me and Clarity, his face pained.

"It's ok. I'll take her back."

I glanced at Mac, surprised, but he was looking at Trey.

"You stay with Clare," he added.

"Thanks, Mac," Trey said, his voice rough.

I tried to get to my feet and my legs wobbled. Mac grabbed my arm and helped me stand. He had to wrap an arm around my ribs and half carry me down the stairs so I didn't tumble down like a drunk. I could hear coughing from multiple rooms and made a note to come back later and check the other brothel workers. They'd gotten better about asking for my help when sick or injured, but many of them still tried to handle it on their own. By the time we got to Violet, my knees were buckling, and my vision was fading in and out.

"Mac." I gripped Violet's mane for support as I stood facing her, shivering. I hated asking for help, but the horse seemed impossibly tall all of a sudden. "I don't think…I can…"

"It's ok," he said, his voice calm and steady. "Can you step on my hands again?"

I managed to get my foot in his hands, and he slowly stood, lifting me so I didn't have to pull myself up as much. The whole world spun, and for a moment I thought I'd be sick, but suddenly I was sitting on the horse. Mac swung up behind me and wrapped his arm around me again. Thank the gods he did, because as soon as Violet started moving, I tipped sideways and would have fallen right off.

"It's ok," Mac repeated, his arm tightening around my waist. "I got you."

"I'm sorry if I puke on you," I muttered.

He chuckled, or maybe I just imagined it. "I can handle it, Bones."

I let my head fall back, wincing as it thudded hard against his shoulder. "Sorry."

"Stop apologizing," he said, but he didn't sound mad.

"I'm sorry," I mumbled, my eyes closing.

He shifted and one of his hands slid under the wild strands of hair that had escaped my braid to press against my forehead.

"I'm fine." I tried to reassure him that I didn't have a burnout fever.

"Course you are," he said dryly, dropping his hand to hold me more securely.

"Just tired." My words slurred like a drunk.

"Hush."

"Don't 'hush' me," I grumbled, insulted.

I thought I heard him chuckle again as I slipped under.

୭ଚ

I woke up to someone taking my boots off. I bolted straight up, my heart seizing, to see Mac staring at me with eyebrows raised, one hand still gripping my ankle.

"It's just me, Bones." He sounded irritated. "Didn't want you to get mud all over your bed."

I lay on my mattress at the clinic. I glanced up at the loft out of habit to see several little pairs of eyes peering down at us. They looked worried.

"It's ok," I told them, "go back to bed."

They retreated out of sight. All except a little blond head that stubbornly stayed to keep an eye on me. Apple acted so protective of me, and I didn't know how to deal with it. Mac pulled my other boot off and moved to throw more logs in the wood stove.

"Apple, go back to sleep," I said, pulling my blanket over me and laying back down.

"Where's Trey?" she asked, her little voice suspicious.

She'd warmed up to Trey and tolerated Griz and Sam, but she remained very wary of all other men.

"Trey's stayin' with Clarity," Mac answered for me.

I liked it when he talked to the kids. His voice got soft and gentle.

"I'm watching the clinic tonight. That ok, Miss Apple?"

I couldn't make out her expression in the dim light, but I imagined her pursing her little lips in disapproval. A slight smile crossed my lips at the picture in my head, but I fell asleep again before I heard her answer.

It took another three weeks for the sickness to disappear. I'd never been so relieved as I was after I healed the last person and no one else seemed to get sick. Then I slept for two whole days, only waking up to use the outhouse. In the days that followed, I noticed a difference in how the people of the hold treated me. More people said hello or they waved and smiled. A large part of me didn't like it, the attention pricking like needles on my skin, but a small part of me felt soft and light every time someone greeted me with genuine happiness. I tried to squash that part of me down, but it persisted like a stubborn weed.

My strength came back so slowly, much to my annoyance. A couple of times I passed out just from standing up too fast, and I fell asleep anytime I sat. I had to take Violet on rounds, even though I wasn't healing much because the walk exhausted me. I knew I didn't have to keep checking in on people, but it made me feel better to see with my own eyes that no one was sick.

Zip didn't come by the clinic, and while I knew that probably didn't mean anything good, I didn't go see him either.

"Hey, Bones, wake up."

I cracked my eyes open. I'd fallen asleep in the exam chair, attempting to catch up on my medical notes. Trey stood beside the chair, shaking me.

"Come outside," he said, his eyes alight with excitement. "I wanna show you something."

I mumbled an ok and let him help me to my feet. He pulled me over to the door and then paused, looking down at me.

"Ok, close your eyes."

"What?" I asked, deadpan.

"C'mon, Bones. It'll be worth it, I swear. We're gonna get on Violet and I'll tell you when we get there."

I grumbled but closed my eyes, hoping I didn't fall asleep on my fucking feet. Trey curled his hand around mine and pulled me through the door. The cold night air hit my face, but it wasn't the painful cold of the past few weeks. In the last couple of days, the weather had warmed up enough that most of the snow had melted, leaving just enough left to crunch beneath my boots. I heard Violet nicker at the sight of me, the sound comforting. When we reached her, Trey placed my hands on her warm side to orient me.

"Ready? he asked. "I'll give you a boost."

I let him lift my foot and place it on his knee and used him as a step to haul myself up onto Vi's back. The familiar move was easy to do, even with my eyes closed. He swung up behind me, his arms going around me to reach for the reins.

"I might fall asleep," I mumbled.

He laughed softly. "That's ok. I'll wake you up when we get there."

It struck me that a couple of months ago I never would have trusted him like this. Now I didn't even think twice. I'd passed out from healing so many times during this sickness, often waking up to Trey carrying me back or sitting behind me on Violet so I didn't fall off or tucking me into my bed at the clinic. He'd had so many opportunities to hurt me, and he hadn't even once. And I could be confident about that because Apple watched him like a hawk when I was unconscious.

So I let myself lean back into him, my head resting on his shoulder. His arms tightened on my waist, reassuring me he wouldn't let me fall off. The warmth of his body soothed me, and I melted into him, letting myself drift off again.

"Bones, we're here."

I startled awake again. Gods, I was so—

"Look up."

Trey still sat behind me on the horse. As I blinked at the surroundings, I realized we were on one of the smaller ridges outside the hold. My heart started beating faster. We were *outside* the walls.

"Bones, look up," Trey repeated.

I lifted my eyes and sucked in a gasp, all thoughts of escape vanishing from my mind.

In the night sky, ribbons of green and purple lights were *dancing*.

I watched them move gracefully across the sky, my mouth agape. Trey chuckled behind me, but I didn't care. This was *magic*. It had to be.

"They're called the Northern Lights," Trey said.

"How?" I asked, my eyes never leaving the sky.

"Dunno," he admitted. "I just know that's what they're called."

We sat in silence for a few minutes just watching. My eyes drank in the dancing lights like I couldn't get enough of them. It was the most beautiful thing I'd ever seen.

"Do you think it's magic?" I whispered.

He didn't answer for a moment. "You know, a few months ago I would've said no. But now that I met you, I think anything's possible."

My cheeks heated but in a pleasant kind of way. Everything about him felt warm and steady, from his chest against my back to his arms around my waist to his hands resting on top of my thighs. As the lights began to fade from the sky, the emotion that welled in my chest threatened to drown me. I couldn't deny my feelings for him were firmly rooted in my heart. I took a shaky breath.

"You ok?" Trey asked, sounding concerned.

"Yeah," I whispered. "I just—" I struggled to describe what I felt. "Thank you for showing me that."

I could hear the smile in his voice. "You're welcome. I thought you might like it."

When the last of the lights faded, he turned Vi's head with the reins and clucked his tongue at her to get her to start walking. I tried to get a hold of myself, but the emotion lingered, pressing against my lungs. He was always so kind to me, and I didn't deserve it, that was for damn sure.

"How'd you feel today?" Trey asked.

"Still tired."

"Well, I'd expect you to be tired for a while after all that healing you did. Guess we can't do much else but wait and see if it gets better."

I hummed a noise of agreement.

"You healed somebody today, didn't you?"

"Yeah." I tried to focus. "Um, that guy from the kitchen."

"Nabu?"

"Yeah. Just about cut his thumb off."

"Did it still hurt? Healin' him?"

I frowned. "A little. But less than yesterday I think."

"Well, that's good." He sounded relieved. "Maybe it'll get a little better every day."

"It'll be fine. You don't have to worry. I can work—"

"Bones," he interrupted, "I'm worried about *you*, not your work."

I fell silent, my face warming again. When he sighed, his warm breath ghosted down my neck.

"Madame arrested a few more people today."

I stiffened, nausea trying to crawl up my throat. I hadn't been summoned to Madame's dungeon since before the sickness, and I'd almost convinced myself that maybe I wouldn't have to help her torture people anymore.

"I'm sorry," he murmured. "Gods, I wish I could do something to make her stop."

I remembered Apple telling me Trey had been one of the rebels. The fear that I'd enter that dungeon room to see him restrained to the chair surged back.

"Don't," I choked out, my voice laced with panic.

"Don't what?" he asked, sounding alarmed.

"Don't...don't—" Gods, was that the only word in my head? "Don't make her mad," I managed to say.

He paused. "Why?"

"I can't—" My voice cracked and I squeezed my eyes shut, trying to force all the emotion in my chest back down where it belonged.

"Bones, talk to me."

"I can't watch her hurt you." The shaky words slipped out of my mouth before I could stop them, and my eyes burned. *Well, fuck.*

He let go of the reins with one hand so he could wrap that arm around me, squeezing me tight. "It's ok, Bones. I'm not gonna do anything stupid," he said so gently that my stupid eyes overflowed. "I promise."

We rode in silence as I swiped at my wet cheeks and tried to get a hold of myself. His arm stayed tight around my waist and his solid comfort helped. As we neared the gate, a figure peered over the wall.

"That was way fucking longer than ten minutes," a familiar voice grumbled. "Hurry up, the guard is gonna change soon."

The gate opened, and Trey urged Violet through. Sam glared as he shut the gate behind us.

"Thanks for the help, Sam," Trey said, a smile in his voice.

"Bones is givin' me enough grey hairs. I don't need you chippin' in," Sam muttered.

"I'll help you pluck 'em out," Trey said.

"You owe me." Sam pointed a finger at Trey. "It's a good thing Bones is my favorite person on this crew."

"Since when?" I asked, raising an eyebrow.

"Since Griz ate the last piece of bacon this morning."

"Oh, I see how it is," I said.

Trey laughed.

"You see the lights, Shortcake?" Sam changed topics as we headed for the stables.

"Yeah." My voice warmed, remembering how beautiful they'd been. "They were the most beautiful thing I've ever seen."

"See?" Trey sounded smug. "Worth it."

"Fine," Sam grumbled, then scowled up at me. "You know, Shortcake, I'm a little offended 'cause nothing could be more beautiful than *these.*" He flexed his biceps and Trey groaned.

They continued bickering all the way to the stable, and I found myself fighting a smile. I slid off Violet and watched Trey get her ready for the night. Sam threw his arm around my shoulders, and I didn't mind it.

It wasn't until I lay in my bed in the dark that I realized these people were starting to feel like a family. It made my eyes well up and panic grip my lungs all at once. Wolf tried to snarl something at me, but he sounded fainter. I pressed my face into my pillow, hoping Trey wouldn't hear my unsteady breaths as I tried to ignore both Wolf's warnings and my desperate longing that it could be true.

CHAPTER 14

The next morning, the door opened, and Zip's massive form filled the doorway.

"Hey, Doc!" he boomed, and all the kids in the loft vanished out of sight. "You feelin' better?"

The unease surged back, my mind attempting to piece together how he wanted me to respond. Trey and Sam bristled by the exam table, but thank the gods, they didn't say anything. It took more effort than I expected to go up to Zip. When I reached him, he pulled me into an aggressive kiss. I could sense the sharp edge of his energy, and it made me more anxious.

"Yeah, I am," I answered, hoping my voice sounded steady.

"You up for Mootzie's tonight?" His hands traveled down from my waist to my hips.

"Sure." I tried to muster a smile and failed.

"Pick you up after the dinner bell then." It sounded more like a threat than a promise, and he kissed me again, all rough beard and teeth, his hands gripping my ass. When he pulled back, he gave me a look that made my stomach churn with dread.

After he left, the silence felt heavy with judgment. I moved awkwardly back to the sink where I'd been washing some tools, avoiding Trey and Sam's gaze.

"You still with Zip, then?" Sam asked, a sharp edge to his voice.

I shrugged, distracted by the anxiety coursing through me.

"If you're into the big burly look, you could at least go with Griz," Sam muttered, and my face warmed.

Trey stayed quiet, and after a few minutes, he strode outside. Sam followed him, casting heavy glances my way. The pit of dread in my stomach grew harder to ignore.

The day flew by, and soon the dinner bell rang. Zip showed up minutes later, and I had to force myself not to jerk away when he grabbed my hand. Most of the snow had melted, leaving just a few large piles from where it'd been shoveled out of the paths. Someone had sprinkled woodchips on the path in an attempt to combat the mud. Zip towed me along in silence, and I retreated into myself like a dog following a familiar path home. Then I realized where we were heading.

I came to an abrupt stop. "Why are we goin' to your place?"

His eyes darkened, sending a familiar chill down my spine. "Thought we could have some fun first."

My heart started beating faster. No way in hell was I having sex with him while both of us were sober. "I want to go to Mootzie's first."

He grinned, but it didn't reach his eyes. "C'mon, baby. I missed you."

Fuck. I had not missed this balancing act.

"I had a long day." I gave him my best pleading look. "I need a drink."

His grin vanished, and my heart leapt into my throat.

"You still my girl, Bones?" he finally asked, darkness flickering in his eyes.

"Yes, but your girl needs a drink."

"You know I thought you'd come see me." He tugged me closer and wrapped both arms around me, trapping me against him.

I tried to keep my voice light, but my temper rose. "When?"

Careful, Wolf warned.

"I've been back for almost two months." His face darkened at my tone.

"I was a little busy," I said, my voice getting sharper, "tryin' to make sure the whole hold didn't fuckin' die."

Control your temper! Wolf barked.

Zip lowered his head to kiss me, but I jerked my head back. He stared down at me, eyes darkening even further. "You wanna play games?"

"No," I tried to temper my voice. "I want to go to Mootzie's, have a drink, and go back to your place later."

"I fuckin' waited for you. I didn't even visit the brothel. And this is the thanks I get?"

"I never asked you to do that."

Something ugly flashed across his face. "What does that mean? You been sleepin' around?"

"When the fuck would I have time to sleep around?" I snapped. "I was practically killin' myself trying to heal everybody!"

He released me, but only to grab both of my upper arms. I tried to pull away, but he tightened his grasp, his fingers digging into my skin.

"You're hurting me." I tried softening my voice to a plea. "Let go."

"Good," he sneered, "'cause I want you to pay attention."

"Zip, stop." I tried to jerk away again.

"I told you from the beginning. I don't share," he snarled.

"I haven't been with anyone!"

"I think you're lyin'," he growled and my stomach dropped.

"Zip—" I jerked hard, but he still didn't let go.

"You know, I saw you the other night—" he started, but a furious little voice rang out.

"Let Bones go!"

We both glanced down, startled, and my panic surged as I met Apple's furious gaze. She stood in the path, her little hands balled into fists as she glared up at Zip.

Zip stared down at her, seemingly shocked into silence.

"Apple, I'm fine," I insisted. "Go back to the clinic."

"She doesn't want to go with you." Apple ignored me, focused on glaring up at Zip.

Zip started laughing, but it wasn't a nice laugh. My stomach twisted into a knot.

"You got a little army of brats now?" he asked, turning to look at me. He still held my arm in a tight grip.

"They work for me. Madame approved it."

Zip turned his gaze back on Apple. "Get outta the way, girl."

"No," Apple spit out.

"Apple!" I snapped, my heart pounding. "Go home."

"Let her go," she repeated, her chin tilting up.

Gods, I had no idea how to de-escalate this situation. I could probably get myself out of this, but I didn't know how to get Apple out of it without making things worse. Didn't she fucking know better?

Before I could act, Zip released me and moved, and the sound of him backhanding Apple across the face seemed to echo like a gunshot. She went sprawling into the mud as I stood there, frozen in horror.

"You need to mind your place, girl," Zip growled.

Apple scrambled to her feet, looking furious as her cheek turned bright red.

"Apple, go home." I heard myself snarl, terror over what Zip could do next crackling through me like lightning. "Right now, or you're losing your place in the clinic."

She stared at me and pain and betrayal filled those blue eyes. I knew it wasn't so much over getting hit as it was me speaking to her like that. My chest ached at her expression, but I would rather she hate me than get killed by Zip. Tears spilled down her cheeks as she turned and took off. Relief surged through me but faded to white hot shame. I should have protected her, and instead, I just fucking stood there when Zip hit her.

"C'mon, Bones." Zip grabbed my arm again and started pulling me down the path toward his shack.

I went with him for a few steps, but then I stopped again, digging my heels in. "I changed my mind." My voice came out angry, but I couldn't temper it. "I don't want to go out tonight."

He let out a harsh laugh. "You think I'm just gonna let you go back and fuck Trey?"

"What?" I said through my teeth, my hold on my temper growing dangerously thin.

"You've been spending a lot of time with him."

"Yeah, 'cause I needed help! Did you miss the part where I was healin' people until I literally couldn't walk by myself?"

He stepped into my space, and I flinched. Something hard and cruel crossed his face at the sight. He grabbed my braid with his free hand and wrapped it around his fist, and my stomach dropped.

"Know what I didn't miss? I saw you the other night," he said in a low voice that scared me more than his yelling. "Sneakin' back into the hold with Trey. You two looked awful cozy together on that horse. You've been fuckin' him, haven't you? You little slut."

Maybe it was his complete dismissal of what I'd done to save everyone's lives from the sickness. Maybe it was the fact he dragged Trey into this. Maybe Sam was right and I just didn't know how to de-escalate shit. Whatever the reason, I lost my temper.

"You are even dumber than you look—"

He pressed his lips against mine. I tried to pull away, but he had a tight hold of my hair. My fists pounded against his chest, but he didn't even flinch. He kissed me roughly, and I started getting flashbacks to Pike pinning me down in the clinic. So I used the same move and bit his lip as hard as I could.

He jerked his head back, swearing. Bright red blood dripped into his beard, and his eyes darkened with rage. I tried to brace myself, but his fist connected with the side of my face and I hit the ground hard enough that everything went dark and fuzzy for a while. I fumbled to pull my little knife out of my boot, gripping it hard so I didn't drop it. When I managed to focus on the world again, I blinked in confusion at the body standing between me and Zip.

"Touch her again, and I'll put a bullet between your eyes," Trey said in a dark voice I'd never heard him use before.

A long, charged silence fell. Part of me wanted to burst into tears at the fact he was protecting me again. He'd promised to be my backup all those months ago, and he'd done it again and again. I could protect myself. I'd been fully prepared to stab Zip with my little knife if it came to that, but I was so relieved it didn't.

The other part of me wanted to scream at Trey to get out of here. I doubted Zip would forget this, and I didn't want Trey to get hurt. Plus, I didn't *deserve* his protection. Not after I watched Apple get hit and didn't do a damn thing to stop it.

"Whatever. I don't fuckin' need this." Zip growled and turned on his heel to stride in the direction of Mootzie's.

I pulled myself shakily up to my feet and brushed wet muddy woodchips from my clothes. Trey glanced at me, but he didn't move from where he stood with his gun drawn and pointed at Zip's retreating back.

"You ok?" he asked, his voice strained.

"I'm fine. Thanks," I muttered, feeling a confusing mix of humiliation and gratitude and shame and that warmth blooming in my chest again. My feelings for Trey were out of control. I tried to distract myself by tenderly prodding my swelling cheek.

Zip disappeared between the ramshackle homes, and Trey holstered his gun and turned around. He studied me for a moment before sighing.

"C'mon." He started back down the path in the direction of the clinic.

I didn't move. I needed…I needed to think. Or maybe not think? I had to get my head on straight, and I needed space to do it. I couldn't go back to the clinic with Trey, and I couldn't face Apple right now.

Trey eventually realized I wasn't following and walked back up to me.

"What's wrong?"

"I'm going to Hydro," I turned to head toward the other dive on the east side of the hold.

"Why?" Trey asked, walking next to me.

"Go make sure Apple's ok," I said instead of answering.

"Bones—" He started to protest.

"Trey, I want to be alone, ok? Just leave," I turned and snapped at him.

He didn't try to hide the hurt on his face, but I turned and strode away, pausing only to scoop up a mostly clean handful of snow from one of the remaining piles to hold against my face. I felt like absolute shit treating him like that, but gods, these emotions I had for him scared me. They were too strong to rip out now, rooted deep in my chest. I no longer had Zip to use as a shield against my feelings toward Trey. I couldn't rely on him getting jealous and pushing people away for me, and I just felt so godsdamned relieved. I swore under my breath.

Maybe it was the coward's way out, but I fully planned on seeing if I could drown these emotions in moonshine.

※

Madame's guards made up the majority of the clientele at Hydro. The door opened smoothly unlike Mootzie's door that wobbled on half-broken hinges. The stools didn't wobble either, and the bar counter looked like it'd actually been cleaned in the past month. I chugged my first drink. The bartender raised his eyebrows at me but didn't comment as he refilled my glass.

I tried hard not to think about it, but I kept seeing Apple's face, the betrayal, the hurt. Gods, why hadn't I stopped Zip? I deserved Zip's anger. Apple didn't. I finished off my second drink and slid my glass to the bartender for another. I was working on my third when a guard named Ritz plopped down in the seat next to me, her face flushed and eyes bright.

"Hey, Doc!" she slurred. "You catch any of the show?"

I wasn't sure if people started calling me "Doc" because Zip did, but at least enough people did it now that it didn't make me think of Zip too much. I finished off my drink, feeling much lighter, and frowned in confusion.

"What show?"

"Gods, you've never been here for sentencing have you?"

"What the fuck are you talking about?"

She grinned and grabbed my arm. "C'mon, it's still going!"

I let her drag me outside into the chilly air. We went deeper into the south side of the hold, through the slums, to where I'd never been before. There were no residences here, just workshops. The buildings were ramshackle, and it smelled like shit, but a crowd of people had formed. A roar of voices filled the air, growing louder as we approached a ring of large pine trees. Ritz pulled me to the edge of the crowd, and I stared in drunken shock at the muddy pit that appeared in front of us. A giant of a man I'd never seen before stood below, bare-chested and streaked with blood. He exchanged blows with a scrawny-looking man who appeared to be losing badly.

"The big one's Brimstone!" Ritz yelled in my ear to be heard over the crowd.

"Who's the other one?" I yelled back.

"Dunno!"

Before I could ask more, Brimstone charged and caught the other man around the neck. His meaty hands twisted and before I could even blink, a loud crack sounded as he snapped the man's neck. The crowd roared, but I barely heard it. I stared horrified at the limp body that Brimstone casually dropped back into the mud. What the fuck was this?

I went to ask Ritz, but she'd vanished, swallowed by the frenzied crowd. I turned back, my eyes darting around. Across the pit from me, several men pulled a small person from a collection of cages. She screamed and fought, but the men dragging her didn't hesitate before they pitched her into the pit with Brimstone. She landed on her hands and knees in the mud, but she leapt up fast and tried to scramble up the side of the pit. A swift kick from someone standing on the edge sent her sliding back down on all fours. She turned in my direction, her eyes wide and frantic, and horror washed over me.

She couldn't be older than sixteen years. Her hair had been crudely shaved from her head and her lip split open. She sobbed as she begged for help, but the crowd around me fucking *laughed.*

"Help me! Please!" I screamed, but the only response was the laughter from the guards outside the tent.

"She's a kid," I said out loud.

"If they're old enough to fuck, they're old enough to take their medicine," someone next to me jeered.

Fury roared through me, hot and blinding. *Fuck that.* I'd failed Apple, and I couldn't just stand here and watch another little girl get hurt by a fucking man.

Don't— Wolf tried to growl.

I jumped down into the pit and landed near the girl, the thick bloody mud sucking at my boots. The girl's head swiveled toward me, terror in her face. Brimstone crossed his arms where he stood near the opposite edge of the pit, eyebrows raised. The crowd quieted slightly, watching with interest.

"What the fuck is this?" I shouted at the giant. "She's just a kid!"

Brimstone sneered at me.

"Get the fuck out of there, Bones. She's been sentenced."

I looked up at the edge of the pit to see the asshole guard, Lem. He glared down at me, and I noticed the cages stacked behind him were empty. The girl must have been the last one.

I glared back at him, fury and alcohol raging through my blood. "She's a kid!"

The girl clung to my shirt with icy, shaking fingers. "Please," she begged. "Please help me."

"Bones!" Lem bellowed. "Get out!"

In answer, I pushed the girl behind me, bent, and drew the small knife in my boot. I flicked it open, my eyes on Brimstone.

"The fuck is wrong with you? You gotta death wish?" Lem yelled. "You better get out 'fore Brimstone kills you!"

I kept my eyes on the giant, but maybe I did have a death wish because I yelled back, "Yeah, and what'll Madame do to *you* if he kills me?"

Brimstone let out an angry roar and charged. The girl took off behind me with a terrified scream. I managed to dodge the giant's first blow and caught a glimpse of Lem's eyes bulging in fear. The giant charged again, and I sidestepped as Wolf taught me, somehow managing to land a long gash in his arm with my little knife. The girl attempted to claw her way up the side of the pit again, but the crowd pitched her back, wild with bloodlust.

Brimstone feinted and in my drunken haze, I fell for it. The next thing I knew, I hit the ground hard, my ears ringing. Before I could even register the pain, Brimstone hauled me up by my jacket. He roared in my face and fueled by adrenaline and fear, I swung my knife and plunged it into his shoulder up to the hilt. He didn't even seem to notice, and my stomach flipped in panic. He threw me back down into the mud where I landed hard on my back and kicked a booted foot into my ribs. I tried to curl up into a defensive position, but he punched me in the head and bright white light blinded me. He rained down blows and kicks as the crowd roared. A bone cracked in my arm and the pain ripped a scream out of me, but my cry cut off when his hands closed around my neck and squeezed.

The girl leapt onto his back, screaming like a wildcat and clawing at his eyes. Brimstone let go of me long enough to pull her off his back and throw her like a doll across the pit. I didn't see her land because he hauled me up by the neck and held me there. I clawed at his hands with the arm that wasn't dangling uselessly at my side, but he didn't even flinch as I drew blood. All I could see were his beady little eyes watching me choke with satisfaction. Black spots dotted my vision and panic surged up my spine. This was it. I was going to die in this filthy pit, failing to save someone *again*.

A gunshot echoed, and Brimstone released me as blood sprayed across my face. I hit the ground hard and lay on my back, gulping in air like a fish with my vision fading in and out. People were shouting, a dull roar in the background. I turned my head slightly to see Brimstone lying crumpled in the mud just a foot away. He stared at me with dead, empty eyes as blood leaked from the hole in his head. Lem appeared above me, swearing, his face white with terror. His eyes darted back and forth, and then he turned and ran.

I couldn't see anyone else, and I didn't move. I wasn't sure if I could. The ice-cold mud did nothing to numb the pain screaming throughout my entire body. I summoned just enough strength to lift my head to glance down at my arm. A bloody bone poked through the skin of my left arm.

I must've passed out because the next thing I knew, I opened my eyes to a freezing mix of slushy rain falling on my face. I shivered uncontrollably in the dark, and my hair fanned out around me as the pit turned into a frigid muddy puddle. I let my eyes fall shut again.

"Bones!"

I pried my eyes back open, staring at the battered and bloody face leaning over me.

"Bones, please don't die," the girl cried. "Whaddo I do? Bones!"

"Trey." I barely managed to get the word out. I couldn't keep my heavy eyelids open.

"No, Bones, please don't—"

Blissful dark swallowed me whole again.

⁂

I jolted back with a cry when pain shot through me like lightning. Someone had picked me up, my broken arm lying limply across my stomach. My head rolled and came to rest on a solid warm chest. I panted through my teeth as I tried to contain my scream of pain.

"Hold on, darlin'. I got you."

I managed to roll my head back to look up. The freezing slush had plastered Trey's hair to his face, and emotion rolled through his eyes like a storm as he stared down at me.

"Get her to the clinic." I heard Mac's voice in the background. "We're right behind you."

Trey started moving and every step felt like agony. I vaguely heard him murmuring gently to me, but then everything went dark again.

⁂

Somebody screamed and as I gasped in a breath, I realized it was me. Trey held my shoulders down as someone else tried to maneuver my broken arm back into the right position.

"She needs a healer," someone cried.

"She *is* the healer!" somebody, maybe Griz, snapped.

Someone moved my broken arm again, and I strained against

Trey's hold, a hoarse scream ripping out of my throat.

"I'm sorry, Bones," Trey said in a low voice laced with panic.

"Get a narc," someone yelled and panic sliced through me.

"No!" I wheezed.

I'd been thirteen years old the first time I broke that arm, and that'd been my first experience with narcs. I still didn't fully understand what happened to me while drugged, but I did know I would rather endure terrible pain than go through that again.

I choked, coughing as I struggled to get a deep breath that wouldn't come. My lungs seized in agony, and my brain flashed back to Brimstone choking me in the muddy pit.

"What's wrong with her?" I heard someone demand.

Collapsed lung, some very removed part of me thought clinically.

"Bones, can you breathe?!"

I managed to focus on Sam's anxious face above me, but I couldn't get enough air to answer.

"Her lips are turning blue!"

I moved my eyes in a panic, searching faces until I found Trey. He had mud and blood smeared across his face, and he stared down at me with wide, horrified eyes. A tear rolled down my cheek as I stared back at him, slowly suffocating. Everything I'd done to push him away felt so fucking stupid now. The regret hurt as much as the pain. I couldn't even say goodbye.

"No!" Trey's eyes narrowed, full of fury and fear. "Bones, don't you dare—"

"Bones, can you try to heal yourself?" Someone grabbed my good hand. "Come on, what if you direct it through me? Like electricity?"

I strained to pay attention. I didn't know. I'd never tried something like that.

"Try! C'mon, godsdamnit!" the voice ordered.

They squeezed my hand hard, and I tried to send that warmth up through my arm and into their hand. They wrapped their other hand around my broken arm, making me jolt in pain.

"Keep going!"

I was running out of air, but I desperately focused on spooling out that warmth. Somebody yelled, but the hand tightened on mine.

"Keep! Going!"

I kept going, pushing my powers up through my arm and into the hand holding mine. Everything blurred and went dark around the edges, but Wolf still yelled at me to keep going so I did, right up until everything faded away again.

༄

I woke up in my bed in the soft light of morning. A vague panic lurked on the edge of my mind, but I couldn't figure out why. I turned my head, my eyes automatically looking toward Trey's bed across the room, but I was startled to see him right next to me. He sat on the floor, half slumped over on my mattress like he'd accidentally fallen asleep there. One of his hands rested on top of mine. I sat up and stared at him, confused.

A slight noise caught my attention and I whipped my head around to see Mac sitting on a chair beside a cot. A body lay in the cot, but I couldn't see them. Mac got to his feet and strode toward me with an expression I couldn't read. I watched him warily as he crouched on the opposite side from where Trey still slept.

"Do you feel strong enough to get up?" he whispered, and something in his tone made dread slip through my veins.

I nodded, confused because I felt fine. I slid out of the bed, trying not to wake Trey, but paused when I noticed my clothes. They were stiff with dried mud and blood, and now that I noticed, so was my hair. I frowned, but then it all came roaring back to me. Zip. Brimstone. The Pit. The girl I'd tried to save. The pain.

My gaze snapped to my arm, remembering the jagged bone and blood, but it was perfectly whole save for a new scar in the middle of my forearm. I prodded my ribs, remembering struggling to breathe, but there was no pain. I looked up at Mac, my eyes wide.

"How?" I demanded in a whisper.

He beckoned me to follow him. I got to my feet, my mind whirling. He led me over to the other cot and I stared blankly down at the person laying in it.

I started shaking my head like I could deny what my eyes were seeing. Sam lay on the cot with his eyes closed, his skin grey and his face gaunt. If I hadn't seen his chest rise, I would have thought he was dead. I stared horrified at him for a moment before my brain jerked into gear. I dropped to his side and grabbed his bare arm. My powers flowed down my arms, but instead of seeping into him, they hit a wall, and it *hurt*. I couldn't help my gasp of pain as I let go, shaking my hands. Mac crouched beside me, his eyes sharp.

"What is it?" he asked.

"I don't know," I whispered, horrified. "It's like I can't...I can't heal him."

Mac's eyes filled with pain, the most emotion I'd ever seen from him.

"What happened?" I demanded.

"He had you direct your power through him to heal yourself."

I stared at him, speechless. That wasn't possible. I looked back down at Sam, noting how it looked like the very life had been drained from him. I had done that? Why had he...how could...

"Bones," Mac's hand wrapped around my upper arm, and I jumped, "it was his choice."

I jerked my arm away. *Fuck that.* I would not let this dumbass die. Mac called my name, but I ignored him and focused as I took Sam's arm again. I called the warmth and tried to direct it into Sam. My power slammed into that invisible barrier, and I winced. Mac called my name louder, but I still ignored him. I tried pushing gently, then harder. It felt like the healing power built in my hands with no outlet and *burned* from the inside out. I gritted my teeth and kept pushing, even as tears of pain started spilling down my cheeks. Then someone grabbed the back of my jacket and jerked me away from Sam.

I fell backward and as soon as my fingers left Sam's skin, light shot from my hands like a flame thrower, filling the clinic with a blinding golden light before vanishing. As I blinked, trying to rid my vision of white dots, I realized someone's body was curled around mine like a shield.

"Bones!" The arms tightened around my waist. "Bones, you ok?"

It took my brain a second to register that it was Mac holding me and calling my name. The pain had vanished as soon as the golden light shot from my hands.

"I'm ok," I gasped. "Are you ok?"

"I'm ok."

Mac sat up, pulling me with him, and we both sat huddled together squinting and blinking. As soon as my vision cleared I checked on Sam first. He still lay there like a corpse, but he didn't seem to be hurt worse. I looked up at the loft next, terrified for the kids, but it looked empty.

"We sent the kids to our bunkhouse," Mac said, his gaze following mine. "They're safe."

"Bones?"

I swung my head around to see Trey sitting up and blinking at us.

"Trey, you ok?" Mac demanded.

"Yeah," he said, sounding dazed.

Trey's eyes focused on the thick bandage around his arm, and he started unwrapping it as Mac and I got to our feet. I moved to Trey's side, concerned about the amount of blood staining the bandage, but when it fell off, all three of us stared at his uninjured arm. Mac swore.

"What?" I asked, confused.

Trey's eyes were wide. "You healed me. You healed me without touching me."

"What?"

"I had a big gash in my arm from the pit." Trey looked as shocked as I felt. "And now it's gone."

The three of us stared at the faint pink scar. My mind whirled. I'd never thrown my power like that. I'd never healed someone from a distance. And I'd certainly never healed myself before.

"Sam?" Trey asked, bringing me back to the present.

"She can't heal him," Mac answered before I could say anything.

Trey's face creased with pain, and I felt that pain stab in my chest. I turned and marched back to Sam's side, determined to try again, but Mac caught my arm and yanked me back.

"Bones, stop. You can't heal him," he said sharply.

"I can still try!" I tried to jerk my arm free, but he held tight.

"It was hurting you," Mac argued.

"I don't care!" I fired back.

"Bones," Mac said in a soft voice I had never heard him use toward me before.

I squeezed my eyes shut, trying to hold back the flood of tears. "Stop," I choked out, "just let me…I can do it."

I felt Mac step closer, and I opened my eyes as he pulled me into him, wrapping his arms around me. I stiffened, but as he pulled me into a hug, all the fight went out of me. I sagged against his chest, sobbing into his shirt. His arms tightened around me as I cried.

"Why did you let him—" I sobbed.

"Bones, he wanted to save you. You were dying," Mac murmured.

"I don't care," I gasped. "He shouldn't have—"

"Any of us would have done it," Trey added, and I felt his hand rest on my shoulder.

"The fuck is everybody crying about?"

I jumped at the hoarse voice coming from the cot and pulled away from Mac to see Sam staring up at us. His eyes were glassy, but he grinned weakly.

"You! What the fuck were you thinking?" I dropped to my knees, grabbing his arm so I could take his pulse as I glared at him through my tears.

"Aww, Shortcake, you *do* care!" Sam's grin widened.

"Don't ever do that again, Sam!" I tried to snap, but a sob choked me halfway through.

"I knew all those mugs of broth were the key to your heart," Sam rasped.

"Sam—" I couldn't even finish, my throat closing up.

"How do you feel, Sam?" Mac asked.

Sam made a face. "Not great."

"I can't heal you," I whispered, and then my face crumpled again.

I buried my face in my arms on the side of his cot. I hated this. A dam had burst, and all this emotion was pouring out and drowning me. I should be taking care of him, not falling apart. Sam gave my head a feeble pat.

"C'mon, Shortcake," he mumbled. "S' ok."

I wanted to snap at him. I wanted to sit up and force my healing power to fix him. I wanted to do a lot of things, but instead, I just cried. Sam's hand found mine and I gripped it back without lifting my head. I felt people move around us, whispering. After I seemed to cry myself out, I raised my head, my breath coming in hiccupy gasps. Sam had fallen asleep again, his hand still curled in mine. I counted his breaths as I stayed there, kneeling beside his cot. He looked so sick.

"I'm gonna go check on Sky and Raven," I heard Mac say.

The door shut behind him, and I turned my head to see Trey standing at the foot of the cot.

"Who's Sky?" I whispered.

He blinked. "The girl you jumped in the pit to save. You didn't know who she was?"

I felt my cheeks warm and shook my head.

"She's Raven's cousin," he said. "We thought you knew that and that's why you saved her."

I rested my cheek on my folded arms. "She's just a kid."

Trey moved around the cot, crouching beside me so he could look me in the eyes. The depth of emotion in his eyes made my own start to burn again.

"Bones," he said and his voice sounded exasperated and somehow fond at the same time.

"What?" I mumbled a little defensively.

His face grew serious. He started to say something and stopped, dragging a hand through his hair. Then he reached out, asking for my hands without a word. I surprised myself by giving them to him without hesitation and he pulled me to my feet with him. We stood facing each other for a moment. He didn't let go of my hands, and I didn't pull away.

He took a deep breath and tried again. "When I saw you laying in that pit," he said, his voice low and rough, "I thought you were dead."

I blinked, feeling shaky, and his hands tightened on mine.

"I swear my heart stopped," he said, even quieter. "And then when you were on the table and you couldn't breathe and you looked at me like that, like you were sayin' goodbye—"

He broke off, that muscle ticking in his jaw as he studied my face. "Bones, why do you have to save everybody but yourself?"

My eyes closed in a desperate attempt to hide my tears. Those words wrapped a fist around my heart and squeezed. I didn't know what to say.

"I want you to live," he added, his voice hoarse with emotion. "And yeah, it's partly 'cause I'm a selfish bastard. I just can't stand the thought of livin' in a world without you in it."

I opened my damp eyes in surprise, and he gave me that sweet smile, stepping closer. I had to tip my head back a little to hold his gaze. He stood so close to me, but I didn't want to move away. I wanted to lean in, to be enveloped in him. I remembered the regret I felt when I couldn't breathe. The tender emotions in my chest were slowly but surely emerging from the dirt, and gods, I was tired of fighting them.

"Can't you see how much you mean to me?" He let go of one of my hands to reach out and brush a stray hair out of my face, tucking it behind my ear.

My lips trembled.

"You might act like you don't care, but I *see* you." He brought his other hand up to join the first in cradling my face. "You're brave and you're kind and you care so damn much." His eyes were so earnest as they held mine captive. "An' I think you believe that makes you weak, but darlin', it makes you strong."

My eyes overflowed and he wiped away tears with his thumbs like a gentle caress.

"I don't know if anybody else would jump in the pit and fight Brimstone to try and save someone they don't even know."

You would. I wanted to say, but I didn't trust myself to speak. I leaned closer to him, drawn to his warmth like a moth to a flame.

"I know you're used to people wanting your power, but gods, Bones, all I want is *you*."

My heart pounded so loud it drowned out everything else. The defenses I'd spent my life building felt paper thin compared to the strength of my feelings for Trey.

"You'll get hurt." My voice quavered as I threw up the last defense I had left.

"Good thing you can heal me then," he grinned.

I tried to glare at him, tears still slipping down my cheeks, but my mouth curled up into a smile. I saw his gaze sharpen on my lips, surprise and then delight in his eyes.

"You dumbass," I said fiercely, then I pushed myself up on my toes and kissed him.

His lips were gentle on mine, still holding my face like something precious. My arms entwined around his neck, pulling myself even closer, pressing our bodies together. I felt him smile against my lips and then his hands slid into my hair to the back of my head, angling my face and deepening the kiss in a way that made my stomach swoop and—

"Fuckin' hell."

We jerked apart and looked down at Sam who glared through cracked eyes.

"I am *trying* to sleep here."

"Sorry, Sam," Trey said with a grin, not sounding sorry at all.

"How come I save your life and he gets the kiss?" Sam muttered.

I felt unsteady, and I couldn't stop smiling. I crouched next to Sam and pressed a kiss to his forehead. The shock on his face made an actual laugh escape my lips, and his mouth dropped open.

"Did you know she could laugh?" he asked Trey.

"She can do anything," Trey replied.

I glanced over at Trey, my face warming, to see him smiling at me in a way that made me feel like I really could do anything. I had to look away before I burst into tears again. So I focused on Sam, noting how sweat beaded on his forehead.

"How do you feel?" I asked, slipping back into the familiar healer role. "Does anything hurt?"

Sam frowned. "I feel...weak. Like I've been sick for a long time or somethin'. It doesn't hurt. It did when your power was going through me, but now I just feel tired."

I frowned back. His breathing appeared shallow. I took his pulse and found his heart rate too fast. I hated that I couldn't just use my power to heal him. It made me think of sitting in that hot med tent in the desert, watching people die from a fever, unable to save them. I released his wrist and took his hand, squeezing.

"You should sleep some more," I said, trying to sound confident, "and later, I'll bring *you* some broth."

He grinned, but his eyes were already half closed. "Alright, Shortcake."

He fell asleep in seconds. His skin felt clammy and his color still looked far too grey. I tried to shove my anxiety down. I couldn't do anything besides wait.

"How are you feelin'?" Trey asked.

I took a second to think about it. "Don't yell at me, but I promise I actually feel fine."

He laughed out loud, and I couldn't help the smile that crossed my face again in response. His laugh felt like sunshine, and I was the godsdamned fool soaking it up like I was starving for it.

"C'mere." He reached out with his hand.

I let him pull me up and wrap me in his arms. I hadn't felt so safe in someone's arms since I was a child. When I looked up at him, he lowered his head to kiss me and—

The door burst open, startling both of us. Mac stood in the doorway breathing heavily.

"Madame's men are comin' to arrest Bones."

Both of us stood there staring at him for a breath before Trey seemed to panic.

"We can't just let them take her!" he snapped.

Mac let out a frustrated noise. "Trey, what the fuck do you expect me to do?"

"I don't know, Mac, but you know this isn't gonna end well."

"I know." Mac's brow was taut, his lips pressed tightly together.

"She's not gonna kill me," I tried to reassure them, but they glared at me.

"I'm not worried about her *killin'* you, Bones," Trey retorted.

"Bones—" Mac bit out.

"I know she's probably gonna have me beaten, ok?" I tried to keep my voice calm and even. "I can take it."

"No, Bones—" Fear coated Trey's voice, and hearing it made me feel sick.

The sound of boots on the porch made all of us look at the door. Sax came in first, his face hard. Lem sneered behind him, but I didn't miss the surprise that flashed across his face at the sight of me uninjured. Unease swirled in my stomach. Gods, if Madame somehow found out what I could do to people by healing myself through them—

"You're under arrest, Bones," Sax said in his gravelly voice.

Trey still gripped my hand.

"Ok." I hoped I sounded calm.

"Turn around," Sax ordered, producing a set of handcuffs.

Trey tensed.

"It's ok, Trey." I turned to him and tried to smile. "It's ok."

He pulled me into his arms, wrapping me in a tight hug. I could feel his heart pounding. "Please be careful," he murmured in my ear.

I gave him a nod as I pulled back, hesitated, then pushed myself up on my tiptoes to kiss him again. I tried to pour confidence into it. I was gonna be ok. I had to be ok.

Sax grabbed my arm and jerked me away from Trey, snapping the cuffs on my wrists. As he started towing me out of the clinic, I glanced behind me to see Mac gripping Trey's arm like he had to physically hold him back, but then the door slammed shut and they were gone.

CHAPTER 15

I expected to go to the dungeon, but instead, we went upstairs to the meeting room. Madame sat alone at the table, reclining in her chair and watching me. A dozen or so of her men stood along the wall behind her. Sax hauled me in to stand in front of the table, keeping a tight grip on my arm.

"You interfered in the sentencing, Bones," Madame said, "and because of that, Lem had to put down my enforcer."

Gods, she said it like Brimstone wasn't even a human being. For the first time, I felt a flicker of pity for the giant. Madame wasn't as angry as I'd expected, but her calm demeanor scared me more.

"Do you think you're special, Bones? You think the rules don't apply to you?"

I swallowed hard, unsure of what she wanted me to say. I wished she'd just tell me my punishment so we could get it over with.

"No."

Madame raised her eyebrows, studying me for what felt like a very long time. I couldn't help shifting uncomfortably in the silence. Gods, what was taking so long?

"I think you need some time to sit on that," she finally said, a cold smile crossing her face. "Someplace nice and quiet where you can reflect as you await your punishment."

What the fuck did that mean? I stared at her, but Sax grabbed my arm and dragged me toward the door.

"Have fun, Bones," Lem taunted as we passed him in the hallway.

My sense of dread ratcheted up. Sax headed for the stairs that led down to the dungeon. I started breathing fast and panicky as the door to the dungeon room came into view, but Sax dragged me past the dungeon, past the cells full of gawking people, and toward another set of stairs I hadn't noticed before.

"Where are we going?" I choked out.

"Solitary," Sax growled.

I didn't know what that meant, but we kept going deeper and deeper underground. The air smelled stale and increasingly like damp dirt. We reached the end of the electric lights, but the corridor continued. Sax clicked on a flashlight, revealing that the walls were growing rougher and more like a rock cavern than something man-made. My skin began to crawl. Finally, we stopped, and Sax unlocked an iron bar door to a small single cell that looked like it'd been carved out of the mountain. I winced as he wrenched me around to remove the handcuffs. Then he shoved me in, slammed the door behind me, and locked it while I stood there staring at him in silent panic. He didn't even bother saying anything before he strode away, taking the only light with him.

I had to bite my cheek to keep from calling after him, begging him to leave the flashlight. I listened to the sound of his footsteps growing fainter until I couldn't hear them anymore. I stood there for a long time, trying to get my eyes to adjust to the darkness, but I couldn't see anything. Panic began buzzing in my head, and I tried to take deep breaths and calm down as I sank to the floor, feeling blindly around the cell. The small space probably wasn't even large enough for a tall person to fully stretch out. The floor and walls were rough rock. Not like the outside of the watchtower, but like I touched the very roots of the mountain. A bucket stood in the corner, and from the smell, I guessed it was the toilet.

I folded myself into a ball against the cold rock wall and tried not to panic about the silent pressing darkness.

I couldn't keep track of the time passing. I tried counting in my head for a while but eventually gave up. It reminded me of being locked inside Wrangler's safe, but at least there my eyes were able to adjust to the dark.

It's gonna be ok. The darkness felt like it weighed on my lungs, making each breath difficult. *She can't keep me down here for long. I have to work.*

I grew less sure about that as time crawled onward.

I told you, don't get involved, Wolf snarled in my head. *Keep your head down.*

"Fuck off," I muttered out loud.

You're smarter than this, he persisted. *You know better.*

"I'm not apologizing for trying to save that girl."

You know she's probably dead. All you did was delay her death a little. So what good did any of that fuckin' do?

I closed my eyes, not that it made any difference. It was just as dark when my eyes were open.

She's probably gonna hurt Trey now. Or one of the kids. Is that what you wanted?

Nausea curdled in my stomach.

You don't need them. You have me.

"No, I fucking don't," I snapped. "You're not here, so stop."

Gods, maybe I'd gone insane a long time ago. I was having a full argument with my brother's voice in my head.

Wolf went silent, and my thoughts drifted back to Sam's grey face. A chill brushed across my skin and I shivered. How had I hurt him? Had I accidentally taken some of his life force? Had my powers harmed him because he wasn't injured? But why couldn't I heal him?

The last time I failed to heal someone—

I slammed those thoughts back down.

I remembered that golden light pouring from my hands like sunbeams and lifted a palm, calling on my powers. They began to flow, giving me a brief moment of hope, but then vanished as though my body knew I wasn't trying to heal someone. I frowned. Had I been able to throw my power like that because Trey was there, and it just sought the nearest injury like a magnet? If that was the case, how far could it reach?

Trey. Just thinking his name made my stomach flutter with either dread or longing, maybe both. I brushed a finger across my lips, remembering how his mouth had perfectly fit with mine. That was the problem with Trey, wasn't it? I wasn't just attracted to him. Being with him felt like we were two halves coming together, and the rightness of it was something powerful, something dangerous.

What if Madame hurt him?

I shouldn't have kissed him.

Fuck.

I lay down and tried to force myself to sleep a little. To have little difference between being awake and being asleep nibbled away at my sanity. As time passed the line between being awake and asleep began to blur even further. I tried again and again to summon my powers, desperate for some light to break up the darkness, but nothing happened.

Sometimes as I lay on the ground, I would swear I could feel things crawling over my skin. I tried not to think about what sort of bugs and creatures would live this far underground.

How long had I been in here?

My stomach ached with hunger, but the thirst worried me more. I started having flashbacks of stumbling through the desert with dry, chapped lips, desperately trying to stay on my feet.

Was Sam still alive?

Did Madame kill that girl, Sky?

Were people dying because I wasn't there to heal them?

What was Madame going to do? *"I think you need some time to sit on that."* I knew what she was doing. She thought I would sit here and panic about all the ways she could punish me, and I hated that I was doing exactly that. Bloody memories tried to raise their heads and I fought to shove them back down.

What would she do? Go after Trey? The kids?

You know better, Wolf reminded me again, and I bit back the urge to scream.

When I first heard the footsteps, I thought I imagined them. They were so quiet that they seemed like a dream. Then a tiny glow of light appeared, and I scrambled up on my knees and gripped the iron bars of the cell. It grew bigger, and I tried to convince myself I would be strong enough to keep from begging Sax to leave me a light.

Finally, a body appeared holding a flashlight. It shone into my eyes and I squeezed them shut, a sharp pain shooting through my head. Somebody cursed, and the light dropped down as they darted forward. Then Trey knelt outside the cell, his arms reaching through the bars to grab my shoulders.

"Bones!" he gasped. "Bones, darlin', are you alright?"

My hands came up to grasp his wrists. "Are you hurt?" I

demanded, my voice raspy.

He frowned at me. "What? No, I'm fine. Are *you* hurt?"

Relief and dread filled me as I shook my head. Madame hadn't hurt him, but that meant she also hadn't taken action yet.

"How long have I been in here?" My voice trembled.

"Three days," he answered, anger clear in his voice. "I brought you some water." He reached into the pack he was carrying and handed a bottle of water through the bars.

I gulped it down.

"I have a second one too."

"Is Sam ok?" I asked as soon as I came up for air.

"He's weak, but he's not getting worse," Trey's hands were moving across my face and body like he had to see for himself I wasn't hurt.

I leaned my forehead against the metal bars, and after he finished his examination, he did the same, pressing our heads together as much as possible with the iron bars between us. The physical contact and closeness made my eyes well up.

"I have some food too."

"What's happening?" I whispered.

"Madame is refusing to tell anybody where you are, but Mac knew she'd probably stuck you down here. She's been keeping the corridor guarded, but I was finally able to sneak down here. I don't have a lot of time, but godsdamnit, I'm gonna get you out of here somehow." He pulled out what felt like dried meat wrapped in a cloth and passed it through the bars to me, and I tore into it. "Sorry, it's not much. I had to be real careful. She's watching me like a fuckin' hawk."

"You shouldn't be down here." With a little food and water, it felt like my brain shifted back into gear. " Trey, if she catches you—"

"I don't fuckin' care," Trey interrupted, his voice tight.

"Trey!" My panic swelled. "You can't—"

"No, Bones, you don't—"

"She'll punish you! Trey, please!"

I heard him take a deep breath, and then he gently took my face in his hands.

"She's already punishin' me," he murmured.

My heart leapt into my throat, but then he continued.

"She knows you bein' in here is killin' me."

"Just please, don't...don't provoke her," I begged.

"It's ok, Bones," he whispered. "I'll be fine. It's you I'm worried about."

A radio crackled and then Mac's voice came through. "Trey, time's up."

Trey swore, and I couldn't help clinging to him again. "I'll be back, ok?" he promised. "Me or Mac. We're gonna get you out." He passed me the second bottle of water. "When you finish this, chuck it down the corridor so no one sees it."

I tried hard not to cry. "Ok."

"Fuck," he muttered.

"Can you leave the light?"

"I'm afraid if Sax or Madame sees it they'll know you had help," he said. "I'm so sorry, Bones."

I tried to push past the panic at the thought of being swallowed by darkness again.

"I'm sorry, darlin'." Trey sounded wrecked. "I'm so sorry."

"Trey!" Mac's angry voice came through the radio.

Trey grabbed the radio and hissed into it, "I'm comin'!" He turned back to me. "I gotta go. We'll get you out, I swear it."

I listened to his footsteps fade away, and the absence of him made the darkness feel even worse than before.

⁖

I tried to ration my dried meat and water, but all too soon they were gone. Did Madame expect people to smuggle me water or did she want me to die? I could go a while without food but only a few days without water. I tried not to think about how many people probably died in this horrible cell.

It wasn't too long after Trey's visit that I woke up *freezing*. I sat up and realized everything was damp—the walls, the floor, my clothes. Water dripped somewhere, and after so much silence the sound felt painful. I huddled in my corner, damp and miserable. A regular person would probably get sick from sitting in these conditions, and I hoped my powers would keep me from falling ill.

Gods, if I just had a light, I could bear this. I tried to summon my powers again, begging any light to appear, but nothing happened.

I started to feel like a fraying rope. The strands broke one by one until only a single strand held me together. My entire body ached for water, and my lips were dry and cracked. I tried to wring some of the water from my clothes, despite knowing it would probably make me sick, but there wasn't enough.

If I screamed would anyone hear it?

I tried to get myself under control, but maybe that last strand snapped because the next thing I knew I was sobbing. I wanted to grip the bars of the cell and scream and scream, but if there was anything I knew how to do, it was how to break *quietly*.

What would Madame do to me? How would she punish me? Would she hurt Trey? Or Apple? Gods, I couldn't handle that. I couldn't.

I wished Trey were here, and I hated that I wished it. I knew I shouldn't let myself get dependent on him, but I couldn't fucking help myself.

It took me a while to realize the darkness had begun to lighten. When I did, I tried to stuff my sobs back down so Sax wouldn't see me crying, but I'd lost control of my own body. I settled for hiding my face in my knees.

"Bones?"

The sharp voice made me raise my head, and I met Mac's eyes glinting in the light of the flashlight. He looked furious, as usual, but my entire self dissolved into relief.

I lunged to the bars, reaching out for him. "Mac," I sobbed.

He crouched and took my hand, eyes widening at my reaction. I gripped his hand with both of mine, clinging to it, and he set the flashlight on the floor so he could wrap his other hand over the top of mine.

"I brought you some food and water." His voice was quiet, but anger still sparked in his eyes.

"Get me out," I choked out, apparently not too proud to let Mac see me break down. "Please get me out of here."

"We're trying," he promised.

I couldn't respond, too busy trying to regain control of myself. He let go of my hand with one of his and reached through the bars to press it against my forehead. Did I have a fever? I didn't think so. I was just so fucking damp and cold. He frowned.

"Your hands are like ice," he muttered, his eyes scanning the small cell. "Do you have a blanket?"

I shook my head, and that muscle ticked in his jaw. He started to pull his hand away, and I tightened my grip in panic. He paused, meeting my gaze.

"I'm gonna give you my jacket," he explained. "I'm not leavin' yet."

I released him, and he shrugged off his jacket and pushed it through the bars. My hands shook as I put it on, and he reached through the bars to button it for me. His jacket was still warm from his body heat, and the relief was immediate.

"Here," he handed me a bottle of water, "drink somethin'."

My hands shook so hard, I couldn't hold the bottle still, and water spilled down my chin. He reached through the bars again to put his hands over mine, helping me hold the bottle steady. I drank the whole thing, the cool water like bliss on my dry, chapped throat. He took the bottle back when I finished, then offered his hand through the bars, palm facing up. I clutched it tightly with both of mine again.

"Nemo is pushin' hard to get you out," he said. "Madame's gonna have to make a decision soon if she wants to keep the peace."

"How's Sam?" I asked.

"He's ok." He squeezed my hands.

"How long has it been?"

His face darkened. "Almost six days."

"Mac, I can't—" My voice came out panicked as tears started flowing down my face again. "I can't do this anymore."

That muscle ticked in his jaw again. "I know." He leaned in closer to where I pressed my forehead against the bars. "So let it out, Bones. I can take it. I want you to let it all out now so when she releases you, you can look her in the eye and show her this didn't break you."

"I think this *is* breakin' me."

"This won't break you."

"I'm serious, Mac, I really can't—" I couldn't finish, an escaped sob choking me.

"You're a river, Bones," he said, squeezing my hands hard to get my attention. "You don't break, you bend. If someone tries to control you, you find a new way around. People might think you're just water, might think they have you contained, but you're strong enough to cut a path through mountain rock and wild enough to wash everythin' away when you rage."

I stared at him through the tears streaming down my face, trying to hold my breath to keep the sobs contained. I never would have expected Mac to say something so beautiful.

"This won't break you, Bones," he repeated, his eyes flashing. "Let it out."

As though he opened a doorway, my sobs broke free. He gripped my hands as I sobbed uncontrollably, anchoring me through it. He didn't say anything else, but whenever I looked up at him, he held my gaze. I thought the well of pain and fear inside me would never end, but eventually, the sobs began to ease, leaving me exhausted. I slumped against the iron bars of the cell, still clinging to him as shaky gasping sobs wracked my body every so often. I watched his thumb slowly stroke the top of my hand, and I had to fight a sudden, insane urge to laugh.

Who the hell are you, and what have you done with the real Mac? I wanted to ask, but I didn't.

He freed one of his hands so he could pass me a small bundle of food and another bottle of water, and then he said the words I'd been dreading.

"I gotta go back up."

I forced myself to release his other hand and started to unbutton his jacket, but he caught my wrist, halting me.

"No, you keep it."

"She'll know you came down here if I keep it," I worried.

Something flashed through his eyes. "Let her know."

"Mac—"

"No, I mean it, Bones. Keep it. I'll be fine."

We stared at each other for a few breaths, but finally, I nodded and he released my wrist.

"We'll get you out," he promised as he stood.

I nodded, my lips pressed together to keep from begging him to stay. He gave me a final look before he turned and strode away. I wrapped his jacket tighter around myself and attempted to engrave the words he'd given me into my mind.

"You're a river. You don't break, you bend."

CHAPTER 16

Maybe the jacket, food, and water helped or maybe exhaustion just caught up to me, but I managed to get some real sleep. I slept so deeply that I didn't even hear Sax's heavy footsteps approaching. I jerked awake at the sound of the cell door creaking open and panicked at the sight of a large silhouette reaching down to yank me to my feet.

"Get movin'," Sax growled at me.

I obeyed, my legs shaky after days of limited movement. As we passed the cells, I got a glimpse of Mist's pale face peering through the bars and felt a surge of relief and guilt. We continued up to the meeting room on the second floor. Mac waited outside the door, his face impassive. He took my arm from Sax who gestured that we go into the meeting room.

As we began to enter the room, Mac leaned down. "Don't do anything stupid," he muttered in my ear.

Anxiety pulsed in me, and I glanced at him once more as we came to a stop in front of the table. He stood like a soldier once again, with no sign of the man who'd held my hands and let me cry.

Madame sat at the table with Nemo and Zana, and armed men filled the room. I saw Madame take note of the jacket I wore before looking pointedly at Mac. He wore a different jacket, but she *knew*. I didn't dare look at him, keeping my eyes on Madame.

"Well, Bones." Madame looked irritated as she flicked her grey dreads over her shoulder. Her fingers drummed a chaotic beat on the table. She cut her eyes sideways to Nemo for a moment, something like disgust crossing her face. "Time to get back to work."

I glanced at Nemo too. He wore a slight frown, a deep furrow wrinkling his forehead, but he didn't react to the look she'd just given him.

"The council seems to think the people have grown dependent on your healing," Madame continued. "So you may return to the clinic to work, and the rest of your sentence will transfer to Mac."

It took me a moment to register what she'd just said. I looked up at Mac next to me, and then back at Madame, my heart pounding.

"Mac was only allowed to add you to his crew so long as he was willing to take responsibility for your actions, isn't that right, Mac?" Madame asked.

My stomach clenched in horror.

"Yes ma'am," Mac said, his voice flat. "I take full responsibility."

"Good," Madame said with a cruel smile. "Ten lashes."

"No!" I burst out in panic as her men stepped forward.

"Bones!" Mac jerked on my arm, but I ignored him.

"Mac didn't do anything! It was all me! I take responsibility."

"Bones, don't—" Mac growled, his hand tightening even further on my arm, but Madame held up a hand, silencing him.

She studied Mac with those ice-cold eyes, tapping her fingers on the table again.

"He can't work for you if he's injured. I can," I added, and I could feel Mac's fury like the heat of a fire.

"Madame—" Mac tried again.

"Another word out of you and there will be even worse consequences," Madame said in a sharp cruel voice, silencing him once again. When she turned to me, she smiled again, and the hair rose on the back of my neck. "Well, Bones, since you're so desperate to take responsibility, I'll let you have it. You can take Mac's lashes." She turned to her men, waving a hand in our direction lazily. "See to it."

Three of Madame's men with guns drawn forced Mac to release me. Sax grabbed my arm and dragged me out the door. I met Mac's frantic gaze and tried to mouth *"I'll be ok"* before Sax yanked me down the hall.

I went with Sax willingly, my heart pounding in my chest. I'd endured a hundred different tortures, but I'd never been whipped. A crowd had already formed as Sax dragged me toward the whipping post. My eyes searched the faces, hoping I wouldn't see any of the kids or Mac's crew, but I couldn't focus for long. Sax snapped at me to take my jacket off, and I obeyed, shivering in the cold wind. One of the men secured my shaking hands to the chains at the top of the post. I stood there, trying to keep the panic down and trying to brace myself.

Then Sax grabbed the back of my shirt and *ripped* it open.

I gasped, trying to hold the scraps of fabric against my chest, more concerned about the brand than my bare body, but then the first bite of the whip hit my back with an echoing crack. The blinding pain shocked me, but somehow I managed to keep my teeth clenched together. Then the second lash came. My body arched in pain and a scream ripped out of me. Again and again, pain blinded me until it was all I knew. I sagged against the pole, sobbing. I could feel my blood trickling down my back and could see it splattered on the ground and against the post. Ten lashes had seemed like a small number, but it felt like an eternity. When it finally stopped, I dangled from my hands, which felt like agony, but my legs couldn't support my weight. Through my blurred vision, I saw Madame's smiling face. She grasped my chin and her eyes flicked down to the brand on my chest.

"I see Juck left his mark on you," she murmured. "Consider this mine."

Madame released my chin. I heard her saying something to the crowd, her voice loud and commanding, but I couldn't make out the words. My vision went black around the edges and—

"Bones, c'mon, wake up. Please, Bones," someone whispered, their voice ragged.

I cracked my eyes open and at the same time, red-hot pain sliced through me. I gasped and involuntary tears of pain started rolling down my face.

"Mac!" Trey yelled.

"Bones, you gotta heal yourself again." Mac's flinty eyes filled my vision.

The words he spoke rolled around in my head like marbles as awareness came back to me. I lay on my stomach on the exam table and my back was on fire.

"Bones!" Trey's angry voice cut through the pain, and I met his eyes.

I'd never seen him so angry. He grasped my hand, and the slight movement made me groan, my teeth clenched together.

"Heal yourself. Like you did before."

Heal myself? I tried to focus. Images and sounds were flickering through my mind. Sam's grey face. The sound of the whip. Madame's smile.

"Bones." Trey's voice softened.

I felt his thumb brush the back of my hand.

"It's ok. I'll be ok."

Sam. I focused on my memory of Sam's sunken face. *Fuck no.* No. I would not fucking do that again.

"Bones, if you don't heal yourself, we're gonna have to give you a narc," Trey pleaded.

I tensed and then attempted to bite back a scream. The slightest muscle movement felt like someone was pouring acid into an open wound on my back.

"I want to do it," Trey tried again, his voice rough. "Bones, let me do it."

"No," I hissed through my teeth.

"What if I do it?" Mac asked, an undercurrent of desperation running through his voice. "Bones, will you heal yourself through me?"

I didn't answer, trying to breathe through the pain, but I kept choking in short gasps of air. Mac leaned down close enough that his grey eyes were all I could see.

"Bones, let me heal you. You took my lashes, so let me do this," he whispered, something like fear flashing through his eyes. "Please."

I squeezed my eyes shut. "No," I choked out.

A commotion broke out over my head, but the pain pulled my focus away again. My back spasmed and a cry of pain ripped out of me.

"Godsdamnit," someone swore.

Pain pricked in my arm and horror surged through me. I tried to turn my head to look, but the familiar ice cold of the drug moved faster, spreading through my veins until everything faded away.

There you are!

Horror washed over me. I kept my eyes squeezed shut. No. This was just a dream. It was just a nightmare.

I've been looking everywhere for you. Where are you?

It's just a dream. It's just a dream. Tears were burning under my eyelids.

What's wrong? I thought— His voice cut off, and I tried to brace myself.

Open your eyes.

I kept my eyes squeezed shut. In the silence, I could feel the emotion radiating from him, and I braced myself.

You used me. The words were sharp with hurt and betrayal.

I flinched at the touch of phantom hands cupping my face, their touch as icy as the narc.

You should know better than to play with fire. The words brushed against my skin like a caress. *Open your eyes.*

No. My voice trembled, but I said it.

I felt the first wave of anger emanating from him. *Open your eyes.*

No.

Is this how it's gonna be? He sounded amused. *You want to do this the hard way?*

I sucked in a panicked breath through my nose and tried to will my mind to be empty and blank like a book with nothing inside.

He sighed in disappointment like I was a disobedient child, and I winced as his fingers tightened on my face. *The hard way then.*

I tried to fight, but as always, he ripped his way inside my head like claws tearing through paper. He reached in and grabbed, pulling up memories I tried to cling to. I felt him chuckle at my pathetic attempt right before he wrenched them free. Images flashed behind my eyes as I tried to scream in pain.

The knife in Juck's heart. The sneering face of the mercs. The bullets spraying the roof. My bloodied hands pressing against Trey's stomach. Mac's eyes in the rearview mirror.

NO. I fought back, trying to snatch the images away.

It didn't have to be this way. I heard the smile in his words.

Lana pointing the gun at my face. Madame's calculating eyes. Hojo's screams. My reflection in Clarity's mirror as I touched the brand on my chest. Mac's clipped words, "Madame would like to offer you a job here as healer for the Vault."

The Vault. He sounded thoughtful. *You got farther north than I thought.*

I sobbed, terrified.

Did you really think I wouldn't find you? His voice sharpened into something cruel. *Did you think I would just give up?*

My body shook as I tried to keep my mind clear and blank, but Trey's face floated through. I felt him pause. He seized the memory, gripping it in his claws as he examined it. I held my breath, my heart pounding as his rage grew like a thunderstorm.

Who is this? His voice was calm.

I tried to picture the endless desert, the sky blending into the sand.

Who is this?

I focused harder on the sand, panic building in my chest.

Who. Is. This? He ripped into my head again, pulling up every memory I had of Trey's face. His rage felt like a scorching iron against my flesh.

Please, I sobbed. *He's nothing to me!*

You're right. His amusement was sharp and cruel. *He will be nothing soon.*

Please! I almost opened my eyes in desperation, barely keeping myself under control. *I swear, he's—*

When will you learn? he interrupted, his voice dangerous. *You belong to me.*

༄

I stared at a beetle crawling its way across the floor. My brain felt like it'd been packed full of cotton. I lay on my stomach on my mattress, and slowly I became aware of people talking.

"We think this might be the spark—"

"—don't risk it. We can't until they—"

"—could have *killed* her, Mac!"

"I *can't.* You don't have the numbers—"

"Fuck the numbers!"

The last words were yelled so loudly I flinched and a pained cry escaped my lips. I heard the sound of chairs scraping across the wooden floor.

"Bones?"

The beetle disappeared beneath a worn boot and a body crouched next to me. I met Trey's soft eyes.

"Hey," he said, a strained smile on his face. "Good morning, Sleepin' Beauty."

Panic roared through me and his expression grew alarmed.

"What's wrong?" he asked.

Gods, what had I done? My eyes filled with tears.

"Bones, talk to me." He stroked my cheek.

Mac crouched next to him, his expression more steady.

"You promised," I rasped.

Trey's expression shuttered. "You were in so much pain, what—"

"Go away." My hoarse voice was borderline hysterical. "Go away, Trey. Get away from me."

He stared at me like I'd stabbed him through the heart. When he didn't move, I started trying to push myself up to pull away from his gentle touch, but the pain that roared to life in my back made me cry out and freeze, panting. Mac grabbed Trey's arm and hauled him away as I tried to convince myself I could get up without passing out. I started trying to move again, but then Mac reappeared, gripping my arm.

"Bones, no," he snapped, "you can't get up. Your back is still a mess."

"I—"

"You try to get up, and I will give you another fucking narc." His eyes glittered.

I froze in terror, then lowered myself back onto the mattress. He released my arm.

"Trey didn't give you a narc. I did," Mac continued. "He tried to stop me."

It didn't matter. It didn't matter who did it. I wanted to scream and rage, but my strength was vanishing.

"For the record, this is *exactly* what doing something fucking stupid looks like." I hadn't seen Mac this angry since the first moment I met him after our rooftop chase. "What were you thinking? Ten fucking lashes! You could have healed me, and I would have been fine. Why the fuck did you—"

"Wasn't your fault," I interrupted, my eyes welling up.

"I made that deal with Madame. I *knew* what I was fucking signing up for," he hissed.

The panic and pain roaring through me made it hard to think clearly. I'd thought nothing could hurt worse than when Juck had pressed a red-hot piece of metal against my chest, letting it sizzle and burn into my skin, but I'd been wrong.

"You wouldn't heal yourself. So we gave you pain meds," Mac continued, gesturing in a sharp, jerky motion. "What the fuck else were we supposed to do?"

"Nothing," I choked out.

He crouched lower so he could meet my gaze. His grey eyes were full of angry sparks. "If you think *any* of us would just sit here and watch you suffer without doing somethin' about it, you don't know us at all. You want to be mad at someone, be mad at me. Not Trey."

I closed my eyes so I didn't have to see the intensity in his expression. I wanted to tell him we were all fucked, but I couldn't. Not without making everything into a bigger mess.

I heard the cruel voice echoing in my head. *When will you learn?*

You know better, Wolf snarled.

Shut up, I begged. *Just shut up.*

"Bones, are you listenin' to me?" Mac's voice rang with impatient authority, but I refused to open my eyes again.

Eventually, Mac gave up and I managed to fall asleep again, although every tiny movement woke me with a pained gasp. A few times I saw Mac checking on me, but most often it was Apple sitting at my side, her tiny hand resting on mine. I could still see the faint remains of the bruise on her face from where Zip hit her. When I met her eyes, I dreaded seeing that hurt and betrayal again, but she just gave me a small smile.

I wanted to tell her I didn't deserve her forgiveness.

Instead, I just closed my eyes again.

The days passed in a haze of pain. Mac and Griz moved me to my mattress. Sam had been moved to the bunkhouse with the kids and the clinic felt so empty. I refused to speak to Trey, desperate to push him away for good this time. I didn't speak to anyone unless necessary. Maybe it was too late, but my mind kept spinning through frantic plans. If I could escape as soon as I could move, maybe I could get far enough away that he wouldn't bother with the Vault. I could get his attention and hope he chased me instead. It was a gamble, but one I would take without hesitation to keep the people of the Vault from getting caught in the crossfire.

I'd lied to all of them. I wasn't the only powered person in the world.

Either that or I was crazy, but the things I'd seen sure seemed like proof he existed, and I sure as hell wasn't going to take that chance.

Mac's crew did not react well to my sudden turn in behavior, and I couldn't blame them. I struggled to bear their anger, confusion, and *hurt*. Trey's broken promise felt like a wound in my heart, even as the clinical part of me understood why they'd drugged me. I didn't understand why it hurt so badly. A broken promise was nothing new.

ᜆ

"Hey, Boney."

I opened my eyes to see Raven and someone else striding into the clinic. I tensed, and then bit back a groan of pain. I didn't want to deal with Raven and whoever—

My thoughts came to a halt as I recognized the girl I'd saved from Brimstone. *Sky.* Her hair had been buzzed short and even, fixing the crude way it had been cut, and dark bruises lingered on her face. She stood there, her eyes wide and tears rolling down her cheeks as she stared at me. I was still stuck lying on my stomach on my mattress. I could get up and move around a little, but it hurt like hell and I needed help. I'd had a few truly humiliating moments with Griz attempting to use the outhouse, but I preferred them over the humiliating moments using a bedpan.

"Sky, don't be a little bitch," Raven snapped, startling me. "You wanted to help, so quit crying."

I winced at her harsh tone, but to my surprise, Sky wiped her cheeks and raised her chin.

"Thank you, Bones." Her voice quavered, but she pushed through. "You saved my life, and I can't ever repay you, but I'd like to help you recover if that's ok."

I stared at her, then flicked my eyes to Raven.

"Yeah, me too. Griz is tired of seeing your naked ass," she grumbled, "so we get to play nursemaids."

I swallowed down the "hell no" I longed to spit out, reminding myself it didn't matter. So I gave a short nod and then winced at the movement.

"Gods, stop moving your head. They didn't shred up your tongue. Use that, dumbass!" Raven snapped open the blanket she'd been carrying. It was a quilt, worn and faded, but much thicker than the pathetic blanket I had. She laid it over me without a word, tucking it in around my body in a gentle, maternal move that startled me.

I brushed my fingers over the soft material. It smelled good, like my lavender soap and something…something that reminded me of Trey.

Raven turned on her heel and started cleaning the clinic, giving Sky orders as she went. I was taken aback at the effort she put into making sure everything was spotless. After about an hour, she and Sky managed to get me up and take me to the outhouse. It wasn't any less humiliating to have Raven pulling down my pants and helping me position on the outhouse hole, but she surprised me again by not making any cruel comments about my vulnerable state.

"With Sam and the kids at the bunkhouse, it's pretty crowded in there," she said like I wasn't struggling to wipe my own ass. "So me, Sky, and Griz are moving into the clinic for now. Trey, Jax, and Mac are in charge of Sam and the kids."

I didn't miss the way her eyes cut to my face when she said Trey's name.

"I'm sure Apple will be here most days. That child is obsessed with you. Trey had to promise she could come help during the day before she stopped sneaking out at night and coming over here."

I remembered all the times I'd woken in a haze of pain to see Apple sitting with me and bit back a sigh of exasperation. I didn't know she'd been sneaking out.

"We got the kids out before they brought you back, so they didn't have to see your back hanging off your bones like bloody ribbons."

I blanched and she laughed humorlessly.

"You think it's bad *hearing* about it? I had to help piece you back together. Hard to stitch someone up when there's not much left to stitch to."

My stomach turned, but she helped me stand and pulled up my pants for me.

"We gotta get you a skirt," she muttered. "Course the boys never thought of that, the idiots."

Once I lay on my mattress again, she sent Sky out to find me a skirt and yelled at Griz to get his ass inside to help change the dressing on my back.

"Hey, Bones," Griz said as he stepped into the clinic, "is Raven behavin' herself?"

"Don't you start," Raven snapped. "I'm here, ain't I?"

I stayed quiet, my cheek resting on my flat pillow. The short walk to the outhouse and back had left me exhausted. I needed to get my strength up.

Griz and Raven crouched on opposite sides of my mattress and helped me sit up enough to start unwinding the bandage around my torso. The dressing had to be changed twice a day. The first time Griz did it, I just about lost my shit. If it'd been anyone else, I don't know if I would've let them without an actual fight, but Griz remained patient and calm, explaining until I let him continue. He kept his eyes averted from my chest and had me lay down on my stomach again as soon as he removed the bandage. When he changed the dressing, I passed out from the pain, so I wasn't uncomfortable for long.

Now having done this routine half a dozen times, I'd gotten slightly used to sitting with my whole fucking chest exposed. *Slightly.* Raven's eyes dipped to the brand on my chest and my face burned, but she didn't say anything. Half the fucking hold had probably seen it along with most of my chest when I got whipped. I didn't care so much about my naked body. A body was a body, and I'd seen many working as a healer. But the brand on my chest wasn't just a scar. It would forever be a mark of pain, humiliation, and shame.

"This is so fucked up," Raven muttered as Griz showed her how to peel the old dressing off.

It hurt like hell, but I stayed conscious.

"To put it lightly," Griz muttered back.

"You don't have to—" I mumbled.

"Bones, shut the fuck up," Raven interrupted. "You can't do this by yourself so don't even fucking go there."

I swallowed hard.

"It's ok, Bones," Griz murmured, "Raven's mad at Madame, not you."

Raven made an angry noise through her teeth that confused me further.

They finished, wrapped me back up, and helped me lay back down. I started to drift off right away, completely spent. I heard them cleaning up by the sink, and I listened with my eyes closed, comforted by the familiar sounds.

"How's Trey?" Raven whispered.

Griz sighed. "Wrecked."

"Honestly what the fuck else—"

"I know," Griz interrupted. "Don't wake her up."

"I've half a mind to wake her up and *make* her explain," Raven muttered.

"Raven," Griz said, his voice a warning.

"I'm not gonna," Raven snapped, "but I want to."

They were quiet for a while and I used the little energy I had left to keep the tears rolling down my face as silent as possible.

"Did she tell him *why?*" Raven asked.

"She said it hurts her, but Trey said she looked terrified."

"That doesn't make any fuckin' sense," Raven grumbled.

"I dunno." Griz sighed. "Just, let's focus on gettin' her back on her feet, ok?"

"Ten fuckin' lashes," Raven muttered, "on the one person she won't heal. What a fuckin' dumbass."

"I just hope they don't get infected." Griz sounded worried.

"That's how Mac's dad died, isn't it?" Raven's voice sounded *soft*.

"Yeah."

"Fuck."

In the silence that followed, I tried to force my miserable self to stay awake in case they said anything else, but exhaustion pulled me under again.

"Trey's been teaching the kids how to fight," Raven said.

I glanced up from where I sat in the exam chair, sewing a tear in one of my shirts. It'd been just over a week since I got whipped and I still couldn't stand for long.

Raven looked amused at the look on my face. "He's not training them to fight in the Pit, just how to defend themselves."

A little bit of the tension left my shoulders.

"Bones, am I doin' this right?" Sky worried.

I looked over at where she watched golden oil drip through a cloth into a small glass jar. I had her straining my Calendula flower oil infusion to make an ointment for dry skin. The cold winter wind left people's skin cracked this time of year, and I'd found a recipe for the salve in the old healer's notebook.

"Pick up the cloth and squeeze the flowers real hard to get all the oil out," I instructed and watched as she did what I said. "Now do a couple more jars."

"You know that weed patch right beside the clinic?" Raven asked, continuing when I hummed an affirming noise. "Trey said it used to be an herb garden for the clinic. He's gonna try to fix it up for you this spring so you can grow your own herbs and shit."

I kept my eyes on my sewing, hating the warmth that spread through me at the idea of having my own little garden. I had to remind myself that didn't matter, I wasn't gonna be here that long.

"Trey said it'll be a good project for him and Jax," Raven continued.

I had to fight the urge to roll my eyes at her. She talked about Trey *all the time*. It wasn't subtle, but then nothing about Raven was subtle. Trey came by every few days, and I ignored him. The hurt and sorrow in his eyes cut me straight to the bone, but I forced myself to endure it. I had to stop before I got him killed.

I didn't stop constantly replaying the beautiful things he'd said to me though, even though they hurt as bad as my back.

"Ok," Raven barked, startling me. "What the fuck happens to you when you get a narc?"

I winced. I'd been expecting this. She'd held it in longer than I would have guessed.

"I don't want to talk about it, Raven." I forced my voice to be even.

"Well too bad," she snapped. "This isn't just about you. So start talkin'."

I bent my head farther over my mending and stayed silent. I could feel her frustration building like a physical force.

"You wanna know what I think?"

"No," I muttered, knowing she'd ignore me.

"I don't think anything happens to you."

I focused hard on my stitches.

"Did you *want* to break Trey's heart, is that it?"

"Raven!" Sky hissed.

"If you don't want to be with him, just fucking *tell* him that," Raven continued ranting. "Stop stringing him along and then dropping him whenever you feel like it."

My eyes were burning, but I *refused* to let any tears fall.

"Trey's a good person. Might be the best damn person I know, and he does not fuckin' deserve this."

That was true. Trey didn't deserve this, and I would never forgive myself for what I'd done to him.

"Really?" She sounded furious. "You're not gonna say *anything?* You're such a selfish bitch!"

I heard her stride to the door and leave, slamming it hard enough to make the windows rattle. The silence she left behind felt awkward as I struggled not to cry and Sky nervously continued straining the flowers. Only about a minute passed before the door opened again. I glanced up, bracing myself for Raven to yell some more, but instead, I met Mac's grave face.

"Madame wants you."

CHAPTER 17

I stared at Mac, trying to process what he'd just said.
"In the dungeon?" I asked.

He nodded, his eyes stormy with anger. I couldn't stand for longer than ten minutes, but I knew Madame wouldn't give a shit.

"Ok." I gingerly stood, leaving my blanket and the shirt I'd been mending. I wore the long brown skirt Sky had found for me, and I had to admit Raven had been right. It made using the outhouse *much* easier.

"The dungeon?" Sky repeated in a tiny voice.

I glanced at her, shame souring my stomach at the fear and surprise on her face. As far as I could tell, most people were unaware of what exactly Madame did in the dungeon. Madame had never told me to keep it quiet, but maybe she knew my role in what she did wasn't something I would ever voluntarily share.

"You gonna be able to walk all the way there?" Mac asked. "I can go get a horse, but it'll make us more late." His expression stayed even, but I could hear the worry in his voice.

"I dunno," I said and then paused, startled at my honest answer. "I'll be fine."

That muscle in his jaw ticked. "Let's go then."

I made it almost halfway before I had to stop, leaning on a tree with stabbing pains shooting up and down my back. My puffs of breath made clouds in the cold air, and the wind made my eyes water, stinging against my skin. Mac swore under his breath, running a hand through his dark hair.

"I can sit on the floor when I get there if I have to," I said, dazed by the pain. "I just gotta get there."

"She's doin' this on purpose," Mac said in a low voice. "She knows you're not healed enough."

"I figured," I muttered.

"I don't know how to help without hurting you."

I looked up at him. He fidgeted where he stood, his eyes darting between me and the Watchtower. I'd never seen him look so anxious, and it forced me to swallow my pride.

"I'm gonna hurt no matter what. Might as well just get me there."

"Do you think you could climb on my back?"

"Like a kid?" I hoped I understood him right.

He nodded, turning his back to me and crouching.

I hiked up my skirt, leaned onto him, and wrapped my arms around his neck. It hurt, putting strain on my back. He reached back to loop his arms under my thighs and carefully stood, which hurt worse. I had a sudden memory of Wolf carrying me like this and my eyes burned.

"You ok?" Mac asked.

"Yeah."

He started moving quickly, and I clenched my jaw shut. Each step sent a stabbing pain through my back, but I refused to make any noise. The walk seemed to take forever, but finally, the watchtower loomed ahead of us. Seeing our destination didn't bring any relief though, and as Mac set me on my feet outside the door, I considered clinging to his neck and begging him to get me out of there.

Instead, I forced myself to take slow painful steps down the stairs to where screams already echoed off the walls.

When we entered the room, I stopped short in the doorway. Mist sat in the chair again, looking gaunt and sobbing. Her blonde hair hung around her face in greasy clumps and blood dripped onto the hay, but she wasn't the only person there. Hawk, the leader of the other Safeguard crew, stood in chains attached to a hook on the wall.

Madame had her long grey dreads in a knot on top of her head as she cut into Mist's arm. Hawk strained against his chains, his jaw clenched, and a vein pulsing in his forehead. His wide eyes swung to us, and the flicker of hope that lit in his eyes at the sight of me made me want to die.

"Took your sweet time, Bones," Madame stated, those cold eyes flicking to me.

I didn't answer. I wasn't going to apologize. Her eyes narrowed on me, but then Hawk yanking on his chains distracted her.

"You know you don't have to watch this," Madame crooned to Hawk, gesturing at Mist with her bloody knife. "All I need is a name."

"I'm so…so sorry, Hawk," Mist sobbed.

I fought the urge to be sick. Was Madame torturing Mist in front of Hawk to try and get him to talk? I'd only had a few interactions with Hawk, but he'd seemed nice enough. Now his bloody face looked anguished. He'd been roughed up, but Mist looked terrible.

"Bones, clean her up," Madame ordered.

Hawk met my eyes, looking expectant, but I dropped mine to the floor. He didn't know my role here wasn't actually to heal but to prolong the torture session until Madame got bored.

I moved forward and placed my hands on Mist's bleeding arm. As I healed her, I made the mistake of meeting her gaze. I expected to see hate and fury directed at me, but her hazel eyes only held deep pain and sorrow and a horrible kind of understanding. My eyes welled, tears spilling down my cheeks.

I'm sorry. I'm so sorry. I thought toward her as I healed her arm.

When I stepped back and Madame stepped forward, her sugary scent wafting over me, the realization dawned across Hawk's handsome face. His eyes flashed to me, anger and betrayal shining there. I'd expected that look, but it still hurt. I dropped my eyes, feeling so helpless.

"Who did you report to Hawk?" Madame asked.

"Fuck you!" Hawk hissed.

Madame placed her knife against Mist's chest, just under her shoulder, and slowly pressed. As the sharp knife pierced Mist's skin, blood began to trickle down her chest. The trickle became a stream as the knife went further in. Madame did it so slowly it must have been agonizing, but Mist just squeezed her eyes shut, breathing through clenched teeth. Madame stopped when the knife was buried almost to the hilt, and then she began to turn it.

A scream ripped out of Mist and Hawk screamed with her. All the blood drained from my face at the sound. My knees buckled and the ground raced up to meet me. Next thing I knew I lay on my side in the bloody straw with Mac crouched next to me.

—"tapped out, Madame," Mac was saying, his voice even, but I could see the anger in the tight lines of his jaw. "If you want Mist to live, you'll have to let Bones heal some more."

Madame said something, but it sounded garbled. I closed my eyes, hoping the room would stop spinning.

"Bones." Mac shook me. "Can you heal Mist one more time?"

"Yeah," I mumbled, hoping I could.

He half lifted me to my feet, and the pain in my back made me nauseous. Hawk glared at me, tears on his face. Madame had pulled her knife from Mist's shoulder. Mist's eyes were closed, her face deathly pale. I knew from just a glance that if I didn't heal her, she'd be dead in a few minutes.

I placed my shaking hands on the wound and tried my best to focus. My healing power flowed with a sharp pain, a warning of an approaching burnout, and my stomach dropped in panic. Mac stood at my side, and it wasn't long before I depended on him for support. His hands tightened on my hips, holding me upright. My healing power slowed to a thin thread, but I kept going, watching with blurry vision as the wound slowly closed. When it did, I could have cried from relief. Madame spoke—maybe to me—but I used all my remaining energy to keep myself upright. Mac half carried, half dragged me out of the room. He hesitated at the stairs, then swore.

"I'm so sorry, Bones," he said, then scooped me up into his arms. I couldn't help the cry that escaped my lips, pain stabbing through my back and—

༄

"It's alright, darlin'." A low, comforting voice.

A cool cloth moved across my forehead.

"I can't," I whimpered. "I can't do it anymore."

"I know. I know, Bones," that voice murmured.

"Please don't—" I choked on a sob. I didn't know what I was saying. This felt like a dream.

"You want me to go?"

I squinted, bringing Trey's blurry face into focus. I lay on my stomach on the hard metal table again, chills shaking me and making pain lance across my back with the movement. Panic surged through me like I'd just grabbed an electric fence.

"No," I gasped, trying to reach for him. "Don't go. Please don't go."

"Ok. It's ok. I'm right here." His warm hand gripped mine and squeezed. "I'm not goin' anywhere, darlin'."

"Fuck, some of these stitches ripped," someone said.

"You sure we can't—"

"No. Absolutely not."

"Well, you better get ready to fucking hold her down."

I didn't understand what they meant, but the next thing I knew, my back burned in agony, and I screamed until darkness swallowed me again.

〰

"—she doing?"

"She's still unconscious."

"This has to stop." The words were whispered like a secret.

In the silence, I struggled to pry my eyes open. I lay on my stomach on my mattress again, my body aching.

"I brought some broth. I know she drinks it often."

"Thank you," Griz said. "She'll really appreciate that."

"Tell her….tell her I'm sorry."

"I'll do that."

I heard the door open and close. I tried to lick my lips to get some moisture into them. A head popped into my vision, startling me.

"Griz, she's awake!" Apple called. Then she glanced back at me, her little hand resting over mine. "Hi, Bones, how you feeling?"

Griz appeared beside Apple, relief clear in his dark eyes. "There you are."

"Water?" I croaked.

Apple grabbed something next to her, holding up a large jug of water with a clear tube sticking out of it. She placed the tube at my lips. "Here. Drink," she ordered.

I obeyed, the cool water like a balm on my dry throat.

"What happened?" I mumbled after I drank my fill.

"You passed out while Mac was carrying you back," Griz explained. "When he got you home, your back was bleeding, so we had to check the stitches. Some of 'em were torn, so we sewed you back up.

You had a burnout fever on top of all that. You were unconscious for almost two days."

I closed my eyes, trying to process all that. I had vague recollections of crying and pain and a warm hand squeezing mine.

"How you feelin'?" Griz asked.

"Like shit," I muttered without opening my eyes.

"Did you just answer honestly?"

The surprise in Griz's voice made me drag my eyes open again.

He smirked, but his eyes were worried. "I can't tell if that means you're dying or if you're just actually starting to trust me."

I rolled my eyes or tried to.

"Should I tell the others?" Apple asked, and I blinked in surprise at her hand resting on his thick arm without fear.

"Yeah, peanut. Go tell 'em." He smiled.

"I'll be back, Bones," she promised as she bounded to the door.

Griz pulled up a chair to the side of my mattress and— *Wait.* A chair? How was he eye level with me? I reached over the edge of the mattress. Normally I'd immediately touch the floor, but now my fingers touched only air.

"We made you a bed frame with some cinder blocks," Griz said, noticing my hand. "Makes it a lot easier to take care of your back when you're up a little higher."

Something clenched in my chest, but I wasn't sure whether it was gratitude for the gift or guilt that they were taking care of *me.*

"You got lots of visitors," Griz added. "Seems most people are takin' your side."

Anxiety swirled in my stomach. "Side?"

"They think Madame was wrong," he said, his eyes studying me.

My heart started beating faster, clearing the cobwebs in my head a little.

"They think she needs to be stopped."

"Don't tell me that," I whispered.

"I'm just repeatin' what they said."

"I can't...I can't know. I don't...Madame will—" I broke off, my lips trembling. Didn't they know they'd end up in that fucking chair in Madame's dungeon if they said shit like that? And then Madame would force me to help her torture them and I couldn't—

"Ok." Griz covered my shaking hand with his steady one. "It's ok.

I won't tell you." He still sounded calm but something like disappointment flashed across his face.

I wanted to beg him to tell people to just keep their fucking heads down, but the words caught in my throat.

Don't get involved, Wolf growled. *Just get out of there.*

⌒

After a few days, it became clear I was involved no matter how I felt about it. People kept dropping by the clinic, bringing little gifts or food. They would whisper to me or Mac's crew that Madame needed to be stopped, that she'd gone too far. Everyone seemed to share knowing glances and nods, and panic built in my chest. A wildfire could take off from a single spark, and I was helplessly watching it happen.

The wounds on my back healed, pulling tight on my back as the muscles tried to knit themselves back together. I would have horrible scars, Madame's mark as she promised, but I tried not to dwell on that.

"I think you're healing faster than most people," Griz said one day as he changed the dressing on my back. "Do you always heal fast?"

It sure as hell didn't feel fast. "I dunno. I don't get sick."

"What about injuries?"

I tried to think back to my major injuries. When I broke my arm the first time, it had healed pretty quick, but I figured my young age played into that. I'd had cuts I had to stitch closed myself, but I hadn't paid much attention to how fast they healed. I'd always been able to get up and work after a beating, but I hadn't had any other choice. The brand on my chest had healed in a month, but I didn't know if that was abnormal. The wound on my shoulder Trey had stitched up *had* healed quickly and normally a giant head wound wouldn't scab over by itself, but mine had.

"Maybe?" I admitted.

He made a thoughtful humming sound.

"Why?"

"I'm just wondering if maybe you *do* heal yourself. It's just slower than other people. Maybe that's why you reached burnout so fast when you healed Mist. Cause your powers have been workin' nonstop trying to heal your back."

I lay there thinking that over, uneasy for some reason. No, not uneasy, *guilty.* Not being able to heal myself seemed like balance for all the things I'd done. Every death stained my soul, and my own suffering felt like retribution.

Maybe if you stopped trying to be a godsdamn martyr, you'd see that.

I shoved all those thoughts away. I hated how often Mac's words floated through my mind. I hated how often they taunted me at night when I tried to sleep.

"You ok?" Griz asked.

I forced my tense muscles to relax and the shrieking pain in my back dulled. "I'm fine."

꙳

I woke up one morning to find a new small table sitting beside my bed. On the table lay the little knife Trey had given me. I'd assumed it'd been lost after I left it buried in Brimstone's shoulder. Warmth and sorrow flooded me. All my feelings for Trey were still there, like an entire fucking garden of dreams I could see, but not touch. I would just have to find a way to live with them.

"You're a river. You don't break, you bend."

Sometimes I had a flash of brown eyes holding me steady as pain lanced through me in my memories. I wondered if I'd dreamed about Trey while unconscious like I'd summoned him to comfort me. Sometimes I could swear I could hear his voice calling me "darlin'."

In reality, Trey stayed away, and even though I needed him to do that, it still hurt. I kept looking for him by the door, kept thinking about the kiss we'd shared, kept missing him. I tried to withdraw from the others, but it was harder to push Raven and Griz away since they'd moved in, and I relied on them so much just to move and perform basic tasks. Mostly I just got quieter and quieter, curled up in my quilt. Griz and Raven continued to try and include me in conversation, Griz looking worried and Raven looking angry. I hated the hurt in their eyes, and I hated how much I hated it. I didn't understand why it was so *hard* to push them all away. Surely I hadn't dropped my guard that much?

I warned you. Wolf was a constant presence in my head these days.

Get better. Get out. I reminded myself daily. *Get better. Get out.*

꙳

"Boney, someone's here to see you," Raven shouted as she pushed the door open.

I turned, my movements still stiff as I tried to avoid using most of my back muscles, to see Clarity walk in the door behind Raven. My heart dropped at how pale and thin and *ill* she looked. I hadn't seen her since I healed her from the sickness. I moved across the room, guilt choking me that I hadn't checked up on her, and she finally looked up and met my eyes.

"I'm ok," she said, like she could read my frantic thoughts. "I'm not sick." She seemed to force a smile. "I just wanted to visit you."

I stopped in front of her, narrowing my eyes to a suspicious glare. I tried to take her arm and let my magic check for itself, but she shifted away like she didn't want me to touch her. I pulled my hand back. I knew we weren't exactly *friends* but she'd let me heal her before.

"I promise," she said. "I'm not sick."

"You look like shit," I said, perhaps more harshly than necessary.

To my surprise she smiled slightly, glancing at Raven. "I think you've been spending too much time with Ray."

Raven glared at her, but something soft in her eyes made me pause. I'd never seen Raven look at anyone like that.

"Ray?" I couldn't help asking.

Raven's icy blue eyes snapped to mine. "Only Clarity gets to call me that. Anyone else tries and they end up bleeding."

"How are you feeling?" Clarity asked.

"I'll be fine," I said, looking warily from Raven to study Clarity again.

Her cheekbones stood out from her thin face and her normally warm brown skin looked like a dull ashy grey. Even her eyes looked sunken.

"Why do you—"

"How come you're not talking to Trey?" she interrupted me, a gleam of determination lighting in her hollow eyes.

I forced all my turbulent emotions to the very back of my mind and willed my face to be blank. "Clarity—"

"Don't bother, Clare," Raven said, glaring at me. "She's a stubborn bitch."

I narrowed my eyes at Raven, my temper rising. Whatever goodwill we'd managed to achieve after my whipping had been slowly evaporating as the days went by.

"I'm allowed to have my own personal business."

"Bones, he cares about you so much."

Clarity's soft and pained voice speared me through the heart. I turned away and went back to disinfecting medical tools.

"Told you," Raven said, and I had to grit my teeth to keep from snapping at her.

"He told me about the narc." Clarity sounded like she'd moved a few steps closer, but I didn't turn around. "Maybe if you just…explain what happens—"

"I don't owe any of you an explanation." I interrupted, trying to blink away tears.

"No, but we're friends." Clarity stood at my elbow, but I refused to look at her. "Friends talk to each other when they're hurting."

Maybe I hadn't had many friends in my life, but I felt more like a deadly virus than a friend. I *knew* getting close to people got them killed, but I couldn't seem to stop fucking doing it. I blinked furiously, trying to keep the tears at bay. If I could just—

Clarity laid her hand on my arm, and my healing magic *jolted.* I couldn't help the gasp that escaped and Clarity jerked her hand back as though I'd burned her. Her eyes widened and we stared at each other for a moment, then she turned and *fled* out of the clinic.

"The fuck did you do?" Raven snarled, but she darted after Clarity before I could answer.

Not that I had an answer to give her. I rubbed my arm, trying to erase the sensation of spiders crawling across my skin. I had no idea what just happened, but my magic had never done anything like that before.

⁓

Three weeks after my whipping, I stumbled on a plan to escape.

I started going for walks as soon as I could, forcing myself to go longer every day as I tried to get my strength up. On one of those morning walks I noticed the loggers removing the wheels from the hauling wagons and replacing them with long skids to go over the snow. Through eavesdropping, I learned they planned to leave at dawn. The sickness had used up more of the hold's supply of lumber than expected, so the loggers were being sent back out to gather more. I watched them cover all their tools in the sleighs with heavy tarps to keep the snow off, creating a perfect place to hide.

I knew I couldn't pass up this opportunity. My back still ached sharply, but the open wounds had closed, and it no longer required a bandage or dressing. It would just be pain, and I could push through pain.

I'd been collecting a little bag of supplies that I stashed inside my mattress. I'd cut a small slice in the bottom and while it wasn't comfortable to lay on, no one noticed. Not that I had many visitors. Clarity didn't return and Raven went back to silently glaring at me. Sometimes that sensation of spiders would crawl across my skin again and my powers would flare in response, but then it would vanish. I had no idea what it meant, but I didn't have time to dwell on it. My plan had to be perfect. If Madame caught me—

I shuddered. Madame could *not* catch me.

That night I stood in the middle of the clinic and allowed myself a moment of grief. It swept over me with a surprising intensity. The kids slept in their beds upstairs and the fire crackled in the wood stove. If I *could* choose, Mac's crew would be the kind of people I'd want for a family. My eyes prickled as my heart ached. This could have been something so *good.*

I clung to a delusional sort of hope that Madame wouldn't punish anyone too severely for my escape. I hated being forced to choose between the chance that Madame punished Mac's crew and the chance that the powered person murdered the entire hold.

I had to believe that Trey would be ok. I had to—

Mac opened the door. The dark expression on his face gave me a second of panic that he knew my plan, but then he spoke.

"Madame wants you."

My stomach twisted.

I followed him through the dark, quiet hold, our boots crunching in the snow. Mac didn't speak to me, and I couldn't tell what that meant. My dread rose as we entered the watch tower and went straight down to the dungeon. I hadn't seen Madame since I'd passed out down here weeks ago.

Inside the torture room, stood Madame, five of her lackeys, and Zana, the third member of the council. I glanced at the chair and my heart stuttered in shock at the sight of Nemo restrained in it. He'd been stripped of his shirt and blood dripped down his bruised face, but there was a defiant fire in his expression as he held Madame's gaze. I glanced back at Mac, but as usual, I couldn't read his expressionless face.

"Hello, Bones." Madame smiled that unhinged smile. "We caught a big fish today."

I looked at Nemo again. His torso was tanned from the sun like he often worked outside without a shirt. He had strange tattoos across one arm and his lean body was more muscular than I'd guessed. Blood matted in his greying hair. He turned his head toward me, making eye contact. He frowned at me, but then Madame spoke, and he turned his attention back to her.

"The question is, *how* big?" She tapped her knife on the palm of her hand. "Have we finally reached the top of this ridiculous *little rebellion,* Nemo?"

Nemo didn't answer.

"Oh good." Madame's smile made me feel sick. "I was hoping you'd do this the hard way."

I swallowed down the bile rising in my throat as she sliced open his chest from his collarbone down to his navel. He screamed hoarsely like he'd been screaming for a while. I healed him with shaking hands when she gestured at me with the bloody knife, trying to breathe through my mouth to avoid the sickly-sweet scent mixed with blood.

"Who is the leader?" Madame asked him once I finished.

He didn't answer, and she grinned as she lifted her knife again. Panic gripped me as I realized this might be a long night.

Sure enough, Madame carved him up for hours. Eventually, she seemed to get bored and had her men start beating him. I healed him again and again, my ears ringing with the sounds of Nemo's screams. My jaw clenched so tightly it ached.

You're getting out of here. You're getting out of here, I repeated in my head over and over.

It had to be close to dawn by the time she stopped. Nemo never said a word, but by the end he slumped in the chair, gasping in ragged breaths and half-conscious.

"Get him out of here," Madame said. "We'll do this again tomorrow."

The men started unbuckling Nemo to drag him back to his cell. I didn't wait to be dismissed. I didn't care if it pissed her off. I turned on my heel and strode out the door, avoiding Mac's gaze as I passed him.

She didn't yell after me, but I heard her voice demanding that Mac stay. As soon as I got out of the watchtower, I started to run.

When I reached the clinic, I slipped in as quietly as I could and changed out of my bloody clothes, throwing on my warmest gear. Then I reached into my mattress and pulled out my small stash of supplies, shoving it into a pack I'd swiped from a house visit. Last but not least I folded up the quilt I'd grown so attached to and shoved it inside. I hadn't been able to figure out how to steal a bedroll, so the quilt would have to do. I hesitated a moment, but then grabbed the little wooden dandelion and packed it too.

As soon as I had everything, I slipped back out the door. Thank the gods, the sun hadn't risen yet, but it would any second. The loggers had packed up the sleighs last night. I'd been sure to walk past to see so I knew exactly where I needed to go. The horses nickered at me as I entered the stable, and Violet poked her head over the stall door. A lump rose in my throat, but I just darted to the sleigh that waited to be hitched up to the horses and slid under the heavy tarp. I crawled across the sleigh bed, edging past the sharp tools. Finally, I reached the wooden panel at the front, curled into the smallest ball I could, and waited, trying to ignore the dull pain in my back.

Only two minutes later, the tarp shifted and someone started crawling in just like I had. I reached down to my boot, sliding my knife out. My entire self recoiled in horror at the idea of using it, but I could not let this chance get away from me. My fist clenched on the knife handle, but then the person got closer and I let out all my breath in a shaky rush.

Trey reached me, dressed in his warmest gear with a leather pack completely with a bedroll strapped underneath it. He met my furious and shocked gaze with a calm expression.

"What the fuck are you doing?" I hissed.

"Goin' with you," he said.

I gaped at him. "What?"

His eyes were so solemn. "I'm goin' with you, Bones."

"You can't—" I started to growl, but then we both heard footsteps approaching and I went silent.

The loggers grumbled to each other as they got the horses out and hitched them up. I stared at Trey, my brain spinning. When the sleigh jerked forward, I slid sideways, bumping right up against him with the movement. He reached out and caught my arm, but then he didn't let go. I glared at him as hard as I could, but he just studied my expression with a small smile creeping over his face.

"It's ok," he mouthed.

We heard the loggers greeting the guards at the watchtower and both tensed, but then the gate groaned open. The sleigh started moving again and I let out a tiny shaky breath. We'd made it through the gate. From what I'd gathered, the loggers were traveling to a spot about three days away. I planned on slipping out and disappearing when they stopped for the first night, but until then I had to wait.

It's ok? Honestly, what the fuck was Trey thinking? What about Clarity? What about the kids at the clinic? What about Mac and the rest of the crew? Why would he leave all of them? He couldn't come with me. He couldn't be anywhere near me. The whole point of this escape was to get as far away from Trey and everyone else at the Vault as possible.

Even worse, a selfish part of me wanted to cry with relief that I didn't have to leave him behind.

CHAPTER 18

The hours dragged by. I wanted to get answers from Trey, but I didn't dare talk more than necessary. Every time I glared at him, he just met my angry gaze with his calm one, which made me want to throttle him. Eventually, I fell asleep, exhausted after my sleepless night of healing Nemo, but my dreams were full of blood and screams and the flash of Madame's knife. I jolted awake with a gasp when someone shook me and met Trey's eyes. He held a finger up to his mouth and then slid closer to me, pressing his lips practically against my ear.

"You were starting to talk in your sleep," he whispered.

I nodded to let him know I understood, my heart lurching. If he hadn't been here, I could've easily given myself away. I started to shift away, but he slid an arm around my waist and pulled me against him. I looked up at him, startled, and he leaned forward to speak close to my ear again.

"You can go back to sleep," he said softly. "I'll wake you up if you start talking again."

I lay there stiffly for a moment, knowing I *should* shove him away, but instead, I found myself curling into his warmth. *Just 'cause it's cold.* I lied to myself. My nose pressed against his neck and he rested his chin on top of my head. Every breath I took flooded me with his scent, the lavender soap from the clinic, the oil he used to clean his gun, and something just inexplicably Trey. It melted my angry defenses and I let out a shaky breath, my eyes prickling.

"It's ok, darlin'," he murmured in my ear. "I got you."

Some final hardened part of me cracked in a way I knew I'd never be able to repair, that lonely garden in my chest stretching and growing and turning toward him like he was the godsdamned sun. If he noticed the tears that slid down my face, he didn't say anything. He just held me until I fell asleep again.

Trey woke me up several times when my dreams made me start muttering or thrashing in my sleep, but I dozed on and off until nightfall. We both lay awake and alert in the darkness when the sleigh began to slow. The loggers complained about sore asses and having to go out again. Our sleigh held the logging equipment while the other sleigh held the tents and food supplies. I'd been banking on the hope that they wouldn't need anything from this sleigh until they arrived where they planned to harvest lumber. Trey seemed to have the same idea, but both of us were tense as we listened to the loggers make camp for the night. At one point someone flipped back the tarp of our sleigh and my heart lurched in terror, but they just grabbed a couple of axes near the back and then secured the tarp back down.

I released Trey's arm that I'd grasped and he let out a slow relieved breath. We waited until the noise died down and eventually, a single pair of boots crunched in the snow, and the sleigh seat creaked as the night watch guard settled in. I squinted at Trey's face, barely able to make out his features in the darkness.

"Ten more minutes," he breathed in my ear.

I counted in my head and before I'd even reached six minutes, we heard the low snore of the guard. Trey grinned, his teeth flashing. He grabbed something beside him I couldn't quite make out and led the way. We slithered on our bellies to the back of the sleigh, moving agonizingly slow to avoid knocking over any tools. Trey dropped down into the snow first. I waited until he signaled and then followed.

Together we crept toward the woods, but then I paused glancing back at the obvious footprints we left in the snow. I shrugged out of my jacket and backtracked so I could sweep it behind us to at least partially erase our tracks. When I reached Trey again, he gave me an approving nod. Once we reached the woods and traveled for a few minutes I shook the snow off my jacket and slipped it back on. Both of us stood for a few breaths just listening, but no sound came from the camp. Trey grinned, but I couldn't return it. Our successful escape should have been a relief, but it made me feel uneasy.

"Here." Trey held out the wooden thing he carried.

I took it but stared in confusion. It had a frame of two pieces of wood shaped like long ovals and some sort of leather latticework inside. Trey dropped his on the ground and set his foot on it, crouching to tie them onto his boot with the attached leather ties.

"Snowshoes," he whispered.

I dropped mine into the snow, copying the direction his snowshoes pointed. Before I could bend to start tying them, Trey turned and started doing it for me. He tapped my boot with a gloved hand and I lifted it so he could access the ties, resting my hands on his broad shoulders for balance.

When he straightened, he gave me a warm grin. "Like this," he whispered, showing me how to take wide strides to avoid stepping on the sides of the snowshoes.

I followed a bit awkwardly, but it wasn't hard to fall into a rhythm and the snowshoes kept us on top of the snow instead of sinking to our knees. It would have been hard, slow work to wade through the snow, especially with my sore back. Gods, why did he have to be so thoughtful? It made it a lot harder to stay mad. As we walked, I glanced back in the direction we'd come. I wanted to get a little farther away from the logger's camp before I lit into him. I wanted to—

I got a glimpse of movement to my left and managed to half turn, my heart leaping into my throat before a hand grabbed my arm and jerked me against a massive body.

"Well, what have we here?" growled Zip.

My heart thundered in my throat, and I didn't answer. He held me so my back pressed against his chest, and I couldn't see his face. His arms pinned my arms to my sides like bands of steel. My snowshoes tangled on top of each other and one had been ripped partially off my boot. Trey had stopped a few steps away. He stood casually, but I could see his body coiled like a spring. He didn't look at me, keeping his eyes fixed on Zip.

"Whatcha doing here, Bones?" Zip asked, his low voice rumbling through me.

"Lookin' for you," I lied, trying to keep my voice steady.

He huffed a dark laugh. "I don't think so, baby. You tryin' to run?"

My mind raced trying to come up with a way out of this situation. If he yelled, he'd wake the whole camp and we'd never escape all two dozen of them.

"See I'm thinkin' it looks like you're tryin' to run. And I'm also thinkin' Madame would reward me handsomely if I brought you back."

"Don't hurt yourself now," my stupid mouth said before I could think better of it.

His arms tightened around me, making my back twinge in pain. "You always did think you were smarter than me, didn't you?" he growled. "You know, Bones, we got some unfinished business, you and me."

Fear settled like ice in my stomach. Trey's face stayed expressionless, but his eyes dipped to mine for a brief second.

"You know, the boys get awful lonesome on these long trips. Having a pretty girl along would be a real treat." One of his hands started moving, drifting across my body, and my stomach turned. "*Or,* I could make sure no one *else* touches you, Bones."

My hands trembled, but Wolf started snarling.

Survive. Do what you have to do to survive.

My mind seemed to hollow out, locking away everything except for the determination to get through this one moment. I knew I'd survived for years by thinking this way, but it felt even more horrible than I remembered.

"You swear it?" I asked, trying to put as much steel into my voice as possible. "I let you have me and you won't let anyone else touch me or Trey."

"Bones." Trey's voice came out soft but full of fury.

"I swear it, baby," Zip said, "on my mother's grave."

"Bones," Trey said again, but I couldn't look at him.

"Ok," I said hollowly.

Zip spun me around in his arms, fully ripping off one snowshoe and forcing me to balance precariously. The victorious grin on his face made me retreat farther into myself.

"Good girl," he said in a low, cruel voice.

He pushed my jacket and pack off my shoulders, letting them fall to the snowy ground. His freezing hands slid under my shirt, slowly pulling it up. I raised my arms, desperately trying to push my mind somewhere far, far away. He pulled my shirt off and then stopped, eyes narrowing at the brand on my chest.

"What the fuck is—"

A strange *pffft* noise sounded and his entire body jerked. I leapt backward and stumbled over my jacket and pack and single snowshoe, landing on my ass in the snow. I caught a glimpse of the blood spurting from the hole that'd opened up in his forehead before he fell over backward with a dull thud and Trey hauled me up and wrapped his arms around me.

"You ok?" He sounded frantic, so at odds with how expressionless he'd been a second ago. "Fuck, I'm sorry. I had to wait until he was distracted."

"I'm ok," I said, dazed as I stared down at Zip's motionless body. "You shot him."

"I told him I would if he touched you again," he said darkly, releasing me to grab my discarded shirt from the ground and shake the snow out of it. He handed it to me and turned his back, giving me some privacy to pull my shirt back on.

"How was it so quiet?" I whispered as I dressed, my brain still trying to figure out what the hell had just happened.

"Silencer." He turned, holding up the gun to show me the strange long barrel. "Madame had a few of these locked away. I helped myself to one before I left."

I'd never seen something like that before. "He knew you were armed; he just thought you wouldn't shoot him 'cause of the noise." I realized.

"I was banking on him being a cocky asshole. Wasn't too much to hope for." He snagged my fallen jacket and pack and handed them to me, then bent to retrieve my snowshoe. "Come on, we better move fast before someone comes looking for him."

"Are we just gonna leave him here?" I asked, shrugging my jacket and pack back on and lifting my foot so he could tie the snowshoe back on.

"Not much else we can do," he said, getting back to his feet. "C'mon."

We set off at a quick pace, trying to step in spots of frozen snow to avoid leaving tracks. The snowshoes kept us from leaving obvious human-shaped footprints, but they still left tracks. The nearly full moon shone in the cloudless sky, giving us dim light to see by. Wolves howled somewhere in the distance, making the hair on the back of my neck stand up.

"They're not close enough that we need to worry, yet," Trey said when I glanced at him, wide-eyed.

Soon the ground began to slope up. Trey showed me how to kick the front of the snowshoe into the snow and use it like a step. I stumbled more than once as I struggled to get the movement down. It wasn't long before my legs started to burn, and my breathing grew heavier. We had moved far enough away that I could yell at him now, but for some reason, I didn't. We hiked in silence for what must have been a couple of hours before Trey spoke.

"He'd never seen the brand before?" His voice sounded cautiously curious.

My face heated. "Not while sober."

"Ah," he said quietly, then, "Can I ask somethin' of you?"

I turned to see him staring at me, his face grave.

"Don't ever let someone hurt you 'cause you're trying to protect me, ok?"

I looked away, shame curdling in my stomach. "I didn't have a whole lot of options, Trey."

"Bones," he said gently, and my eyes burned, "you gotta start trying to save yourself too."

"I'm a healer, Trey. Saving other people is what I *do,*" I snapped.

"I know," he said, still in that gentle voice, "but the way you throw yourself into the line of fire, Bones, it's like you think your life isn't worth as much as other people's lives."

"It's not," I spit out without thinking.

"It *is,*" he countered. "People love you, Bones. If you can't try to save yourself for you, do it for them. Next time you think about throwing yourself in harm's way, think about Apple."

I flinched, but he wasn't done.

"She watches you. Everything you do. You're teaching her what to think about herself by how you think about *you.* Why do you think she tried to take on Zip all by herself? Fighting for what's right, that's a great thing, but do you want her to throw herself on top of a live grenade when she didn't have to? When there were other options if she worked *with* people who were trying to help?"

"Sometimes there *aren't* people, Trey." I couldn't look at him, anger and guilt shimmering in my veins. "You know how many bikers Juck had? Over a hundred. That many people and not a single damn one ever—" I broke off, my voice shaking.

He snagged my arm, jerking me to a halt. "You went through hell, Bones, and gods I'm just grateful you made it out of there, but we're *not* the Reapers. We've been tryin' to show you that for the past, what, six months? I know you didn't have people then, but you do now."

Don't trust 'em. Wolf snarled, but he sounded quieter.

We're not the Reapers. He talked about the crew like they were here and a part of this. Clearly, they'd been making their own plans.

"So what, they sent you along so you could try to convince me to go back? Is that it?" I finally looked at him, trying to hold onto my anger to avoid giving in to the tears that threatened in my eyes.

"Gods, no," he exclaimed. "Bones, we knew you were planning on running. We knew you had a secret stash of supplies in your mattress. We knew you were gonna try to leave with the loggers. And darlin', all any of us wanted was to *help* you."

I stared at him. *How?* I wanted to ask, but I feared what the answer might be.

"So Mac sent you to keep an eye on me." My voice came out ragged. "You're here to make sure I don't disappear. So I can't—"

"Godsdamnit, Bones, I'm here 'cause I *love* you," he interrupted in a burst of emotion that shocked me into silence. "Have loved you practically since you saved my life on that rooftop. And I'm not expecting anything of you, but I'm here 'cause I *want* to be here *with you*."

His voice grew hoarse and one of the tears I tried to hold back slid down my cheek.

He took a step closer to me and wiped it away, his hands cold on my heated face. "I'm here 'cause those couple times you let me in before you got scared and pushed me away, I saw how much you cared. Then I watched you build those walls back up because you were afraid. And I don't know if you're afraid that I'll hurt you or if you're afraid that you'll hurt me, but I will give it my all showin' you that you can trust me." His hand lingered on my cheek, thumb brushing across my cheekbone. "If you don't want me, I'll find a way to live with that, but I'm willin' to risk my heart just in case the only thing holdin' you back is that fear."

I had no idea what to say. My heart pounded in my throat. The feelings in my chest grew, putting out new leaves and tiny flower buds, but at the same time, guilt drowned me. He didn't know the danger he was in. He was willing to risk everything, but he had no idea how big the risk was.

"There's something you don't know," I whispered before I lost my nerve, more tears sliding down my face.

"Ok," he murmured, dropping his hand from my face, "I'm listening."

My entire body trembled. "I'm not the only powered person."

Surprise filled his eyes.

"I don't know who he is, but he can get in my head. Not all the time, but whenever—" I swallowed hard. "Whenever I'm drugged."

A horrified understanding dawned on his face.

"He gets in and he can see all my memories. He knows what I can do, and he's been trying to find me since I was thirteen. I don't understand what his power is exactly, but I think he...he somehow was behind everything that happened with the Reapers turning on each other. Like he was in their heads too."

Trey remained steady and silent.

"Juck d-drugged me after...after—" I made a helpless gesture to my chest. "He saw what happened. I *let* him see what happened because I didn't care anymore. And he was angry. He said I b-belonged to him and that he was gonna kill them all."

I'd turned that day over and over in my head hundreds of times, but it still didn't make any sense. Forty-five of the Reapers had died from the fever a month earlier. I hadn't been able to save a single one without my powers. Tensions were high, and Vulture was stirring shit up, trying to get the gang on his side.

"Vulture acted so...so weird. Like he wasn't himself. He called a gathering and just...just *told* them about my powers and that Juck had kept me all to himself, but he sounded so...he sounded like he was pretending to be someone else. And then...they *turned* on each other. Everyone was shooting, but it didn't make any sense why they were attacking each other. Everything just went to shit so fast and I—"

I had to stop for a second, trying to breathe. Trey took one of my hands, squeezing it.

"Juck was gonna take me and run, but Vulture caught up to us. Juck shot him and tried to leave with me...and I...I stabbed Juck and ran." I gulped in a shaky breath. "I don't know how, but I think *he* did it. He killed them…and he did it without even *being there*."

"You killed Juck?"

I nodded, trying to read his expression.

"I'm glad he's dead, but I'm sorry you had to resort to that."

I wasn't even surprised that he immediately knew I hated doing it, even after everything Juck had done to me.

"So this person, he saw you again when we gave you the narc after you got whipped."

It wasn't a question, but I nodded again anyway.

"He saw where you were."

"He's angry. He thinks I used him to get away from the Reapers. And maybe…maybe I did. I didn't mean to but…" My voice trailed off for a second. "I thought if I could draw him away—"

"You're using yourself as bait?" A hint of anger entered his voice.

"He could kill *everyone*, Trey—"

"What will he do to you if he catches you?"

I wanted to shake him. Was he not listening? "I don't know, but I don't think he wants to kill *me*."

"No, he probably wants to do something worse." Trey's eyes darkened.

"Trey!" I needed him to understand. "He's after *you*. He wants to kill *you*."

He stared down at me for a few breaths. Then he did the *last* thing I expected, and his face broke into a giant fucking grin. I gaped at him.

"Did you not hear me?" I demanded. "Trey—"

"He wants to kill me 'cause you *care* about me," he said, his tone *gleeful*.

I sputtered furiously for a second. "*That's* what you're latchin' on to? You can't come with me! He's gonna *kill* you, dumbass!"

"He can try."

I was gonna kill him. "Trey—"

"Look, Mac and I knew there was somebody else trying to find you. Somebody who scared you. We thought it was maybe a warlord or something, but it doesn't matter who it is. I'm not gonna just bail on you and make you face whoever it is all by yourself."

"He has powers! And I have no idea what he can do!"

"Ok, so we'll be careful."

I threw my arms up, frustrated. "Trey!"

"I'm not leaving, Bones." He stepped closer, into my space, and his voice softened. "You hear me? This is my decision and I'm not leaving."

I stared up at him helplessly, my heart in my throat, but he smiled that sweet, gentle smile.

"C'mon, we better keep moving."

CHAPTER 19

We walked in silence for another hour while everything Trey said played through my head on repeat. He said he loved me, and as much as I wanted to dismiss it, gods help me, I couldn't. He'd shown me he loved me over and over again before he said the words out loud. Tears burned in my eyes. I tried for a brief moment to peer into my feelings, but the intense emotion there immediately overwhelmed me, and I had to slam everything back down. I couldn't delve into my feelings about Trey right now. I had to stay in control.

"Mac's gonna take care of the kids," Trey said from behind me. "He won't let anythin' happen to them."

Gratitude swelled in my chest. My fear for the kids had been so sharp that it hurt. The only comfort I had was knowing they'd be in more danger *with* me. They might never forgive me for abandoning them, especially Apple, but knowing Mac's crew would protect them made it easier. The pang of sorrow in my chest surprised me. I hated to admit it, but I'd miss them, even fucking Raven. Then another thought occurred to me, and my heart sank.

"What about Clarity?"

"She's the one who figured out you were leaving," he said. "She didn't ask me to, but when I told her I was goin' with you, she was so relieved."

I glanced back at him and he offered me a slight smile.

"I'll miss her, of course, but this is where I'm meant to be."

I turned back around. My emotions swirled through me like a storm. I knew how much his sister and Mac and the rest of the crew meant to him, and Clarity loved her brother. Why the hell would she *want* him to leave with me?

"How did she know?" I asked to distract myself.

"She wouldn't say."

I looked again to see him frowning, a slight furrow between his eyes.

"But Mac and I checked your mattress, so we knew she was right."

I frowned too, remembering how strange Clarity had been the last time I'd seen her. Had she already known my plans? Had she snooped through my stuff? Raven probably would have let her. She liked Clarity a hell of a lot more than she liked me.

"Madame will put a bounty out on us when she discovers we're gone. Mac is gonna try to cover for us as long as possible, but most likely she's gonna know soon."

I shuddered, my fear over what Madame might do to the crew surging back.

"Will she take it out on Mac and the crew?"

"There's a chance, yeah," Trey said, "but they know that."

We fell silent again. I tried not to dwell on what Madame might do to them. I didn't know how to process that they accepted that risk just to help me. It made leaving them behind so much harder.

Soon I had to focus all my energy on hiking up the damn mountain. I had recovered some of my strength but my walks around the hold did little to prepare me for snowy mountain terrain. My steps grew clumsier as I tired and the pain in my back worsened. It wasn't long before I stumbled and fell, sliding down the hill and into Trey, who somehow managed to stop me without being knocked down the mountainside.

"Whoa, you ok?" he said, helping me back up to my feet.

"Yeah," I said between heavy breaths, "sorry."

"It's ok. Let's take a break."

"You don't have to—"

"C'mon, we can eat a little something too."

I gave up and let him usher me over to a fallen tree, watching as he brushed the snow off. He sat next to me, close enough that our thighs pressed together, but I didn't feel trapped, not with Trey.

"Ok, I got some dried meat and some apples. How about you?" he asked, digging through his pack.

"I got dried meat too." I fished out the small satchel I'd been storing bits of food in. "And I got *this.*" I pulled out a full wedge of hard cheese and his face broke into a grin.

"How the hell did you get that?" he demanded.

"I stole it," I admitted, flushing slightly. "Neena has a thing for Griz. I sent him to the kitchen on a fake errand. She was so distracted by him that I was able to slip into the root cellar and grab it."

"You tricky little thing, you." That sunshine smile lit up the whole damn woods.

"It's also how I was able to get this." I pulled a chunk of cornbread out wrapped in a clean cloth.

"Well, you win this round." He held up a withered apple with a playful grimace.

We ate in companionable silence. The woods had grown even darker, which meant dawn wasn't too far off. Wolf growled in my head, but I did my best to ignore him.

You're gonna watch him die, Wolf whispered. *Don't you remember?*

The horrific, bloody images flashed through my mind and I flinched like I could get away from my own memories.

"What's wrong?" Trey stiffened, his eyes scanning me.

I tried to get a hold of myself, but Wolf had opened a floodgate of memories I did my best to keep locked away. My heart seized in my chest and my lungs turned to stone.

"Bones?"

"I can't watch you die." The words slipped out, harsh and panicked.

"Well, I don't plan on dyin' anytime soon," he said, nudging my leg with his.

I couldn't respond because I used up all my air to get that one sentence out.

"Hey," he laid his hand over mine where my fingers dug into my leg.

When I didn't pull away, he flipped my hand over and laced his fingers through mine. I gripped them, trying to pull some of his steady strength and calm through our joined hands.

"You want to talk about it?" he murmured. "Or would you like a distraction?"

"Distraction," I managed to get out.

"Alright," he said with no judgment, "when Mac and I were about thirteen we stole a bottle of moonshine and got shitfaced. Then 'cause we were shitfaced we thought it'd be a good idea to challenge each other to climb the watchtower."

"The outside?" I choked, thinking of the rough concrete exterior.

"The outside," he confirmed with a grin. "Course we got probably twenty feet up and panicked. So then we had to cling to the wall and yell for help, which brought all the guards running. They had to go fetch ladders to get us down. My mom was so furious at us that Madame let her pick our punishment. We had outhouse duty for two weeks."

Tight bands still wrapped around my chest, but my lungs breathed a little easier. "What happened to Mac's parents?"

He hesitated for a moment, then sighed. "Mac's mom died when he was three. His dad was one of the leaders of the early rebellion, but Madame caught wind of it and had the leaders whipped." He squeezed my hand a little tighter, his voice rough with pain. "Fifty lashes each."

My back spasmed in pain at the thought. "Fifty?" I gasped.

"It wasn't a punishment they were meant to survive," Trey murmured. "That scar on Mac's face? That was from the whip. He tried to get to his dad during the whipping and took a lash to the face. Just a little bit higher and he would've lost his eye."

"How old was he?" I asked, feeling sick.

"Seven. Somehow his dad survived, but he died a few days later. The wounds got infected and he'd lost so much blood."

I swallowed hard, remembering Mac's fury at me for taking his lashes, his desperation that I heal myself through him. It made more sense now.

"How old are you?" I asked.

"Twenty-seven," he replied. "You?"

"Twenty-two. So how old were you when Clarity was born?"

"I was, let's see, nine. Mac was eight."

"You're older?"

"By eighteen months and yes, I *do* pull the oldest brother card whenever I can."

My heart twinged again, but then I realized something. "Clarity's only eighteen?" I whispered.

He let out a heavy sigh. "Yeah."

She seemed older than that, but it wasn't too surprising. Life in a brothel tended to make people grow up fast.

"I'll carry guilt about her being in there for the rest of my life," Trey confessed in a low voice.

"How come?"

"When our mom died, her dad, Reed, was still alive. I was old enough that I could've taken her in, but Mac and I were training hard to get into the Safeguard. I let Reed take her instead, even though I knew he had a bad gambling problem. He got in a drunken bar fight and got himself stabbed. He owed a lot of debts, so Madame took Clarity in payment. She didn't go right into...*serving* people, but they worked her so hard makin' her clean and cook. She started getting sick a lot, and she never seemed to fully recover. And I know she was exposed to, well, a lot of shit that a kid shouldn't be exposed to. She was always beautiful, and she attracted attention." His face was so dark. "By the time I convinced Madame to let me take her out, she wouldn't leave. She got it in her head that staying where she was would protect *me.*"

I remembered Clarity's battered face and hot anger coursed through me. He must have sensed it because he glanced down at me and squeezed my hand again.

"I know. I fucking hate it too." He sighed. "But while she might be physically kinda fragile, she's so damn smart. Smarter than me and Mac put together. I've tried so hard to get her to leave, but she thinks she'd just be a burden. And to be fair, she's created a real community there. There used to be fights between...the brothel workers."

I noted how he seemed to avoid using words like "prostitute" and "whore."

"The woman in charge encouraged grudges and pitted them against each other all the time. Mostly for her own amusement, I think. Clarity slowly changed that. And the others have her back, as much as they can anyway."

I sat quiet for a while, thinking about everything he'd said. After a few minutes, I realized the iron vise on my lungs had disappeared.

"Thank you," I said, looking back up at him.

He smiled, his eyes so full of warmth. "You're welcome."

He released my hand, and I noticed that I didn't want him to let go.

ଚଚ

We set out walking again and slowly the darkness lightened. The sun rose over the mountain, bathing the snow in a pink and orange glow, before Trey spoke again.

"So where are we going?" he asked cheerfully.

"As far away as possible." I hadn't planned that far ahead. My only focus had been to get *out*.

"Oh good, nice and vague." I could hear his grin.

"Feel free to go back if you don't like it."

"Awww, you say that like you wouldn't miss me," he teased.

"I wouldn't," I lied.

He laughed. "You think I can't tell when you're lying by now?"

I flashed a rude hand signal behind me without turning to look at him and he laughed again.

"Sorry, darlin', you're stuck with me."

My stupid heart did a little skip at "darlin."

"Cause first you kissed me and then, even worse, I heard you *laugh*. An' I knew I wouldn't be able to rest until I heard it again."

Thank the gods he walked behind me so he couldn't see the ridiculous fucking smile that managed to creep across my face. "Don't hold your breath."

"Don't worry," he said lightly, "I'm a very patient man."

He was more patient than anyone I'd ever met. Far more patient than I deserved.

"So do you want to join a different hold or a gang? Or are you hoping to just lone wolf with me, your lovable sidekick?"

My smile grew so wide that it hurt my cheeks. "Doesn't havin' a sidekick defeat the purpose of a lone wolf?"

"You can define 'lone wolf' however you want, darlin'."

Gods, every time he called me that, my heart jolted in a way that made me feel warm down to my toes. I thought back to his original question, trying to figure out a somewhat honest answer as I trudged through the snow.

"I dunno," I finally said. "I just want to be in charge of my own life for once. I want to heal people without hurtin' them and I want to keep *him* away from the Vault."

In the silence, the crunch of our snowshoes in the snow sounded loud. "Those are all things I'd feel good about fightin' for."

I opened my mouth, but he beat me to it.

"And don't say I don't have to."

I turned around to glare at him, but he just laughed.

"I know I don't have to. I want to," he said. "You're worth fighting for, Bones."

Gods. I wasn't sure when it happened, but my feelings for him hadn't been lying dormant. They'd moved on to my defenses, viny tendrils working their way through the cracks, and now as they grew again, my walls crumbled down. I didn't know what to say, so I just kept walking. Trey let me walk in silence for maybe ten minutes before he started talking again.

"What's your favorite color?" he asked.

I glanced back at him again, confused. "Why the fuck do you want to know that?"

"This is called getting to know each other better, Bones," he teased.

"I don't have one," I said.

"Oh come on, everybody has a favorite color."

I sighed and searched my mind, immediately thinking of the warm brown of his eyes, but I wasn't going to say that. "Yellow, I guess."

"What kinda yellow?" he pushed.

"What the hell do you mean what kinda yellow?" I twisted to glare at him.

He grinned. "There's a shit ton of yellows, Bones. You gotta be more specific."

I blew out an annoyed breath. "Uh, I dunno, dandelion yellow, I guess."

He hummed. "Mine is green, by the way. Green like those glass bottles you had at the clinic."

I pretended not to notice *he'd* named the exact color of my eyes as I struggled to kick my snowshoe into the hard snow.

"Ok, what's your favorite food?"

"Are you serious?"

"Deadly."

"How many more of these questions do you have?"

"Probably an endless supply."

"I shoulda let you bleed out on that rooftop."

"You and I both know you would never do that." He said it teasingly, but my amusement vanished.

"You have no idea what I'm capable of doing."

Silence fell for a minute. "So tell me," he finally said.

"Tell you what?"

"Tell me the worst thing you've ever done."

The memories that tried to escape again made me feel nauseous. I picked up my pace, trying to put more distance between us, but he kept up with his long legs. My throat felt dry as sand. He'd been so vulnerable earlier, telling me about Clarity and the guilt he carried.

Don't show weakness, Wolf ordered.

"My favorite food is fried dough rolled in cinnamon sugar."

"Well, well, well," he said, and I glanced back to see him smiling like I hadn't just refused to open up. Again. "Bones has a sweet tooth."

I kept walking, trying to push down the guilt. He didn't speak for a bit, and I started to feel relieved that maybe he'd finished with the questions.

"What's your favorite animal?"

I covered my face and groaned.

"C'mon," he wheedled, "I know you have one."

I sighed and gave up. "Horses."

"Mine's horses too!"

I thought of Violet and a pang of sadness ran through me. I wished I could've taken her with me. It'd be nice to have a horse right about now.

"Favorite season?" Trey asked.

I frowned. "Summer I guess."

"I like fall. Smells the best."

Well, I couldn't argue with that.

He went on and on and I began to worry that he actually did have an endless supply of questions. I told him how I loved the rain so long as I didn't have to ride a bike in it, the smell of lavender and fresh baked bread and pine needles, the moment when the sun first peeked over the mountains and made everything pink, neatly organized medical supplies, the feel of a body mending itself under my hands.

He told me he loved the chill of autumn nights, sitting beside a campfire watching the embers burn, the smell of apples and peppermint and lavender, the feel of galloping on a horse with the wind in his hair, and the adrenaline of sparring with an evenly matched partner. Then he paused, and I glanced back to see him staring ahead with a furrowed brow.

"Damn. I can't think of any more."

"Pity," I said dryly.

He laughed. "Oh, I'll think of another eventually."

"I don't doubt it."

"I know you'll be on the edge of your seat til then."

"Don't know how I'll sleep at night."

I stole another glance back to see he wore that sunshine smile, and I realized how much I liked being the one to put it on his face.

It took several hours to reach the ridge we'd been walking up to. The mountain grade got even steeper, the snow powdery one moment and frozen solid the next. I moved slow, breathing hard and trying not to wince at the pain in my back with each step. Trey stayed behind me just in case I fell again. In the last bit, we had to take off the snowshoes to climb over huge rocky boulders. As I slid down from the last one and stepped out onto the top, my body trembled with exhaustion. We both sat, catching our breath and gazed out at the valley below. The snowy view *was* beautiful. We could see for miles up here, and it was *almost* worth the way my back ached and my legs burned. I couldn't help turning to look back the way we'd come. Mountains and trees had swallowed the Vault. I couldn't even see the watchtower. Several plumes of smoke coming from behind the mountains were the only hint it existed.

"See that smoke over there?" Trey pointed to our left as I turned back around.

I followed his finger to see the faint wisps of smoke curling up from behind a thick grove of trees.

"That's a trading post. There's a family who lives there and runs it. It's not huge, just one building that has a store and lodging up above. It'd be a good place to spend the night."

"Tonight?" I asked, looking at the long, long way down the mountainside.

"No, that's too far to make before nightfall. I assumed we'd camp tonight."

"I was hoping Madame would think I went South." Anxiety slid through me that my barely thought-out plan was too simple. "Since it'd be easier traveling. That's why I'm going North."

"That's smart." Trey grinned. "I think you're right."

My cheeks warmed under his praise.

"Well if you want to keep going north, I know there's a big settlement that way. We'd need to find some sort of transportation though 'cause it'll get deadly cold and it takes a couple of weeks to get there on wheels. Probably longer on horseback. Otherwise, if we go Northwest there's a smaller settlement. There's less snow and cold that way, but more mountains to cross. It's a shorter distance but might take the same amount of time due to the mountain passes."

My gratitude for him surged as I realized exactly how unprepared I'd been. I hadn't even tried to steal a map. I'd approached this escape the same way I'd approached my escape from Juck, focusing only on the first step, getting out. If Trey hadn't been here, I probably would've gotten myself lost in the snowy wilderness.

"I'd vote northwest," I said. "Maybe we could get some horses."

"That's my vote too. How's your back feeling?"

I fought back the instinctual urge to dismiss the pain. "It hurts," I admitted.

His eyebrows rose, the only indication that my honesty surprised him. "Going downhill will be easier. Maybe we go until noon and then make camp?"

I squinted up at the sky. The sun was still a few hours from noon, but I could do that. "Ok."

୬ଦ

Trey was so wrong.

Going downhill on snowshoes was *worse* than going up. I slipped and slid more times than I could count, stopping only when I crashed into something, usually Trey. My wrists rubbed raw from frozen bits of snow under my coat sleeves, and my socks soaked up the melted snow in my boots. The cold seeped through my skin and into my very bones, and my back ached in a way that made me nauseous. Trey fared better, but I knocked him over a few times when I crashed into him. The only bright side was with all the sliding, we got farther than expected by noon.

"You see those big boulders?" Trey pointed up ahead to where I could see large rocks between the trees. "Probably a good place to find some shelter."

We made our way there. The deep snow would have been up to my waist if I didn't have the snowshoes. Four or five giant boulders were nestled in the snow, standing at least three times Trey's height. I followed him, watching as he inspected each one. He picked one that sat at an angle, creating a clear area at its base.

"This one is perfect." He grinned at me.

"What can I do?" I asked, shivering.

"You want to dig out some of this snow to make the clear space a little bigger while I go cut some wood?"

I nodded and shrugged off my pack before sliding down the small incline to the base of the boulder. Both of us worked quietly for a while and soon I had a larger space cleared out and Trey had wood for a campfire. He peeled off strips of wood with a large knife to make a small pile of kindling.

"So I'm guessin' you don't have a bedroll," Trey said.

I flushed slightly. "No."

He smiled slightly down at the wood. "Lemme guess, you were planning on surviving the cold out of pure stubbornness?"

"I woulda been fine," I grumbled.

"Sure," he teased, "if by 'fine' you mean 'frozen to death.'"

"I have a blanket. And I know how to build a fire." I glared at him.

"Then why am I doin' all the work?" He lifted his head, grinning at me.

"Isn't this why you came?" I raised an eyebrow. "To help?"

His grin widened into that sunshine smile. "You actually accepting help for once?"

"I accept help all the time!"

He laughed out loud. "That's the most ridiculous lie you've told yet."

I rolled my eyes and grabbed a couple of skinny sticks to break into pieces as he coaxed a spark into a fire. He'd taken off his gloves, placing them on the ground beside him as he fed small pieces of wood into the fire.

"Gimme your gloves," I said, holding out my hand.

He handed them over, watching as I put them on my sticks and stuck them in the snow close to the fire so they could dry out.

"Thanks." He smiled that sweet soft smile he seemed to save for me, and my heart did another stupid little skip.

I did the same thing with my gloves, then held my cold fingers over the flames, trying to warm them up as he built up the fire. After a while, he had me take over. I fed the flames and watched as Trey stabbed some pieces of wood into the snow on the sides of the rock to create makeshift walls that blocked the wind a little and gave us at least some protection from predators. The heat bounced off the rock that leaned over us, making a nice warm bubble.

Trey broke larger fallen pieces of wood by sticking one end between two trees close together and pushing on the other end until the wood broke with a loud crack that made me jump.

"Sorry!" he called, smiling.

An answering smile curled around my lips in response. Things felt...different between us. Maybe because we were outside the hold. Maybe because I'd been honest with him about the danger, and he still stayed. Maybe because he'd told me he loved me. Or maybe Trey had gotten into my heart and put down roots a long time ago and if I was honest, there was no way of fully ripping him out. I couldn't deny I was so *glad* he came. Godsdamnit, I liked him so much it terrified me. He'd taken off his coat and the sweater under it as he worked, leaving him in just a T-shirt as he built up a small woodpile, and I couldn't help but admire him, the muscles in his arms as he pushed the logs until they broke, the way his wavy brown hair fell against his face.

Gods, I wanted to kiss him again and run my fingers through that hair. Why hadn't I done that the first time?

He glanced over and caught me staring, one side of his mouth lifting in a slight smirk. My face warmed and I went back to concentrating on the fire. I'd cleared enough room at the bottom of the rock for both of us. I glanced at Trey's bedroll. He would try to make me take it. I'd bet anything on it. I glanced at our little shelter again. How *were* we gonna do this? I sure as hell wasn't gonna take his bedroll and make him sleep in the cold.

What was the point of still pushing him away? He knew about the danger. He was here. He'd been honest about how he felt. Was he right and just my fear stood between us?

My heart pounded, but gods, I didn't want to fight this anymore.

"I'll be right back!" Trey called, unaware of the mental battle I waged.

I listened to his boots crunching away. I wasn't sure if it was a testament to Trey's persistence or to how weak my defenses had become that we'd only been out here for a day and I'd given up.

Don't— Wolf tried to snap.

No. I shoved him back down. *No, I'm making my own damn decisions.*

I heard Trey coming back and my heart fluttered in my chest. I looked up when he came around the side of his makeshift walls and blinked in confusion. He had an armful of large rocks. He looked amused at my expression as he crouched and placed four rocks into the fire.

"You makin' rocks for dinner?" I couldn't help asking.

"No, smartass." He grinned. "I'm heating up rocks so we can dry out our boots."

"How do you know all this shit?" I asked, impressed again.

"Part of the training to join the Safeguard. The Vault is pretty isolated, so members of the Safeguard crews gotta be able to survive the elements when we're traveling on missions."

I remembered him saying he and Mac had trained hard to join. "Why the Safeguard?" I asked.

"We wanted to get outside the walls, see what else was out there." He paused. "Well, that was my motivation anyway." Pain flashed across his face. "Mac was forced to join the guards super young. Madame wanted to keep a close eye on him after what his dad did. He worked his way up from the inside. He had a much more brutal training experience than I did. He used to come home covered in blood from the other guards beating on him. But he—" he hesitated, "he eventually established himself as someone people didn't want to mess with, and he worked his ass off to move up through the ranks. He impressed Madame enough that she offered him the position of her second, so he woulda been one under Sax. That's when he asked if he could start a Safeguard crew instead, which was a few steps down in power, but she let him."

Guilt pricked me that I hadn't bothered to learn any of this while at the Vault. I'd made assumptions about all of them, but probably the most assumptions about Mac.

We fell into silence as we ate another small meal and drank the last of our water. Trey had a small metal pot that he put over the fire and filled with snow to melt and boil so we could refill our bottles.

"You can have the bedroll," Trey said, just like I thought he would.

"No." I had to suppress a grin.

"If you think I'm gonna sleep in it and watch you—"

"Let's sleep together."

He cut off mid-sentence and stared at me. The shock on his face made one corner of my mouth curl up in amusement.

"What?" he asked in a choked voice.

"Let's sleep together," I repeated. My amused smirk grew, and his eyes kept darting down to my mouth.

"You and me?"

"No, me and that other dumbass who tagged along."

His eyes narrowed. "Are you gonna run off again in the morning?"

I winced, but I deserved that. I shrugged. "Didn't work to get rid of you the first time, did it?"

He glared, but his eyes sparkled now. "I *knew* that's what you were doin'."

"And you call *me* stubborn." I rolled my eyes.

He stared at me like he wanted to read every thought in my head. "K, I'm gonna need you to be real clear, Bones. Are you sayin' you want to share a bedroll just to keep warm or do you want to share a bedroll to be with me?"

He was giving me an out, even though I could see how desperately he hoped I wouldn't take it. It made my eyes burn again and I had to swallow hard.

"I want to be with you," I said.

He shifted closer, his eyes warmer than the fire. "I know I already said this, but just in case there's any confusion, I want to be with you too. I've wanted to be with you for a long time now."

I opened my mouth to say something sarcastic, but the last of my defenses crumbled down as every single one of those damn flowers in my chest bloomed all at once, and I ended up whispering, "I'm sorry I made you wait."

His cool fingers cradled the side of my face, his thumb brushing gently over my lips. "I'd wait a thousand years for you."

"You'd be long dead in a thousand years," I said dryly even though my heart pounded.

"It'd still be worth it," he whispered, and then he kissed me.

CHAPTER 20

H e kissed me like he'd been dying, and I was the only thing who could save him. It wasn't like the gentle, soft kisses we shared before. This kiss was hard and desperate like he wanted to devour me. And for the first time in a very long time, maybe the first time *ever,* I just let go.

I kissed him back just as fiercely, gently nipping at his lip and letting his tongue sweep through my mouth. I wasn't sure how I'd ended up in his lap, straddling him, but I wasn't complaining. His cold hands slid up under my jacket and my shirt until they found my bare skin. I jumped at the cold touch, and he stopped.

"This ok?" he murmured against my lips.

"Yes," I breathed. "Your hands are just cold."

His lips curled against mine. "Sorry."

"I'll warm them up for you," I added, and he pulled back to grin at me, heat sparking in his eyes.

He helped me slide my jacket down my shoulders and then returned to slide his hands across the skin of my stomach. They were freezing but warmed against my heated skin. I could feel the calluses on his palms, but his touch was so gentle it made my eyes prickle.

"Tell me to stop at any time," he said. "If you feel uncomfortable —"

I interrupted him by finally getting my hands in his hair just like I'd wanted, sliding my fingers through the soft waves before gathering a handful at the back of his head and tugging. He groaned against my mouth in a way that made heat pool in my stomach. His hands traveled upward under my shirt, tracing the shape of my body like he wanted to memorize me. When he palmed my breasts, those calluses scraped against my nipples and I whimpered.

"Gods, Bones," he said in a low groan.

A brief flash of self-consciousness went through me. All of me was small, and the Reapers had made plenty of comments about how I lacked curves. But that unease vanished almost as quickly as it came as his hands roamed the slopes of my breasts. His lips trailed down my jaw to my neck, and I couldn't even feel the cold anymore, only him. Then I felt his fingers tracing the horrible brand on my chest and I stilled, my cheeks heating with discomfort again.

"I'm sorry," I found myself saying faintly. "I know it's so ugly and —"

He swiftly pulled away so he could meet my gaze. His eyes looked almost black and there was no mistaking the desire there.

"Nothin' about you is ugly." He pressed his entire palm flat against the brand on my chest. "Not this." His other hand traveled around to my back, gently running over the thick healing scars and rough flesh that still ached with pain. "Not this. You don't ever need to apologize for your scars."

"But—" I tried to protest, feeling shaky.

"These scars are proof you survived," he interrupted softly. "That you walked through fire, and you came out the other side. You're a godsdamned warrior, Bones, and the most beautiful woman I've ever seen."

My eyes welled up and his other hand slid around to my back to gently pull me closer again, his head dipping to press a kiss to the brand on my chest.

"How are you real?" I whispered, my heart so full of joy and want and sorrow and longing that it hurt.

"I'm real," he murmured with a soft smile, straightening so he could kiss my lips again, this time gently. "This is real, darlin'."

"I don't know if I believe it."

He smiled against my lips. "Let me try and prove it to you then." His hands tunneled into my hair, cupping the back of my head and deepening the kiss.

I melted into him, tilting my head to give him better access, my arms twining around his neck, pressing our bodies even closer together. I couldn't get enough of him, wasn't sure if I'd *ever* get enough of him. I'd never felt this way from a kiss, so out of control and so steady at the same time. Everything about this felt right, and it made me realize with a sudden clarity that being with Trey would be something new. I'd never been with someone just because I *wanted* to be with them. There were no desperate plans in my head, no ulterior motives. It felt like surrendering, but I had no idea a surrender could feel so beautiful. When he pulled back minutes, maybe hours later, a noise of protest escaped my lips. He chuckled.

"Not here," he murmured. "I want you in a place that's warm so I can see every beautiful inch of you without worryin' about you getting frostbite."

My toes curled inside my boots and I thought of the trading post we planned to sleep at tomorrow night. The heat sparking in his eyes told me he was thinking about it too. I was sitting in his lap, facing him, my legs stretching out behind him. His fingers ran through my hair.

"Your hair is so beautiful," he said softly. "When you came out of the brothel with Clarity and you had it down, I just about forgot myself."

My cheeks warmed but in a pleasant, heady way.

His hand left my hair to cradle my face, brushing his thumbs across my cheekbones. "And don't even get me started on your freckles."

My blush deepened and he smirked a little when he noticed.

"Or your eyes."

I couldn't resist the giddy smile that crossed my face, so I leaned forward and buried my face in his shoulder. He wrapped his arms around me, resting gently on my sore back. I took a deep breath. No wonder I'd grown attached to that quilt. It smelled so much like Trey and Trey—

I took a shaky breath, the realization hitting me. "You smell like home."

"The lavender soap?"

"No," I whispered, "just you." That's why I loved his scent so much. My eyes prickled. I wondered how long I'd been making that association without realizing it.

His arms tightened around me and he pressed a kiss to my temple. His voice came out rough with emotion when he spoke, "I'll be your home as long as you need."

We stayed that way for a while, wrapped up together and listening to the sounds of the forest. After a few minutes, he shifted.

"Let's take off our boots so we can get these rocks in there to dry 'em out."

I reluctantly left his lap, unlacing my shoes and pulling my wet woolen socks off as he did the same. My feet were bright red with cold and I winced, trying to rub some warmth back into them. Trey maneuvered the warm rocks into our socks with sticks as I held them open. Steam rose from the socks as he held them up.

"Now we put these in our boots. You got a spare pair of socks?"

I dug around in my bag, searching for the pair I'd grabbed, pulling things out as I searched. When I held them up, he was staring at me with a soft knowing smile.

"What?" I asked, confused.

"I thought for sure you'd take my quilt and stuff it down the outhouse hole or something."

I looked down at the quilt I'd pulled out of my pack and then back up at him. "Raven gave it to me."

"Yeah, I asked her to. You were shivering with that shitty blanket you had so I gave you my winter one." His eyes were so beautiful in the firelight. "My mom made that quilt."

My fingers trailed over the soft surface of the blanket, emotion overwhelming me that he trusted me with something so precious. "It's beautiful," I whispered. "I loved it because it smelled like you." My cheeks warmed again with the realization that he had indeed been *home* for a while. "I guess that makes sense now."

He beamed at me, brighter than the sun.

After we got everything ready in our little camp for us to sleep, we curled up together in the middle of the bedroll, adding the quilt on top before Trey rolled the sides back up around us. I took a deep breath, loving that his scent surrounded me now. We'd both taken off our jackets, comfortably warm in our little shelter with our legs entwined and arms wrapped around each other. Trey had piled the wood where he could reach it to throw more on the fire when it began to die down. It felt a little strange to be trying to sleep in the middle of the day, but I wasn't about to complain.

He kissed my forehead and I tilted my head up so he could capture my lips again. He kissed me like he wanted to savor the taste of me. I wasn't sure when I began to move against him, when his arms tightened around me, or when our kisses turned greedy and wanting, but the warmth that spread through me seemed to settle between my legs. I wanted *more,* and I'd never felt this way before. Being intimate with Vulture had been pleasurable enough, but calculated. Being intimate with Zip had sometimes been pleasurable, but more felt like a task that I had to get through. Being intimate with Trey felt…intimate.

"I know I said I wanted to wait," he said roughly, "but gods, I want to touch you."

"Yes," I breathed, "please."

He chuckled a low sound that made me want to shiver. "Where do you want me to touch you, Bones?"

"Everywhere," I murmured, but my fingers glided over the top of his to pull his hand down toward the front of my pants.

He groaned what might have been a curse, and when I released him, his hand slid slowly down the front of my pants. His fingers were cold, but they blazed a trail of heat across my skin. At the first touch of his fingers between my legs, I whimpered out loud and he froze again.

"Is that—" he started to say, concerned.

"Don't stop," I whispered.

I tilted my head up to look at him and the heat that sparked in those warm brown eyes made me feel like I was on fire. His lips curled into a crooked smile as he began to move his fingers again, stroking and circling, picking up speed. I arched toward him, my breath catching as the pleasure increased. I tried to slide a hand down between us, desperate to feel the hard length of him pressing against my thigh, but he caught my wrist with his free hand.

"It's *my* turn." His teeth flashed in a lazy grin and his thumb pressed down exactly where I wanted it, making me jolt with a gasp of pleasure.

I needed to do *something* with my hands, so I slid my arms up around his neck and pulled his head down to kiss him. His free hand slid up my shirt, across my stomach to my breasts as he slipped a finger inside of me.

"Oh gods, Trey," I moaned, desperate for *more* and hot enough to burst into flames.

"Fuck," he swore as I moved against him, whining with pleasure as he worked in a second, "Bones." He said my name like a low groan of desire.

I wanted to hear my name on his lips like that forever. No, I wanted to hear my *real* name—

The heat built to something almost unbearable. "Trey," I gasped, my fingernails digging into his shoulder, "please." I didn't even know what I asked for, just that I needed more of him, all of him.

"Let go, darlin'," he said, low and husky. "I got you."

His fingers curled inside me and I swore to the gods I saw stars. My muscles clenched, my legs shook, and the pleasure that rushed through me felt like nothing I'd ever experienced before. I babbled his name, clutching his shirt in both fists. When the wave of pleasure faded, I felt like a rag that'd been wrung out, boneless. He withdrew his hands, and I looked up at him as I caught my breath to see him grinning.

"Your eyes were glowing," he said smugly.

I stared at him, certain I'd heard him wrong. "Glowing?" I asked.

"Glowing," he repeated. "They looked like liquid gold."

I stared at him, my mouth slightly open in astonishment. That had never happened before, but I'd certainly *felt* like liquid gold. His grin widened at my expression.

"Well that's new," I said.

He looked so pleased with himself that I started giggling, still reeling from the heady pleasure that had coursed through me. Pure delight lit up his eyes.

"I don't think I'll ever get enough of hearin' you laugh." He met my gaze and his eyes grew dark with desire again. "Or hearin' you say my name like that when I'm touchin' you."

I had to force myself to breathe evenly. His smug smile reappeared as if he knew exactly how his words affected me and he ducked his head to kiss me.

"Consider that a warmup for later," he murmured against my lips.

"Isn't it my turn now?" I raised my eyebrows and he laughed.

"Now it's time to sleep. You'll have to wait."

I glared at him, but uncertainty slid through me. "You don't feel… frustrated?"

His smug expression melted into his sweet smile. "No, darlin'." He pressed his lips to my forehead. "That was all for you."

I curled into him, my head on his shoulder as he pulled me close. I'd never met anyone like Trey. I still didn't understand why he loved me, but gods, I *knew* it.

Tell him.

I wasn't sure if that soft voice in my head meant my real name or that I loved him too, but either way, I pressed my lips together and tried not to feel like a damn coward. I just needed a little more time.

৩৶

"Bones, darlin', wake up. You're just dreamin'."

My eyes jerked open with a gasp. I was sitting straight up, half out of the bedroll, terror tensing every muscle in my body. Trey sat next to me, not touching me, but speaking in a low gentle voice. Night had fallen. I focused on him in the light of the campfire, trying to calm the raging panic in my chest.

"Sorry," I got out between gulping gasps of air.

"S' ok," Trey murmured, "can I touch you?"

I nodded, confused. He caught my hand, squeezing it tight, and tugged me a little closer. I shivered, but not just from the cold.

"I tried to touch you earlier and you panicked," he explained. "You were talkin' about a wolf."

I stiffened in fear, and his eyes narrowed on my face. For a long moment, neither of us spoke.

"Bones," he whispered, slipping his arms around me, "please let me in."

I stayed stiff in his arms for several breaths, but as his warmth seeped into me, my body slowly relaxed and melted into his. I needed to open up. I *wanted* to, even as my hands started trembling.

"Not *a* wolf," I said before I lost my nerve. "Wolf. My oldest brother."

He paused. "Who's Dune?" he finally asked.

Panic began roaring in my ears, but to my shock, I heard myself say, "My other older brother."

"What happened to them?"

I squeezed my eyes shut, tears burning at the back of my throat. "I killed Dune."

In the silence, I startled at his fingers under my chin, tilting my head up. I opened my eyes to see so much compassion and kindness in his eyes.

"Tell me about it?" he asked.

I stared at him, silent for a long time, but the words begged to be released—the secret I'd never told a soul.

"Dune was a couple years older than me, and he was the only one who knew what I could do," I whispered as though afraid to speak any louder. "He was trying to help me get better at healing. He'd bring me injured animals and he came to me whenever he had a scrape or cut. But he wanted me to push myself and I was too scared. Sometimes…the animals that were really hurt still died. And I didn't want to…" I sucked in a ragged breath. At some point, my gaze had dropped to his chest instead of his face, afraid of what I might see in his eyes. "So one day we were arguin' about it and he got so *angry*. And…" I had to stop and breathe for a moment. "I know it sounds crazy, but he *stabbed* himself in the gut. I tried to stop him, but he…he did it, and then when I tried to heal him…" It got harder to push the words out, my throat tightening. "I don't know what happened. It was like something went wrong and my powers *hurt* him instead of healing him. He started screaming like I was torturing him and the bleeding wouldn't stop and then…then…he just *died*."

In the silence, I didn't dare look at his face. Maybe he'd change his mind. Maybe he'd decide to leave. What kind of person killed their own brother? Maybe he didn't believe Dune had done it himself. Wolf sure as hell didn't. No one in their right mind would just stab themselves—

"Bones." Trey's voice sounded so gentle, and suddenly I was more afraid of his forgiveness than I was of him pushing me away.

"No." I squeezed my eyes shut again. "Don't. I *killed* him."

"Sounds like you tried to heal him to me," Trey said, his warm hands on my face.

I tried to push away the images that bubbled up, but it seemed I'd released them just by speaking Dune's name. I could see his sandy blond hair blowing around his face in the hot summer breeze, the weird determined gleam in his blue eyes, and the flash of the knife. I could smell the blood that dribbled out between his hands. I could hear his screams of pain when my healing power flowed into him, my desperate cries for help, and then Dune's pleas for me to stop, but I couldn't stop because he was *dying* and I knew if I didn't heal him with my power, he'd *die*.

I could see Wolf's face when he found us, the rage on his face when Dune cried his name, his horror at the blood and the knife, and the way he looked at me like I was a monster as he tried to stop the bleeding. Then Dune gave an awful shudder and went still, and the silence was worse. I stared numbly at his empty blue eyes, convinced at any moment he would blink and laugh at me for being so scared.

I remembered Wolf snarling at me through his sobs, the feel of the hot rooftop beneath my bare feet when I panicked and tried to run, Wolf's body crashing into me, knocking me to the roof so hard I couldn't breathe for a moment, his voice screaming in my ear, asking me what the fuck I'd done. And I had no answers because I *didn't fucking know.* I didn't know. But Dune was dead. He was dead and he was never coming back, and his blood coated my hands and my clothes, and I'd killed him.

"Why would Dune fucking stab himself in the gut?" Wolf roared at me as I sat curled in a tiny ball in the cell that smelled like vomit. "That doesn't make any sense! I saw you! You *stabbed him."*

"I didn't. I didn't do it. I was tryin' to help him." I was struggling to breathe, I was crying so hard.

"You're lying."

I'd never seen him so angry. I'd never seen my oldest brother look at me like he hated me like he wished I'd been the one to bleed to death on the rooftop.

"Come, Wolf." Pa's voice sounded cold and hard as he dragged Wolf away. He wouldn't even look at me, no matter how much I begged him to. "The council will decide what to do with her."

Wolf jerked himself free, slamming into the bars so hard I shrieked. "I don't understand. Tell me why you did it! Why would you kill him? He loved you!"

"Hey."

I came back to the present. Trey cupped my face as tears rolled down my cheeks. I tried to duck my head, embarrassed, but he held my face still.

"Bones," he said, "it wasn't your fault."

"You don't know that," I bit out. "You weren't there."

"Maybe not," he said, refusing to let me look away. "But I know you, an' I've seen how far you'll go when you're trying to save someone. So I *know* it wasn't your fault."

"It was—"

"You just about killed yourself to heal everybody in the hold from that sickness, even people I *know* you hate, people who have *hurt* you. We were fucking *abducting* you and you still healed me. You saved my life, and you did it 'cause you're a *good* person who cares about people. So no, I don't think you murdered your brother, Bones. I think it was a horrible accident, and I'm so sorry you had to go through that."

"Stop it," I snapped at him, jerking my head free.

"Stop what? Stop tryin' to show you how everyone else sees you? Cause no, I'm not gonna stop doin' that." He smiled.

I closed my eyes and more tears rolled down my cheeks.

"C'mon. Let's try and get a few more hours of sleep, ok?"

When he tugged me, I went with him, sliding back into the bedroll and his arms. The wolves started howling again, but they sounded farther away. I could hear Trey's heart beating in his chest and it soothed me. He believed me. He was the first person to believe me about what happened that awful day. I felt foolish now for thinking he wouldn't. Trey had never wavered, despite everything.

"You're a river. You don't break, you bend."

Well if I was a roaring river, shifting and unpredictable, Trey was the very mountain below us, steady and constant.

When I woke up in the morning, frost coated Trey's long eyelashes and my nose felt numb with cold, but entangled together inside the bedroll we were toasty warm. Our fire had died to glowing coals, but we needed to get moving anyway. His eyes blinked open, and I watched him focus on my face and smile that sweet, warm smile.

"You're still here," he murmured.

I slid my hands up his chest to twine around his neck, watching his pupils expand in surprise. When I stretched up to kiss him, his arms tightened around me, his lips meeting mine. Kissing him was addictive. I didn't want to stop. Gods, I was so fucked.

I forced myself to pull away after a few minutes. "C'mon, we better get moving," I whispered.

We packed up our small campsite and buried our fire in the snow in case anybody tracked us here. I knew they would be tracking us eventually. I just hoped we'd be able to get far enough away. When we started walking again, Trey reached out and grabbed my hand with a grin. I raised an eyebrow at him as we walked hand in hand.

"So, you and me, we're a thing now, right?" he asked.

"Depends. What's 'a thing' mean?"

"Means you're mine and I'm yours. We don't make love with anybody else."

"Make love," I repeated, amused, but I couldn't deny that was exactly what he'd done last night.

He gave me a playful glare. "It also means I get to take care of you. No more 'I'm fine' shit."

"What if I *am* fine?"

"Ok, smartass, you can say you're fine if you're actually fine. I mean no lying. It means that I get all of you and you get all of me. The good and the bad. It means I'll always have your back. No matter what."

Blooms filled my chest again. "Do I get to kiss you whenever I want?"

He grinned, delighted. "You sure do."

"I'll think about it."

His outraged face made me burst out laughing, and he lit up. "Gods, I love your laugh." He pulled me close, eyes dancing as I tripped over both our snowshoes.

"I guess if we're gonna be a thing, you get to hear me laugh." I grinned.

"It'd be an honor, darlin'."

When he kissed me, the warmth that ran through me felt as pure and golden as my healing powers.

CHAPTER 21

Despite making, or more accurately falling, a good distance yesterday, the hike to the outpost would still take all day. My leg muscles were sore and my back ached, but I pushed through it.

"Tell me more about your mom?" I asked after an hour or so, fiddling with the ends of my hair. It'd been so long since I wanted to be close to someone and know everything about them that I'd half forgotten how to do it.

Trey's eyebrows raised but he smiled. "Her name was Ana Mason, and she was the best person I've ever known. She worked as a seamstress, and we never had much, but she made everything seem magical. She loved everybody, saw the best in everybody. She made me and Mac and Clarity those quilts using leftover bits of fabric she saved for a whole year."

I smiled.

"She died when I was twelve. She'd gotten pregnant again with Clarity's dad, Reed. They were kinda on and off, but she wanted to make it work. I think she thought it'd give us all some more stability. She was getting older though and somethin' went wrong. The baby got stuck I think." He swallowed hard. "There was so much blood. I knew it was bad."

My eyes prickled. "I'm sorry you lost her. She sounds like an amazing person." I paused. "She sounds a lot like you."

He smiled, his eyes wet. "What about your mom?"

"I never knew her." I shrugged. "She died in childbirth with me, but I survived. Everybody always said I looked a lot like her. I know she was strong-willed and she loved collecting books, but that's about it."

"Sorry to hear that. What about your dad?"

I took a breath, resisting the urge to change the subject. *"Please let me in."* He'd asked last night, and I was gonna try. Trey deserved that much.

"He was gone a lot and when he was around, he avoided me. Wolf," I swallowed past the lump in my throat, "used to say it was 'cause I looked so much like Mom, but I think he never forgave me for being the only one to survive."

Sam's grey face flashed through my mind. Maybe I *had* killed her, just like I'd almost killed Sam. A chill walked down my spine.

"So who took care of you?"

"Wolf. He practically raised me and D-Dune."

"What happened after Dune died?" he asked.

I balled up my trembling hands. "They exiled me."

Trey came to a sudden stop, startling me. "What? How old were you?" he asked, his eyes a storm again.

"Ten," I whispered.

"They exiled a fuckin' ten-year-old child?"

He looked furious. It felt obvious now, but it struck me that I'd never really thought about it like I was a *child.* In my head, they exiled a murderer, which made perfect sense. But now I tried to picture one of the older kids being locked outside the Vault and told to leave and my stomach clenched. I would never let that happen.

And now that I thought about it, why *did* everyone in my old hometown let it happen? People *were* strict there, but I could think of quite a few people who I would've expected to protest. Or maybe they just stopped seeing me as a child as soon as I was covered in my brother's blood.

"What about Wolf?" Trey asked. "He didn't try to stop it?"

My breath caught, the memory flashing across my vision as clearly as if I relived it.

I woke up to someone shaking me, hard. I gasped at the sight of Pa leaning over me where I lay in the dirty straw. I had a brief moment of hope that he would take me out of the cells and tell me everything would be ok, but that died as soon as I saw the cold look on his face. He didn't untie my hands, just gripped my arm in a bruising grip and dragged me out. The sun hadn't even risen yet, the hold quiet and dark. When he brought me to one of the side gates of the hold, I couldn't keep quiet any longer.

"Pa—" I started, my voice hoarse from crying.

"Shut up," he snarled at me, and I flinched.

We'd never had a close relationship, me and Pa. As a busy member of the council, I didn't see him much. Wolf always said I looked so much like Mom that Pa struggled to be around me. Wolf looked like Mom too, but being a girl made it worse. Despite all that, Pa had never been cruel or hateful toward me, not till now.

He unbolted the side gate and dragged me outside the hold. Goosebumps rose on my arms in the chilly morning air, and I shivered. He finally turned and looked down at me, his blue eyes, Dune's eyes, glittering with fury.

"You've been exiled," he said in a harsh voice.

I immediately started to cry. "Pa! I didn't—"

I stumbled backward when he slapped me hard across the face, my cheek stinging.

"You've been exiled," he hissed, spittle flying from his mouth. "You will start walking and you will never come back here. If you do, I will kill you myself."

"Where's Wolf?" I choked out. Wolf would never let this happen. He wouldn't. Right? The memory of his face twisted in fury and hate flashed through my mind and I had to swallow a panicked sob. No, he was still my brother. He wouldn't—

"Wolf isn't gonna save you. He wants you dead," Pa said, still in that harsh voice. He drew a knife and my heart leapt into my throat, choking me, but he just grabbed my shoulder and spun me around to cut through the ropes on my wrists. "So you better start runnin', girl, 'cause he's gonna come after you, and not even the gods will be able to save you if he catches you."

The ropes fell off my wrists, and he shoved me forward so hard I sprawled face-first in the sand. I scrambled to my feet, shaking in terror, but he just stared at me with hatred.

"Wolf wouldn't—" I started, my voice small and trembling.

"You ever seen a wolf get a hold of a rabbit?"

Tears poured down my face. Wolf couldn't hate me. He couldn't.

Could he? He was my brother. I needed him. I couldn't do—

"Run, lil rabbit." Pa smiled cruelly. "Before Wolf tears you apart."

I started walking backward away from him, terrified. Once a safe distance away, I turned and ran. The last time I glanced back before I disappeared into the scrub, he still stood there, a shadow in the dark, watching me flee.

"Bones?"

I snapped back to myself. Trey stood in front of me, his hands on my shoulders, concern shining in his eyes. I was breathing in short pants, my chest constricting.

"You back with me?" he asked.

I stepped forward into him and he immediately wrapped me in his arms. For a long time, we just stood there—me breathing in his familiar comforting scent and Trey holding me tight.

"Sorry," I mumbled once I breathed more normal.

"It's alright. What happened to you was fucked up, Bones, and you're allowed to have feelings about it. I sure as hell do. They never should've done that. You were just a kid."

We stood in silence for a few more minutes.

"How the fuck did you survive?"

I took a shaky breath. "I was in the desert for about a week, just walking, trying to get as far away as possible. Then Juck found me."

His arms tightened around me, and his voice sounded anguished. "Gods, Bones."

"It wasn't so bad," I lied.

"Don't lie," he admonished, but gently. "Griz said you learned how to heal like a regular healer from books?"

"Yeah. Vulture scavenged some for me, and I just read them over and over until I had 'em memorized. On long rides, I'd recite all the stuff in my head."

He pulled away, still gripping my shoulders so he could look down at me. "So you were a ten-year-old kid and you taught yourself how to be a fucking healer by reading books." His eyes shone with admiration. "First of all, you're incredible. Second, all of that is fucked up and you did not deserve any of it."

I had to press my lips together to keep from admitting that I thought maybe I *did* deserve it. I'd killed my brother, my best friend.

Maybe everything that happened afterward was exactly what I deserved. Suffering in retribution was the whole point of exile being a punishment. I wasn't sure how much suffering atonement required, but—

"No. You did *not* deserve it," Trey said sternly, startling me. He smiled when I looked up. "Yeah, I thought that was probably what you were thinking."

"What are you, a mind reader?" I grumbled.

He grinned, releasing my shoulders to grab my hand again as we continued on. We traveled in silence for a while. The grade grew less steep and I got the hang of the snowshoes. The quiet, peaceful woods were so still, but also so damn cold. My face burned when the wind blew.

"How's your back today?" he asked.

"Still hurts, but I'm getting used to it."

He quieted for a bit, something dark and haunted flitting across his face.

"You ok?"

"Yeah." He sighed, his hand tightening on mine. "I'm just not sure I'll ever be able to get the image of you dangling from the whipping post covered in blood out of my head."

I winced. "I'm sorry."

"Not something you need to apologize for, darlin'. You know, Madame didn't used to be quite so bad. After her partner, Viper, died it was like it broke something in her. She got cruel. She seemed to enjoy punishing people, hurting 'em. To my knowledge, she never tortured people until about three months before we brought you back."

My stomach turned. I did not want to think about Madame or rebellions or torture. Trey glanced at my face and read all my thoughts *again.*

"What Madame made you do, it wasn't your fault, Bones."

I looked away. "I could've refused to do it."

"She probably would've just hurt you until you gave in," he retorted.

I couldn't contain the shudder that went through me, goosebumps rising on my arms.

Trey squeezed my hand. "I keep thinkin' I know how low she'll go, and then she surprises me by goin' even lower."

I knew why. Trey couldn't help but look for the good in people. It was his nature. I wasn't sure what my nature would have been, but I did know that sort of optimism had been beaten out of me.

"Tell me more about your brothers?" Trey asked.

My stomach constricted with panic, and apparently, I couldn't keep anything secret from him anymore because his thumb stroked the top of my gloved hand, comforting.

"I was closer with Dune." I finally managed to get out, my heart pounding in my chest. "He was my best friend. Wolf—" Gods, I would not cry. "Wolf and I fought a lot. He had to be more my dad than my brother, and I hated that. But he taught me how to defend myself, how to survive. He'd make me get up at dawn and practice, and I hated that too." I swallowed hard. "He's the reason I've survived this long." My lips twisted in a bitter smile. "Which is funny since now he wants to kill me for what I did."

"How do you know that?" Trey asked.

"My dad told me when I was exiled."

He squeezed my hand. "I'm sorry."

"We're a lot alike I think." I surprised myself by continuing. "We even look the same. Both of us got our mom's eyes, hair, and freckles. Dune looked like our dad. He was blond and blue-eyed." I took a deep breath. "Wolf was paranoid about everything. It's why he trained me so hard. Dune was softer, more gentle. He loved animals. He hated that he had to go hunting, and I hated that I couldn't go hunting 'cause I'm a girl."

Trey stared at me, his brow furrowed in confusion. "Cause you're a girl?"

I grimaced. "The place I grew up was different. They thought a woman's place was in the home, raising babies, and cooking and cleaning."

"So a servant." Trey frowned.

"Basically."

"Well, that's fuckin' stupid."

A startled grin crossed my face. "Yeah. It was fuckin' stupid."

He grinned back at me. "Raven is a better shot than me *by far*."

I made a face. "Gods, good thing I left before she pulled a gun on me."

He tilted his head. "Did you know Raven's the one who told us what Lana had done?"

I looked up at him. I thought he was joking, but I couldn't find a hint of teasing on his face.

"Gonna guess that's a no."

"I thought they were friends," I said.

"They were. They were like sisters, but when Lana confided in Raven about what she arranged, what those men were gonna do to you, Raven ran across the whole damn hold to get me and Mac. It's how we were able to get to the clinic before—" That muscle in his jaw flexed. "Gods, when I saw that asshole on top of you if I'd had my gun, I would've shot him without a second thought."

I swallowed hard. I'd been unconscious for that part.

"I'm so sorry that happened, Bones. I'll never forgive myself—"

"Trey." I tugged him to a stop. "It wasn't your fault."

He met my gaze, looking anguished. "I trusted Lana when—"

"It's not your fault," I repeated, squeezing his hand. "I don't blame you." I hesitated, remembering with shame the awful things I'd said to them. "I was lyin' when I said I'd rather be with Juck. I...I only said it 'cause I knew it'd hurt all of you." I took a breath. "You *were* different. That's part of why I was so angry. I'd been tryin' not to believe it, but I'd started to, and then..." Gods, this was fucking hard. "I was mad at myself. For darin' to hope that maybe this could be different."

He held my gaze, opened his mouth, then closed it with a grimace.

I waited.

He sucked in a deep breath and blew it back out and tried again. "You told Mac that you knew how to handle it." His voice sounded pained. "Had...something like that happened before?"

My heart rate picked up and my mouth went dry. I didn't know if I could speak without my voice breaking, so I just nodded. Fury flashed through his eyes.

"Juck?" he asked.

I nodded again, a chill that had nothing to do with the cold creeping over me.

"Fuck," he muttered through his teeth, squeezing his eyes shut. When he opened them again, they met mine with a furious sorrow. "I wish I could bring him back to life so I could kill him. Slowly. And painfully."

I forced a slight smile, remembering the pain on Juck's face as he drowned in the blood pouring into his lungs. "Oh, his death was painful. I stabbed him at least six times."

He stepped forward, dropping my hand so he could cradle my face in his gloved hands. "Good. I hate that he hurt you. I hate that he ever touched you. I hate that no one fucking stopped him. And I hate that you had to kill him to get away." Tears glimmered in his eyes. "An' I'm so glad you became a part of our crew."

We're not the Reapers. We've been tryin' to show you that for the past, what six months? I know you didn't have people then, but you do now. His earlier words ran through my head again and my eyes prickled.

"I still don't..."

"You don't what?" he asked.

"I know I'm a pain in the ass." I tried to lighten the mood, but my pathetic attempt at a joke fell flat.

His eyes saddened, and I hated that I'd put that expression on his face. "I wish I could show you how I see you, Bones. How we all see you. You're so smart and brave." He flashed that crooked grin. "An' yeah, sometimes a pain in the ass, but despite all the horrible shit you've been through, you still care so much about people. Most people woulda stopped caring a long time ago."

"You wouldn't."

His smile was sad. "We've lived very different lives, darlin'. Sure mine hasn't always been easy, but I didn't go through hell like you did. I'm not sure what kinda person I woulda been after all that."

The lump in my throat choked me. "You wanna know the worst thing I've ever done? I convinced a boy in the Reapers to run away with me. His name was Rally. We were friends—actual friends—and I realized he wanted more. I didn't feel that way toward him, but I saw an opportunity. So I told him I loved him, told him anything he wanted to hear, just so I could get him to take me away on his bike. I knew it was a death sentence for him if he got caught, but I did it anyway." I blinked, trying to keep my eyes from overflowing. "After they caught us a couple of days later, Juck made me watch the Reapers torture him to death." The tears escaped, the horrible memory overwhelming me. "They tore him apart."

"And what happened to you?" Trey asked softly.

More tears escaped and my voice shook. "That was, um, the first time. With Juck."

His face darkened with fury again. "How old were you?"

"About fourteen," I whispered.

That muscle ticked in his jaw like he was grinding his teeth. He didn't say anything, just pulled me into him and held me. I gripped him, and for a long time, we just stood there. Telling him all this stuff brought a strange mix of panic and relief. The combination made me nauseous.

"I still think you're a good person. You were a kid in a horrible situation." He pressed a kiss to my hair. "The fact you've been carryin' all that guilt with you? It proves that you're *good.*"

I started to protest, but he interrupted me.

"A bad person wouldn't think of Rally again. A bad person would never call it the worst thing they've ever done." He pulled back enough to gaze down at me, sincerity shining in his eyes. "You are *not* a bad person, darlin'."

I love you. I wanted to say, but I didn't.

"We should keep goin'," I said instead, "or we're gonna be walkin' in the dark."

The sun moved across the sky as we trudged along. The cluster of trees with the smoke rising above it grew closer. By the time the sun began to set, it took all my energy to keep putting one foot in front of the other. The pain in my back jolted through me with every step. I tried to distract myself by thinking of ingredients I could use to make a salve for my back. My go-to had been a salve made from comfrey and plantain for years, and I knew plantain grew wild here. The salve Griz and Raven used on my back was a recipe from the old healer's notebook that had horsetail in it. Maybe the trading post would have some dried plants I could use and some sunflower oil. It wouldn't be too hard to make an oil infusion. Not quite the same as the salve, but close.

I didn't have any experience with whip wounds so I didn't know if it was normal to have lingering pain. The wounds hadn't gotten infected, whether from the salve or my healing powers. Some parts of the scars seemed like they would heal pretty flat, but other parts seemed like they would be thicker and raised. Those were the ones that seemed to ache—

"Bones?"

I blinked and glanced over at Trey.

"You ok?" he asked. "You were lost in thought over there."

"Just thinking about salves."

A grin spread across his face. "Salves, huh?"

"Don't you ever think about salves?" I raised an eyebrow.

"I think I can honestly say I have only thought about salves one time and that was when we were reading the healer notebook to find something to put on your wounds."

"Well you picked a good one," I said, trying to chase away the memories that darkened his face.

"That's lucky 'cause I think we picked the very first one that had ingredients we could find."

"It had horsetail in it."

He looked nervous, and I grinned.

"Horsetail was a good choice."

"How come?"

"It reduces inflammation and helps wounds close faster."

"Well, that's fucking cool." He grinned back at me. "Why were you thinkin' about salves?"

"I was thinkin' if the trading post had the right ingredients, I might be able to make an oil infusion for my back."

"Is your back hurtin' bad?" he asked, studying my expression like he was waiting for me to lie.

I bit back the compulsion to do just that. "Yeah."

"Then we'll do that. We should be there soon."

"Do you think they'll have plumbing?"

"I'm not sure. I hope so. A hot bath would be nice."

"A hot bath would be fuckin' incredible," I corrected him, and he chuckled.

In the distance, the wolves started howling again.

"How far away are they?" I asked, shuddering.

"Pretty far." Trey glanced up at the setting sun. "But I'm still glad we're gonna have some better shelter tonight."

We walked in silence for a few minutes, and when I adjusted my pack for the fourth time on my aching back, Trey stopped me.

"Let me take it," he said, holding out a hand. "We don't have much farther to go."

I hesitated, but gods, my back hurt. I slipped my pack off my shoulders and handed it to him, mumbling my thanks.

"Look at you accepting help," he teased as we started walking again.

"Don't make me take it back," I muttered.

He laughed and reached out to snag my hand again.

"We shouldn't use our real names at the trading post."

"Ok," he agreed. "What name do you want to use?"

Tell him.

The fear that rose choked me.

Nobody will be looking for that name. I tried to convince myself, but a louder, sharper voice prevailed.

You don't know that.

"Sara," I finally got out, hating myself for my cowardice. "That was my mom's name."

"Sara," he repeated, smiling. "That's good. I'll be Flint." His smile turned sad. "That was Mac's dad's name."

"Flint and Sara," I murmured.

"Flint and Sara."

CHAPTER 22

The huge man standing behind the counter in the trading post looked like a bear pretending to be a human with thick black hair that seemed to cover his entire body. His brows rose when we walked in, and his eyes narrowed as he scanned us.

"Howdy," he said. "Awful late for you folks to be out."

"We're just passin' through," Trey said. "You have an open room we could rent for the night?"

He stared at us a moment longer and then nodded. "I do. Not many people passing through in the winter."

"We like it that way." Trey smiled, all calm confidence. "Nice and quiet."

A smile tugged at the giant man's mouth. "Well, that's for damn sure. I'm Zeke. You looking for one bed or two?"

"One," Trey said without hesitation.

Butterflies erupted in my stomach, remembering what he'd said last night. *I want you in a place that's warm so I can see every beautiful inch of you without worryin' about you getting frostbite.*

"I'm Flint, and this is my wife Sara."

My wife.

I managed a smile when Zeke's eyes landed on me, my heart still pounding.

Zeke surprised me by smiling back. "I got just the room for you." He turned and grabbed a key off the wall behind him. "Number 3.

Normally we charge extra if you want hot water, but I'll throw it in for free tonight."

The surprise on Trey's face matched my own.

"Thank you. That's very generous," I said, hoping he understood how much of a gift he'd just given us.

His smile softened, the expression at odds with his stature. "My pleasure, miss. You folks need anything else?"

When we said no, he pointed to the stairs on the other side of the room and wished us a good night. We climbed up the squeaky stairs and made our way down the hall to the door with a large number three painted on it. Trey unlocked the door and we stepped into the prettiest room I'd ever seen. Old faded floral wallpaper covered the walls and a thick green rug lay over the wood floors. In the corner stood a metal radiator, then a large bed with four wooden posts sticking up in the air, and a small dresser. Trey locked the door behind us, and I kicked off my boots before moving through the room to peer into the small adjoining room to find a bathroom, complete with a working toilet and a large clawfoot tub. I turned and looked at Trey in astonishment.

"This is incredible."

He grinned. "I'm glad you like it. I wish we could stay longer, but it's just a little too close to the hold for comfort."

I grinned back, warmth sparking through me. "We'll just have to make the most of it then."

His eyebrows raised, his eyes sharpening on me as they darkened with desire. "You sure you don't want to get some sleep? Or a bath?" he asked carefully.

Gods, this man. I loved him. I loved him so much that it made my heart ache with the beauty of it.

"I just want you."

The emotion that flooded his face made my eyes burn. He crossed the short distance between us in just a few quick strides, and then he kissed me so fiercely it made me realize how much he'd been holding himself back before. I ran my fingers through his hair again, exploring what made him groan against my mouth or made his breath hitch. He broke away from my mouth to trail burning kisses down my neck, his tongue dipping into my collarbone as he worked my jacket off my shoulders at the same time. As soon as my jacket hit the floor, I did the same to his, taking the opportunity to splay my hands across his broad chest. My head tipped back, knocking against the wall as he continued to torment my neck. Already my breath came in short pants and my skin buzzed in anticipation.

His hands gripped the hem of my shirt, and he pulled back just enough to catch my eyes, silently checking. I raised my hands, holding his gaze and hoping he could see the desperate want that roared through me. He gave me a truly sinful smirk and slowly pulled my shirt up and off, letting it drop to the floor. He went still, eyes drifting across my chest, and while I still felt flickers of insecurity about the awful brand on my chest, they were easier to ignore when he gazed at me with so much blatant hunger.

I slid my hands under his shirt, my fingers searching until I felt the small raised scar on his stomach. That desperate moment when I'd pressed my hands against the bloody wound seemed like another lifetime ago.

"That's my favorite scar," he said, his voice low in a way that did something pleasant to my insides.

I rucked his shirt up, but he was too tall for me to pull it off. He grinned and pulled it the rest of the way off, and I let my eyes drift across his naked chest, admiring the lean muscle. His breathing quickened as my hands trailed up, tracing the same path my eyes had taken, across his chest and shoulders and then down his arm until my fingers brushed the faint scar in the shape of my teeth marks from where I'd bitten him.

"Not this one?" I purred, a sly grin crossing my face.

His answering grin was downright dangerous. He caught my hand and brought it up to his mouth, kissing down to the middle of my forearm. "I could give you a matching one if you want." He sank his teeth into my forearm just hard enough that I let out a little gasp. Then he swirled his tongue over the mark, warm and soothing, his eyes still locked on mine.

Gods, I felt drunk, intoxicated by him. "I can think of better places for you to put your mouth."

He made a strangled noise, surprise mixing with the blazing heat of his eyes, and then he kissed me again. His hips shoved into mine, pushing me back into the wall. He wasn't holding any of it back now, pouring all of his emotion and need into how he touched me and kissed me.

Let go, I reminded myself. *Let him in.*

"I lied to you earlier," I breathed, and he pulled back to look at me, wariness in his eyes. "My favorite color is the color of your eyes."

His eyebrows raised, but that sunshine smile chased away the concern. "Brown?"

"Yes," I gasped as his fingers brushed over my nipples. "I've never wanted to get lost in someone's eyes before I met you."

"I can understand the feeling," he said hoarsely, watching my face, "because I've never seen eyes as beautiful as yours."

"Green like glass bottles," I teased, arching toward him.

"You saw right through that, didn't you?" His smile turned sheepish.

"You're not very good at hiding how you feel," I murmured with a smile, reaching up to brush his wavy hair out of his eyes. "You live everything you believe out loud."

He grinned, then dipped his head and caught one of my nipples in his mouth making me gasp, and the next few minutes were lost to the sensations of his tongue and teeth and hands on my breasts. He slowed as he moved upward, pressing his lips to the brand on my chest like he had last night. I leaned my head back against the wall, tears burning in my throat at how reverently he kissed the part of my body I thought no one would ever look at with anything but disgust.

His hands trailed down to the waistband of my jeans, lazily undoing the buttons and sliding my pants and undergarments off my hips torturously slow. As soon as they hit the floor, however, he hauled me up into his arms. I sucked in a breath at the sudden movement, wrapping my legs around his waist as he made his way toward the bed. He laid me down and then took a step back, staring at me, every bare inch just like he'd promised.

"Beautiful," he said in that low, rough voice.

I smiled wide, and those blooms in my chest felt like a whole damn garden.

I rolled onto my side, watching him undress further and blatantly admiring him as more of his lean muscled body came into view, and as he dropped his pants, I could *see* how much he wanted me.

"Have I ever told you," I asked in a conversational tone, "that you are the most handsome man I've ever seen?"

He prowled back toward the bed, and the heat in his gaze almost made me shiver.

"I never had a chance in hell tryin' to push you away. Especially when you look at me like that."

He grinned as he reached the bed, but he didn't join me. Instead he gently but firmly grasped my ankles and tugged hard enough that I tipped onto my back and slid across the bed with a gasp.

"Have I ever told you," he asked in a matching casual tone as he sank to his knees at the side of the bed, pulling my legs over his shoulders. "That I have dreams about doing this." He shifted forward, pressing a kiss to my inner thigh, and I shuddered. "And when I wake up," His lips ghosted across my opposite leg. "I can't remember your taste." His teeth scraped the skin of my inner thigh and a cry escaped my lips. "Just that I couldn't get enough." Another kiss and I whined with frustration. He raised his head and met my eyes, looking so fucking smug.

"Trey," I pleaded.

His warm breath glided across my skin as he chuckled, but then his arms wrapped around my thighs and pulled me even closer as his tongue flicked across my slit.

"Fuck," I gasped, my hands clenching handfuls of the blanket and my hips bucking, but his arms tightened around my legs, holding me in place.

His tongue moved in slow, languid strokes like he had all the time in the world, and he hummed deep in his throat. My legs trembled, toes curling.

"Oh my gods," I gasped.

His tongue delved inside, licking and swirling. When his mouth moved upwards, his fingers replaced his tongue, and I cried out, straining against his hold on my legs. I panted, trying to keep my moans quiet, but then his tongue swirled over my clit, and he sucked and I dissolved into pleasure. His fingers kept pumping, tongue flicking until my release faded. He emerged from between my legs, that smug smile firmly on his face.

"Better," he said.

"What?" I was still trying to catch my breath.

"You taste even better than I dreamed," he rasped, crawling up my body to claim my lips again.

I could taste myself on his lips and tongue, but it wasn't unpleasant. I wrapped a hand around his cock, and he groaned against my lips.

"I want you," I breathed, stroking him and making him shudder.

"You sure?" he asked, staring me in the eyes, and I could see his desire as well as his restraint written all over his face. "We don't *have* to do anything you don't feel comfortable—"

"Trey," I interrupted, a soft smile on my lips, "I love you."

He went so still I was half afraid he stopped breathing.

"I love you, Trey, and I want you," I repeated in a whisper, my eyes prickling.

"I love you." His voice sounded rough with emotion, and then he captured my lips in a desperate, bruising kiss that made our teeth click together.

This time when I moved, he moved with me. His cock sank into me, and the pleasant burn made me gasp, He paused, looking worried.

"Are you—" he started to say.

"Trey," I interrupted him again, my voice a demand as I gripped his hips, "I want you to fuck me."

His smirk crackled with heat. With one thrust, he sank himself fully inside me, and I dug my fingernails into his hips with a moan. He began to move, rolling his hips slowly, and I threw a leg over his hip to try and pull him even deeper. I wanted him, all of him. His smirk deepened and he drove into me deeper and faster, our hips snapping together. The coiling tension in my center built like a fire.

"Tell me what you want, Bones," he rasped.

"More," I moaned. I couldn't get enough.

He suddenly gripped my upper arms and hauled me up, his cock still buried inside me as he kneeled on the bed with me sitting in his lap. I gasped at the new angle, the new pleasure.

"Fuck." My head tipped back as his hips set a rhythm.

"You're so beautiful," Trey breathed, and then his lips were on my breast, his tongue swirling around my pert nipple and I went over the edge again. The burning was both pleasure and pain until it built to the point where I instinctively let go.

"Bones, open your eyes," Trey gasped, stilling.

I hadn't even realized I'd closed them, but when I opened my eyes, I froze. I was *glowing.* All of me. Glowing. As though sunshine ran through my veins and beamed through my skin in a warm golden light.

"Oh my gods," I got out.

"Beautiful."

I met Trey's wide eyes and in the light of my skin, they looked like honey. I could see my eyes reflected in his, wide with shock and fully glowing golden, no white or pupil to be seen. My heart lurched at how jarring, how *inhuman* it looked. I bent down, pressing a kiss to his neck so I couldn't see my reflection anymore. His breathing hitched, so I did it again, scraping my teeth lightly over his pulse point.

"Bones," he groaned.

I slid my hands back into his hair and he suddenly tipped us until my back hit the bed, pushing my knees up against my chest. He pounded into me, his hand reaching between our bodies and teasing my clit, and I cried out as pleasure barreled through me again. Shortly after, Trey gasped out a string of swear words mixed with my name and shuddered. He dropped his forehead to mine, both of us gasping for breath and covered in a sheen of sweat.

"Am I still glowing?" I murmured, dazed.

He pulled back to glance down at me and grinned. "Just a little."

I held up a hand and stared at my skin. It glowed faintly, but it was still glowing.

"What the fuck?" I breathed.

"Good thing you didn't light up the forest like a beacon yesterday."

"Oh my gods, this would happen to me when I'm trying to disappear."

"I'd say I'm sorry, but I'd be lying."

"You *will* be sorry when you can't have me again unless we're in a windowless room."

"Oh shit." His smug grin vanished into a forlorn expression, and for some reason that's what did me in.

I started laughing, and it wasn't long before he joined me, both of us dissolving into manic laughter. By the time we managed to stop, the glow had faded to my relief. I curled into him, tilting my head up to gaze at him.

"I love you." My voice caught.

His hands came up to cup my face, stroking my cheekbones with his thumbs. His beautiful eyes glimmered. "I love you, Bones."

We lay there tangled together for a while, our hearts returning to a normal rhythm. I started to drift off when Trey shifted.

"You still want a bath?" he murmured.

"Yeah," I mumbled.

I heard him chuckle. "Only if you promise not to fall asleep and drown."

"You better come in with me just to make sure."

He grinned. "Safety first."

Hot water poured from the faucet, sending steam billowing around the room. From what I knew, this used to be a mundane, normal thing in the Before, but to me, it seemed almost magical.

"Could the Vault have hot water?" I asked.

"Technically parts of it could, but we've never been able to get the water heaters workin'," Trey answered. "There's some parts missin' or broken that we haven't been able to jerry-rig with scavenged parts."

"You ever think about what it must've been like in the Before?"

Trey leaned over the tub, one hand in the running water. I admired the way the warm light from the candles we'd found played across his lean body. His summer tan had faded, but I could still see the faint tan lines around his neck and waist.

"Oh of course," Trey answered. "I love lookin' at any books from Before that I can find. Seems impossible this is the same place."

"I saw one of those airplanes once. It crashed in the desert. It was in pieces and gutted, but it was so fuckin' big. I dunno how they built somethin' that big."

"I dunno how they got those things up in the air," Trey said.

"Me either," I agreed, thinking about how huge and heavy even the smallest piece of the plane had been.

"So what's the story you were told?" Trey asked. When I stared back in confusion, he clarified, "Why the world ended."

I made a face. "Punishment from the gods."

Trey made a face too. "Sounds like some pretty shitty gods to me."

"What about you?"

"Oh, we heard all sorts of stories. I remember my dad telling me there was a war and everybody just killed each other. There was a real old lady in the Vault when I was a kid named Bugs. She seemed *ancient* so we were pretty sure she must've been there. Mac and I both asked her at different times and got two wildly different stories. She told me that monsters as big as mountains came from the sea and destroyed everythin', but she told Mac everyone got sick with a disease that made them *eat* each other."

I wrinkled my nose. "The Reapers had stories more like those. One of 'em was that everybody *melted* except for all the people who hid underground. That one scared the shit out of me."

"Gross." Trey chuckled.

When I climbed into the tub, I moaned. The hot water soothed my sore back and muscles. Trey climbed in behind me, the tub large enough for both of us, especially once Trey sat with his back against one end of the tub and I settled in between his legs, leaning back against his chest.

"Well this is nice," he said, and I could hear the smile in his voice.

"This is amazing," I corrected him.

"Does it feel ok on your back?"

"Yeah, it's helping."

"Here, lean forward a minute," he said, and I did, feeling a tiny flash of insecurity at baring my scarred back to him. He gently ran his hands across the healing scars. "Does it hurt everywhere?"

"You see the really thick scars?" I asked, and when he made a sound of agreement, I continued, "Those seem to hurt the most. But after walking so much, pretty much everythin' hurts."

He pressed into my back with his thumbs, avoiding the thickest scars. "Does that feel good or bad?"

"Mostly good."

"Tell me if it hurts."

He rubbed my sore muscles, and so long as he avoided the thick scars, it ached pleasantly.

"Tomorrow I'll ask Zeke if he has any dried herbs or flowers," I mumbled.

"I'm sure Zeke will have somethin' you can use." His hands left my back to wrap around me again. "Did that help at all?"

I smiled, leaning back into him. My back still ached, but it seemed looser. "I think it did. Thank you."

Between the comfort of his body and the warmth of the water, my eyelids grew heavy. His fingertips brushed across my bare skin.

"Will you tell me about this?" Trey asked, his fingers landing on the brand on my chest. I stiffened, and he added, "You don't have to, darlin'."

I didn't want to, but I doubted I'd ever *want* to talk about that day. I tried to steady myself, taking a few deep breaths. In the silence, we could hear the wind gusting against the house.

"The only people who knew what I could do were Juck, Vulture, and a man named Grip. After Grip died, Vulture started wantin' more—more power, more control. Normally, Juck would've shut that shit down right away, but he couldn't cause Vulture knew my secret and he wasn't afraid of threatening to reveal it. It started gettin' real tense between the two. Juck tried to get him killed a couple of times, but Vulture survived. So Vulture got real friendly with the gang. He was good at that—bein' charismatic and charming to get what he wanted. It reached a point where Juck knew if he killed him, the gang might revolt. And I—"

I sucked in a shaky breath. Trey's arms tightened around me, his head dipping to press a kiss to my shoulder.

"Vulture wasn't a good person, but he'd been less cruel to me than Juck. So I figured if I was gonna pick a side, I'd rather it be his. So I started sneaking out to see him." My eyes burned, ashamed to admit the next part. "I did the same thing as before…with Rally, that boy I ran away with. I told him whatever he wanted to hear and did whatever he wanted to do. But Juck caught us together one night." My voice trembled, remembering the panic and terror of that moment. "He dragged us out of Vulture's tent. He was so fuckin' angry, I thought he was gonna kill both of us. Instead, he had his men hold me down while he got some metal fencing and bent it into a 'J.' He put it in the fire until it was red-hot and then he made Vulture watch while he burned it into my chest so no one would ever forget that I belonged to only him."

"Gods, Bones." Trey sounded stricken and his arms tightened around me again.

"I passed out from the pain." I felt numb as I recounted the story. "While I was out, he beat Vulture nearly to death. I don't know why he didn't kill him. Maybe he thought I loved Vulture so he could use him to control me or maybe it was the other way around, I dunno. I woke up in so much pain, and he drugged me even though I was beggin' him not to. And, well, you know what happened next."

"How much time passed between that night and when the revolt happened?" Trey asked, his voice dark and quiet.

"Four days."

"So then Vulture told everyone about your powers and they all started fighting each other?" When I nodded, he continued. "And then Juck shot Vulture and tried to get away and that's when you stabbed him?" I nodded again, trying not to remember the blood coating my hands. "Was Vulture conscious when you left?"

"Yeah. He watched me kill Juck. He thought I did it to help him win. When he realized I was leaving him to die—" I could see the rage and the betrayal on his face as if it'd happened yesterday. "If he's alive, he's someone we don't want to run into."

"He's someone who doesn't want to run into *me*," Trey growled.

"I'd prefer to never see him again," I said, my voice faint.

"Well the good news is, last we heard, the few Reapers left were heading south. Hopefully for good. If he's still alive, he probably went with 'em." He pressed a kiss to my temple, then lingered there, speaking low and soft in my ear. "Thank you for tellin' me."

We sat in silence for a while, just soaking in the warm water. The sick feeling in my stomach from talking about that awful day began to fade. My head rested back against Trey's shoulder, and his arms held me against his chest. I could feel his heart beating.

"We should try to get some sleep," he eventually said, and I agreed.

Entwined together in the bed, his hand carded through my damp hair. I'd never experienced the intimacy of laying skin-to-skin with someone after being vulnerable in a different way than just sex. It still scared me, but it felt...it felt like *healing*, as though Trey had his own kind of healing power that flowed through me, piecing together all the broken parts of my soul.

CHAPTER 23

The next morning, I woke to the soft sunrise shining through the curtains. Trey slept beside me, one arm draped over my hips. I propped myself up on one elbow and just gazed at him for a while, admiring his long lashes and the way his wavy hair framed his sleeping face. I remembered waking up with him in the clinic all those months ago and fleeing as if I could somehow outrun my feelings for him. It was selfish, but I was glad it didn't work. I didn't want to run from him ever again.

"You keep starin' at me like that, and I'm gonna have to kiss you," he murmured without even opening his eyes, one corner of his mouth curling up.

I smiled. "Is that a promise?"

He cracked his eyes open, a lazy grin spreading across his face. "It *is* a promise."

When he grabbed me and pulled me on top of him, I let out a little shriek of surprise, but then his lips were on mine, and I melted. I would never get enough of this, of him.

He groaned against my mouth as I wiggled my hips. We were both still naked and I could feel the hardness of him against my body. I grinned and did it again, and his eyes opened, dark with want.

"We should probably get up and get goin'," he murmured.

"We probably should," I agreed, dipping my head to gently bite his collarbone.

His fingers tightened on my hips, another groan escaping him. "Gods, Bones."

"Or we could see where this goes," I countered with a grin.

"I like that option better," he said, pulling my head back down to kiss me again.

A few hours passed before we managed to get dressed and leave that peaceful little room. I wished we could stay and take our time. Maybe someday we could afford that luxury.

Zeke smiled when we came down the stairs. "Mornin'. You folks sleep alright?"

"Yes, thanks." Trey smiled back. "You've got a real nice place here."

"Been in the family a long time," Zeke said, pleased. "The hot water work for yah?"

"It did," I answered. "Thank you. It was lovely to take a hot bath."

Zeke's smile softened again as he glanced at me. "I lost my wife a couple years back to a fever. We had nearly twenty-seven years together, but it still feels too short." He looked at Trey. "Don't take a single moment for granted."

Trey's hand found mine and squeezed. "I'm so sorry for your loss," he said to Zeke and I nodded in agreement. "That's good advice," Trey continued, smiling down at me. "I know I haven't stopped thankin' my lucky stars I met her, and I'm not sure I ever will."

My eyes prickled and Zeke beamed, his eyes bright.

"Nice to see a young couple in love," he said, his voice gruff with emotion.

"Do you have any dried flowers or herbs in stock?" I asked, desperate to change the subject. "And some oil? Sunflower would work."

Zeke cleared his throat. "Got some sunflower oil over there on the shelf," he said, gesturing. "We got several dried herbs. You'll find those in the jars to your left."

I found calendula and wild plantain and a small amount of horsetail plus the sunflower oil and a small bottle to put it in. When I brought my supplies up to the front, Zeke had left.

"Got us a horse." Trey grinned.

"How are you payin' for all this?" I asked, lowering my voice.

"With the silencer," Trey answered. "It coulda got us two horses, but Zeke's only got one extra right now. So he gave me the rest back in gold."

I blinked in quiet astonishment. It made sense that silencers were so valuable since I'd never seen one before. The Reapers had what I assumed must be every single weapon and then some, but none of them had silencers.

"He's saddlin' the horse up now." Trey glanced at my hands. "You find somethin' that'll work? Zeke said if you wanted to make your infusion you were welcome to use the kitchen. I'm gonna see if Zeke needs any help."

 જી

Zeke's kitchen looked worn, but tidy. As I began to rub the dried herbs between my hands to release more of the oils before dropping them in the jar, a slight noise made me glance down at my feet. Somehow, I managed to avoid swearing as I jumped at the sight of little eyes peeking out at me from between the tabletop and the bench pushed underneath.

"Oh you scared me," I said, trying to calm down my heart.

"Who are you?" a little voice demanded.

"I'm B— uh, Sara." I stumbled a bit. "Is Zeke your dad?"

"Yeah. Why are you back here? Dad don't let people in the kitchen."

"Oh," I said, surprised, "he said I could come back here to mix up an oil infusion."

The eyes disappeared and then a little boy with messy dark curls scooted out from under the table. "A magic potion?" he asked, eyes wide.

I slipped into that familiar healer role as I studied him. He looked to be around six or seven, but the terrible thinness of his body made him look frail. I could see his blue veins through his pale skin and dark circles framed his sunken eyes.

"It's kind of like a magic potion," I said, crouching to his eye level. "What's your name?"

"Roe," he answered. "Can I help? I'm ten so I'm good at helpin'."

I did a double take at his age but forced myself to smile. "Sure."

Roe pulled the bench out so he could climb up on it to see the table. I showed him how to rub the dried herbs in my hands. Roe began to enthusiastically copy me, asking millions of questions that I answered patiently. I didn't need my powers to know he was ill. I kept seeing a single word from the medical textbooks in my head. *Terminal.*

I was helping Roe pour the oil over the top of the herbs when the door opened, and Zeke and Trey came in.

"We're makin' a magic potion!" Roe chirped to his dad, who looked startled to see him.

"Roe, you're supposed to be in bed," the large man scolded. "You're gonna give yourself another bad spell."

Trey smiled at us, but I could see him noting the boy's condition too.

"A bad spell?" I repeated.

Sorrow flashed across Zeke's face as he came and picked Roe up. The boy wrapped his arms around his dad's neck, burying his face in his shoulder. "He's been sick since before he could walk. We've seen many different healers, but no one can give us any real answers. Sometimes he has bad spells where he is so sick and weak that he can't even get out of bed."

I glanced at Trey. I almost expected to see him shaking his head, warning me not to do anything to blow our cover. Instead, I found him already looking at me, his eyes soft.

"*Your choice,*" he mouthed, and my heart swelled again.

I knew the risk in healing Roe, and a few months ago I might have kept my head down and continued on my way. Maybe Trey's faith in people had rubbed off on me, but I wanted to believe if I healed his son, Zeke would keep my secret. And even if he didn't, I couldn't walk away without trying.

"I'm a healer," I told Zeke. "Could I try examinin' him?"

Zeke gave me a long look, and I held his gaze, waiting for his decision. Finally, he turned to the boy. "Roe, is it ok with you if Sara examines you?"

Roe grimaced. "There gonna be needles?"

"No," I said, smiling. "No needles."

"Oh! Ok then." The boy smiled back at me.

"Can I see your hands?" I asked, and the boy put his hands in mine with a trust that made my throat ache. "Now I'll need you to be just a little bit patient, ok?"

When he nodded, I sent thin tendrils of my healing power flowing down my arms and into him. He jolted a bit as they reached him, his eyes widening.

"What—" I heard Zeke demand, but Trey murmured something and he quieted.

I kept my eyes on Roe's face, concentrating on what I could feel through my powers. The illness seemed to be everywhere, in his blood and bones and flesh. I'd never healed anything like it, but as usual, my powers knew what to do. They spread through his body as though they needed to immerse him, requiring me to funnel more and more power into him. When his pale skin began to glow faintly, I watched his face for any signs of distress. I didn't think it would hurt him, but I'd never done anything like this before, and I couldn't help but remember what Sam's body had looked like after funneling a large amount of my power. So far, he didn't seem to be experiencing any pain. His wide eyes stared into mine. Zeke hovered at my side, and I could hear Trey continuing to reassure him.

It felt strange to heal something so severe after healing people with the fever. Especially because as much as this taxed my power, it didn't feel alien. I could tell parts of his body weren't quite right, as though they'd mutated, but those mutations were still made from his body. As my power flooded through him, each individual mutated cell seemed to need healing. It drained me more than I'd anticipated, but I kept going.

As I finally neared the end, the color and health began to return to his face, transforming him from looking pallid and fragile to a healthy child. He'd probably always be small for his age, and he'd have to pack on some fat and muscle, but I did not doubt he would. Zeke let out a choked sound, and I spared a glance up at him to see tears flowing down the giant man's face.

"Dad?" Roe asked, looking worried.

"It's workin', son." Zeke beamed through his tears. "I think it's workin'."

As I healed the very last mutations, I knew without a doubt this disease would have killed him before summer's end. Gratitude flooded me that we'd come here, and that Zeke let me use the kitchen. When I finished and released him, I tucked my hands into my pockets to hide their trembling.

For a while, no one spoke. Zeke gently touched Roe's face where his cheeks glowed a rosy pink, studying him as though afraid what he saw wasn't real.

"Nothin' hurts anymore," Roe whispered, his expression a mix of shock and wonder. "Dad, am I better?"

Zeke folded his son in his arms, silent sobs shaking his shoulders. Trey moved next to me, slipping an arm around my ribs and pressing a kiss to my head.

"How is this possible?" Zeke managed to ask.

"Sara has an incredible gift," Trey explained. "But we are gonna have to ask you to keep this quiet."

"You're on the run," Zeke said. It wasn't a question, but both Trey and I nodded. "What do I owe you—"

I cut him off. "You don't owe us anything. You showed us so much kindness, an' I'm just glad there was somethin' I could do to repay it."

Zeke stayed quiet for a moment before he nodded, swiping at his wet face. "At least let me send you with some more provisions."

When we relented, he began to move around the kitchen, gathering food and wrapping it for us to take.

"How did you do that?" Roe asked, tugging on my jacket to get my attention.

I hesitated, unsure how much I should tell a child who might accidentally give away my secret. "You were right," I said finally. "I *do* make magic, just not potions."

His eyes widened. "You fixed me with *magic?*"

"Yes, but you gotta keep it a secret, ok?"

He nodded, and I smiled.

"You feel better?"

"Yeah!" he said. "I feel great!"

Zeke sniffled from where he stuffed several apples into a bag. "Your secret is safe with us, right, buddy?"

"Right!" Roe agreed.

Zeke pressed the bag of food into Trey's hands and then startled me by enveloping me in a giant hug. "He's the last piece of Wren I have, and I'll never be able to thank you enough for what you did," he whispered.

"It's alright," I whispered back, my throat tight with emotion. "I'm glad I could help."

Zeke pulled away and shook Trey's hand. We exited into the frigid air, heading toward where a white horse with black spots stood saddled and ready, our meager possessions already strapped on. I didn't mind that we only had one horse. Trey and I had been riding together on one horse for so long that riding alone would feel, well, lonely.

As we began to ride away, I twisted back. I could just make out Zeke and Roe standing in the window watching. I raised my hand and waved, a soft happiness rising in my chest when they both waved back.

"You're incredible," Trey murmured into my hair.

My cheeks warmed. "Thank you for lettin' me make the decision."

"Bones, you can always make your own decisions about healing people." Trey's voice was firm. "It's not my power, and I have no right to try and dictate what you do with it."

A soft and strong emotion swept through me and brought tears to my eyes. I laced my gloved fingers through his resting on my thigh. "This is all I want to do. I just want to heal people like Roe."

"We'll find a way for you to do that then."

"Do you think he'll keep our secret?"

I expected him to answer right away, and when he didn't, I twisted to glance up at him.

He sighed. "I think he will unless someone threatens Roe."

A chill walked down my spine. I knew he was right, but I couldn't judge Zeke. I already knew I'd sell out the whole rebellion to save Trey. It made me feel unsettled that I hadn't thought of that possibility because normally I would. Wolf's voice rose from the depths of my mind, growling warnings.

"We can't control what other people do," Trey said, squeezing my hand, "just our own actions."

I grimaced. I knew he meant it to be comforting, but it made me feel sick to my stomach.

"Whatcha thinkin' about?" Trey asked after a few minutes of silence.

"Doesn't that scare you?" I asked.

"That I can't control what other people do?"

I nodded.

"I find it more liberating than anythin'. I don't have to be responsible for other people's actions, just mine." He paused. "Does it scare you?"

"Yeah."

His arms tightened around me. "I'd guess that might be 'cause you're *always* tryin' to control what people are gonna do."

"I am not."

"Bones." He sounded exasperated. "You pushed everybody away, and when you finally let me in a little bit, you ran straight to Zip just to get rid of me. That's control."

"No." My voice grew sharper. "That was survival."

"Survival for who?"

"Me. You. Everybody."

"You don't get to make those decisions for other people, though, darlin'."

"Trey, people who get close to me end up *dead*," I snapped.

"So it's better to just refuse to let anyone ever get close to you again?"

Fear turned my stomach. "Yes."

"So what's the point then?" he asked. "What are you surviving *for?*"

I couldn't answer him. I didn't want to admit that I asked myself that same question constantly, or tell him I'd spent the last twelve years only thinking about one day at a time, on trying to survive from dawn to dusk, and I had no idea how to see further than that. I didn't want to tell him I survived because Wolf's voice in my head demanded I keep going or that I still clung to a tiny delusional shred of hope that maybe I could atone for Dune's death.

So instead I shot back at him, "What are *you* surviving for?"

"Well," he said, "I want to make my mom proud. I want to help make this world a better place. And maybe you don't know this, but there's this beautiful healer that I've kinda fallen in love with, and I want to start a life with her."

I tried to stay mad, but my eyes prickled.

He leaned forward, his cold nose pressing against my ear. "That's you."

I let my head thud back against his chest, huffing out a heavy breath. "Even if that life is always on the run?" I asked, my voice low.

"Yes," he said without hesitation.

"Even if you never get to go back to the Vault?"

He hesitated for a split second. "Yes."

"Trey," I said, my stomach sinking at that tiny hesitation, "you deserve better—"

"No," he interrupted with conviction, "Bones, you don't get to decide what's best for me. There's that control again. I've made my decisions. I'm where I want to be."

My eyes burned and I blinked back tears. I wasn't trying to control him. I just wanted him to be safe. I swallowed hard and tried to push Rally's screams from my head. I hadn't loved Rally in a romantic way, but I'd loved him as a friend, and it broke me to see him tortured to death. I had no idea how long a body could go before it took its last breath, how much pain a person would be forced to endure in the meantime.

"You did this to him, Angel." Juck had hissed in my ear. *"So don't you dare close your eyes."*

We rode in silence for a long time. When we stopped for a break, the space between us felt stiff. I hated it. Trey still gave me a smile when I glanced at him, but it didn't reach his eyes. I went to relieve my bladder, and on my way back, I noticed he was staring into space with a frown.

Gods, I didn't want to spend this time fighting with him. I crouched and grabbed a handful of wet snow, packing it into a ball shape. When I chucked it at him, I expected to miss. Instead, my snowball smacked into the side of his head. I covered my mouth with my gloved hands, trying not to laugh. He leapt to his feet, his eyes narrowing at me as he wiped snow from his face.

"You did not—" he growled, but his eyes sparkled, "—just throw a snowball at my head."

"I would never."

"Cause I'll have you know—" He crouched, scooping up a handful of snow, "—I always win snowball fights."

I couldn't resist the grin on my face any longer. "Those are some big words."

"You don't believe me?" He raised an eyebrow as he packed the snow into a tight ball.

I scooped up another handful of snow, monitoring him as I grinned. "I'm just sayin' that's a lot of talk with little to back it up."

"I can't believe—" he started, but then he charged mid-sentence.

I shrieked and chucked my snowball at him, missing by a mile, and turned and ran. His snowball hit me in the back of the head and a second later he tackled me into the snow. I got a faceful of cold wet snow, and when he flipped me over, he laughed at the snow coating my face.

"You believe me now?" he asked, full of smug confidence that he'd won, but he didn't know my brother taught me to fight dirty.

I smashed two handfuls of snow into his face.

He sputtered, and I dissolved into laughter. Most of the snow dripped off his face right away, but some stayed stuck to his eyebrows and the stubble on his face, making him look like an old man. He glared down at me for a moment as I laughed at him, but then his lips crushed into mine, silencing me. I wrapped my arms around his neck and kissed him back.

The earlier tension between us melted away as swiftly as the snow.

CHAPTER 24

We rode until dusk, stopping to make camp near a small river so the horse could get a drink. The horse shifted nervously when the wolves began howling again. They didn't sound any closer, but they also didn't sound farther away. Both Trey and I stopped making camp to stand and listen.

"Do you think they're followin' us?" I asked Trey in a low voice.

He frowned. "They should have plenty to hunt without needin' to track us down, but I've heard stories of packs sometimes gettin' bored and goin' after humans just for the challenge."

I shuddered, the hair on the back of my neck rising.

"It's ok," he said, reaching over to squeeze my gloved hand. "They're still not close enough to be a threat."

"And if they get close enough to be a threat?"

That muscle in his jaw flexed once. "Then we'll have to be prepared to fight." He looked down at me, his eyes sharp. "You know how to shoot?"

"Yeah. Well, I didn't get much practice with Juck, but Wolf taught me."

"I've only got the one pistol, but hold on."

He moved into the trees, searching for something while I stood with the horse. A loud crack sounded, and the horse and I both startled.

Trey returned holding a large dead branch. "We'll make this into a torch. Animals have an instinctive fear of fire, so that can be an effective weapon."

I nodded as we moved back to our campfire, taking a seat beside him as he stripped some of the smaller branches off.

"If the horse takes off, let her." He glanced at our horse, regret clear on his face. "The wolves will probably go after her instead of us. They *want* their prey to run, so no matter what, *don't run*."

Nausea swirled in my stomach, but I nodded.

"And if I tell you to climb a tree, you gotta promise you'll do it, even if it means leavin' me behind."

My eyes shot to his face. "No."

"Bones—"

"No," I snapped.

"Bones—" he tried again, reaching over to grab my hand, but I jerked away.

"No." I fixed him with a fierce look. "I'm not gonna leave you behind. So don't you dare fuckin' ask me to do that."

He stared at me for a moment and then sighed, bringing his hand up to rub his face. "Just, can you at least promise that you'll try to stay safe? Remember you can heal me, but if you get hurt," his voice broke, "I can't do a damn thing about it." He dropped his hand, and the worry in his eyes made my throat tighten.

"I'll try to stay uninjured, but please don't ask me to promise anythin' else," I allowed.

He took a deep breath, and I watched him swallow the argument he wanted to have. "Ok," he muttered. "Ok."

In the silence, the fire crackled and the horse chewed her oats. We studied each other, and I wondered if he also wished we were still back in our warm, safe room at Zeke's outpost like I did.

"Why wouldn't you heal yourself after you were whipped?" he asked.

I narrowed my eyes. "What do you mean, why? You saw what it did to Sam."

"So, what, you're never gonna do that again? Even if the alternative is dying?" His voice sounded even, but a strong emotion flickered in his eyes.

"Yes," I said a little shortly. I didn't know why the hell we were even having this conversation.

"Bones," he pleaded, and I recognized the emotion in his eyes. It was fear.

"Trey, I'm not gonna drain the life out of someone to save my own skin." I tried to soften my voice. "Sam almost died. He was still mostly bedridden even when we left."

That muscle in his jaw flexed again.

"Would you honestly do it?" I pressed, and he didn't respond, but we both knew what the answer would be.

"I just can't watch you get hurt again," he finally confessed, "and be fuckin' helpless to do anything."

"Trey." My eyes prickled at the emotion in his voice. I'd never seen him like this before. I stood from the log we were sitting on and moved to stand between his long legs, crouching to meet his gaze. "It's gonna be ok."

He stared at me, his jaw tight. I cradled his face with my bare hands. The stubble on his face had grown thick enough to be called a beard now. His eyes locked on mine.

"It's gonna be ok," I repeated.

He sucked in a deep breath, then turned his head to press a kiss into my palm. "Sorry. I just—" He cleared his throat. "I saw my dad's body after he was killed by that bear, and I just keep picturing it happenin' to you."

I ran my fingers through his hair, and his long eyelashes fluttered closed. "I'll be careful."

He smirked, his eyes still closed. "S'not really reassurin' comin' from you."

I rolled my eyes. "I've never promised to be careful, so don't go actin' like that's a promise I've broken."

He cracked his eyes open, his grin widening. "Sorry. You're right. But if you bein' careful actually looks like bein' careful, I will eat my damn hat."

I glanced up at his knit hat, raising my eyebrows. "Hope you're hungry."

His arms snaked around me, pulling me tight against him. "I *am* hungry," he said in a low voice that made my blood heat, "but not for that."

I grinned and pulled his head down so I could kiss him deeply, sucking his bottom lip into my mouth. He groaned and pulled me even tighter, but the eerie sound of a wolf howling made us both freeze again.

"Did that one sound closer?" I asked, dread spreading through me like ice.

"Yeah," he muttered, staring out into the darkness as answering howls sounded.

"Do we wait or do we go?"

Trey hesitated. "Probably better to go. If we travel through the night, maybe we can put some distance between us without pushin' the horse too much."

I nodded, getting to my feet. Together we packed up the few things we'd set out. The horse shifted, staring out into the darkness. When we set out, she moved forward at a trot like she was eager to leave. Thick clouds swallowed the moon, and the darkness pressed in on us, our small lantern only illuminating a few feet in front of us. I could feel the tension in Trey's body, and I wished I could do something to get his mind off animal attacks. I remembered him telling me that story about him and Mac when they were teenagers. I frowned, trying to think of a lighthearted story. I didn't have very many, but then a memory surfaced.

"For a while when I was really little, Dune used to insist he had a friend named Ash. Any time he got in trouble for somethin' he'd try to say it was Ash who did it. Used to drive Wolf crazy, I guess. Then it kinda became a joke between the three of us. If somethin' unusual happened, we'd always say, 'Must've been Ash.'"

I hadn't thought of that in a long, long time. It made my eyes prickle. I tried to avoid thinking about the good memories I had with my brothers because it hurt so bad it made it hard to breathe. For the first few months with the Reapers, I'd been haunted by those memories. I missed them so much that I started contemplating turning myself in so Wolf could kill me. They could bury me beside Dune, and I wouldn't hurt anymore. That was about the time when Wolf's lessons on survival started manifesting in his voice growling at me in my head. One night as I lay crying in my bedroll, I realized I couldn't hold onto those memories *and* survive. So I forced myself to shove them all down and pretend they didn't exist. I got so good at it that sometimes I did forget.

Trey's arms around me tightened. "Ash," he repeated in an amused voice. "Me an' Mac tried to blame Clarity for a broken lamp once."

"Did your mom believe you?" I asked.

He chuckled. "No cause Clarity couldn't even sit up by herself, much less throw a ball."

I grinned, trying to picture them as kids.

"I don't remember which one of us came up with the idea, but it wasn't our best."

"So I guess you've always been a bad liar."

"Hey," he said, indignant. "I'm not a bad liar."

I let out an amused huff. "Sure."

"I just don't lie much."

"Cause you're bad at it."

"I bet I could tell you a lie right now and you'd believe it."

"Try me." I grinned.

"Alright. I'm gonna tell you three things and one of 'em will be a lie and you have to guess which one."

"Ok."

He paused for a moment, thinking. "I hate mice. I don't like goat cheese. I can't swim."

I had to resist laughing. His voice changed on the last statement, a clear tell, and besides that I doubted the Safeguard training would neglect swim lessons. "You can swim."

"How did you know that?" he demanded.

"You're a bad liar," I repeated, tilting my head back to grin at him. "It's ok. I love that about you."

He glared playfully down at me.

"You don't like—

A howl interrupted me and we both fell silent. The horse's ears flicked back, listening. They still sounded close, but not *closer.*

"Should we be quiet?" I whispered.

"Probably wouldn't hurt," he muttered.

I tried not to think about the wolves, but they kept howling like they wanted to remind us they were there. I couldn't help thinking how horribly fitting it would be if I spent most of my life afraid of Wolf killing me only to be killed by actual wolves.

The night seemed to stretch on forever. I dozed off a few times, usually jerking awake in a panic and startling the horse and Trey. He kept insisting I could sleep, but I didn't want to make him stay awake alone, so I fought it the best I could. The wolves howled until the sky began to lighten. Our poor horse plodded through the snow. We would have to take a break soon. As the sun rose, we listened for the wolves, but the mountains had fallen silent again.

"Hey, look!" Trey said, pointing a hand in front of us.

I followed his finger to see faint plumes of white smoke rising from behind the next rise. My heart seized in anxiety. "Is that a fire?"

"No." I glanced up to see him grinning. "I'm gonna make it a surprise if you don't know."

"Ok," I said with suspicion.

It took us several more hours to reach the white smoke, but we didn't hear the wolves at all. As we drew nearer, I wrinkled my nose. Something smelled *foul*.

"What is that smell?"

"Well, it's part of the surprise," Trey admitted.

I twisted to look at him, eyebrows raised.

"I promise it's a good surprise."

"A good surprise that smells like that?" I asked, but he just laughed.

When the source of the smoke came into view, my mouth dropped open. It wasn't smoke. It was *steam*. About halfway down the hill from us a waterfall seemed to be coming from the ground, spilling down into several deep rock pools that led to a small river snaking through the valley. The river had chunks of ice along the edges, but the clear pools of water steamed like a hot bath.

"It's called a hot spring. The water's hot all year round, but they all smell like this, unfortunately."

"How?"

"Dunno. Just comes up from the ground that way. You wanna soak? It'll give the horse a chance to rest and I'm pretty sure the wolves are doing the same since they've gone quiet."

I grinned and nodded.

Trey took the horse down to the river to get a drink and give her more oats while I stayed by the pool with our supplies. I ate some of the food Zeke sent with us as I slipped my boots and socks off, rolling up my pant legs to dip my toes in the hot water. A moan escaped my lips. I couldn't wait to get my stiff, sore body in there.

As soon as Trey made his way back up, I handed him the rest of the food I'd been eating, then shrugged off my jacket and pulled my shirt over my head. When he came back into view, I almost laughed. He was watching me undress with dark eyes, a smile playing across his lips, and his hand frozen halfway to his mouth as though he'd completely forgotten about the bread he'd been about to bite.

"You better finish that so you can join me." I grinned as I pulled down my pants.

He immediately stuffed the whole thing into his mouth, and I laughed. I waded naked into the pool, trying to avoid slipping on the rocky bottom. Standing in the middle, the water came up to my chest, and it felt incredible, especially on my back. When I turned to glance at Trey again, he was already wading in after me.

"This is amazing," I said as he neared.

"*You're* amazing," he said in a rough voice and his lips crashed into mine.

I matched his energy, our tongues rolling over each other. I'd never wanted someone like this. Would it always be like this, like I would never get enough?

His beard scratched pleasantly against my skin. I slid my hand down between us, grasping the length of him in the water, and his fingers tightened on my skin as his breathing hitched. Our lips broke apart and I watched his face as I brushed my thumb across the velvet tip of his cock and he shuddered, his hips thrusting into my hand as he swore. I stroked him for a while, exploring what made his breathing hitch and what made him groan my name. He tried to slide his hands to my breasts, but I stopped him.

"It's *my* turn." I smugly echoed back his words from that night in the woods.

He huffed a laugh, then swore again as I continued stroking him.

"You keep doin' that, and I won't be able to last much longer," he rasped.

I grinned, releasing him and he swiftly bent to wrap his arms around my waist. My feet left the rocky bottom as he stood straight up, and I wrapped my legs around his waist.

"I want to hear you moanin' my name again." His lips ghosted over the shell of my ear as he lined himself up at my entrance. "I want to see you glowin' and comin' undone."

I shivered, my heart racing, then gasped as he abruptly slid inside with one hard thrust.

"Fuck, Trey," I choked out.

He began lazily rolling his hips, and my arm muscles strained as I tried to lift myself so I could increase the pace. I growled in frustration, and he chuckled.

"Trey," I begged, "please."

"What do you want, Bones?" he teased, tilting his head back to see my face.

The steam rose around us in gauzy ribbons. Sweat beaded on his forehead and tendrils of his hair clung to his face, damp from my wet hands dragging through it.

"Is this what you want?" he murmured before I could answer, pulling my hips down hard and making waves of water crest over the rocks.

My fingers dug into the sinewy muscles of his shoulders. "Yes."

He did it again, harder, and I knew I'd probably have bruises on my hips from his hands.

"Don't stop," I whimpered, heat coiling through me.

"Gods, I love you," he groaned, slamming into me and making the water choppy with waves from the movement.

"Trey," I gasped.

My blood buzzed through my veins, and I could feel my power building with the pleasure.

He continued his brutal pace, making me keen through my teeth. My skin began to glow faintly, and a devilish smile crossed his face. My head tipped back, my breath coming in fast pants, as electricity *sizzled* through me.

"Oh my gods," I gasped, "right there."

He pulled my hips down onto him even harder. "Right there?"

"Gods, Trey," I managed to gasp before the entire pool filled with soft golden light.

"Fuck, darlin'." His pace grew even more frantic and desperate.

I looked at him, bathed in the golden light that emanated from me, and thought he was the most beautiful thing I'd ever seen. I watched the pleasure shatter across his face, his muscles clenching as he panted. I'd never get tired of seeing him like that.

As he stilled, I wrapped my arms around his neck and pulled him in to kiss him again. I meant for it to be a soft, gentle kiss, but his arms pulled me tightly against him. He sucked my tongue into his mouth, demanding and needy like he couldn't get enough even though his cock was still buried inside of me. I kissed him back just as fiercely, and soon

I *felt* him harden inside of me again. I grinned against his lips.

"What, that wasn't enough for you?"

"This is what you do to me," he murmured, rolling his hips. "I will never get enough of you, Bones."

"Well, you make me literally *glow.*" My breath hitched.

That smug smile returned. He continued to slowly thrust into me, and a tiny whine escaped my lips.

"I love those noises you make," he rasped, increasing his pace.

"I love *you.*"

His sunshine smile shone as bright as the golden light beaming from my skin.

৬৩

We spent a couple of hours in the hot spring pool, soaking and enjoying each other's bodies. Again, I never wanted to leave, but as we lingered, reality kept creeping closer.

Eventually, I sighed and wrapped myself around him. "I wish we had more time."

"I know. Hopefully soon we'll have all the time in the world."

"Might not be enough," I said, pressing my cold nose against his neck.

He laughed. "Might not be."

"I'd rather not get eaten by a wolf though."

"Same."

I forced myself to let go of him and make my way out of the pool. My skin still glowed faintly and as I stepped into the cold air steam rose from my body.

"You look like a fallen star," Trey said in a low voice.

I turned to see him gazing at me, and I wished I had one of the cameras from Before. I wanted to memorialize that expression on his face so I could always remember him staring at me with awe and love and desire. It made my eyes burn with emotion, but then the icy wind gusted, and I scrambled for my clothes.

"Gods, I didn't think about how cold it would be to get out," I said through chattering teeth.

"Yeah, that's always the worst part," Trey said, emerging next to me, his skin also steaming.

"Do you think we could start a fire?" I asked as we quickly

dressed.

Trey hesitated, glancing out at the quiet landscape. "I'd feel better if we put some more distance between us and the wolves."

We made our way down the hill to where the horse dozed on her feet. Trey saddled her back up and we ate a little more before starting out again. Trey handed me a small metal compass and showed me how to make sure we were heading west. Mountains and trees spread as far as I could see under the huge blue sky.

"Once we get through these mountains we'll come to a large river," Trey explained as we followed a small deer trail in the snow. "If we follow it south, we'll come to a dam. We can cross there and keep goin' west."

"Have you been this far before?" I asked.

"I've been to the dam, but that's as far as I've gone."

"What were you doing at the dam?"

"There was a group of people livin' inside the dam, but they went radio silent. So Madame sent us out to go check on 'em."

"Really?" It surprised me Madame would care.

"Well, she wasn't so much concerned with their well-being," Trey clarified. "They were people who used to be at the Vault, but Madame thought controlling the only crossing for miles and miles would be advantageous. So she sent a team to do that. I was just a kid when they left. They ran the damn for years, demanding payment from people who wanted to cross."

"What happened?" I asked, already guessing the answer.

"They were all dead," Trey answered, confirming my suspicion. "Either some group didn't want to pay the toll or they were tryin' to take control of the dam. Looked like a massive firefight, and none of our people survived." He sighed. "So we collected whatever hadn't been looted, burned the bodies, and left. After that Madame decided the dam was too far away from the Vault to maintain."

"Do you think the wolves are still followin' us?" I asked after a pause, rubbing my gritty eyes and trying to stifle another yawn.

"Not sure," he said tensely. "I hope not."

As much as I tried to stay awake, I must have passed out because the next thing I knew, Trey was shaking me, and the sun was disappearing behind the mountains.

"How long was I asleep?" I mumbled, disoriented and annoyed at myself.

"A while," Trey said, but he didn't sound mad. He dismounted and I realized we'd stopped to make camp for the night.

"Have you heard the wolves at all?" I asked anxiously as I slid off the horse.

"No," he said, but he didn't look happy about it. "I don't know if that's good or bad."

I studied him as we started setting up our campsite. He moved slower than normal, his face lined with exhaustion.

"Trey, you should sleep, and I'll take the first watch."

He looked like he wanted to argue for a moment, but then he just nodded. "Alright." He cracked a weary smile. "Do I look as tired as I feel?"

I smiled. "You look pretty damn tired."

He made a face. "Guess I do then."

I had to hassle him into only doing the bare necessities so he could get to sleep. He insisted on finding a big dry stick to use as a torch, building a small wood pile for the fire, and showing me how to use his pistol, but then he collapsed into the bedroll and immediately passed out. I settled myself next to his head, holding my cold hands out to our crackling fire with his gun in my lap. The woods were quiet and still. Our poor horse had started dozing almost as soon as we'd dismounted. I hoped we were able to give her enough rest tonight.

My thoughts drifted back to the Vault as I stared at the fire, full of bittersweet wishes and wants that I knew better than to have. It took me a while to name the emotion clogging my throat. I was *homesick*.

That realization hurt like a physical blow. I hadn't had a *home* in twelve years, partly due to living with a roaming bike gang, but even if the Reapers had stayed in one place, it never would have felt like *home*. Not like the Vault. The Vault felt like home because of the people I'd left behind. People I'd probably never see again.

I let myself cry for a little while, but I didn't want to wake Trey, so after a few minutes I wiped my face and tried to stop. The shame for wanting Trey enough to let him come with me rose, reminding me of its existence.

How would I get *his* attention? I couldn't just take a narc because he'd get in my head and see Trey. Fear gripped my lungs. Despite my best efforts, he would find out about Trey eventually. We would be running for the rest of our lives. Did Trey understand the toll of that kind of life? I did. I knew exactly how it felt to be constantly looking over my shoulder and suspecting everyone of ill intent. Would Trey be able to live like that? Gods, would this leave him as broken as me?

The wind blowing in the trees almost sounded like a howl, and it made the hair on my arms stand on end. I curled my gloved hand around Trey's gun and stared into the darkness, listening and trying my hardest to stop thinking, but my brain latched onto all my guilt and anxiety and would not let it go. When Trey woke up a few hours later, I tried to stuff the emotion back down to hide it.

"Hey," he yawned as he sat up, "any trouble?"

"Nope." I thought I did a passable job of sounding normal, but his eyes snapped to my face.

"What's wrong?"

"Nothin'." I tried to smile. "Just tired."

"Bones, don't do that. What's wrong?"

"Don't do what?" I crossed my arms.

"Don't shut me out," he said, frustration clear on his face.

"I'm not," I said more shortly than necessary.

He gave me an incredulous look. "Something is clearly wrong, and you're lying about it."

"I'm fine!"

"No!" He shoved his feet in his boots, that muscle ticking in his jaw. "We're not doin' that anymore, remember?"

I gritted my teeth, my temper rising. "What, so that means I *have to* tell you everything?"

He stood, frowning down at me. "No, it means you can be honest with me. You don't have to carry shit by yourself."

"Trey." I tried to sound reassuring. "I really am fine. I can handle stuff on my own, I promise."

He stepped in front of me and crouched, his eyes glittering with emotion. "You wanna know how I know that's a lie?" He didn't wait for me to say anything before barreling ahead. "I know that's a lie cause every single time you've had a burnout fever, it's like you're a different person. You don't try to hide how scared or lonely or hurt you are. You ask me to stay with you. Even after you refused to talk to me, when you got that burnout fever tryin' to heal Mist, you were inconsolable askin' for me until Griz finally came and got me. And then you *clung* to me and begged me not to leave. That's when I realized those fevers were the only time I saw how you were actually feelin'. And it killed me to know how much you were hurtin' inside, but you wouldn't fuckin' let me or anyone else help you." He paused, his eyes searching my face. "I probably could've asked you anythin' when you were feverish and you would've been honest with me, but I didn't. I want you to tell me shit 'cause you trust me."

I stared at him as my eyes welled up. I remembered that time after the fire when I asked him if I said shit while delirious, and he lied. Now I knew why. I wanted to be mad. I *was* mad, horrified that I'd been vulnerable without even knowing, but that didn't explain the pain in my chest. I knew he wasn't lying. Besides the fact he was a horrible liar, he'd worked so hard for my trust, and no one in my life had ever done that before.

"I don't—"

"Bones." Trey grabbed my hands and squeezed them, his voice thick with emotion. "It's ok to need people. It's ok."

My eyes overflowed and he tugged me forward into his chest, wrapping his arms around me.

"Let people in, darlin'. You gotta let 'em in. There are *good* people out there. Not perfect, but people who are tryin' to do the right thing and they *want* to help. You don't have to be strong all the time. You can lean on me."

"I'm just so scared," I whispered through the tears.

"There's a lot of scary shit out here," he murmured. "Everyone's scared. Hell, I'm scared half to death most of the time."

I scoffed.

"I am." He squeezed me tighter. "Especially when the woman I love is out jumping into pits to fight fuckin' giants with just a tiny knife."

I choked on a tearful laugh.

"I know it's a risk, but gods, Bones, don't you want to live for something else besides just survivin'? What's the point if you're too scared to experience all the things that make life worth living? I *am* scared—fuckin' terrified, of losing you. I don't know how much time we have, but I *do* know I don't want to miss a single second of lovin' you."

I wrapped my arms around his neck, pulling him tight against me.

"I'm—" my voice broke, "I'm tryin'. I s-swear."

"That's all I'm askin'."

I sniffled. I hated that this was so hard for me, that I was frustrating him, that I was so fucking damaged and he had to work so hard—

He pulled back to look at me, eyes glowing in the firelight. "This is the part where you tell me what's goin' on in your head. What's scarin' you?"

Fear clogged my throat, and for a moment we stared at each other as I struggled.

"I just...so much of me is...is broken." My fingers twitched with the urge to touch the brand on my chest.

"Bones—"

"No, Trey, listen," I interrupted, "you...bein' with you feels like... like *you're* healin' *me*. But I'm so scared if I lose you...if somethin' happens to you—"

"Don't go down that path."

"Trey, it's...I've lost *everyone* I ever cared about. I'm stuck on this fuckin' path."

"You're only stuck if you believe you're stuck." He looked so calmly confident.

"Trey," I said, frustrated, "it's not that easy. I can't just *believe* things are different and then they magically are."

"Why not?" he asked. "Maybe if you put good things out into the world, good things will find you."

We stared at each other for a few breaths before I spoke.

"That is the stupidest thing I've ever heard."

He took my hands and squeezed them. "Bones, you can heal people just by touching them. A year ago, if somebody had asked me if I believed that kinda magic existed, I would've *laughed*. Magic exists, so maybe it *is* that simple."

"If it's that simple, then why do good people go through shit?" I demanded.

"I dunno," he said like it didn't terrify him to not have answers. "But I don't think anythin' bad can come from being a good person." He waited, but I stayed silent, so after a minute he just sighed. "C'mon, you should get some sleep now."

I pulled off my boots and climbed into the abandoned bedroll, watching him put more wood on the fire. My thoughts rattled around in my head like rocks. I didn't know how to explain to him that he was putting the pieces of me back together, but if I lost him, I would break again. And I wasn't sure there'd be anything left of me.

CHAPTER 25

After two nights of not hearing the wolves, we began to relax that maybe they'd given up and turned back. We emerged from the mountains to find the remains of a paved road that wound along beside the large beautiful river stretching out in front of us. I understood why Madame wanted to control the bridge. The river was huge and wide. If the dam wasn't there, a person would have to travel far out of their way trying to find a way around. Swimming seemed risky and would be straight-up foolish during the cold months.

The horse's hooves sounded too loud on the pavement, echoing off the growing cliff walls to our left. It put me on edge. We could see the dam in the distance, but I couldn't tell what kind of state it was in from so far away. I wondered how long it would last. What would happen when it broke down?

It took half the day to reach the dam. The road had been carved out of the rocky cliffs and fallen rocks littered the ground, ranging from pebbles to giant boulders. We had to dismount and walk for most of it. I went first, trying to find a safe path, and Trey followed, leading the horse. The horse threw her head back and snorted, often fighting to pull away from Trey when rocks would move and shift underneath her hooves, but he coaxed her through it. On the right side of us, the ground dropped into a steep hill down to the river. I tried to ignore my anxiety about being trapped between the rocky wall and the edge of a cliff.

When we got closer, I stared at the giant wall of concrete,

speechless at the enormous size of the thing. How had they built something so huge? How had they kept the river back so they *could* build it?

"How did they—" I started to ask.

The horse turned her head and jumped sideways a second before something leapt out from behind a giant boulder. A giant wolf narrowly missed us with its snapping jaw and the horse let out a terrified noise and took off at a gallop. I shrieked, clinging to the saddle horn, and Trey swore as he grabbed onto me with one arm and fumbled for his gun with the other. Behind us howling and barks filled the air, spurring the horse on even faster, and I managed to glance behind to see more than half a dozen huge grey wolves pursuing us.

"Hold on!" Trey yelled over the sound. "Let the horse go and just hold on!"

He twisted backwards and the first gunshot made my ears ring. One of the wolves yelped, and maybe I imagined it, but the howls and barks seemed *angrier.*

We flew down the rocky road, and I prayed to any gods listening that the horse wouldn't fall on the loose rocks. My eyes watered and I squinted through the wind to see the dam rapidly approaching. The horse ran as fast as she could, but the wolves easily kept pace. Trey continued to shoot, and I heard a few yelps, but I had no idea if he'd managed to kill any of them.

"Try to steer her onto the bridge!" Trey yelled in my ear, and then I heard the telltale click of an empty gun.

I knew he had more ammo in his jacket, but I wasn't sure if he could reach it. I seized the reins. The turn for the bridge appeared, and I started pulling to the side, hoping the horse would understand that I wanted her to turn. She seemed to get the idea and began to turn toward the bridge, but then she stumbled. For a second, I thought she would be able to right herself and keep going, but then we were falling.

Trey grabbed me around the waist and for a sickening moment, we were both airborne before the ground slammed into us hard. The horse screamed, a horrible cry of fear and pain, and I knew without looking that we'd lost her. Trey recovered before I did, hauling me to my feet, but a blur of grey fur crashed into him and knocked him back to the ground. The gun clattered across the ground, and I screamed in terror. Trey grappled on the ground with a wolf that was attempting to rip his throat out. He'd managed to get an arm up so the wolf's jaw crushed his forearm instead of his neck, but blood sprayed, and I could *hear* the cracking of bone as he screamed. Still, he fought back, attempting to wrestle the wolf to the ground and get the upper hand.

I started to run for the gun but then remembered it was empty. After a frantic glance around me, I grabbed some of the large rocks that littered the ground and threw them at the wolf as hard as I could, screaming. After a few misses, I managed to get the wolf squarely in the jaw, and it released Trey's arm, turning toward me with a snarl. Trey gasped on the ground, his face pale and his arm a bloody, gory mess. The wolf stalked toward me, its muzzle covered in Trey's blood, and I clutched the rock in my hand tighter as I raised my arm.

"Get out of here!" I screamed at the wolf. "Get out!"

The wolf didn't stop and as Trey cried my name and the horse's screams faded, I knew we were about to die. The smell of blood filled the air along with the awful sound of the wolves beginning to tear into the horse's flesh.

The wolf lunged at me, and I threw the rock as hard as I could at its head with a scream of helpless fury.

A gunshot rang out and the wolf twisted in the air, the fierce light abruptly extinguished from its eyes. I gasped in a breath and then it hit me, knocking me off my feet and pinning me to the ground. As I struggled to escape from under the dead wolf, more bullets whistled around us. I managed to shove it off and spared a glance at the dam to see a group of people in dark tactical gear approaching as they fired, picking off the wolves, but then I crashed down on my knees at Trey's side.

His eyes met mine, full of fear and pain. His arm was *shredded*, and I didn't waste any time. I ripped my gloves off and wrapped my hands around his arm, the warmth of my healing powers rushing down my arms and into him. I gasped in panicked sobs as I watched the broken bone, ruptured muscles, and torn tendons and ligaments slowly mend.

His good hand suddenly gripped my arm, squeezing, and I looked up at his face.

"S'alright darlin'," he whispered, which only made me cry harder. "Bones, it's alright."

The wound finally closed into an enormous, jagged scar, but I didn't let go, running my fingers around it and moving his arm so I could see for sure that it healed.

"Are you hurt?" Trey asked, letting me examine him as his eyes scanned my body.

"No," I sobbed.

"I'm ok, Bones." He pulled his arm free from my grip and sat up so he could wrap his arms around me. "I'm ok."

I clung to him, shaking. I could hear boots on the pavement, and I knew whoever had saved us was approaching, but I didn't look up. Trey was ok. He was ok. We were alive.

"Don't make any sudden moves," Trey whispered urgently in my ear.

I raised my head in alarm. A dozen armed people surrounded us, and while they weren't pointing guns *at* us, they also hadn't holstered their weapons. I scanned their faces, but I didn't recognize any of them. Their grim expressions made my stomach flip with anxiety but they *had* saved our lives.

"Thanks for the assist," Trey said carefully.

They just stared at us, and then a familiar voice rang out.

"Angel."

I twisted in panic, hoping I heard wrong, but the circle of armed men parted and Vulture stepped into view.

He looked the same, but somehow different at the same time. He'd always been wiry, but he seemed thinner than I remembered. His dark blond hair hung long, covering his ears, and his narrow face was still good-looking, but it had a harder edge to it now. His eyes looked almost *black.* They'd been blue before, hadn't they?

I stared at him, my heart pounding with fear. This wasn't possible. I had to be hallucinating. He couldn't be here, how the fuck was he *here?* Trey's arms had tightened around me, both of us silent and tense. Vulture stepped closer, crouching an arm's length away so he could peer into my eyes.

"Not expectin' to see me, were you?" Vulture drawled. "Guess you were probably expectin' me to be as dead as Juck, huh?"

I couldn't look past his dark eyes. I expected them to be full of fury and vengeance, but they were strangely empty. It wasn't reassuring though. It made my skin crawl.

"When I saw the bounty out on your head, I jumped at the chance to track you down," he said. He glanced at Trey and *there,* some emotion flashed through those dark eyes.

"Vulture—" I tried, my voice shaking, but he held up a hand, stopping me.

"Nah, I'm not interested in your lies, Angel."

"I'm sorry," I whispered anyway.

He stared at me for a few breaths. "Which part are you sorry for? For all the lies or for leavin' me to die?"

"All of it," I choked out.

It scared me so much more that he wasn't yelling. I'd seen him angry. He had a temper to rival mine, and I knew how to handle that. I didn't know what to do with this terrifying blank version of Vulture.

He stood. "So are you gonna come nicely or is this gonna be a fight?"

"Come where?" My voice shook.

He grinned, showing all his teeth. "Back to the Vault."

I gasped in fast and panicked breaths, trying to think straight. This couldn't be happening. Gods, I almost wished the wolves had killed us.

"Let's cooperate for now," Trey breathed into my ear, his lips concealed by my hair. "Try to relax their guard."

"I'll come nicely if you promise you and your men won't hurt him," I said, ignoring the frustrated noise Trey made.

Vulture's grin widened. "Deal."

"Bones," Trey growled, "the fuck are you doin'?"

I turned to look at him. "I love you," I whispered.

That muscle in his jaw ticked and desperate fury shone in his eyes. "I love you too."

I forced myself to pull away, to leave the safety and comfort of his arms, to stand and walk over to where Vulture waited. His men moved in, grabbing Trey, hauling him to his feet, and binding his hands behind his back. I stopped an arm's length away from Vulture, eying him. I'd not included my own safety in that deal on purpose, hoping he would seize on that technicality. I *expected* him to hurt me. I'd left him to bleed to death in the hot desert, but this was between me and Vulture, and I wanted to keep Trey out of it.

Vulture studied me with an unexpected intensity like he was looking for something. When he stepped forward, I tried hard not to flinch but didn't quite succeed, and he raised an eyebrow with a smirk. He slowly stroked a knuckle down my face.

"I missed you," he murmured.

My skin crawled, but then a sharp pain stung in my arm and I jumped. I looked down to see that with his free hand, he'd stabbed a syringe into my arm. The icy drug rushed through my blood, and I stumbled back a step, swinging my panicked gaze to Trey. It looked like he was fighting the men holding him and yelling, his furious and worried eyes on me. A deafening buzzing drowned out everything. I tried to get my lips to move, but the ground rushed up to meet me.

The ominous silence loomed over me.

My body floated in darkness, suspended in something not quite like water and not quite like air.

I waited, terrified, for that cold voice to speak. I didn't dare open my eyes.

The silence stretched on as I waited.

And waited.

And waited.

And waited.

I sat straight up with a gasp of panic.

"There she is." Vulture crouched in front of me in the snow, that empty smirk still on his face.

I stared at him blankly, still gasping in panicked breaths. He held another syringe, so he must have injected me with something to wake me up. I could feel it, the adrenaline surging through me, but my mind and body felt sluggish, still caught in the narc's web.

"Get her up," said a cold voice that I recognized with a rush of terror.

Vulture hauled me to my feet and shoved me forward. I stumbled a few steps, my legs and feet still numb, and glanced around disoriented. A huge crowd of people surrounded us, full of familiar faces. We were back at the Vault. How the fuck were we back at the Vault? My thoughts felt like they moved through thick, sticky honey.

The entire hold appeared to be here, held back by Madame's men with their guns drawn and ready. My eyes found Mac and the horror and fear on his face felt like a reflection of my own. Griz stood next to him looking panicked, an expression I'd never seen before on his face. Where were the others? They had to be—

"Bones."

I turned at Madame's sharp call and my heart stopped.

Madame stood about ten feet away from me and in front of her Trey knelt in the snow, his arms still bound behind him, his eyes fixed on me. In one smooth movement, Madame drew the pistol holstered at her waist and pressed it directly to the side of Trey's head.

You're gonna wanna pay attention, Bones," Madame said in that cold voice. "I want you to remember this the next time you think about runnin'."

"No!" I gasped in horror, lunging a step forward, only to halt when she flicked the safety off the gun.

I could hear people in the crowd also shouting and crying out, but I couldn't make out what they said through my panic.

"Please, Madame, I'll do anythin'—"

"Bones," Trey interrupted, his eyes never leaving mine, "let 'em in."

"Madame!" I couldn't even begin to process what Trey just said, and what it implied. This was all happening so fast—too fast—and I needed to *think*, but the heavy drugs clouded my mind. "Madame!" I tried to keep my voice calm, but it shook. "Please! Please wait! Please can't we just talk—"

"Bones, darlin'."

My gaze snapped back to Trey's face, and the love and regret and *acceptance* in his face made the panic roar even louder in my head.

"No!" I cried, terrified tears rolling down my face. "Trey! Please don't—"

"Darlin'," he interrupted, his voice rough with emotion, "I'll find you again in another lifetime. Maybe there we'll have more time." His voice cracked. "I love you."

"Trey, please!" Oh gods, I couldn't breathe. I couldn't breathe.

"How sweet." Madame's voice was ice-cold.

"Madame! Please!" I sobbed. "Just let me—"

"I love—"

She pulled the trigger.

෨

In one blink Trey was looking at and speaking to me and in the next his body jerked backward, slumping over. Half his skull was gone, blood and gore everywhere. Part of my brain couldn't accept what my eyes had seen. I couldn't understand how someone so full of life could be snuffed out just like that. The snow underneath him quickly turned red.

Vaguely I could hear the crowd yelling behind me. People sobbed. Madame spoke to them, her voice harsh, but I wasn't listening. I forced my body to move and fell to my knees beside Trey, trying to avoid looking at the gaping hole in the side of his head. His beautiful brown eyes stared blankly at the sky, but all the warmth that shone in them had gone out.

"Trey, please. Please, no." I repeated, my voice cracking, as I cradled his bloody face. I knew it was pointless, but I couldn't help trying to heal him. The warmth seemed to pour from my hands and then evaporate into the cold air instead of seeping into his skin. No life remained in him for me to heal. I couldn't bring him back. I'd never been able to bring back the dead, and the gods knew I'd tried.

Something in me broke, and I suddenly understood the woman who had screamed for her child after the Reapers tore them apart from each other. My own scream ripped out of me. I couldn't have controlled it if I tried. I screamed as the pain tore me apart, as all the beauty and hope Trey had coaxed to life inside of me shattered.

I managed to somewhat silence myself by folding in half and pressing my face against Trey's motionless chest. My hands fisted in his jacket. He still smelled like Trey, like home, even as the metallic tang of blood filled my senses. I heard Madame's men driving the restless, agitated crowd back. I could hear them shouting for a long time, a dull roar in the background. The cold snow seeped into my pants, freezing against my skin until I couldn't feel it anymore.

"Please don't. Don't leave me. Please." I sobbed into his chest. Why hadn't I told him I loved him from the first moment I knew? Why had I wasted so much time trying to push him away? We could have had more time, gods, I just wanted a little more time.

When a heavy hand clapped down on my shoulder, a feral part of me came loose.

I put my whole body and all my fury into the punch, landing a solid blow to the side of Vulture's face. He went down with a surprised expression. His men rushed me and I fought them, screaming and clawing and spitting like a wild animal until finally one of them raised a rifle and swung the butt of it hard at my head and then I knew nothing at all.

CHAPTER 26

I woke up with a manacle on my ankle, chained up inside the clinic like a damn dog. I sat up, my head aching.

"Well, look who's up."

I glanced over to see Vulture sitting in one of the chairs, watching me. He had a dark bruise under his eye. It matched the stabbing pain in my right hand from punching him. A brief flame of that feral rage flickered in my chest before it died under the crushing weight of grief.

"Me and my men are in charge of the clinic now," Vulture continued, his voice devoid of emotion. "So don't try anythin' stupid, Angel."

I laid back down on my mattress, turning my back to him. Every breath felt like agony, worse than when my lung had collapsed. I knew I wasn't physically hurt. I'd felt this same pain after Dune died, like a literal piece of my heart had been torn from my chest. There was no cure for this pain, nothing to be done to ease it.

I just wished it could kill me.

I watched the sunlight dim through the loft windows.

One of Vulture's men entered the clinic with dinner rations, setting mine near my mattress. I didn't move or acknowledge it. The rest of his men filed in as night fell, six in total counting Vulture. They weren't Reapers and they weren't from the Vault. They brought in chairs and drank and laughed and told crude jokes and played cards. I sensed them looking at me every so often, but no one spoke to me. Vulture stayed separate from his men, staring silently from the chair by the door.

Every time I closed my eyes, I saw the blood spray from the bullet going through Trey's skull.

Gods, I wished she'd shot me instead.

Why hadn't I *done* something? I should've fought, I should've thought faster, lied my ass off about knowing shit about the rebellion, *anything*.

"Bones, please let me in."

"I don't know how much time we have, but I do know I don't want to miss a single second of lovin' you."

"You don't have to be strong all the time. You can lean on me."

I stared ahead, tears streaming from my eyes. I let him in. I loved him. And I lost him.

A hand grabbed my shoulder and rolled me over. I stared through swollen eyes at Vulture glaring down at me. He could do whatever the fuck he wanted to me, and no one would stop him, but I couldn't find the energy to care.

"Eat your food," he snapped.

I jerked away from him, rolling back over.

"Angel!"

I waited for him to grab me again, but he didn't.

"You think I don't know what you're doin'?"

I didn't care.

"I'm watchin' you. Don't forget that."

I heard him walk back over to the door and sit where Trey used to sit. I would never be able to glance at that chair and see Trey brightening the whole room with that sunshine smile again.

The pain in my chest crushed my lungs. I understood why they called it heartbreak. My heart had fractured into tiny pieces and every single one of them hurt like hell. Worse than when Juck had branded me, worse than Brimstone snapping my arm, worse than when Sax ripped the skin off my back with that whip.

I squeezed my eyes shut.

"I love you, Bones."

The gunshot cracked like thunder and I screamed—

Someone grabbed my arm and shook me hard. I opened my eyes with a gasp to see the dark clinic, and for a brief second, I thought maybe *all* of it had been a nightmare, maybe Trey was about to—

"Shut up, Angel," Vulture's voice growled instead.

He loomed over me like a dark shadow. I rolled away, curled into a ball, and stuffed the blanket into my mouth to muffle my sobs. After a minute, I heard him walk back to the chair. I squeezed my eyes shut again.

"You're a river. You don't break, you bend."

Mac's comforting words rang hollow now. I couldn't find a way to bend this time because I didn't break, I shattered.

Someone yanked on the chain connected to my manacle, and I opened my eyes to see daylight streaming in the windows. I moved my head just enough to see Vulture standing at the foot of my mattress with a woman holding a bloodied rag to her head.

"Time to get to work," Vulture ordered.

I got up, washed my hands, and performed the necessary steps to stitch up the woman's head in a numb haze broken only by the sound of the chain clanking along behind me. The injured woman perched on the exam chair watching me with wide eyes. She looked familiar, and I knew if I thought about it, I'd remember her name, but I couldn't summon the energy or the desire to try. As I cleaned the wound, she made a soft sound that had me glancing down to her face out of habit. Her wide eyes glimmering with tears met mine.

"I'm so sorry, Bones," she whispered.

I kept working, trying to shove those kind words deep down where I couldn't think about them, but they festered like an infected splinter. She didn't try to speak to me again, but right before I finished, she managed to catch my hand, squeezing it for such a brief moment that I almost thought I imagined it. After she left, I numbly cleaned up my workspace until Vulture cleared his throat. I glanced over at where he stood near the door, leaning against the wall. He nodded toward my mattress where my breakfast ration sat on the floor.

I finished sterilizing my tools, washed my hands, and curled up on my mattress again without touching it.

Most people who came in to be healed were grave and quiet. Their eyes flickered between me and Vulture. Some of them murmured condolences that burned into my skin like the brand on my chest. I didn't respond to them, but they didn't seem upset by it. Madame's guards, on the other hand, came in grinning and laughing. I almost refused to heal the few who walked in with injuries, but that tiny lick of fire flickered out again before I could do anything with it. So I just did my job and ignored the cruel comments they threw at me. I knew they wanted to get a reaction, and I hadn't spent twelve years being taunted by the Reapers for nothing.

I refused my dinner ration again. Vulture glared at me, his dark eyes glittering, but he didn't say anything.

Twice a day Vulture let me off the chain to use the outhouse. I moved through the days like a dead person walking. Nothing seemed real. People continued to come in for healing, but I didn't see any of Mac's crew. I wasn't sure if they'd been forbidden to come or if they just couldn't stand to see me. If they hated me now, I couldn't blame them. Trey had been their family, and because of me, he was dead.

Every night I woke up screaming, Trey's bloody face etched on the back of my eyelids, and every night Vulture snarled at me to shut up, so I did. I kept waiting for him to do *something* to me, to get his revenge for my betrayal, but he didn't. Maybe Madame had told him not to touch me.

Vulture let me go almost four days without eating before he jerked me upright one evening. He leaned in from where he crouched beside my mattress. "You're not allowed to starve yourself to death, Angel." He snarled, dropping a plate in my lap. "You keep this up and I'll put a fucking tube down your throat and force-feed you."

I stared at the plate in my lap and made myself pick up some of the food and take a bite. I didn't taste it at all, chewing and swallowing out of habit. Vulture stayed where he crouched, watching me close enough that my skin began to crawl a little. We'd been something like friends once. When I first snuck into his tent and dropped to my knees in front of him, his eyes widened with surprise, but he hadn't hesitated.

He knew the means to power and control were a dangerous game, but his earlier words at the dam echoed through my head. *"Which part are you sorry for? For all the lies or for leavin' me to die?"*

I would never forget that moment of raw pain and betrayal in his eyes when I left him for dead. I'd hesitated at that moment, startled by his reaction, but even if he had meant *something* to me, I never loved him.

Not like I loved Trey.

Trey's dead, empty eyes flashed through my mind, and I dropped the rest of the food back onto the plate, feeling sick. No, anything I'd ever felt for Vulture was as dead as the man I loved. Maybe he didn't pull the trigger, but he killed Trey just as much as Madame did.

As much as you did. A small voice whispered in my head and bile rose in my throat.

I shoved the plate away from me, covering my mouth with my hand and breathing in through my nose like Sam had taught me. Vulture stared hard at me for a moment, but then he took it away and returned to his post by the door.

After that, I ate just enough to keep Vulture off my back. I slept most of the time even though blood and the gaping hole in the side of Trey's head filled my dreams. I woke up screaming more often than not, but being awake was worse than being asleep. At least when I slept, sometimes I didn't have nightmares. Being awake was one long, unending nightmare I knew I would never wake up from. So I stayed on my mattress, chasing that escape of nothingness. I got better at waking up with my jaw clenched tight so I didn't scream out loud. The people of the Vault who came in for healing kept whispering concerned questions, but I still didn't answer them. Maybe I couldn't. I rarely spoke at all and despite sleeping most of the time, the exhaustion never eased. I wondered where the kids had gone, but I didn't ask. They were probably dead too.

Six days after Trey's death, Lem showed up at the door and announced that Madame summoned me.

We went down the stairs to the dungeon torture room and stepped through the door to see Nemo sitting in the chair again. He looked thin, his pale face covered in dark bruises. Madame stood in front of him and gestured to him with her clean knife when I entered.

"Get him back to full health," Madame ordered like nothing had happened, like she hadn't put a gun to Trey's head and killed him.

I didn't move.

"Bones," Madame ordered.

"No." The word came out hoarse, but it came out.

The temperature of the room seemed to plummet. Everyone stared at me, Nemo included. I met his pained eyes for a second.

"What did you just say?" Madame asked, her voice dangerous.

"I said no," I said louder.

Madame stared hard at me for a moment before looking at her men. "Looks like Bones needs another reminder."

Lem stepped forward, grinning. His first blow knocked me flat on my back. I didn't even bother trying to get up. Lem hauled me up anyway so he could put a fist in my gut. I doubled over wheezing.

"You ready to heal him now, Bones?" Madame asked, her voice sharp as broken glass.

"No," I rasped out.

After the third time I refused, a part of me seemed to snap. I was on my hands and knees in the dirty hay, watching a string of blood drip from my mouth to the floor, when I started *laughing*. The entire room went still. I pushed myself up onto my knees, grinning around a mouthful of blood.

"Something funny, Bones?" Madame asked, her voice almost shrill.

"Fuck you," I said, still grinning like a maniac. "I'm not doing shit for you anymore." I pointed a finger at her, my hand steady despite the pain. "You better fuckin' pray you never get hurt or sick ever again, 'cause if you do, I'm watchin' you die."

Fury and maybe a little bit of fear flashed in her eyes, and she gave Sax a sharp order to take over from Lem. Sax looked unnerved as I knelt there grinning up at him with blood dribbling down my chin. Maybe it was his idea of mercy or maybe he just didn't like it when people weren't scared of him, but his first blow hit me hard in the temple and knocked me right out.

CHAPTER 27

E ight days after Trey's death, Griz walked into the clinic, his arm wrapped in a bloody bandage. When I looked up and saw his face, my stomach flipped with a brief nauseating mix of surprise, hope, desperation, and guilt. But his expression didn't change, staying blank and flat, and my emotions died as quickly as they'd come. Vulture didn't move to stop him, so Mac's crew must not have been forbidden from seeing me. They hadn't come *on purpose*.

I moved forward, the chain around my ankle clanking along behind me. I still sported a dark purple black eye, but the swelling had gone down enough for me to open it. More bruises ranging from purple to green in color were littered across my face and the rest of my body. I knew I looked rough since most people who walked in gasped out loud at the sight of me. I braced for Griz's reaction, but he just walked straight up to me and held his bandaged arm out without a word. I focused on that to avoid meeting his gaze. I reached for the bandage so I could unwrap it and see the wound, but his good hand snaked out and caught my wrist.

"Wait," he said, low.

I looked up at him, taken aback. His eyebrows creased and his eyes gleamed with pain, making worry burst in my head like a flare. I tried to reach for the bandage again, but his fingers tightened on my wrist, halting me for the second time.

"Bones, *wait,*" he growled.

I gave up and tried to pull my arm back, but he didn't let go of my wrist. My gaze shot back to his face, a familiar fear tightening in my gut. Griz shifted sideways so that his bulky body blocked Vulture's view.

"It's ok, Bones," he breathed as his thumb stroked my arm, "just hold on a sec."

Gunshots erupted outside, and screams filled the air. I jumped with a gasp, but Griz just spun, shoving me behind him and putting three bullets in Vulture before I even realized he had a gun in his hand. He turned and trained his gun up at the loft.

"Anyone up there?" he asked. "Bones, is anyone up there?" he repeated sharply when I didn't answer.

"No," I finally managed to answer from where I stood frozen, staring at Vulture sliding to the floor and leaving a large bloody streak on the wall behind him.

He stared back at me, gasping wetly. "Angel, he got...I'm not... please..." he choked out, his face lined in panic and pain.

If I ran forward, I could heal him and save his life, but for the second time, I just stood there staring at him as he bled out. Griz locked the door and then shoved the exam chair in front of it, propping it to make it harder to enter. Vulture's choked pleas trailed off. His blue eyes locked on me, swirling with a multitude of emotions. Griz finished blockading the door and moved back to where I stood. He knocked the metal exam table onto its side and got behind it, looking up at me.

"Bones, c'mere," he snapped.

Outside the screams and gunshots grew louder. I glanced at my mattress and strongly considered just lying down again. Griz swore and leapt up, grabbing my arm and yanking me down behind the table.

"I need you to focus. This is it. We're gonna stop Madame for good."

That should have made me feel something, but it didn't. "Are you actually hurt?" I rasped out, still eying the bandage.

"Nope," he said, eyes scanning my injured face. A muscle in his jaw flexed several times. "Just needed an excuse to get in here. Are you ok?"

I just stared at him, unable to muster the energy to tell him that was a stupid fucking question. Pain flashed across his face, but before he could say anything else, someone started trying to break the door down.

Griz shoved me down and I tried to make myself as small as

possible as he got up on his knees to aim over the table, waiting. Pieces of the door went flying over the table as they slammed into it. Griz fired off a shot and someone let out a strangled scream. Then bullets slammed into the table and the wall over our heads. The next few moments passed by in a blur of Griz popping up to fire shots and ducking down as bullets whistled around us. Judging by how often screams followed his shots, Griz was a pretty damn good marksman. Finally there seemed to be a pause and Griz dropped back down, breathing heavily, and flipped up his jacket. Underneath he had an insane amount of ammo strapped to his chest. I must have made some sort of noise because he peered at me as he reloaded.

"You didn't get hit, did you?" he asked.

I shook my head. He started to say something else, but then bullets peppered the wall behind us again. As soon as they stopped, Griz leapt up and returned fire. Outside I could hear gunshots and screams from what sounded like every direction now. This wasn't just a "little rebellion" as Madame had called it. This was an all-out war.

"Gods, they better hurry the fuck up before the clinic falls apart," Griz said the next time he dropped down to reload.

I eyed the wall behind us, noting the many holes and splintered wood. A tiny part of me flickered painfully to life at the sight of the clinic being torn apart, but then it died.

"Don't worry," Griz said with forced lightness, "we'll fix it."

The floor creaked and Griz twisted to peer over the table. I jumped as he leapt to his feet and fired off a round of shots at the two men who had crept through the broken door. His body jerked, blood spraying, as bullets went through the right side of his abdomen and upper thigh, but he only took a single step backward, continuing to fire. I heard bodies thud to the floor, and Griz dropped back down, pressing a hand to his bloody side with a grimace.

"Don't suppose—" he gasped out.

I was already scrambling over to him in a panic, pressing my shaking hands to his side, and trying to heal him as quickly as possible. Trey's bloody face and empty eyes kept flashing through my head. Griz covered my hands with one of his large ones and squeezed.

"It's alright, Bones," he said, his voice so gentle it made my eyes burn. "You got this. I'm gonna be fine."

Someone yelled outside, and then bullets slammed into the other side of the clinic. I flinched, trying to focus on healing. Griz kept his hand over mine the entire time, and finally, the wound in his side and the wound in his leg both closed. Outside someone started screaming a horrible devastated scream, but then a gunshot echoed and the sound cut off. I swallowed, wrapping my trembling hands around my body again as my panic over Griz's injuries faded away to that empty nothingness again.

Somewhere in the distance some sort of automatic weapon started firing and the windows in the loft rattled.

"That'd be the machine gun in the watchtower," Griz said grimly. "Let's hope the rebels got to it first."

Gods, how many people were dead? Or injured? And here I was with the power to save them, just hiding in the clinic like a fucking coward. I *was* a fucking coward. I'd always been too afraid to act, too afraid to risk my own survival, and I couldn't live with that anymore.

I stood and Griz grabbed my arm, yanking me back down.

"What the fuck are you doing?" he growled.

"There's probably hurt people out there," I said. "I'm not just gonna sit in here and hide."

He glared at me. "You serious?"

"You don't have to come."

"For fucks sake, Bones," he gave me an incredulous look. "There's no way in fuck I'd let you go out there alone."

I stood again, feeling so strangely detached and calm. "Then let's go."

"You still have a fucking manacle—"

I crossed the clinic quickly, the chain clanking behind me, to where Vulture's dead body slumped against the wall. I tried not to notice how many dead bodies littered the floor. To my relief, Vulture's eyes had closed, and I didn't hesitate before crouching and fishing through his shirt pocket where I knew he kept the key. Griz arrived at my side a second later, gun held ready and swearing under his breath. My fingers closed around the cold metal and I pulled the key out, bending to unlock the manacle on my ankle.

"You need any tools?" Griz asked.

"No," I answered, shoving my boots on and standing. I wasn't gonna deal with tourniquets and stitches and shit right now. I'd just use my powers. I was at least good for one thing—healing people—and that's what I would do.

"Don't burn out," Griz warned, but I pretended not to hear him.

ॐ

We stepped out into a grim scene. Bloody bodies lay collapsed in the snow, limbs contorted grotesquely. I didn't have to go far to find one still alive. A young teenage boy I didn't recognize had dragged his body halfway behind a barrel. He had his bloody hands pressed against the gunshot wound in his chest. His eyes widened in terror when he noticed us, but he didn't say a word. I crouched beside him, but Griz grabbed my shoulder.

"He's one of Madame's," he said in a low voice.

I stared at the boy, and he stared back at me, his nostrils flaring as he struggled to breathe. I could *feel* death creeping closer, like an icy breath on the back of my neck.

"Take his weapons then," I said to Griz as I leaned forward and pried his hands away from the wound, replacing them with my own.

The boy started crying as my healing powers flowed into him, mending his body back together. Griz didn't try to stop me, he just disarmed the boy of his gun and several knives.

"It's ok," I hoped I sounded comforting. "You're gonna be ok."

"I'm sorry," he sobbed, thin shoulders shaking.

"It's ok," I murmured, watching the wound close. "Go home, alright?"

He nodded. As soon as the wound healed, I helped him up, grabbing him as he swayed. He glanced between me and Griz and swallowed hard, his throat bobbing.

"I was just followin' orders," he whispered.

As he stumbled away, Griz murmured, "I shot him. He was trying to get into the clinic."

Gods, what was wrong with me? I felt *nothing*.

I didn't respond, turning and picking a direction at random. We'd only made it about half a dozen steps when a gunshot sounded from behind us and a bullet whizzed past my ear, so close the heat of it brushed my skin. Griz tackled me to the ground, shielding me with his body as more bullets flew around us. He twisted as we fell and returned fire. A strangled cry rang out, then silence. Griz leapt off me and darted over to a fallen body, checking for a pulse. I dragged myself to my feet and followed him, staring down at the dead eyes of the boy I'd *just* healed.

"Bones!" Griz snapped, standing back up and scanning me. "Are you ok?"

"He missed," I mumbled.

"He must've grabbed another gun from one of the bodies." Griz's eyes flashed with anger.

I turned and started moving again. I knew I should feel angry or betrayed that the boy I'd just risked to save had still tried to kill me, but all I felt was tired. Griz walked behind me, almost on top of me he hovered so close.

"I'm sorry, Bones."

I picked up my pace a little, hoping he'd get the point that I didn't want to talk, but he kept up with me.

"You're a good person for givin' him a second chance."

You'd think I would've learned by now that good people just ended up dead.

"It's what Trey would've done."

A sharp pain cut through the numbness, and I whirled on him. "Don't."

He stared down at me, his face grave. "He wouldn't want—"

Thank the gods we both heard the sound of pained sobs at the same time. I took off, following the sound and trying to convince myself I wasn't running away from whatever Griz had been about to say. I slipped between buildings and spotted a man lying on the ground, clutching his leg. It looked like someone had shot his kneecap out. He twisted to look as we approached, and I stopped in my tracks when I recognized Lem. Behind me, Griz halted as well.

"Bones," Lem said, his voice shaky, "help me. Please."

I stared at him, and the bruises he'd put on my face seemed to pulse with pain.

"Bones, please," he pleaded.

He'd smiled the entire time he beat me. I knew his type well, men who enjoyed hurting anyone smaller or weaker than them. I didn't know the details of what he'd done to Sky, but it had left her terrified of most men. Despite all that, I still felt nothing. After a moment, I just turned around and walked back the way I'd come.

"Bones!" Lem shouted. "Please! I'm sorry!"

"You want me to take care of him?" Griz asked in a low voice as I passed him.

"I don't care."

"Bones!" Lem screamed. "I'm sorry! Please! No, don't—"

I flinched at the gunshot, but I didn't stop.

ᏋᏋ

I kept going and all the faces blurred together. I healed everyone I found unless I recognized one of Madame's guards who delighted in afflicting hurt. Most of the fighting seemed to be around the watchtower now. The sound of the machine gun rattled inside my rib cage. I didn't know who the rebels were, so I couldn't tell which side had the most dead bodies littering the ground.

I wasn't aiming for the watchtower, but as I followed the bodies, we got closer and closer. I froze when bullets peppered the ground around me. One grazed my arm before Griz grabbed me and dragged me between the buildings. As he peered around the edge, returning fire, I inspected the shallow wound. I used my teeth to tear a strip off my shirt, wrapping it around the wound and called that good. As the gunfire continued, I leaned against the side of the building and closed my eyes. Exhaustion swept through me, but I wasn't at burnout. Not yet.

"Bones?"

I opened my eyes to see Griz moving toward me. He took my arm, examining my sloppy bandage job. He looked worried.

"Your arm ok?"

"It's fine. Shallow."

He frowned. "You at burnout?"

I shook my head, pushing myself off the wall and ignoring the sharp look he gave me. I thought he might argue, but all he said was, "You stay behind me."

We crept through the hold, heading toward the market. None of these bodies still breathed. I tried not to notice their faces, but I recognized people, people I'd healed, people whose names I knew. As we entered the market, a slight sound from one of the booths caught our attention. I moved forward, but Griz grabbed my arm and pulled me back behind him. I followed as he approached the booth, gun raised. He stepped inside, and a strangled cry rang out. Griz lowered his gun, eyes widening.

"Jax!" He dropped down out of my sight, and I darted into the booth after him.

Griz knelt beside Jax who sat propped up on the side of the booth. His shoulder oozed blood and based on the amount covering his shirt and the floor, it'd been bleeding for a while.

"Don't scare me like that," Jax mumbled. "Almost shot you."

I glanced at his hand lying in the dirt and gripping a pistol.

"Sorry, kid," Griz said, peeling his torn shirt back to get a look at the wound. "Looks like the bullet's still in there."

I crouched, nudging Griz out of the way.

"Bones?" Jax's eyes widened as he scanned me. "Your face—"

"It's fine," I interrupted, placing my hands over the wound on his shoulder and trying to ignore how much he looked like Dune.

"Where's Mac?" Griz asked.

"Watchtower," Jax rasped. "Madame's holed up in her office."

Thank the gods the bullet hadn't come out. It probably saved his life, preventing him from bleeding out. My healing power warmed my cold hands as I watched the bullet push its way out of Jax's skin until it dropped into the dirt. A couple of seconds later only a pink scar remained.

"That's so fuckin' weird," Griz breathed, and I glanced at him to see awe on his face. He'd seen me heal a lot of wounds, but seeing a bullet come out by itself *was* something else to behold.

I sat back on my heels, tucking my icy shaking hands between my thighs. Jax touched the new scar on his shoulder with just the tips of his fingers, his eyes even wider.

"You ok to walk?" Griz asked him.

"I think so," he said, giving me a hesitant smile. "Thanks, Bones."

The machine gun started going off again, making all of us jump.

"That's Raven," Jax said, grunting as Griz helped him to his feet.

I wearily pulled myself up too, trying to ignore how everything spun.

"You getting close to burnout?" Griz asked, and I glanced at him to see his sharp eyes studying me.

"I'm fine," I said.

Griz frowned, looking hurt. "We really goin' back to that shit again?"

I didn't have time for this. "Let's go," I muttered, moving to push past him, but he caught my arm in a tight grip.

He studied my battered face. His brown eyes were so different from Trey's eyes. While Trey's eyes had been so full of warmth and sunshine, Griz's eyes were cool like pebbles in a mountain stream. I didn't know what he was looking for, so I waited, staring back at him. After a few seconds, he sighed and pulled me back so he could walk first.

"Stay behind me."

I nodded and he released my arm, stepping out of the booth to lead the way. Jax followed behind him, leaving me to bring up the rear. As we left the market, the number of dead bodies increased. These looked like they'd been ripped apart, littered with bullet holes from the machine gun. The carnage and the smell of blood made me want to gag, despite all my experience.

One of the bodies let out a wet-sounding noise, and I quickly followed the sound to find an older woman gasping her last breaths. She had a huge fucking hole in her abdomen. I crouched beside her, then hesitated and glanced up at Griz.

"I don't know," he answered my unspoken question of which side she fought for.

I looked back down at her. She had precious seconds left. I wasn't even sure if she could see me. Her eyes stared at the sky, unfocused and taking on that glossy sheen of death as she wheezed.

It's what Trey would've done.

I laid my hands on the gaping wound and let my power flow as quickly as I dared. It took a long time to close the wound, draining me of energy and power as I very narrowly saved her life. When I finished, I pulled my trembling hands back, swiping my bleeding nose with my filthy sleeve.

"Bones?"

I met the woman's eyes, now clear and focused.

"You healed me."

"Yes."

"Don't waste it," Griz growled at her, bending to take my elbow and help me up.

The woman swallowed hard, her eyes glimmering with tears. "Thank you."

I tried to take a step away and swayed. Griz's hand tightened on my elbow.

"Jax, cover us," he said, jerking his head toward the woman.

Jax raised his pistol, keeping the woman in his sights as we moved up to the watchtower. Griz didn't let go of my arm, and I didn't argue. My legs wobbled like a newborn calf.

"How many more?" Griz asked once we managed to get up alongside the watchtower.

"What?" I asked, trying to catch my breath.

"How many more can you heal? And don't give me that 'I'm fine' bullshit."

I leaned against the cool stone wall. "One. Maybe two."

He nodded. "That's what I guessed. Kid, can you—"

Bullets slammed into the tower around us. Before I could react, Griz darted in front of me, taking the bullet meant for me. I tried to hold him up as he began to fall, but a sharp pain in my leg made me stumble, bringing both of us down. On the other side of Griz, Jax let out a horrible gurgling cry.

The machine gun roared to life in the tower, deafening me as bullets sprayed into the alley where the shots came from, tearing through everything in their path. I clapped my hands to my ears as I frantically scanned Griz. He clutched his abdomen, blood oozing, his nostrils flaring in pain. On the other side of him, Jax held his neck, choking as blood spurted between his fingers. Panic seized control of my lungs. Both wounds would kill them in a matter of minutes.

I moved without thinking, grabbing Jax and yanking him down beside Griz.

"Jax first," Griz groaned, but I ignored him.

I put one hand on Jax's neck and the other on Griz's stomach. I'd never tried to heal two people at the same time before, but I didn't have time to second-guess myself. My healing power flowed differently, thinner, as I directed it into both of them. It hurt—a dull ache that grew sharper as I continued. Blood started trickling over my lips from my nose again.

"Bones!" Griz tried to pull away.

"Griz, don't move!" I snapped at him, then out of desperation added, "Please!"

Thank the gods he listened. The bullet wound in his stomach began to close, but slowly. The wound in Jax's neck did the same, but as I looked at his blue lips, I had another surge of panic. It wasn't fast enough. He would run out of air before I could finish healing him, but I couldn't stop healing Griz to focus on Jax because Griz would die in the time it took for me to heal Jax.

I clenched my jaw, determination flooding through me. I would *not* choose one to sacrifice. I could do this. I would do this. And if it killed me, so be it.

"You gotta start trying to save yourself too."

I pushed Trey's soft voice somewhere far, far away where I couldn't hear it anymore, but it did nothing to stop the tears welling up in my eyes.

I closed my eyes, focusing on the healing power inside of me, and instead of just letting it flow, I *pulled*. It fucking hurt, but I just yanked up handful after handful of that power, forcing it to flow faster. I heard Griz gasp a curse and I opened my eyes to see nothing but blinding golden light like the sun had fallen to earth in front of us. I couldn't see Griz or Jax, but I could still feel them under my hands. I could still sense their injuries healing, their bodies knitting themselves back together faster. Tears of pain rolled down my face, but I didn't stop until I reached for more and grasped nothing but wisps of smoke.

It had to be enough because I couldn't live in a world where I failed to save another person I loved.

I stopped pulling, and the pain vanished, but an icy cold rushed in to take its place. My body seized.

I remembered Trey saying my healing power felt like sunshine. I remembered the warm honey of his eyes in the light of my golden skin. I remembered him touching me gently, murmuring that I was beautiful. I heard shouting, but as the golden light began to fade, darkness roared up and swallowed me whole.

CHAPTER 28

I stared blankly at the clinic ceiling.

I lay on my bed as soft morning light streamed in the windows. I couldn't remember how I got here. Did Trey—

Pain lanced through my chest and I sucked in a sharp breath through my teeth. Immediately a familiar face appeared above mine.

"Bones?" Griz asked with a strange desperation. "Hey, how you feelin'?"

I remembered Griz bleeding. In a panic, I struggled to sit up, my eyes dropping down to his stomach. He reached out and gripped my shoulder, halting me.

"I'm ok," he said. "Jax is ok too. You healed us both."

I let out a shaky breath and relaxed back down onto the mattress, the panic fading.

"When you're feelin' better I'm gonna yell at you for scarin' the shit out of me." Griz's large hand released my shoulder and took my limp one. "You've been unconscious for almost four days."

He waited for a reaction, but I had none.

"Madame is behind bars," Griz added.

That should have made me feel *something,* but it didn't.

"We got all the kids into homes after you left. They're all safe."

I was sinking underwater and drowning on dry ground. I'd been called heartless before but now it was true. A giant hole gaped in my chest where my heart used to be.

"Things are gonna be different now." He squeezed my hand. "Nemo's in charge. He's makin' changes, big changes. We're gonna make this place better." He paused, his voice growing gruffer with emotion. "We're gonna make it what Trey wanted it to be."

That awful pain shot through my chest again, and I had to focus on breathing in and out. The silence stretched on, waiting, but I had nothing left to give.

"Bones," Griz said soft and pained, "please talk to me."

About what? I wanted to ask but the words sat in my chest heavy like rocks.

"I miss him too."

The emotion in his voice made my throat ache, but I just closed my eyes.

❧

I must've drifted off because I woke with a gasp, struggling to keep my scream locked in my throat.

"Hey, you ok?"

I blinked away Trey's bloody face, trying to get my bearings. I was sitting straight up in my bed and beside me, Mac sat in the chair staring at me with wide, alarmed eyes.

"Bones?"

"I'm fine," I said, my voice hoarse.

I pulled the blankets off and scooted my way to the edge of the bed. Mac stood, getting out of the way.

"Careful," he warned, "you had a fever for a long time, and you've got a bullet wound in your leg."

I didn't remember getting hit, but as I stood, my legs trembling, a sharp ache came to life in my left calf. I started limping toward the door.

"You need the outhouse?" Mac asked, and I realized he was walking with me, hovering close.

I nodded.

"Can I help you walk?" he added, an edge to his voice.

"I can do it," I muttered.

While I sat in the outhouse, I pulled up the skirt I wore to see my leg. It had been cleaned and bandaged, and I wondered who did it, now that Trey—

I sucked in a sharp breath and forced myself to shove the memory of his bloodied face and empty eyes back down.

When I came out, a small crowd of people stood in front of the clinic. Mac took my arm without asking if I needed help, and I didn't argue about it. As we approached, the crowd shifted, revealing Nemo. He leaned heavily on a cane, his face pale, but he smiled at the sight of me.

"Good to see you up, Bones. I'm sure you heard I'm taking over, but I just wanted to make sure you knew you're an important part of the hold and your place here is solid."

I didn't say anything. Did he think he needed to remind me that I belonged to the Vault? Clearly, I knew. I'd learned my place. An awkward silence fell, but finally, Nemo said something about letting me rest and left. The crowd of people followed him, and I watched them leave. Mac still had my arm tucked in his.

"Bones?" Mac asked.

I flicked my eyes up to him. I couldn't find the energy to do much else. His brow furrowed as he studied me.

"Are you hurt?" he asked.

I shook my head.

"Are you sure?" he pushed. "I mean besides your leg."

I shook my head again and looked away. I hurt inside and out, but he couldn't do a thing about it. We stood there for a while, and my mind wandered away again.

"Bones, you can talk to me. Nobody expects you to be ok right now." Mac finally said in a low, urgent voice.

I wasn't ok, and I wasn't trying to pretend anything different. I was just *empty*. I didn't understand what they wanted from me.

"You want to go see some of the kids?"

I shook my head.

"Did Griz tell you that you healed fifteen people at once with that burst of power?"

Fifteen people, but not Trey. Not Dune.

The silence stretched as we stood there, watching people move about the hold. The bodies had been removed and people moved about cleaning up debris and patching the damaged buildings. The clinic had already been put back together, and the wooden building resembled Trey's quilt with its many patches of different colored wood and materials.

"I loved him too," Mac's voice sounded low and rough. "I miss him every damn day."

Unshed tears ached in my throat.

"We buried him," he added, releasing my arm to gently wrap my cold hand in his. "Took a long time to get through the ground 'cause it's still a little frozen, but I can take you to his grave whenever you're ready. If you want."

His grave.

I pulled my hand free. When I turned and limped back inside the clinic, he let me go.

The next day I sent Griz on a fake errand and went straight to the watchtower. None of Nemo's men questioned me when I said I'd been sent to see Madame. One of the guards, a big burly man named Smith, took me down to the cells.

"Never got to properly thank you for healing my family from the sickness," he said as we walked. "Thank you."

I mumbled a response, hoping he wouldn't keep talking. He seemed to pick up on that and stayed quiet until we reached the cells. Madame sat against the wall, her cold eyes glinting with anger. Her grey dreads were covered in blood, her face bruised, and her lip split open. Someone had wrapped a bloody bandage around her upper thigh.

Smith unlocked the door and let me in, locking it behind me. "Just holler when you're done," he said.

I stood just inside the door, listening to Smith's footsteps fade away.

"Come to heal me?" Madame sneered. "Of course, Nemo *would* send you. He was always soft."

I stared down at her, feeling so damn hollow. I remembered Trey saying that when Madame's lover died it broke something in her, and I wondered if the same thing had happened to me. I sure as hell felt broken. I moved forward and knelt at her side, looking directly into her icy blue eyes. Desperation lurked behind her glare, like an animal caught in a trap. I could still smell that sugary scent that always surrounded her, partially hidden under sweat, dirt, and blood.

I leaned forward, resting one of my hands on her shoulder. "Nemo didn't send me."

Madame's eyes narrowed. "Then what—"

I brought my other hand up and slashed the knife Trey had given me into her throat.

Everything slowed, just like it had when I'd stabbed that knife into Juck's chest. My mind seemed to go somewhere else as the sharp little knife cut deep. Dark red blood began to run down her neck.

Jugular. My brain supplied.

I kept going, pressing harder as she tried to jerk away, her head thudding into the wall. She let out a horrible gasping noise.

Trachea.

Warm bright red blood sprayed with such force I felt it hit my face. I didn't even flinch.

Carotid.

I pulled the knife free. Her eyes widened in panic and fear as she began to suffocate on the blood pouring into her airway, but I just knelt there and watched her die like I'd promised. Her wide eyes stayed locked on mine until they glazed over and her body slumped to the side. Madame was dead.

I wasn't sure if her death made me feel any better, but it sure as hell wasn't gonna make me feel any worse.

I turned and sat against the wall next to her body, tilting my head back to lean against the cool stones. I tried not to think about anything at all, but I just kept hearing Trey's last words. *I love you, Bones.* When the guards came back to check on me, all hell broke loose.

A flurry of noise and activity exploded. They hauled me to my feet and wrestled my knife from my clenched fist. The others knelt beside Madame's body, examining her. They stared up at me wide-eyed when they saw the bloody slash in her throat.

"Did you do this?" the one feeling for a pulse on Madame's bloody neck asked.

I didn't answer.

"Bones, did you do this?" Smith demanded, but I stayed silent.

"She's dead," the one on the floor announced like it wasn't fucking obvious.

"Somebody get Nemo!"

"Did you kill Madame?"

"What happened?"

The questions blurred into noise.

"Bones?"

I looked up to see Nemo staring at me, his brow furrowed. He looked between me and Madame's body and then up at Smith.

"Sorry, sir, we just weren't sure what to do with her," Smith said.

Nemo studied me a moment longer before gesturing at me to follow him. "Come on, Bones. Let's go upstairs."

"Do you want me to—" Smith produced a pair of handcuffs.

"No, that won't be necessary, but fetch Mac, will you?"

I followed Nemo up the stairs, pretending not to notice the concerned glances I received. The remains of Madame's office door leaned against the wall, peppered with bullet holes, and hacked to pieces. Inside Madame's office still looked the same, except for a box on the bloodstained floor full of papers.

"Sorry, I was just startin' to clean things out in here," Nemo said.

I stood numbly in the middle of the room. He took a seat behind the desk and motioned toward the other chair. I hesitated a moment longer, but then I sat. He leaned back in his chair, steepling his fingers together and studying me.

"I gotta say, that was unexpected."

I waited.

"You're not in trouble, Bones," he said. "We were gonna have a public execution. Not my choice, but that was what the majority voted. Some folks might be disappointed, but I don't think anybody is gonna blame you for what you did."

I stared at my hands covered in dried streaks of Madame's blood.

"I certainly don't."

I glanced up at him, and he offered me a half smile.

"I'd like to talk to you more about all of this later, but I don't think now is the right time."

As if on cue, running footsteps grew louder, and then Mac burst through the open doorway, looking uncharacteristically panicked. His eyes sought me out first, scanning me before turning toward Nemo.

"It's alright, Mac," Nemo said. "Could you take Bones back to the clinic?"

Mac stared at him, breathing hard like he'd run all the way here. "That's it?"

"That's it," Nemo replied.

Mac grabbed my arm, pulling me to my feet and propelling me out the door like he feared Nemo might change his mind. Once we were outside, he glanced down at me, his grey eyes sparking.

"Why the fuck would you go and do something so reckless?" he snarled at me.

I didn't bother answering. He swore under his breath and marched me back to the clinic. When he towed me inside, we found Griz and Raven waiting.

"Did you really just kill Madame?" Raven asked, her entire face alight with surprise and something like pride.

"Raven," Griz warned.

"She did," Mac answered for me, his voice still tight with anger.

"Damn." Raven actually grinned. "Good."

"Raven," Mac snapped at her as he tugged me over to the sink.

I looked in the mirror to see blood smeared across my cheek.

"You should clean yourself up," Mac muttered.

I glanced at his reflection in the mirror and caught his dark eyes watching me, anger still tight in the lines of his jaw.

I turned the water on, washing my hands and my face as he turned away to reply to Griz and Raven's questions with short one or two word answers. My sunken eyes stared back at me in the mirror, dull and empty. Someone came in with a sprained wrist, giving me something to do, but none of Mac's crew left. They spent the rest of the day casually hanging around the clinic and trying to pretend they weren't watching me like they feared I would snap and kill someone else.

If I had the energy, I would have reassured them that I was done. That was it, the whole of my plan for vengeance.

Now there was just nothing.

CHAPTER 29

L ife continued as normal after I killed Madame. No one even really spoke to me about it. A few people muttered to themselves when I walked past and even more stared at me with a new wariness, but nothing more. It was so anticlimactic that sometimes I wondered if I'd actually done it or if it'd all been a dream. I'd been prepared to be locked up for murder, and to have nothing happen made what I'd done feel less like vengeance and more like just fresh, pointless blood on my hands.

Apple showed up the very next day. When I turned to see her step through the door, I froze. For a long moment, we just stood there, staring at each other. She deserved so many explanations and apologies, but none of them made it past my lips. Finally, she walked toward me and wrapped her arms around my legs. My eyes burned and my hand dropped to rest on her blonde head. After a minute, she let go and went straight to the sink and washed her hands like I'd taught her. Numbly I went back to what I'd been doing, moving around the clinic like a silent ghost as I worked, but she didn't seem to mind. She just hovered near me the entire day, quiet and watching, helping with small tasks and bringing me a glass of water every so often.

She watches you. Everything you do. You're teaching her what to think about herself by how you think about you. Trey's words stabbed through my head.

I'd planned on being a better person for Apple and all the kids, but mostly I wanted to be better for Trey. What was the fucking point? Why try to be a good person when all the best people I knew just ended up dead?

"I don't think anythin' bad can come from being a good person."

I should've known that was bullshit.

I'd been afraid, terrified, that this would happen, but I hadn't realized until now that I'd also been in denial that it *could* happen. Trey had just seemed so different, like he was somehow exempt from the awful reality I'd seen, like he couldn't end up dead like everyone else because he was so full of life. There couldn't be a time *after* Trey just like there couldn't be a time *after* the sun.

Yet here I found myself, lost in that after with no idea how to keep going.

I looked up from my miserable thoughts to see Apple talking happily to Griz as she leaned against the wall, one foot up and resting on the wall behind her just like how Trey used to stand, and it struck me like a fucking bullet. The glasses of water, the company, the help, they were all her attempts to fill Trey's shoes for me.

My lungs stopped working. I dropped the bandage I'd been wrapping around a young man's arm and darted toward the door.

"Bones?" Griz's voice sharpened with alarm as he caught up to me by the door.

"Can you finish?" I managed to gasp, gesturing to the patient who stared wide-eyed at me, before fleeing outside.

My feet took me to the stables. Violet nickered at me when I slipped inside her stall. I stroked her, trying to get myself under control, but I lost that battle. I sank into the straw, my arms wrapped around myself as I sobbed. Violet sniffed my hair and nudged me with her nose. When I didn't respond, she stood beside me like a silent sentry as the pain swallowed me whole.

By the time I managed to get control over myself, the sun had set. I pulled my hood over my head and shoved my hands in my pockets, hoping nobody would notice me as I trudged back to the clinic. When I pushed the door open, I froze on the threshold.

Sam stood in the middle of the room.

I hadn't seen him since before Trey and I had left. He looked like a shadow of his former self, thin, still too pale, and *pissed*.

"Where the fuck have you been?" he snapped, striding toward me.

A sliver of guilt trickled in through the numbness. "I'm—"

He pulled me forward into a hug, interrupting me. I could feel his heart pounding in his thin chest.

"You scared me," he said, his voice rough. "Gods, I'm so sorry. I shoulda been here sooner. I just had a bad spell the last few days. Got laid up with a damn cold like an old man."

My arms had instinctively wrapped around him, but he felt like a different person. I could feel all his ribs beneath my fingers, the muscle mass he'd been so vain about had vanished. He felt *fragile*. I almost asked him why he hadn't come to the clinic, but then I remembered I couldn't heal him.

"It's ok," I mumbled.

"Everybody's out lookin' for you." He pulled back, studying my face. "Griz said you freaked out in the middle of bandaging someone."

His scrutiny made me feel far too exposed. "I'm fine," I said, pulling away and making my way to the sink under the pretense of washing my hands. "Sorry I scared you."

The silence thickened, making me afraid to turn around. When I did, he stood by the exam table, his arms crossed, and eyes narrowed.

"So we're back to that bullshit," he bit out. "I didn't believe Griz when he told me."

"Sam—" I tried, but he interrupted.

"I'll go tell everyone you're back." He made his way to the door but paused for a moment. "I missed you, Shortcake," he said quietly before he stepped out the door.

The days slid by, thick and slippery as mud. Nemo *was* a better leader than Madame. He exiled any remaining assholes who liked the way Madame ran things. He opened the canteen up to everyone, regardless of whether they worked or not, but improving housing for everyone remained his top project. With about half the hold dead or gone, there wasn't a housing shortage anymore, so he started moving the rusters out of the slums and into the empty houses.

A few of Madame's top people were unaccounted for, including Sax and Zana. After a few days of combing through the hold, the general consensus was that they had fled during the fight.

Griz and Sam took over guard duties again. Raven came almost every day and bossed Sky and Apple around, but her eyes looked as hollow as mine. Jax still didn't say much around me, but he came by the clinic every day and did odd jobs for me like chopping firewood or wrapping rolls of bandages. Mac worked closely with Nemo, but he made an effort to come by the clinic almost every day. I didn't say much to any of them. I wasn't trying to shut them all out, I was just so damn *tired*. I had to use every ounce of my energy just to get through every day.

They were all more subdued too, but every once and a while they'd get into a stupid argument, and for a second things almost felt normal. In those moments, I found myself looking for Trey, expecting to see him teasing Griz, wrestling Sam, or throwing his arm around Jax. A thousand tiny moments of realizing he was *gone* hadn't done a damn thing to dull the pain.

ॐ

The first time Mac showed up and announced that Nemo had summoned me, anxiety spiked so sharply through the numbness that I had to dart outside the clinic to be sick.

"You ok?" Mac asked, following me outside.

I stayed leaning over, my hands resting on my knees, and tried to convince myself I wasn't about to hurl again.

"Bones?" Mac hovered at my side, sounding worried.

I sucked in another desperate breath through my nose. What would I do if Nemo wanted me to help him torture someone?

"Hey," Mac crouched in front of me so he could look up at my face, "are you sick? I can tell Nemo you can't make it tonight."

"I'm fine," I whispered.

His eyes narrowed into a glare. "Bones."

I forced myself to straighten, smoothing the front of my shirt with trembling fingers. "Are we...are we going to the dungeon?"

He stood with me, and his brow furrowed in confusion for a second before realization dawned on his face. "Oh shit. No. He wants to talk at his place. He's not usin' the dungeon."

"Ever?"

His face darkened, and he stepped into my space to grasp my

shoulders. "Bones, you never have to help torture people ever again." His voice was firm. "And if anybody tries, they'll have to answer to me."

I shuddered, and he squeezed my shoulders gently.

"I'm sorry," he murmured. "I shoulda realized what that sounded like."

I stepped backward and his hands fell back to his sides.

"You ready?" he asked after I didn't say anything.

I nodded, but my anxiety followed me the entire way to Nemo's house. Nemo lived in one of the nicer homes built close to the tower. I'd been there once before to heal Nemo during the sickness, but it looked completely different. Some of the walls had been removed, opening up the room. People stood around tables, pouring over maps, talking about crops, and discussing the best material to use for new roofs.

"Nemo's turning his house into his headquarters. Less intimidatin' than the watchtower," Mac explained quietly.

We went up to the second floor and Mac rapped on one of the doors in the long hallway, entering when Nemo beckoned us inside. Nemo sat behind a desk. He looked up and smiled, and I studied him out of habit. His face had filled out a little and his color was back. Shame cut through me as I realized he never came for healing after his imprisonment. I couldn't blame him if he didn't want anything to do with my healing powers anymore.

"Howdy, Bones, Mac," he said, gesturing at the chairs in front of his desk. "Please, both of you, take a seat." He eyed me as I sat, making me uncomfortable. "How are you doing, Bones?"

"I'm fine," I said, ignoring the annoyed huff Mac gave next to me.

"I'm not gonna beat around the bush. I'm sorry for what Madame did to you." He leaned forward on the desk, his gaze earnest. "I know that might not seem like much, but I am terribly sorry for all of it. We've been working on taking over for a long time, but I hate that so many innocent people got hurt before we could stop her."

I fidgeted with my hands under the table, unsure of what to say.

"I wanted to let you in on what's been going on. This uprising has been brewing for years, but Madame took out the initial wave so brutally that people were scared." Nemo glanced at Mac, and I realized he was talking about Mac's dad. "She wanted to intimidate the people, and it worked. The hold offered them security, and they were terrified of losing that. It took a long time to rebuild the resistance, and as you know all too well, Madame got wind of it somehow."

I swallowed hard, unsure if I should apologize to him for helping Madame torture him. "I'm sorry—"

He held up a hand, stopping me. "You don't need to apologize. I know you didn't have a choice."

I did though. I'd just made it far too late.

"You've been an important figure in the resistance, Bones."

I had to fight to keep my expression even, nausea swirling in my stomach.

"You won the people over. You didn't hesitate to heal the rusters after that fire. You saved everyone's life during the sickness, regardless of where they lived. Jumpin' in the pit to save Sky was another demonstration of how far you were willing to go to save people Madame saw as lesser. When Madame had you whipped for it, it was the final big push we needed to turn people to our side." He sighed and rubbed his chest where I knew a long pink scar ran up his torso from Madame cutting him open like a dead fish. "Course I didn't plan on getting caught by Madame. That threw a wrench in things. I had to rely on the people to riot, which they did after Madame killed Trey."

My entire body stiffened.

"I'm so sorry for your loss," he continued, his voice softening. "Everybody loved Trey, including myself. He was a good man, a kind man. He was also a member of the resistance. When Madame killed him, it was the spark that lit the fire. Those who were a part of the resistance were compelled to act, and the few people who were still afraid were convinced to join them."

Nausea rose, and I swallowed down the urge to puke again. So me and Trey had *both* been pawns.

"I know this might not be much comfort, but Trey wanted to make this place different. I think his soul will rest in peace knowing he had a hand in it."

I gritted my teeth to keep from screaming that I didn't care, that Trey's life had been too high a price to pay.

"I'd like for you to stay here, Bones," Nemo added. "You're a valuable member of this hold. If you need anything, please let me know."

I nodded and that seemed to satisfy him. I knew what it meant to be *valuable*.

"Alright, I'll let you go. Thanks for taking the time to see me. Oh, and we found these. Thought you might want them back."

I reached for my pack and Trey's pack as he pulled them out from behind his desk. I automatically shrugged mine on, the familiar weight settling on my back.

"Have a good night, Bones," Nemo said, and when I glanced at him, his smile looked sad.

❦

In a daze, I returned to the clinic alone since Mac needed to speak privately to Nemo about something. When I got back inside, I set both packs down on my bed and stared at them for a long moment. I did not have the strength to go through Trey's things, so I opened mine instead. Of course, the little wooden dandelion he'd made for me sat on top. I struggled to breathe through the pain in my chest as I took it out and set it aside, but the next thing wasn't much better.

It was his quilt.

I pulled it out, bundling it close to me and pressing my nose to the soft fabric. Tears rolled down my face. It still smelled like him. I clung to it, desperate to breathe him in, knowing the scent would soon fade and then the last little piece of Trey left in the world would be gone.

I curled up on my mattress, my arms wrapped around the quilt, and sobbed until I couldn't breathe.

❦

Hours later, a soft knock sounded at the door and Mac poked his head in.

"Can I come in?" he asked.

I was scrubbing the floor, despite it being nearly midnight, trying to lose myself in mindless work. I shrugged and avoided eye contact, knowing my eyes were still red and swollen. Gods, I hoped he wasn't staying long.

"You want a drink?"

I looked up, surprised. He had a dark expression on his face, but he held up a bottle of liquor.

"Sure."

I put my cleaning supplies away while he poured us two glasses. When I came back over, he handed me one and then downed his drink in one shot. I watched him as I drank mine slower. It burned the whole way down and tasted like ass, but I didn't care. He poured himself a second glass and then leaned on the table, dropping his head down so I couldn't see his face.

"Fuck," he muttered.

"What?"

"Doesn't it piss you off? he asked darkly without looking up.

"What?"

"Bein' used like that? For somebody else's cause?"

I paused, feeling a tiny flicker of rage come to life in my chest. "I'm *always* bein' used for somebody else's cause."

He glanced up at that, his eyes stormy with rage and pain and guilt. He downed his second drink, setting it on the table with a hard thud. "Fuck," he said again.

I tipped my drink back, downing the rest of it like he had. I had a feeling I would need it.

"I did that," Mac said. "I used you for my own cause by bringin' you here." He brought a hand up and rubbed his eyes hard. "I'm so sorry, Bones."

I tried to feel *something*, but even the anger had been snuffed out by the crushing numbness.

"You already apologized," I said, pouring myself a second drink.

"When?" He dropped his hand down, staring at me with an intensity I wasn't drunk enough to handle.

I shot back my second drink. "When you were sick."

He looked wary. "I apologized to you?" When I nodded, he frowned. "I don't remember doin' that."

"You had a real high fever." I shrugged.

"Did I say anythin' else?" he asked.

I thought back to that moment, grateful to the alcohol for making this easier. "You apologized and said you couldn't let Trey d-die." My voice shook. "I told you I knew you didn't have a choice. You asked if I hated you, and I told you I didn't."

He stared at me for a moment longer, that muscle in his jaw jumping, then poured himself a third drink and downed it. "Was that it?"

I hesitated a moment and his eyes sharpened.

"What else?"

"You just wanted to make sure I knew I was a part of your crew," I said, making a snap decision to not tell him how he'd promised not to let anyone hurt me again. I wasn't sure if he'd feel guilty, but I didn't want to risk it. It wasn't a promise anybody could keep.

He looked uneasy, and I couldn't blame him. I remembered when Trey revealed I said things during my burnout fevers that I didn't remember afterward. Maybe I should have kept that whole conversation to myself.

"Why weren't you a part of the rebels?" I blurted out.

He met my eyes for a moment, looking startled, before turning away. "Madame watched me closer than most people. Plus, I didn't know who was in charge, and I wasn't willin' to jeopardize the safety of my crew on the hope that whoever it was would be a better person than Madame."

I couldn't fault him for that.

"After—" His voice broke. "After Trey died, I joined 'cause I knew I'd at the very least be able to get rid of Madame and Vulture."

The pain that stabbed through me at the mention of Trey's name took my breath away for a moment. Would that ever go away? Or would it hurt for the rest of my life?

"I didn't know Vulture found you or that he was bringin' you back. Madame kept it quiet," Mac said, low and pained. "If I'd known I would've done *something*. I hope you know that."

I nodded, hoping he could see the honesty in my face because I *did* know that, but knowing it wouldn't bring back the dead.

We stood in silence for a few moments. Finally, he let out a sigh.

"I better go. Griz is the night guard so let him know if you need anything."

I nodded again, pain and grief still holding my lungs in a vise. After he left, I went to my bed, wrapped myself in Trey's quilt, and tried to ignore how the quiet of the clinic slowly crushed me.

෴

Time kept moving and I kept dragging myself forward with it. Nights were the worst. Griz or Sam usually took night guard duty, but they stayed outside, leaving me alone in the clinic like they thought I wanted privacy. I was somewhat relieved because I could let myself cry into Trey's quilt without worrying about anybody seeing me, but if I was honest with myself, I was so fucking *lonely*. As the sun set every day, I just wanted Trey. I started doing rounds in the evening like I had during the fever, checking in on injured or sick people. Anything just to get out of the fucking clinic. I hated how my eyes constantly strayed to the empty place by the door where his mattress had been. I hated waking up and reaching for someone who wasn't there.

Every night I watched him die in my nightmares. Sometimes I dreamt of other horrible things, but most often it was Trey's death. I watched the light fade from his eyes over and over again until sleeping began to feel like torture. So I stopped sleeping. At night I stayed awake and worked. I re-labeled all the tinctures. I deep cleaned everything. I mended all the tears in my clothes. I caught up on my medical notes. On really bad nights, I went outside and walked alone along the wall of the Vault until my body was too exhausted to keep going. Griz or Sam always asked if I wanted company on those walks, but I always declined.

I pretended not to see Trey's pack sitting in the corner of the room.

In the daytime, I dozed between patients which usually kept me from having a full-fledged nightmare. People got used to shaking me awake when they needed healing. A knot of guilt lodged itself in my stomach as people kept trying to talk to me and kept making an effort, and I couldn't be anything but this empty shell of a person. I kept waiting for people to snap at me or tell me to get over it, but they didn't. They were *kind,* and that was almost worse.

"Nemo approved the plan to start a school for the kids," Leda told me one day as Jet toddled around the clinic. "We're looking at a few buildings, but they're all gonna need some renovations before we can do anything. I'm hoping we can spend the spring and summer working on it and the kids can start in the fall."

"That's great," I murmured.

It took me a bit to realize she'd gone silent, and I looked away from Jet to see Leda studying me.

"Bones, you know you can talk to me anytime, right?" The earnest kindness in her hazel eyes reminded me painfully of Trey. "I'm here for you."

I nodded.

"The grief never goes away," she added after a moment, her voice slightly shaky. "I lost my partner before I even knew I was pregnant. Having Jet helped a little, but the only thing that really dulled the pain was time." She covered my hand on the exam table with her dark one. "Just know it's ok to *feel.*"

After she left, I stood at the exam table for a long time. I had to be broken because most of the time I felt *nothing*. Besides the moments where the grief and pain suddenly came pouring out of my eyes, the emptiness consumed me. I remembered sitting in Madame's cell watching the blood spurting from her neck and feeling nothing at all. Maybe time couldn't fix me. Maybe I was more like Madame than I was like Leda. How much pain could a person take before they went mad? I wasn't sure how much more I could bear.

Mac's crew started going out on missions to get supplies for all the new projects as the snow melted. I wasn't sure if Mac asked people to check in on me, but in the crew's absence, the clinic stayed full of people. Apple and Sky came every day. The two girls had bonded, and I was grateful for that. At least they had each other. Leda and Jet stopped by most days. Even Nemo came by once.

Then one day, the door opened, and Mist walked in.

I froze at the sight of her, an ice-cold guilt filling the numbness. Her face had a little more color to it and she looked less skeletal. She wore her blonde hair down, hiding the awful holes where her ears had once been. Scars covered her arms, scars that I'd helped put there.

Mist smiled, looking nervous, but she came up to me and handed over a bar of soap. "I thought you might be getting low."

I took it, my fingers trembling.

"And I just wanted to make sure you knew, I don't blame you," she added in a whispered rush. "It wasn't your fault, Bones."

I looked down at the soap in my hands. I didn't deserve her forgiveness. Hawk at least agreed with me. I'd seen him a few times around the hold. He hadn't said anything, but the simmering anger in his eyes when he looked at me spoke for him. Hawk hadn't forgiven me for what I'd done, and it made me feel relieved. I would never forgive myself for the torture I'd helped Madame afflict, and it strangely comforted me to know at least one other person out there felt the same way.

"I'm sorry about Trey," Mist added in a trembling whisper. "He was a good man."

My breath caught, and she squeezed my shoulder, her eyes glimmering with tears before she turned and left. I caught a glimpse of Apple and Sky watching, their faces solemn. I had to bite back the impulsive urge to snap at them to leave. They shouldn't be here with me.

They should go help someone better, someone like Leda, where they could learn how to be *good* from people naturally that way. What could they learn from me? How grief could make a person wither away until they crumbled into dust?

I didn't see Clarity at all.

I tried to convince myself it would be disrespectful to go to her. If she didn't want to see me, I could at least honor that. She probably hated me, and I couldn't blame her. Seeing me would probably just cause her more pain, and gods, hadn't I done enough?

CHAPTER 30

I thought the grief would eventually fade like Leda had said, but instead one day I woke up still heartbroken *and* burning with rage. I thought it would go away, but it didn't. The anger crackled under my skin like lightning, burning me from the inside out, but even worse, I was angry at *Trey*. Suddenly the beautiful stories that people told me about Trey grated on my fragile sanity. I tried to avoid talking to anyone as much as possible because I didn't want to hear about how Trey had stayed up all night helping somebody patch a leaking roof or how he'd taken on extra work to help people who were sick. Everyone had a story about Trey, and every single one just made me angrier. The guilt ate me alive. What kind of person did that make me? How could I be angry at the person who died because of me? If anybody knew I felt this way, they'd probably be horrified.

Somehow a couple of months passed. The snow began to melt during the day but still froze at night. Mud coated everything, the kind of mud that sucked at my boots and reminded me far too much of when I'd jumped in the pit to fight Brimstone. I wished I could fight someone like that again. Maybe it would release some of the anger that crackled in the back of my mind like radio static.

I headed back to the clinic alone one night, covered in no small amount of blood from helping a woman give birth to twins. The babies seemed to be strong and healthy, both of them letting out an ear-piercing wail after I patted their backs. Still, coming back a storm grew heavier and heavier in my chest. I couldn't shake the horrible, selfish thought that seeing new life brought into the world just reminded me of the life I'd had ripped away from me. I swore under my breath. What kind of person hated innocent babies just for being alive?

You're a good person, Bones.

If Trey could see me right now, I doubted he'd still say that with such certainty.

I came to an abrupt halt, staring at the little path that led toward the cemetery. I passed it every night, pretending not to see it, but for some reason, I couldn't walk past it now. My feet slowly took me down the path, that empty hole in my chest aching worse with every step. It took me a while to find Trey's grave as I squinted in the moonlight at the names carved in the simple wooden markers. When I finally found it, reading his name hurt a lot worse than I expected. I sank to my knees at the side of his grave, the cold damp mud seeping into my pants.

Despite watching a bullet go through his head, despite being painfully aware of his absence every second, apparently a stupid part of my mind still hadn't actually believed it until now. Now seeing him reduced to a simple, plain grave marker reading "Trey Mason," that last tiny shred of delusional hope shriveled away. Trey was never coming back.

I hated him for leaving. I hated knowing that he probably *would* see his death as a noble sacrifice or some shit. I hated him for charming me with his kindness and for breaking down all my defenses. I hated him for making me fall in love with him and then fucking *leaving* me here alone. What the fuck was I supposed to do now? I leaned forward and dug both my hands into the dirt. Dirt was all that was left of him. I clenched handfuls of it, fighting the urge to fling it at the marker bearing his name.

I knelt there for a long time, shivering and burning with anger as I gripped handfuls of ice-cold dirt. I startled when someone crouched beside me and looked up to see Mac. He still wore his tactical gear, so he must have *just* returned from his latest mission.

"C'mon, Bones," he murmured, "let's go home."

I let him pull me to my feet. He wrapped an arm around me, tucking me against his side. He was taller than Trey had been, I noted numbly. Dirt caked my hands and knees and blood coated my clothes. He noticed the blood and frowned.

"That's not your blood, is it?" he asked, a slight edge to his voice.

"No," I said, "Miss Hatch had her babies."

"Babies?" he repeated with surprise.

"Twins."

"Everybody ok?"

"Yeah," I mumbled.

We didn't speak for the rest of the walk. We entered the clinic to find it empty, but warm, the fire roaring in the wood stove. I wished it could thaw the cold that had settled in my very bones. I went to the sink, washing the dirt off my hands.

"Bones, how can I help?"

I twisted to look at where Mac stood by the exam table. In the dim light, his scar looked like a grim slash across his cheek. His grey eyes glittered but with something softer than his usual fire. He ran a hand through his black hair, shoved both hands in his pockets, and shifted on his feet.

"Please," he added even quieter, "I want to help."

"Help with what?" I asked, my voice hoarse.

"With you." He pinned me in place with those intense eyes.

I turned back around, turning the water off and reaching for a towel, the tears in my eyes and the anger in my chest both burning.

"I don't need—"

"Don't." He strode to my side and grabbed my shoulders. "Don't do that. Don't say you're fine and that you don't need help. I know that's not true."

I tried to jerk away half-heartedly, but he didn't release me. "What the fuck do you want me to say?"

"I dunno, but I *want* to be there for you. If Trey could see you right now, he'd kick my ass."

"Well he's dead, so you don't need to worry about that," I said, my voice getting sharper.

"Bones," he growled, a hint of anger entering his voice, "c'mon, I'm not just doing this for Trey, ok?"

"Mac, I just want to be alone right now." This time when I jerked away, he let me go, his hands dropping to his sides. My temper hung by a thread.

"It's just me." He calmed his voice, but his eyes still snapped with sparks. "You can let it out. I can take it."

I heard the echo of him saying the same thing in that horrible cell below the watchtower when I was coming apart. It made my throat ache, but I couldn't come apart again. If I did, I wasn't sure I'd ever be able to pull myself back together.

"Let *what* out?" I snapped.

"All the shit that's fuckin' eating you alive," he snapped back.

I glared at him, my jaw clenched, and he glared back at me. For a long time, we just stood there as I desperately tried to hold it together.

"Why'd you go to the cemetery tonight?" he asked.

I shrugged, looking away.

"Bones."

I stared at the door, hoping he'd get the message.

"I was there too. I heard what Trey said."

My gaze swung back to him, panic and pain smashing through my self-control. "Don't," I hissed.

"He told you to let them in. He was talking about us, wasn't he?" he asked.

My fists clenched so hard that my nails bit into my palms, and that muscle jumped in his jaw. I had the sudden image of *both* of us teetering on the edge of a cliff.

His voice came out harsh and rough. "You think I don't have to watch him die every night in my dreams? You think I don't hear you screaming when you couldn't heal him? You think any of this is fuckin' *easy*—"

"I *hate* him, is that what you want to hear?" The words poured out of me like vomit. "I *hate* him. I didn't go lookin' for this! I was fuckin' fine just by myself, but he just couldn't leave me be. He had to get in my head and fill it with all this shit about a better world. He made me fall in love with him and then he fuckin' *left* me here alone. And I know it wasn't his fault, I know he didn't choose this. I know he was *murdered* and it was *my* fault it happened. I know I'm a piece of shit for feeling this way, but I'm so fuckin' *angry*."

I broke off, breathing hard, furious tears filling my eyes. Mac hadn't moved from where he stood tensely an arm's distance away, his eyes glittering. The silence roared in my ears.

"It wasn't your fault," Mac finally said, his voice low and rough.

I stared at him, fury running through me again that he picked *that* to harp on. "Are you fuckin' serious?"

"It wasn't your fault," he repeated, his eyes fixed on me.

"It never would've happened if I hadn't let him come with me!" I cried, throwing my arms out in frustrated disbelief.

"You think you *let* him?" Mac's voice rose. "He was dead set on going. You might be stubborn, but Trey was worse, especially when it came to you."

The anger howled freely through me now. I put both palms flat on his chest and *shoved*.

"Stop it." I shouted. "You *know* it's my fault, so don't you dare fuckin' lie to me to try and make me feel better!" I might as well have tried to shove the watchtower over. He didn't move an inch.

"I'm not lying, Bones." His voice sounded rough with emotion but frighteningly honest. "It's not your fault."

"Stop!" I shoved him again, putting more weight into it.

He still didn't move, but he grabbed my shoulders again, squeezing. "I'm angry too," he snapped. "I'm angry at myself for not joinin' the rebellion earlier, for not helpin' Trey make this place better before it killed him. I'm angry at Madame. I'm angry at Nemo, but you wanna know why I'm angry at *you*? It's cause you're closing yourself off to everyone, pushin' all of us away like you're the only one who loved him!"

"I'm not tryin' to push you away!" I said furiously as tears started rolling down my face. "I just don't have anythin' left!"

He stared at me for a few breaths, something softening in the angry lines of his face. "What do you mean?"

"I'm just—" Gods, now that the tears had started I could not get them to stop. "I'm just *empty*. I can't...I can't bend this time. Madame won. She didn't just break me, she d-destroyed me, and there's *nothin'* left."

He stood there holding my shoulders and studying my face as I tried to rein in my hiccupy gasps.

"He was p-puttin' me back together." I whispered. "And now I'm broken just like Madame.

"What do you mean broken like Madame?" he asked.

"Trey said she wasn't as bad before Viper died," I choked out. "He said when Viper died it was like it broke somethin' in her. And that's how I feel, *broken*. Half the time I don't feel anything at all."

Mac let out a heavy sigh and released my shoulders to scrub his hands over his face. "Trey didn't know Madame like I did," he said quietly. "She was always cruel. She always liked hurtin' people, and I've got the scars to prove it. I just never told Trey all of it 'cause I thought keepin' it to myself was all I could do to protect him." Pain sharpened in his voice. "And now I can't help wonderin' if I told him everything from the beginning, maybe he would still be alive."

The pain in his voice broke me. I tried to bring my hands up to cover my face, but before I could, he pulled me into his arms. My face pressed against the hard body armor he wore, and his arms tightened around me, holding me as I sobbed. He breathed raggedly and tears dropped into my hair. I could feel his grief hitting me like a physical force, and gods, he was right. I hadn't thought of anyone else. I was so fucking selfish.

"I'm sorry," I sobbed.

"It's not your fault," he whispered. "You hear me, Bones? It's not your fault."

We stood there for a long time. My arms wrapped around his waist at some point, and even though the body armor wasn't a terribly comfortable thing to be pressed against, I didn't move.

"You should hate me," I mumbled, drunk with exhaustion. "Why don't you hate me?"

"I don't hate you," he murmured, and I realized we were having a strange mirror conversation of the one we'd had during the fever.

"You *did*."

"Yeah, well, I'm an asshole," he said. "That was never about *you* though."

I scoffed, but I still didn't move.

"I was angry at myself for fuckin up the mission, for letting my crew put everything on the line for me and Trey. I wasn't sure if Madame would think finding you was worth everything we lost."

The memory of Madame's knife slicing open his gut flickered across my mind and I shuddered.

"You still cold?" he asked, turning us so the heat of the wood stove warmed my back without letting me go.

"I was just remembering when she cut you open." With the stove at my back and his chest at my front, a little warmth crept through me.

Now *he* shuddered. "Gods, I thought for sure I was gonna die."

I mulled over his words for a minute, surprised. "Did you think I wouldn't heal you?"

"Honestly, I still wasn't fully sure I believed you had powers." He hesitated. "But yeah, a part of me thought you might just let me die for dragging you here."

I tried to imagine what would have happened if I'd refused. Madame probably would have killed both of us. Would it have been better to die then?

"I don't think I could've just stood there and let you die," I confessed, remembering how his wound had reminded me painfully of Dune's. There'd been no hesitation in me when I went to heal him, just desperation.

"I'm sorry for all the times I reminded you of Juck."

I pulled away, looking up at him in horror, and he released me, stuffing his hands back in his pockets. He stared down at me with those flinty grey eyes, something soft and pained in their depths. Something vulnerable that I'd never seen in him before.

"You *never* reminded me of Juck," I said, my voice coming out harsher than I'd meant.

"Didn't I?" he asked darkly.

"No," I said, "you didn't."

We stared at each other for a long time. He didn't look convinced, and I tried to get my brain to piece together a better answer.

"A lot of times I assumed you'd do something like Juck would've done," I finally said, "but you never did."

"Do you still wish you were with him instead of here?" he asked in a low voice.

Guilt stabbed me as I realized he'd been holding onto the lies I threw at him in anger. "I was lyin' when I said that," I admitted with a grimace. "I only said it to hurt you."

His eyes studied mine, but he didn't say anything.

"I watched him do so many horrible things." The words just spilled out of my mouth. "He tortured the people he trafficked. He'd cut their tongues out if they screamed too much, and he'd...he'd do a lot worse if they really pissed him off. If I tried to get him to stop, he'd beat me and then make me go weeks without any food. He branded me after he found out I was sneaking out to see Vulture so I'd never forget I *belonged* to him. He was *evil*." My voice shook so hard I could barely get the words out, but I wanted him to understand he was *nothing* like

Juck. "He...he forced himself on me for the first time when I was fourteen after I tried to run away. He *liked* hurting people, Mac. You're nothin' like him, and—" My voice quavered. "And I'm sorry I made you think you were."

A muscle jumped in his jaw again.

"For the first time?" he repeated in a dangerous voice.

I couldn't get any more words out, so I just nodded, clenching my trembling hands at my sides. I dreaded seeing pity on his face, but only fury shone in his eyes.

"I wish he was still alive so *I* could kill him. Slowly," he muttered.

Trey had said almost the same thing.

Despite the heaviness, the grief, and the horrible memories crowding my mind, I had to fight the urge to smile. Gods, maybe I'd truly lost it. I *was* broken. The harder I tried to keep a straight face, the more the corner of my lips turned up. His eyes focused on my mouth, surprise washing away a little bit of the darkness in his eyes.

I finally gave up and let myself grin like a crazy person. "That might be the nicest thing you've ever said to me."

He blinked, and then an answering slow grin spread across his face. Gods above, Mac had *dimples.* I wasn't sure if I'd ever seen him smile beyond a slight smirk.

"Well, fuck, I better work on that," he said.

Let 'em in.

"I hate bein' alone in here." The words tumbled out of my mouth.

He looked confused for a second, but then understanding flooded his face. "Is that why you haven't been sleeping?"

I frowned. "I've been sleepin'."

He gave me an exasperated look. "At night?"

"Well, no," I admitted, my face warming.

"Then we'll make sure you're not alone in here anymore."

I blinked at him in surprise.

He hesitated a moment, then added, "You want me to stay tonight? I can get a bedroll and sleep on the floor."

A sudden wave of emotion washed over me, and my eyes prickled. "That'd be nice." I managed to get out.

He smiled. "Let me change and grab one. I'll be right back, ok?" He headed for the door, then paused, turning back to look at me. "Bones?"

I glanced at him. The firelight played across his face and

highlighted the golden sparks in his eyes.

"You're a part of my crew," he said in that soft voice I rarely heard, "but you're also my *friend.* You're not alone, ok?"

My eyes burned. "Ok."

He flashed those dimples again. "Be right back."

After he left, I headed up to the loft to change my clothes. The relief coursing through my body made me lightheaded. A few months ago, I would've seen that as weakness. Now I wasn't sure what I'd call it, but maybe it could be something good. A little bit of the fog I'd been living in had cleared. I wouldn't have to be alone anymore, and maybe tonight I could tell Mac about the other powered person. I knew I needed to tell them, but I hadn't been able to think or care past my grief.

I'd only just reached my dresser when I heard the door open. I stopped and turned to walk back to the edge of the loft to see if Mac had forgotten something, but I froze mid-step when the light flicked off. A chill crawled up my spine as I tried to get my eyes to adjust to the dark. That wasn't Mac. He wouldn't shut the light off like that.

I stood in silence, straining my ears when I heard a whisper of a noise to my left. I half turned, panic flooding me, but someone grabbed me, spinning me around and pinning my back against a tall, wiry body. A hand clapped over my mouth, muffling my scream. He wore thick gloves, so when I tried to bite him, I didn't get any skin. I tried to kick his knees, ready to fight, but a low voice spoke harshly in my ear.

"Don't make me do this the hard way, Ember. Your time's up."

My heart stopped beating. Hearing my real name for the first time in twelve years felt like a painful electric shock, but hearing that voice was worse. Even after all this time, I knew it. I'd been dreading hearing it again since I was ten years old.

"Lights," someone said in a low voice from down below, and then a few seconds later the lights came back on.

He spun me around to face him, large hands gripping my shoulders, and I met those green eyes identical to my own. There was no softness, no kindness, no love in my brother's face, just a burning fury that seared through me.

"Think you ran far enough?" asked Wolf.

To be continued…

ACKNOWLEDGMENTS

Ten years ago, I was sitting in a psychiatric ward after a suicide attempt and trying to make a five-year plan. It was the daily activity, and I hated it. My entire life felt like it had shattered, and I didn't want to live another day, much less five whole years. As a nurse gently pushed me to think past tomorrow, I decided to write the dream that felt the most unachievable. I wanted to write a book. It felt laughable at the time. I couldn't even function as a human, so how the hell was I supposed to write a book?

The ten years that followed were full of diagnoses, therapy, psychiatrists, and medication as I tried to untangle the knots in my head and remember who I was through the fog of severe depression. I am here today because of all those things, but I did not do it alone.

First and foremost, I have to thank my best friend and husband, Aaron. You have truly seen me through better and worse and sickness and health. We had the unique opportunity to grow up together due to getting married so young, and I will forever be so grateful that we grew in the same direction. You put up with me being absorbed in writing, distracted thinking about writing, falling asleep while writing, and (possibly your least favorite) sobbing while writing. He *did* try to talk me out of that one thing that happened as I cried all over my keyboard. He was unsuccessful, but I want everyone to know that he tried. Thank you for reluctantly promising to be honest and tell me if my book was terrible as my very first reader and for immediately coming upstairs after reading the first few chapters and telling me with so much excitement that it was *so good*. Thank you for always being willing to get philosophical about atonement or technical about whether or not the internet would exist in my world, and for bringing me a cocktail and not rolling your eyes when I was in dramatic agony over the impossibility of writing my book synopsis. You were my biggest fan from day one and encouraged me and hyped me up every day. You are the best, and I love you so much.

Thank you to my two boys, who were as patient as a six-year-old and two-year-old can be when they wanted a snack and their mom was trying to finish writing a paragraph. You are and will always be the best things I've created. I'm sorry this book is not about *Minecraft* or the singing germs from that one episode of *Curious George* like you hoped. I love you both all the way up to the moon and back.

Thank you to my best friends Amy, Stephanie, and Jason, who freaked out when I casually mentioned I was halfway through writing a book and genuinely wanted to know all about it. You've always been in my corner whether it was visiting me in a psychiatric ward and making me laugh or being excited about my many artistic endeavors. Your steadfast encouragement means the world to me, and I love you all so much. A special thank you to Steph and Amy for not ending our nearly two-decade-long friendship after reading that one chapter. I don't blame you for the "FUCKING HELL KELSEY!!!!!!!" texts you sent. I definitely deserved them.

Thank you to my brother Brad who was the first person to finish the entire book (in what, two days??), and for entertaining me with your stream of commentary. Your enthusiasm was such an incredible boost, and you helped me get over that writer's block I was struggling with in my desperate, competitive attempt to keep up with you.

Thank you to my incredible beta readers, Paula, Florence, Diane, Shannon, Jess, and Abby. You all were so helpful and encouraging and the book is truly better because of you. Paula, you have been such a steadfast supporter and your love for my characters is a dream come true. Shannon, you cheering me on made me cry more than once in the best way. Flo, your artwork of my characters still makes me tear up, and thank you so much for all your help and advice.

Thank you to all my friends and followers on Instagram and TikTok who expressed excitement to read this book. Thank you to all *fifty-three* of you who signed up to get the ARC. That still blows my mind, and your enthusiasm for an indie book from a first time author has been incredible. Thank you for all your messages, your social media posts, and reviews. And oh my god *I'm so sorry*. If you've finished the book, you know what I mean. You have no idea how hard it was for me to not shout major spoilers at you in warning. If it's any consolation, I broke my own heart and it will haunt me forever. And if that doesn't help, feel free to send me angry emails.

Thank you to Max, my therapist, who spent the last ten years helping me understand my own brain and making me passionate about breaking the stigma around mental health.

Thank you to my group of RPG-ers online and in real life who helped me hone my storytelling skills and keep that creative writing spark alive.

Thank you to my parents who raised four kids in the remote mountains of Montana. As an adult, I've realized how unique an experience it was to milk goats in the morning, carry chickens around like baby dolls, and spend most of our time in the woods letting our imaginations run wild. Also, please do not read this book.

Finally, thank *you*, dear reader, for taking a chance on an indie book and making what was once my beautiful, unachievable daydream my reality. Every single one of you matters, and if anyone else feels trapped in a dark place with no way out, I can tell you with absolute certainty, it won't be easy, but it does get better.

Love, Kelsey

ABOUT THE AUTHOR

Kelsey Speer is an author and artist who lives in Minneapolis, Minnesota with her husband and two children, but she grew up in the remote mountains of Montana where the story of *Bones* takes place. With a background in graphic design, she is always creating something. Thanks to that creative spirit, she has explored numerous artistic mediums from embroidery, drawing, costumes, painting, ai art, fancy cakes, and the color of her hair, but the one she always comes back to is writing.

Kelsey started writing her first novel when she was twelve years old. Tragically the pink floppy disc containing it was lost. Since then, she has started writing many different books, and after finally getting officially diagnosed with adhd as an adult, she actually finished one.